PROLOGUE

Thursday 27 August 1992

Sue Melrose was bored. She closed the *Daily Record* and threw it on the floor. Pulling her long dark hair into a scrunchie, she looked out of the window, checking the weather. It was five o'clock and the sun was shining in the sky, making the tarmac steam and shimmer.

The world seemed a happier place for everybody else.

Just not for her.

Despite her own mood, her own frustration, the woods across the road looked green and inviting rather than the dark and threatening gloom of the previous week. Today had been a bloody awful day: waiting in for a roofer who did not appear; losing two fights – one with her mother, one with her husband. Why could they not understand that just once she wanted to get out the house, to eat a meal that somebody else had cooked, put on a nice dress and not get it covered in baby sick?

Just once.

But her mother had refused to watch the kids and Steven had refused to pay for a babysitter, suggesting instead that Sue take the boys out for a walk as he was going to work late.

'Again,' she snapped. And banged the phone down.

There was no point in asking the fat bitch next door to look after the boys – she'd rather ask Myra Hindley.

So Sue put on her new white sundress to cheer herself up. She then pulled the sunflower hat over Bobby's blond curls. George was ready to go. At three years old, he was always ready to go anywhere. The dirtier the better. He was the sort of kid who wouldn't keep clean for more than two seconds. Heidi was at the door, blonde tail wagging, tongue dancing out the side of her mouth. Steven normally took the dog to work, so Heidi was feeling abandoned too. And for what, or for whom?

Sue had a suspicion there was somebody somewhere, undermining her marriage.

She slipped Bobby into his baby wrap, then wound the material round her waist and neck. He settled quickly. Sue combed her hair into long brown curls, picked up her keys and hummed a Carly Simon song to herself.

They were going to pick daisies in the wood.

Sue set out of 2A Altmore Road, the soles of her feet feeling the warmth of the tarmac through her flip-flops as she lifted George by the hand to swing him round. The wee boy spun on one toe, giggling his infectious Little Boy Blue laugh, the sunflowers on his hat dancing this way and that. Letting her dress float out, she spun with him, turning to face the row of cottages with their dark, disapproving faces. So she reversed the spin and headed into the trees, rebuffing her horrible neighbours – May the moaner and Andrew the henpecked hubby. Sue pitied their daughter, wee Lorna with her blonde ponytail, only five, never allowed in her own front door without taking her shoes off, yet they let her sit on the old pervert's knee. He would be watching her now, from the obscurity behind the dirty windows of the big house.

The old guy was never out in the afternoon; his type preferred dawn and twilight. She had seen Andrew Gyle, the henpecked neighbour, go out earlier – going to chop wood, no doubt, but he'd be deep in the forest, nowhere near the Doon. Sue entered the chill of the trees by the gap in the hedge, turning immediately north, up the hill and away from the parade, away from the casual walkers. She had never been as far in as the huge hollow, the Devil's Pulpit, but one day she'd get there and see for herself if it was a bottomless gateway to hell. Beyond that there was the hill by the Big House, and the ruins of the old church. God at the top and the Devil at the bottom; Sue trapped somewhere between.

But that was not for today. Today was for visiting the Doon, getting her good dress covered in mud and stained with grass. They would pick daisies and bluebells, make necklaces and hang them round Bobby's neck. Sue joined George in his happy, skipping dance, losing herself in the thoughts of moving house. George's fingers slipped from hers, Bobby snored gently. It was

RAT RUN

An Anderson and Costello Mystery

Caro Ramsay

This first world edition published 2016
in Great Britain and the USA by
SEVERN HOUSE PUBLISHERS LTD of
19 Cedar Road, Sutton, Surrey, England, SM2 5DA.
Trade paperback edition first published
in Great Britain and the USA 2016 by
SEVERN HOUSE PUBLISHERS LTD

British Library Cataloguing in Publication Data
A CIP catalogue record for this title is available from the British Library.

ISBN-13: 978-0-7278-8619-4 (cased)
ISBN-13: 978-1-84751-720-3 (trade paper)
ISBN-13: 978-1-78010-781-3 (e-book)

All Severn House titles are printed on acid-free paper.

Severn House Publishers support the Forest Stewardship Council™ [FSC™],
the leading international forest certification organisation.
All our titles that are printed on FSC certified paper carry the FSC logo.

MIX
Paper from
responsible sources
FSC   FSC® C013056
www.fsc.org

Typeset by Palimpsest Book Production Ltd.,
Falkirk, Stirlingshire, Scotland.
Printed and bound in Great Britain by
TJ International, Padstow, Cornwall.

wet underfoot now, but it felt rather nice, liberating even, getting her feet damp and filthy. Oh for a house without neighbours, but Steven wouldn't . . . she heard a noise, a quiet mewling from behind her. She turned round.

George wasn't there.

The branches of the trees had locked overhead, blocking out the heat from the sun. The little sunlight that filtered through dappled the path, emphasizing its emptiness. She had not realized that the forest was so dense, so deep, and so black.

'George?' she called out, holding Bobby a little tighter.

No answer except the wind rustling the leaves above her head. A branch creaked. Bobby started to whimper. She cradled his head and set off back along the path, calling for George. Heidi was prancing back and forward along a track that was overgrown, her hackles up, ears pricked.

Sue stood quietly, trying to calm her heart. Just a moment ago, he had been right behind her. Now the lower leaves parted, lifting with the breeze, mocking her that they had taken her son. She turned at a rush of sound, expecting to see George's beaming smile. The undergrowth wavered, and she ducked as a crow flew out, its wings clattering in the air.

Bobby started crying, Sue started shouting, stumbling back the way she had come, the twigs pulling her hair from their roots, and scratching her skin to bleeding.

Then she heard a yelp that translated to *Mum* as she relaxed. The foliage opened and George came stumbling out, covered in dirt, holding late bluebells in his podgy fists. A gift for his mum. She took them and kissed his cheek, letting go of her panic.

Hand in hand, they walked on to the Doon.

'Sore Mummy,' said George, prising her tight grip from his wrist.

'Sorry Georgie.' She relaxed her hold. 'Look, you run on, get Mummy some more flowers.' She could see the Doon now, a sunlight clearing less than ten feet ahead. George bumbled on and starting scrambling up the big stone, moss covered and curved like a claw, in the middle of the ruined wall. It was deathly quiet; the wind seemed to have died in the last few minutes.

It had been a long time since she had last been here. She couldn't recall when, but remembered feeling happy, so that was quite a while ago. She undid the baby wrap and placed Bobby on a flat stone, in the sunshine. He gurgled immediately and kicked his chubby legs in the air. He opened up his fingers and started pulling at the little purple flowers that poked their heads through the moss.

Then he shoved them in his mouth.

Sue walked around, enjoying the sun and the birdsong, leaving Bobby sunbathing on the stone. George was climbing up the ruins, bum in the air, clumsy little shoes scraping on the wall. Heidi pricked her ears up, listening.

Sue closed her eyes, oblivious to her surroundings.

That was her first mistake.

Her second was to turn when somebody called her name.

ONE

It had been raining for weeks. Even for a Scottish summer, this was ridiculous. The windows of 10 Altmore Road were splattered with transparent comets, obliterating the view across the road to the trees. The leaves danced in the wind, the whole forest swaying in a carefully choreographed routine, bending and oscillating before whiplashing back, each in sequence, like a Mexican wave.

It was twenty to six; the gentle light of dawn played on the horizon. The silhouette of Altmore Wood was undulating against the lightening sky. Lynda McMutrie had been awake most of the night, sitting looking out the front window, dressed in her flowered nightgown with her big blue cardie wrapped round her shoulders. Her feet, cosy in red slippers, were warm in front of the fire. An old Agatha Christie lay open on the arm of the chair, an empty bottle of vodka sat on the rug; the glass had rolled to rest against the hearth following the slope of the floor. The crowd of fake Capodimonte ornaments sitting on their dusty carpet on the mantelpiece looked down disapprovingly. Punch and Pantalone were contemptuous. The Blacksmith and the cherubs were reproachful. At least the lady of Lourdes was sympathetic. She knew life could be tough.

Drink was more persuasive than sleep, and sleep was an enemy. The noise of the rain on the roof tiles was a constant irritant; a sudden change of wind direction heralded a full volley on the window glass. Then Lynda was aware of the other noise – a whooshing, and a gentle roaring that crept into her ears. And into her head.

That was her first thought, as the noise was so clear.

Then she looked into the bottom of her glass, a more likely source of her hallucinations. Over the years she had suffered them all: chased by lions, eaten by spiders; once even humiliated at the Eurovision Song Contest. God, the relief when she had woken up from that one.

All due to the demon drink. But she didn't think she was drunk now. Not by her standards.

She eased herself up in the chair, watching the gleaming sheets of water streaming down the road, like the first waves of an early tide racing up grey sand. All that water pouring from the sky.

She relaxed back, thinking about opening another bottle.

But that sound in her ears wasn't for letting up. If anything it was getting louder.

And coming from inside the house. Frowning, she looked out the window, up at the dark sky, out to the woods, to the trees, at the cracked ceiling, at the bubbled wallpaper, and finally at the floor. The noise was coming from down there somewhere. She got up and walked unsteadily to the hall. Her arthritic hands on the back of the chair, then on the sideboard, on the door handle, on the table in the hall, then on the door that concealed the steps to the basement. She didn't trust her knees or her balance these days. The noise crescendoed as soon as she opened the door. She tried the light switch. Nothing but a dry click. She reached out for the wooden handrail, grasping it tightly in her fingers. Feeling the edge of the old wooden steps, down one, two, three; reaching with her toes in their red slippers. Each foot playing catch-up with the other before she dropped another level. Hand over hand on the rail, crabbing her way into the downstairs space. A ninety-degree turn at the bottom, three more steps, then the sole of her foot was wet. The squelch of her bodyweight on the basement carpet gave her a fright.

Then she saw the photographs. Two of them warped and stained with water lying discarded on the bottom step. Both were photos of her first love, in his youth, tall and square-jawed; both pictures taken the day they had had their champagne picnic in the wood. Smiling, a little tearful, she eased herself down and picked them up gently, ignoring the pain in her thumb.

Then she slipped.

Or fell.

Or something.

*   *   *

Jennifer Lawson sat on the old pine chair, nursing the sore backside she had inflicted on herself at five that morning, falling asleep sitting on the loo. Tiredness had finally overcome the noise of the rain battering off the roof. Now she was looking out of the kitchen window of 8 Altmore Road. The rain seemed never-ending. But she was enjoying that rarest of moments; both her children were asleep. Simultaneously.

Gordy had finished eating and had stopped coughing for a moment, allowing him to succumb to his tiredness. Taking advantage of his wee brother being quiet, Robbie had promptly joined him in the land of slumber. With Douglas still dead to the world upstairs, so Jennifer was left awake, as wrung out as a wet rag. Hence the falling asleep on the toilet.

The darkness outside looked as light as it was going to get. She had two washings to go in the machine, another three basketfuls were still damp, and with Gordy being sick during the night there would be his cot cover strewn on the bathroom floor, stinking, and a trail of clothes on the stairs, or wherever she had taken him to try to stop him screaming. She turned her head, listening to the boiler making its loud but ineffectual roar. It had been on full all night but the chill hung in the air, a dampness that clung to the sheets and the clothes and the furniture. Nothing in this house dried out or warmed up. Jennifer looked up at the ceiling, expecting to see icicles hanging from the kitchen light, but it was the usual: dancing cobwebs. She heard her husband's footsteps. It was ten to seven and he was up and about at last. Tiptoeing to the bottom of the stairs, she heard him talking on his mobile. She could only make out low mutterings, not the way he spoke to his staff at the bank. It was the way he used to talk to Jennifer.

She returned to the kitchen table, side-sweeping the dirty plates with her arms so she could rest her head and think about Gordy. He had been sick. His coverlet was stained with little specks of blood. Douglas said it was from the eczema on his fingers and toes. They looked sore, like tiny paper cuts, but when she had tried to examine them, Gordy had started his warp-factor screaming that woke Robbie, who promptly went red in the face and asked to go for a number two monkey as per page five of Painless Toilet Training. So Jennifer had spent the small hours of the morning stumbling round number 8 with one child or the other, cleaning this bit, feeding that bit, soothing the other bits. At some point, Gordy really turned up the volume and Douglas had stomped downstairs and asked politely if she wouldn't mind making that kid 'shut the fuck up'. Then he had felt guilty and put the kettle on. He had handed her a mug of milky tea when he knew she took hers black. He trudged back upstairs, muttering something about how he had an early start in the morning and needed some bloody sleep.

Today was another day, he might be in a better mood.

Nobody could ever say that Jennifer Lawson wasn't an optimist.

Her husband appeared, looking lovely in his crisp designer suit, which was so at odds with his surroundings of old brown wallpaper, mismatched blue carpets and the second-hand black leather suite. He smelled of good aftershave. She smelled of stale sweat and baby sick. He placed his briefcase and laptop at the door, laid his bulky rucksack beside them, his computer and classic car magazines on top.

He could hardly wait to get out.

She could understand that.

'Are you taking more stuff away with you?' she asked.

'Aw pet.' He kissed her on the top of her head, ruffling her unwashed hair.

She muttered an apology for the acrid aroma of dirty nappies that clung to her housecoat, and floated around her head like a cloud of midges on a summer's evening.

'I am at the Edinburgh office today. I did tell you.'

No you didn't.

'Have you had your breakfast yet? You need to keep your strength up, running around after these hooligans all day.'

'Are you offering to make me something? Some scrambled egg? A bacon roll. Some toast, even just warm the bread up a wee bit. I don't mind.' She tried to inject some humour, but it was her heartfelt wish for something hot and tasty to be put in front of her so all she had to do was eat it. With a bit of luck it might even be off a clean plate.

'Sorry babe, I have a breakfast meeting.'

Babe?

He opened his jacket, pulled out his wallet and took out a wad of ten-pound notes, counted out four and placed them on the table in front of her. He folded the rest away. 'God, this house is a mess.' He placed a manicured hand on the radiator. 'Does it ever warm up?'

'No, we need a new boiler.'

'No point in spending any money, it's going to be demolished within the year. We wouldn't get a return on the investment.' He checked his Tag Heuer.

'Maybe not, but at least I could get the washing dry,' she mumbled. 'So is this builder guy—'

'Not "this builder guy"; his name is Gregor. And yes, we are in negotiations, it won't take long. We just need to sit tight, pet.'

'Why can't I sit tight in the Edinburgh flat with you? Are you not coming back tomorrow? Why are you taking all that stuff?' She tried to check on the calendar that it was Friday, but the door had swung closed slightly, blocking her view. It had started to do that. It had a mind of its own these days. Even the bloody house conspired against her.

'I can't work here with those two about, you know that.'

'*Those two* are your sons. And you have an office in Glasgow, like four miles down the road.'

'And a meeting in Edinburgh.' He was fiddling with his cuffs now, unable to meet her eyes. 'And the Edinburgh flat has achieved a twenty per cent gain in value since we bought it, so you can't complain about that, can you?'

Yes.

He leaned over her, his hands on the table, like a teacher talking her through a difficult algebra problem. She looked at his lovely clean fingernails; she had God-knows-what under hers. 'So if I stay there overnight, maybe also tomorrow, I can get so much more done. Then we can have a go at the Artex on Sunday, we can tackle it together.'

She didn't believe him. He knew she didn't believe him. He knew she had no strength to argue. If it was being demolished next year, then why remove the Artex? She walked him to the front door; he patted both sleeping children on their heads as he went past. She held the door open for him and wondered if he remembered their names.

He kissed her on the cheek, keeping his good suit away from the stains on her housecoat. 'Stay inside, you'll get soaked.'

He pressed a button on the Audi keypad and dashed out into the rain, briefcase in hand, rucksack over his shoulder, magazines rolled under his arm. Jennifer watched him go. She raised her hand to wave goodbye, but he drove down towards the parade without a backward glance. She was still standing there when he indicated left and pulled out, disappearing from her view beyond the Altmore Wood. She leaned against the door lintel, breathing in the damp air, wet and biting. It reminded her of being at home on the island.

Bloody August and the air outside the house was warmer than the air inside, so she breathed deeply, closing her eyes, enjoying the delicate new day, watching the rainfall. She wondered if it was possible to fall asleep standing up, like horses. She felt herself drifting, then was whiplashed back to reality as Gordy started to gurgle in the living room behind her. She stayed at the door, keeping her eyes closed, hoping that the baby would fall asleep again. She relished the damp rain, the music of raindrops sprinkling on the long grass, the smell of the woods opposite where the dark trees stood resolutely against the weather, as they had for a hundred years or more. She opened her eyes as Gordy coughed, a deep, racking cough that came from the bottom of his boots. He was gearing up for a screaming fit once he could get his breath. Wee soul. She left him to it; she needed a little time to herself, just watching the water pour from the sky. She tried to see some patterns in the clouds – a cat, or an island, a pork chop – but it wasn't that kind of cloud or that kind of a day. The rhododendrons had lost some of their leaves, discarding them to form crimson footprints over the verdant grass carpet below. So sad to scatter their petals so soon, battered down by the weight of the water over the past few days.

She took a final breath of clean, fresh air, mindful of how smelly the house was. It stunk of baby and toddler, and all kinds of bodily functions and malfunctions – and something else, something that was getting worse. It was a dense, musky smell that seemed more defined when she was on her own; like the smell seemed to know when Douglas went out, and then, sensing his absence, let its own presence be known.

She saw Laura, the gym bunny from number 12 running up the road with their wee poodle. They had on matching outfits, her and the dog, bright pink and waterproof. Jennifer almost cried with envy at somebody with enough energy to go for a run *and* colour-coordinate their dog. Jennifer waved, thinking that it would be nice to shout out: *Why don't you come in for a coffee later, I'll find a clean cup.* She wanted to say, *We are the same age, can we be friends?* Or, *You live two doors up, bloody speak to me.* But Laura was jogging past, her blonde ponytail snaking out of the back of her cap, headphones on, and the small, expensive dog tootled behind, wrapped up in some kind of pink designer cling film.

The wave wasn't returned, so Jennifer closed the door before suffering any further rejection.

Stuck-up cow.

TWO

It was leaving seven thirty by the time Howard Dirk-Huntley had both kids and the retriever on board the Range Rover. Sorrell, climbing in as usual, his school cap screwed up in his pocket, still sticking a slice of jammy toast into his mouth, staining his cheeks blood red; Tabitha, walking sedately round the lawn of number 2 Altmore Road, keeping to the path, holding her school bag over her head to protect her long hair from the onslaught of rain. She slid up on to the front seat beside her dad, pulling her school skirt around her knees before dropping her bag into the footwell. Isla, the retriever, bounced around in excitement behind the grille, shaking and splattering the windows with fine spray in anticipation of a day at the family allotment, playing in the mud and getting filthy.

The interior of the Overfinch stank of damp dog.

Tabitha turned up the heater, steaming up the windows, 'When is this rain going to stop, Daddy? I bet hockey will be cancelled tomorrow.'

Howard put the Range Rover into drive, and contemplated

the luxury of a lie-in on a Saturday morning, a rare event with
a thirteen-year-old daughter who played for her school team,
usually in pouring rain, usually at the other end of the country.
'It will stop when it stops.' He adjusted the de-mister, waiting
for the windscreen to clear. 'You both have money? All your
books? Sorrell, have you got your training shoes and not your
football boots? You will be playing indoors today. Mummy did
tell you that last night. Three times.'

'Yes,' the boy said automatically, then thought for a moment.
'No.'

Howard blasphemed under his breath and put the vehicle
back to park.

'Mummy says you have to pay a pound every time you swear.
Double for the "f" word,' said Tabitha, contemplating the shape
of her eyebrows in the vanity mirror.

'She doesn't have to run you two to school though, does she?
You hang on here, I'll get them.' He slipped his seat belt off
and opened the door, bracing himself to go out into the driving
rain, a quick run up the driveway to the front door where Esther
was now standing, the trainers hanging from the crook of her
first finger of her right hand, a five-pound note in the palm of
her left.

'Three times I reminded him,' her chubby face set in that
no-nonsense gurn that made her look like her mother.

'I might be home earlier if this weather doesn't let up; I'll text
you and let you know. Bye.' He tucked his head down and looked
back to the Range Rover, where Sorrell had taken his cap out of
his pocket and was squeezing it through the grille, goading Isla
to chew it.

Howard bounced into his seat and slammed the door. The
Range Rover squeaked. Metal scraped against metal from the
rear somewhere. 'If she bites that, you are not getting another
one. You will have to go to school with a frayed hat and then
you will feel quite silly, won't you, Sorrell? There will be a
deduction of house points.' And another bloody letter home to
us, he thought. 'For every action there is a consequence, and
you have to be responsible for your own actions, you know
this. We have talked about this before . . .'

'So tell somebody who cares,' said Sorrell, airily. 'Isla's

bored. Can we go to school now? Action: drive. Consequence: we get to school without being bored. Simples.'

Howard cursed again but remembered to do it quietly this time.

The Range Rover groaned a little, giving a small judder. 'Sorrell! Stop making that bloody dog jump about!' shouted Howard.

'That's another pound,' said Tabitha, as her Dad took his hands off the steering wheel, trying to figure out what that slight tremor was. The position of the seat was shifting under his bodyweight. He pulled on the handbrake, sensing the movement but not being able to process it.

Then the Range Rover started moving sideways.

Then backwards.

Howard slipped it into drive, instinct telling him to move the vehicle forwards. He jammed his foot on the accelerator a minute too late. The Range Rover slid backwards, downwards. Howard grabbed on to the steering wheel with one hand, the other arm instinctively reaching out for his daughter. Tabitha braced herself against the back of her seat screaming; Isla started barking as Sorrell shouted, 'Daddy, Daddy!'

In the rear-view mirror, Howard saw the back of the vehicle slide, the rear window obliterated by black, thick mud. The Range Rover creaked and groaned, punctuated by loud banging as clumps of earth hit the roof and the wings. Then it rotated slightly. There was a teeth-grinding screech as the concrete lip chewed the back axle.

All went silent, just the huff-huff of the dog panting and a squeak as the Range Rover swung, seemingly in mid-air.

Tabitha reached for the door.

'Don't Tabs.' Howard put his hand out to stop her, 'Just stay still.'

The vehicle ticked and tocked, tilting back and forth. The rear window bobbed up and down. The view was totally obscured.

'Is everybody OK? You Tab?'

'Yes Daddy.'

'Sorrell?'

'Yes. Isla's OK too, Daddy.'

Howard saw the front door of the house open. Esther appeared, her mouth opened in a scream, both hands up, telling them not to move. She ran across the garden, slipping and sliding in the grass. Howard opened the window to hear Esther shouting . . . *down a hole, sinkhole, get out for God's sake, get out the car* . . .

Esther leaned across the gap from the jagged edge of concrete, pawing thin air, but couldn't reach her son.

'Esther, stop. Everybody stay where you are,' shouted Howard. Even the dog stayed still. The neighbour, Michael Broadfoot, appeared in his peripheral vision, dressed in his jogging bottoms and extra-large He-man T-shirt, eyes full of too-early-in-the-morning confusion.

'Oh my God.' Broadfoot pointed. 'Jesus Christ. Rach? Call 999.'

Rachel, the breadwinner, appeared at their front door, dressed in a dark business suit, mobile in hand, already dialling.

There was a creak and a crumple of metal as the rear of the Range Rover juddered down and sideways another ten inches. Sorrell screamed. All he could see now was dark, muddy walls, streaming with rainwater, all around him.

Broadfoot ran across his front garden, vaulted his eighteen stone over the small hedge and hurried to the vehicle.

'I can't get out; if I do the whole thing will go down. Esther, climb on the front, for God's sake, give it some counterweight.'

Esther stood watching the hole, hearing the swirling, sucking water at the bottom, a grey living entity that rushed up towards her, eating at the sides of the hole, causing it to crumble. It was devouring the earth.

'Esther, you have to move.' Broadfoot pulled her out of the way. 'Sit there, stick your whole bodyweight on it.' He went to the back, reached over the expanse of fresh air, and leant down to open the rear passenger door. The vehicle lurched alarmingly as the boy scrabbled to the side of the seat.

The door held fast. Broadfoot could hear Howard shouting about child locks. 'Put down the window, son.'

Wide eyed, the boy did so, and reached his arms out, not looking down. Broadfoot pulled him clear, swinging him across the gap.

The boy was chanting the dog's name; answering whimpers came from the back as the dog struggled against the grille.

It was crossing Broadfoot's mind to try to get the dog out when the concrete underneath gave way again, another slice slithering into the water below. He jumped back just in time. The dog was out of reach now.

Howard saw Tabitha opening her window, saw Broadfoot's big tattooed hands reach in. He leaned across to shove her up and out through the window as hard as he could. It all went into slow motion, his hands reaching into fresh air and the Range Rover screeching and lurching before it plunged into nothingness.

Jock Aird was mooching about Altmore House, drinking tea and nibbling at ginger nuts. Sleep was not a friend of the elderly, and he always rose early in the summer to get the best of the day, which was a laugh in this weather. He had spent an hour with Betty, his old collie, strolling around Altmore Wood, where as a pup she had chased rats and rabbits. The dog walked slowly now, waddling about with her Marilyn Monroe swagger. She must be about fourteen now, give or take a year or so. Jock was seventy, give or take a year or five.

They took their time to relish the early morning quiet of the world in general and Altmore Road in particular, before the rat run of the little people going from A to B then B to A, the dance of their cars in and out of driveways. It made him laugh.

Every morning they went out the back of the house, down the path, and up round to the Devil's Pulpit, where Betty would slump down, her nose twitching in the air as she scented the nocturnal visitors to her wood. Jock would sit on his stone and roll a cigarette, both of them content with the company of the tiredness in their bones. In her youth, Betty had stood at the top of the Pulpit and, at the scent of a rabbit, dashed over the lip, down into the brambles and the thorns forty feet below, delighting in the thrill of the chase.

Which had always been Jock's philosophy with the fairer sex.

This was a time to reminisce, enjoying a smoke. No matter

how often he sat there, his mind wandered back at some point to that day: the day the woods had lost their innocence; the day Sue Melrose and her two wee boys had been killed.

Twenty-three years ago. Give or take.

The trees had grown dark on that day. The sun never penetrated the canopy now, as if the leaves had covered their shame. Nobody used the woods any more, not the way they used to. People stayed on the perimeter path. Parents kept their kids close. Like the wee refugee at number 8, a young girl stuck with her two wee bairns and a husband that couldn't get out the door quick enough.

Back in those days, Jock and Andrew had managed the wood. They would chop up overgrown trees and collect the fallen branches to feed their fires over the long cold winter. Jock still went out to chop firewood. It took a lot longer now. The winters seemed to last a lot longer, too; the summers were gone in a single breath.

But no matter what the weather was, no matter how his memories hurt, he would return until the day he died. An hour and a half walk, then back in for a pot of mashed tea. Their normal routine. From their viewpoint on the top floor of the house, they could watch all the comings and goings of the rat run below; get to know all the secrets of the little line of cottages that looked on to the woods. His family had owned them all at one time.

In one way or another.

Times change.

People don't.

Today, when Jock came in from the walk, he took off his boots, shook out his waterproofs and left them to dry in the small, unlocked porch at the back. Then he rolled off his thick wool socks to the thin socks underneath. He rubbed Betty with a worn towel, leaving her silverback sticking up and spikey. She then trudged up the stairs to wait in front of the wood-burning stove as he boiled the kettle, made a pot of tea, placed a cup and two packets of ginger biscuits on a tray – dark, chocolate-covered Border biscuits for him, and plain ginger nuts for Betty. Then he came up to join her.

He had his dining table and one chair at the window. Betty's big brown eyes watching from her folded blanket in front of the fire, eyes moving from him to the ginger nuts and back to him as he poured the tea out. The street was shimmering like a rainbow trout today, a glimmering iridescence of blues and yellows.

Most days it was the grey of a hunting shark.

He could spend hours watching his little empire. Brian, the arse with the plastic grass at number 12, who wanted the world to think he owned a Bentley when any idiot could see it was a Chrysler 300. With a Bentley badge on it.

He worked in a gym or something. They had fake tans, him and his skinny missus, who went out running with earphones in and dressed her dog up. They looked like they never ate. His bird might look amazing, but Jock knew what Brian got up to out the back door of number 4.

Nobody seemed happy with themselves nowadays. Everybody wanted to be with someone else or be somewhere else. Either they wanted to move out of this street or to stay here and change it into something that it would never be.

Lynda at number 10 would be slowly drowning her misery in vodka and her detective stories. He wondered if she had heard from her daughter. Barbara had run off to Spain – bloody right, too. Shame, but Lynda could be a right bitch, drunk or sober. She never looked out for her neighbour, the wee refugee with the two bairns. Jennifer? Now that lassie was a worn-out, determined woman. And she was well mannered; said hello sometimes when not fussing over her boys. Her husband was never here. Jock had scraped the snow from her path when he saw her struggling with the wee ones. He hadn't said.

Then there was the posh wanker who had bought Andrew Gyle's old house and the Melrose house next door and knocked back through. Jock had spent a wonderful afternoon once watching them trying to get a Rayburn in the front door when the back of the house had French windows. Then there was the absurdity of the Wednesday firewood delivery when they lived across the road from an overgrown forest. The scarfed harpy had said they didn't like to use up natural resources. Jock couldn't think of an answer to that one.

Jock liked it when Esther, the scarfed harpy, came flying out

the house, charging up Altmore Road like she owned it, ready
to complain with both barrels. They were desperate for the other
houses to refurb, to drive up the property value; then they could
afford to relocate to the country. But, for now, they kept a goat
and some chickens in their back garden and an allotment in
Hardgate. They quoted Scottish heritage and history but it was
all about commodity, something that could be bought and sold.

In his day a home was a home.

The scarfed harpy had dared to come to his door once,
complaining that Betty had given their retriever fleas – working-
class fleas. He had been whittling wood, so he'd had a knife in
his hand when he had gone round the house in response to her
banging the front door that didn't open.

So she'd called the police. Cow . . .

And now Betty was supposed to be on a lead.

No chance. This was her home. It had been in his family for
over three hundred years, give or take. Before that there had
been a smaller house, and beyond that, for a couple of years,
there had been a small church – a simple dry-stone building,
enough for the local community. If the old tales were true, the
church had been washed away and sucked into the Devil's
Pulpit. The graveyard had been on the higher ground, so they
had built the new church up there. If the older tales were true,
the Devil had preached from the Pulpit as the old church was
devoured and then God had chased him. In his haste, the Devil
had left a claw on the floor of the forest, known as the Doon,
or the Dubhan as it appeared on older maps, where Altmore
was Alltmohr. One old map he owned showed Clachan Stone
– the centre of the Doon – as the Devil's Claw. The youngsters
used to inject their heroin there until Jock scared them away.
With his shotgun.

His family had farmed this land for generations; his father
had built the six cottages for the farm workers and the bigger
house at the bottom for the manager. Then they had been swallowed up by the Glasgow sprawl and there was only the street
and the woods left. They were even building on the other side
of the hill now.

At half seven, Jock was supping his second cup of tea. His
teeth were lying on the saucer, so he could suck on the ginger

biscuits without any crumbs getting under his false teeth. He snuggled into his seat and settled down to watch the Friday morning Altmore Road rat run. A toothless grin spread across his face as he heard the sound of a minor earthquake and twisting metal, saw the wanker's Range Rover go backwards into a hole in his front garden. He hadn't seen that happen since Jimmy McGarrigle's ploughshare disappeared in the home field in 1962.

So he settled back to enjoy the spectacle.

THREE

Costello closed the door of her riverside flat and walked awkwardly back to the living room humming 'Private life, drama baby leave me out.' She limped, only weight-bearing on the outside of one foot, keeping her blister clear of the carpet. Then she sat down and put her foot back in the bucket of warm water, staring at the damp towel lying crumpled beside the half-eaten packet of Doritos. She had been enjoying them for breakfast until interrupted by the buzz of the entry system, hobbling to the door in her pyjamas, presuming wrongly that Archie Walker was the only person who would dare to annoy her this early. She had barely recognized Brenda Anderson's voice as she asked to come up as she was 'just passing'. On the morning of the meeting that was going to decide her husband's future? Aye right! Costello had buzzed her in and, sure enough, there was Brenda Anderson, the DCI's missus, suited for work, her red hair neatly cut into a power bob. But her face was pinched and pale. 'Sorry. I need to talk. To you, I mean.'

The conversation that followed was awkward. Costello had put on her dressing gown and made a cup of tea. Brenda had sat with her handbag on her lap, her feet crossed at the ankle as if she were the Queen. Her eyes were fixed on the breakfast TV news as if the towel, the Doritos, and the basin of blood-stained water were perfectly normal.

'Long shift on high heels. Blister,' Costello had explained, and Brenda had given her a look. The look that belonged to sceptical PE teachers and thin women who worked for Weight Watchers.

'This rain is terrible,' said Brenda, looking out through the huge window that looked right down the Clyde.

'It's atrocious; there's some bad flooding in town,' Costello agreed.

Brenda sat still, very stiff, very upright. Then her cup had started to shake. 'Colin will fall apart if they don't let him back.'

Costello had no answer. It had been fourteen months of doctors, psychologists, psychiatrists, occupational health and God knows who else. Peter, the Andersons' son, wouldn't come out of his room. The rumours of their daughter's – Claire's – mental health abounded; Costello had hoped they were untrue, but was too scared to ask.

The conversation had been short and one-sided. Brenda was terrified that her family was falling apart, that Colin would not be able to accept the fact his career was over, if that was the decision. In that case, the marriage would be over as well. Brenda had had enough.

Having told Costello that, she had left.

Costello wriggled her toes in the now lukewarm water. Brenda had thought, wrongly, that Costello had known something, or had some influence.

If the past fourteen months had been hell for the Andersons, it hadn't been a bed of roses for the rest of them. Living the life of a Police Scotland detective who nobody knew what to do with had been frustrating. She had gone to meetings to develop things, looking at spreadsheets, judging people she didn't know on their key performance indicators. People she would never meet and had no wish to judge.

DI Costello preferred to look people in the eye when she decided to dislike them.

She had been dreading this day and had been up most of the night, blaming her sore foot but knowing it was worry about Colin. It was twenty to eight and all the early dawn was revealing to her was a sky full of more bloody rain. Most of it already seemed to be battering against her window, looking for a way in. The Clyde beyond was in a dark and churning mood.

She pulled her foot from its soapy bath and examined the blister. It was huge, filled with blood. She checked her mobile phone – still no word from Archie. If anybody knew, he would.

Today, as the song said, was the day the teddy bears had their picnic. The top brass were meeting DCI Colin Anderson to pass on their considered opinion of whether he was fit to return to work.

Today, either way it went, Anderson would need his friends with him. The team had a lunchtime meeting planned, in a nearby café called Where The Monkey Sleeps, a corner seat booked so they could console or celebrate. It would be the first time they had been together for over a year.

The emotional car crash of the Shadowman had hit them all hard, but Anderson had lost his lover, nearly lost his daughter – and his life. He was now in danger of losing his career and his marriage. He had been diagnosed with PTSD. The top brass were looking for a scapegoat. The family had closed ranks.

Oh yes, the fallout of the Shadowman was like the rain, still falling. Vik Mulholland, their pretty handsome metrosexual DS, had broken his ankle. It had mended, then he had bent the pin. He was still not back on full operational duty. There was a rumour that a certain medical student called Elvie McCulloch was looking after him well in her flat in Glasgow. Supposedly because he couldn't manage the stairs up to his mum's flat.

And Costello believed that as much as she zipped up the back.

She looked at the phone again. Still nothing. Serves her right for expecting a relationship with a married man, a fiscal to boot. A married man with a demented wife, in the medical sense. It could take Archie a long time to get Pippa up and about in the morning. Sometimes she never went to bed, spending the night walking around the bungalow like a caged animal, testing the locks on the doors, muttering that she was looking for Archie, who was always three steps behind her. Whatever demons possessed that woman's mind, they came out to wreak their havoc when darkness fell. It put her own blister into some kind of perspective.

By the end of the day, one way or another, the gang would be back together. Colin, with his own demons of the post-traumatic stress. Vik with his superficial charm. Wyngate, the new dad, with his magnificent spreadsheets. She had met Professor Michael Batten for coffee a few times last year, when Colin had been really bad; not eating and haunted by night-mares. That's when Batten had hinted that Claire had been in a psychiatric ward for self-harming.

Colin was not coping. Brenda, his wife, needed support but had none. And nobody knew what to do.

Today might be the end of their era together.

Costello was not ready for that yet. She had been biding time, believing that Colin was coming back. Her career was on hold; everything was marking time and treading water. Except those who were drowning.

Colin Anderson woke from a sleep that was not his own. His nightmares were those of an unsound mind, where fire had consumed all and he was the only one left alive, stumbling about in a blackened, warped world as his loved ones ran ahead of the flames. They sang joyfully, ignorant of the death that pursued them. He tried to follow but his legs were stuck in the mud, too heavy to pull free. When he looked up, they had gone into the smoke, lost from his sight. Then he heard their screams as flames seared their flesh. He felt their pain as the heat blistered their skin and burned their lungs.

At that point, he usually woke up. Then he would check the house, opening doors, windows, checking escape routes. In the early days, he had pushed all the furniture against the wall so they would have a straight run to the door. He wasn't as bad as that now, but those first few months had been embarrassing for the kids as Peter tried to pull the settee away from the TV screen. Colin had lifted his hand to strike him, then turned on Brenda as she tried to intervene. He could remember his own tears, standing in the middle of the living-room floor, screaming that they would all die if they got caught there.

Brenda just looked at him in stunned, accusatory silence.

The guilt was the worst thing. So Dr Cotter said in her beautiful silky tones. It is what it is. He cannot change the events that happened that night, so he had to *accept*, and until he did that, he would be taunted by images of trees and flames. And pain. He would feel he was being burned. It was his brain reminding him, not of what had happened, but reminding him of what he had not accepted.

It was the way with all post-traumatic stress cases.

The guilt was made worse by the fact that he was a wealthy man now. Materially rich, emotionally empty.

The pain in his leg eased off slightly. The flame was now licking at his skin. He closed his eyes and lessened its power by accepting it, as he had been taught. If he mentally put his hand out to shake hands with the pain, it would go away. There was nothing to be scared of. He took his sertraline and his lorazepam, swallowing them dry.

Then he waited.

Dr Cotter was right. She was always right in daylight, in company. At three o'clock in the morning, sick, alone with a cold sweat, she had no idea how wrong she was.

He stared at the ceiling, putting his hand out and letting his fingers walk across the bed. Brenda was not there, of course she wasn't. But his fingertips found the hairy body of Nesbit. His life might be collapsing around him, but his dog was always true.

There were to be no distractions this morning; he had to keep his mind together.

Today was the day.

The air on the upper landing was still scented with orange shower gel. He would go through his routine as normal. That was what Dr Cotter had recommended: keep things at home as normal as possible, even when he was lying on the bathroom floor curled up in a ball, crying because the pain of invisible flames was too much for any human soul to bear. Even when his daughter was sectioned after slitting her wrists. As the hospital looked after Claire, as the psychologist looked after Colin, Brenda had to keep going for Peter, for some sense of normality.

PTSD was infectious; it worked its way through a family tree like woodworm, eating away at the foundations.

Anderson crossed the hall and paused, Nesbit following him out of the bedroom, snuffling. The house was bathed in the dull daylight. He could hear the rain battering on the roof and it only did that when there was a blow on. Some things don't change.

He paused at his daughter's bedroom. She was going back to school today, just for the afternoon to see how she got on. He wanted to open the door and wish her good luck, tell her not to worry, she would cope. Oh, and by the way, I am sorry for nearly getting you killed and for getting our best friend killed. We both lost someone dear to us and she has left you so much in her will and I can't even tell you that.

Why? Why should he? He admitted to Dr Cotter that he was angry at his daughter for not saying anything of comfort to him. Not one word about the loss of Helena, his lover, her mentor. Why wasn't he allowed to mourn her?

But all this angst was normal according to Dr Cotter; it was all to be expected. Better out than repressed, and it would all return to some kind of new normality in the course of time.

In the course of time.

He wished the violence in him would subside. God knew how many times he'd come close to striking his own children at some imagined slight.

Without realizing it, he had walked to Claire's door and placed the palm of his hand flat on the paint. It was lying slightly open. He listened at the gap; there was no noise from inside, not the gentle breath of a snore, no wheeze of respiration. He removed his hand; he was not allowed in her room now. Until they came to the time when they could talk to each other again.

That was what the doctor said.

He sighed and went into the bathroom, trying to not make a sound.

He needed to get back to work.

He ran the hot tap, filling the sink with steaming water, and dropped his face into the surface, let the heat ease the pain off. He recognized the headache – brutal, throbbing. He had waited eight months for today. It wasn't going to pass without some kind of stress reaction, but pass it would.

He held his breath under the water.

He slowly let the air bubble from the corner of his mouth, then lifted his head from the water and took a deep breath in, shaking the loose water from his hair. He leaned against the mirror, letting the cold glass calm his forehead. And tried to get the pounding in his heart to relax, the skewer in his head to stop twisting.

Today he would know, and at this moment he didn't care which way it went. Anything was better than this no man's land; this endless round of talking, going through it and over it again and again. Dissecting it down into every little decision, like O'Hare teasing out a piece of organic tissue until it was an unrecognizable sliver on a slide.

He lifted his forehead from the mirror and looked at his reflection. His drawn, lined face was alien to him, but the tears coursing over his cheeks were familiar enough.

He blinked slowly, catching a tear before it fell, then opened his eyes at a *click*. Out of the corner of his eye he saw his daughter's door close.

He wasn't the only one who wasn't sleeping.

God knew that his nightmares were bad enough.

Hell only knew how bad hers must be.

FOUR

Number 8 Altmore Road was dark. Midsummer, and Jennifer Lawson was wiggling a light switch, trying to get it to work. The electricity had gone on the blink again and she needed to examine Gordy's throat. He was grimacing, his face going from pink to red, then purple as he went into another coughing fit. Green mucus poured from each nostril; something white was running in two small rivers out of the corners of his mouth. Jennifer sat beside him and wiped away whatever was coming out. Then she put on cream to protect the skin, but that only lasted a couple of minutes before the dribbling and streaming started again. She felt her son's forehead; too hot. The wee one had a sweat on, yet the house was cold. The eczema on his hands and feet had broken out in small, bloodied cuts, and there were a few more specks of red round his nose. Jennifer was beginning to suspect he was allergic to something.

Robbie had pulled his own Pooh Bear duvet up round about him on the settee; it was easier to keep an eye on both of them if they were in the same place. And the nursery, as the back bedroom was jokingly called, was stinking of something. Probably a dirty nappy that Robbie had removed from himself and stuffed somewhere she hadn't thought of looking.

The smell was foul. It shadowed her around the house, like the dampness and the darkness. It had been Douglas's idea to buy this house, knowing from his builder friend that it would sell within minutes at a huge profit once the builder had got planning permission for a through road. These houses would have to be demolished, as would Altmore House, at the top of the road, where the creepy old guy lived. It reminded her of the evil lair in *Masters of the Universe*. It would always be Castle Grayskull to her.

With the money they could pay for the Edinburgh flat outright. It had windows that didn't leak, floors that didn't squeak, and doors that closed and stayed closed. The roof wasn't porous and the bedrooms didn't stink of mould and mildew.

Gordy coughed again – more green globules. As she wiped them away, Gordy smiled, the smile that melted her heart. She looked up at the curtain rail, hanging at an angle, the plaster too damp and old for the screws to have a proper grip. The boys deserved better than this.

Of course it had all come up in the home report, so the property was dirt cheap. It was sold as an old house in need of refurb – a good project; a good investment opportunity to add value. The estate agent hadn't been aware of McGregor Homes' plans to flatten the whole lot. So there had been no refurb, no investment. And Jennifer had agreed to it all. This house was a business decision, hence the nice modern flat in Edinburgh city centre where their future would be. Except it was all taking a long time. And Jennifer suspected Douglas had another interest in Edinburgh, one that did not have a saggy stomach or smell of sick.

But she needed to stay here until the planning came through, taking the kids to the woods opposite, playing in the park, trekking back and forth to the nursery as she wouldn't be able to afford a car. Douglas had splashed the budget on a brand-new Audi.

She had known about the family murdered in the woods in the early Nineties. Sue Melrose had been a mum of two wee boys, just like her. A mum enjoying the woods on a warm summer's evening. Jennifer had never ventured into Altmore Wood. Was it the knowledge of the murders? The fact that her boys and Sue's boys had been about the same age? Or maybe it was the density of the trees? Her constant tiredness? She had pushed the pram on the pavement that skirted the trees but had never walked the overgrown path that went miles into the dark interior.

It looked dangerous.

She pulled Gordy closer to her, thinking how Andrew Gyle had slaughtered Sue and the boys. It made her stomach churn to think about it. But Gyle was serving life without the possibility of parole. He had lived at 2B, his victims next door at 2A, and here was Jennifer cuddling her son while looking out the window of number 8 on to the wood beyond.

The notoriety of the address was another reason the house was so cheap.

It affected her more than she thought it would. Was it because she was left on her own for so many hours in the day, or did the spirits of those two boys know her two boys were in this house and were coming back in some way, their ghosts trying to regain the childhood they had lost. That was bloody nonsense, of course, but it was one explanation for the weird noises, the inconstant smell and the wonky doors.

She wiped Gordy's face again; his eyes were swollen and he was wheezing. She should take him to the doctors' or up to the hospital. It was Friday; if she wanted an appointment, she needed to do it today rather than leave it till over the weekend.

She looked at the weather; she would need to waterproof both of them. Robbie said he needed to go a number one monkey, and pointed to his pot. At least the wee lad was trying. Jennifer lifted him and laid him across her knees, unbuttoning his overnight Babygro as Robbie kicked and wriggled, keen to get free. The minute she pulled his nappy off, he urinated in a tiny arc all over the upper arm of her housecoat. She sat there and let him; he giggled. She picked him up and plonked him on the potty. Gordy coughed again, his face going scarlet. Jennifer held him on her hip and walked into the kitchen through the door that now refused to close. She turned the tap on. Nothing happened. She turned it off and on again. Still nothing. She tried the other tap. A splutter of water, then nothing, then a loud clanging somewhere in a pipe downstairs. It eventually fell silent. She used the little water she had gathered to wash his face, trying to cool him down. She was looking for a clean hand towel when she heard the sirens outside. She stayed rooted to the spot.

The noise came from the end of the road, down at the parade, near where the folk with the Range Rover lived.

The old Melrose house.

So it was someone else's problem. She had enough of her own.

By nine o'clock, Professor Michael Batten was in Kelvingrove Park, listening to the raindrops patter on his umbrella as he splashed in the puddles like a kid. As a forensic psychologist, he was well aware of techniques to control stress, and jumping in puddles was the one that worked well for him. And no one would see him. The park was almost empty. The joggers had jogged off home in the face of the relentless rain. Only the most determined of dog walkers were dragging their reluctant charges around on the end of tight leads. The fat Lab waddling round the fountain seemed more interested in getting back to see if the central heating had been turned on yet.

Batten walked on, alone in the park, taking the long way round. He had consulted on some of the worst crimes imaginable, but the events of last year up on a small bay at Loch Lomond had left him reeling. It had all got a bit too close.

Because he considered DCI Colin Anderson a friend as well as a colleague, he had gone to the meetings, the enquiries, fighting his friend's corner, proving that Colin still had a career in the police service and that PTSD was a condition people recovered from or lived with. But if he told the truth, as his clinical mind saw it, and as the results of the cognitive therapy would prove, Colin Anderson's days as a police officer could be over. The damage was deep. God, even his own wife and children had refused to attend the trauma-focused family therapy sessions.

Anderson was on his own, so Batten had felt compelled to step up to the plate and put his reputation on the line.

It's what a friend would do. But the consequences scared the shit out of him.

He stopped at the fountain and stood to enjoy the water jetting into the air, joining the rain and falling to splash back in the pond again.

He lit a cigarette. He had been off the fags for a few years until the Shadowman case last year. It was never referred to in great detail, just 'The Shadowman'. Since then he had increased to forty a day. The wee glass of whisky at night had become two. Sometimes a third if sleep was particularly evasive.

The Shadowman. Thank God he was only a psychologist. If he had been one of the cops on the team, he would have been into habitual abuse by now. He drew in deeply, letting the smoke infiltrate the deepest pockets of his lungs. Who gave a shit what they said – sometimes he needed a fag. Sometimes he just *did*.

He closed his eyes, happy to be cocooned under his black umbrella.

The conclusion of the Shadowman case had been the result of an unfortunate and unforeseen chain of circumstances. The understanding of such was not the way of big organizations. Police Scotland would want a scapegoat.

At the end of the day, all it ever boiled down to was being in the wrong place at the wrong time. That was all it took. It was your Donald Duck.

Last week five people had died in Glasgow city centre, standing in a bus queue. *If* the two students had been on time for their lecture. *If* the old man had left his haircut for another day. *If* the woman hadn't gone to work, *if* granny had not offered to look after the baby . . .

Batten looked at his watch. Ten o'clock. Anderson would be called in about eleven. There would be a rep from occupational health, the federation rep, the mental health team at Castle Brae, and some top brass, given Colin's rank and the weight of public support that was on his side.

It would look bad if they signed him off and they were cognizant of that. DCI Colin Anderson was an excellent police officer with a record second to none. He was extraordinary in his care for victims and the other members of his team, a great communicator, a team player. He was exactly what Police Scotland aspired their detectives to be.

The media had gone to town on the fact his lover had turned up at the enactment of the crime. Then hastily redrafted when it became clear she had been terminally ill, her clarity of thought impinged by the lesions on her brain. Colin had become some sort of hero.

As Batten saw it, Anderson's best chance of recovery was routine and structure. Normality. He needed that to get his sanity back, but he couldn't return to work until he had his sanity. His world-view was that his job was worthwhile. He helped to stop atrocities.

He needed to work to validate that world-view; he needed his job.

Batten thought he had countered every argument the board might have come up with. Anderson needed familiarity and support around him and he seemed to be getting bugger all from his family. He deserved people he knew he could trust, so Batten recommended that Anderson should get his old team back with a low-key case to work on, something to get his intellect working and restore his confidence. His only restriction would be that he would be office bound, nine to five. Good God, after all the years he had been in the force, surely they owed him that?

Somebody, maybe Costello, had arranged for them to meet Colin for a coffee after the meeting to celebrate the good news. Or catch him if he fell.

FIVE

The recovery vehicle took an hour to secure the chains round the back of the Range Rover as a small crowd of experts scratched their heads about what to do next. Some determined rubberneckers had wandered up from the parade and were watching from the pavement that bordered the woods. The residents of Altmore Road had all gone back indoors. Esther Dirk-Huntley had pulled her children back inside the house, not wanting them to be present if Howard was injured, or if any tough decisions had to be made about Isla. She took no solace from her neighbours. There had been too many fights over the noise of the hens, the stink of the goat and the precise location of the boundary fence for the drama of a life-threatening sinkhole to unite them. The Broadfoots, at number 4, had been told by police to stay inside their house until their driveway could be tested, but their teenage daughter kept creeping out to take photos on her mobile. She chatted flirtatiously to the tall, suntanned man from number 12 until his wife appeared and dragged him back into the house, marching him up past the front garden of number 6, with its ugly display of old mattresses and bits of car engine. The plump girl at number 8 had asked when the road would be open as she needed a taxi to take her baby to the doctor.

The rescue services were chiefly concerned about Howard, who had been stuck in the driver's seat for hours now, unable to get his door open. The vehicle had been secured by two wire cables, so there was no immediate danger to him, but the hole was filling slowly with water and the retriever was still in the back of the Range Rover, panicking and clawing at the grille.

When Jim Mitchell, senior firefighter, saw the TV cameras arrive, he realized there was no way they could let the dog drown. Not a golden retriever. Not the nation's favourite. Not in front of the media. Mitchell was in contact with Howard by his mobile phone and all conversations were now soundtracked by the drone of the helicopter overhead.

'Can you still hear me OK?'

'Yip.' The voice was terse.

'OK, we are going to smash the front window, pass you a rope and a hook. I want you to hook the—'

'Grille in the back, for the dog? I couldn't face the children if we left her here.'

'Yeah. Can you reach? The vehicle is secured, it won't sink any further.'

'How do we get the dog up? How do you get me up?'

'We'll get you up, don't worry. One of the lads is coming down.'

Howard looked up, but all he could see was the dull grey wall of the sinkhole. He waited, talking calmly to the dog, which was squealing in distress. The noise of the water was getting louder and Isla was no longer paddling about in a few inches. Her golden coat now had a thick layer of stinking scum up to her neck.

Howard was terrified to move. He had never really considered he was scared of anything, but this – this was something new. He talked, the dog whimpered. It passed the time as he tried to ignore the deafening rush of the rising water, while holding on to his phone as if his life depended on it. Which it well might. Every so often, the vehicle would give a little bounce, as if the pressure of water was lifting it a little. No gross movement, just a reminder that the next one might be the big one. He worried what the Range Rover was fixed on to at road level. He tried not to think about the fire appliance sliding backwards to crush him at the bottom of the sinkhole.

If the hole got bigger and swallowed the lot of them . . .

He glanced at his watch. If they didn't get out of here in the next few minutes, Isla would drown. And ten minutes later, so would he.

Horrified, he watched the rear-view mirror as Isla was slowly engulfed by dirty, brackish water. There was no daylight now, just the odd wayward beam of a torch dancing on the sinkhole walls. Then he heard a metal clunk right above his head, solid sounding, and the melodic grind of a well-greased engine. The vehicle lifted slightly. Then there was the rattle of chain links and two black waterproofed legs appeared at his side window.

His mobile went again.

'I want you to crouch down in your seat, keep your eyes covered, until we talk again.'

Howard was grateful to curl up like a foetus, thankful for the familiar smell of the warm leather as it caressed his cheek. He waited. Then he heard a quiet tap.

A thousand pieces of glass showered over him.

He thought it would never stop.

The mobile was talking again.

'Slowly get up.'

He could see the soles of the boots braced against the side of the sinkhole. Then a hook, strapping attached, came through the broken windscreen, a gloved hand above swung it back and forth so Howard could reach and catch it on the back swing.

He heard the dog splutter as she went under.

'That hook is for you, secure the belt round your waist.'

Howard heard Isla yelping and gasping for breath, claws and paws scraping at the grille that penned her in. 'Get the dog out first. I'll get the hook on the grille, you pull. She'll jump.' Howard reached up and belted himself round the waist. Then he grabbed the hook. Unclicking his seat belt, he dropped through the gap between the front seats, seeing his son's school cap floating on the black water. He clipped the hook on to the grille. Isla's brown eyes were wide in panic. He was now twisted and trapped, his whole weight on one elbow. It crossed his mind that he might never get out of this. He could feel the arteries pound in his skull, black stars flashed in front of his eyes.

He pulled on the rope.

He had lost the phone somewhere.

'Pull it up,' he shouted into the back seat. 'Up! Up!'

The rope tightened, the grille buckled slightly, then bounced free and smacked him in the face. He pulled his head back as he felt the wet, filthy fur of the dog rush past him and then he felt himself fall, falling into the dark swirling water in the rear foot well, immersed in the dark, churning depths.

*   *   *

By twenty past ten, Colin Anderson was exiting the Clyde
Tunnel, taking the long way round to the city centre. He was
driving slowly, steadily, hoping that his nerve would not fail
him. He felt his heart skip a beat as a siren sounded, a fire
appliance going in the opposite direction. Anderson pulled over
to the pavement to let it pass, narrowly missing a parked car.

With sweating palms, he did a U-turn and drove up to Helena's
house high on the terrace; four storeys in Florentine Renaissance
style, with the attic studio overlooking the Glasgow skyline.

Just as he had done the week before. And the week before
that. He couldn't drive past the place. He heart drummed on
with its irregular beat. *Feel the fear*, he said to himself. Why
was he scared of a house?

Because it was his.

Last month he had sat in front of a lawyer, a very expensive
lawyer, who spoke in mortician measured tones. Anderson could
recall the words exactly. 'So, I conclude that the sum total of
the last will and testament of Helena Grevell McAlpine née
Farrell is left to you, Mr Anderson, including all investments,
pensions, properties, inclusive of the former domicile situated
at Kirklea Terrace and the Gallery Cynae Art Gallery, all paintings and works in progress. There is an advisement that Ella
Welsh is employed and her terms and conditions retained until
such times as . . .'

He didn't want it. Not any of it.

He wanted Helena Grevell McAlpine née Farrell back.

The following day, after another night when his sleep had
been stolen by nightmares, he had phoned the lawyer. Less than
twenty-four hours later, and he had already been smothered
with the thought of the responsibility. There was a business,
people to employ, paintings on loan to galleries, more hanging
on the wall. Memories.

Another thing to taunt him, another thing that he could not
cope with.

'I wouldn't be too concerned, Mr Anderson. Mrs McAlpine
was a very astute businesswoman and has procedures in place.
Mrs Welsh would be the best person to run the gallery for you;
she has been doing so for over a year now. We are having the
properties cleaned and maintained so there is nothing for you

to do until you are ready. I did refer to that when we last spoke, but it can be very difficult to take in.'

The lawyer then went on to chat casually about the individual bequests: her father's medals to his regimental museum; two investment accounts, one for Claire Pauline Anderson, one for Peter Colin Anderson, and the funds those accounts held. 'For their further education. Mrs McAlpine presumed your children would be going on to university.'

At the moment Claire was having difficulty getting out the front door.

'I think you said at the time,' Anderson could see the lawyer in his mind's eye, looking over his half-moon specs as a pudgy hand conducted the conversation by fountain pen, 'that your son was fourteen. I suggest you leave that in trust. I recommend that you get the assistance of a financial adviser and we can help arrange that for you.'

He was numb; he was numb in the office, numb after the phone call, and he felt no better now sitting outside a house he owned.

The lawyer alluded to the library of her work that she had kept, and how that would greatly increase in value now.

Now that she was deceased.

Then the lawyer had added, casually, that the terrace property alone was worth one point one million pounds in today's market. Anderson looked at the front door of the house, matt black with a single gold knocker.

It mocked him – one point one million indeed. More than he would ever earn.

Last night Brenda had asked him to get teabags on the way home. Teabags for their breakfast tomorrow, when he might have a job that he didn't need.

And he realized just how badly he did need it.

The Range Rover was now up on the hard standing, rolling awkwardly on its own wheels as it was winched towards the tracks of the recovery vehicle. Once it was aboard the flat top, it would be driven away for the insurers to argue over. Engineers from Scottish Water had arrived on the scene with their emer- gency vans, and were now knocking on doors to see who had water and who had not. Two civil engineers were already looking at iPads in the dry sanctuary of their cars, following the activity in the hole via a remote camera. Howard Dirk-Huntley was sitting in the back of an ambulance, nursing a fractured shoulder and minor facial injuries. His first action had been to ask for his wife's mobile so he could march up and down on the pavement, screaming at his lawyer. Then Esther had walked Sorrell and Tabitha to the parade, where a friend met them to take them to school. Isla had been locked in the goat's pen until the dog groomer arrived to shampoo her, water permitting. If they had any water by then. The small crowd had dispersed, all wandering away down to the parade where they could dry out, get a cup of tea and hope to get on the telly. The helicopter had disappeared.

Somebody in an orange suit and a hard-hat head-cam was dangling down the sinkhole, suspended by the same apparatus the firefighter had used. He was armed with a hammer and some penetrating ultrasonic equipment to test the walls of the sinkhole, making sure it was a one-off event. At the bottom, the dark muddy water was swirling and eddying, daring him to fall in. The little waves that slurped against the side, making the surface pulse, suggested there was some flow-through. There had been no movement in the walls for over half an hour now but the water level was still steadily rising. A truck had delivered two huge slabs of weathered plastic sheeting, ready to be pulled over once the situation had been stabilized.

The man down the hole worked his way round the wall, his foot secure in a stirrup, dangling like a trapeze artist waiting their turn in the spotlight. The video camera on his helmet recorded every detail. It was the young civil engineer in his car watching his iPad screen who stopped and paused the live feed, rewound it, then played on.

Then rewound and paused.

Not sure of what he was seeing, but aware of a chill running up his spine. He felt vaguely sick. He knew what he was seeing, what his instinct was telling him. He opened the car window to call over the nearest police officer but, as usual, there was never one around when you wanted one.

SIX

By half twelve they were sitting round a table in Where The Monkey Sleeps. DS Vik Mulholland had managed to join them, sneaking away in his lunch break, curious to hear the fate of his old boss. Professor Batten noticed, with the pleasure of seeing a well-known comedy routine, that it had taken less than five minutes before the sniping started between Costello and Mulholland. If he didn't know better, he might think they were married. Costello looked solemn in her customary dark grey and moaning about her foot, Mulholland looking very sharp in a charcoal grey, moaning about his leg.

The chitchat was vacuous, merely marking time until Anderson walked in through the door and informed them of the board's decision. They avoided talking about it, knowing their relief would be heartfelt if Anderson could return, not knowing the appropriate response if he could not.

Batten, for his part, had been glad that his recommendations were positive. Anything else would have seemed disloyal, yet he was still nagged by the fear that his friendship had overruled his professional judgement. He consoled himself with what he knew to be true. Colin needed normality back in his life and his normality was chasing killers. Offering him more atrocities to investigate might overload a mind that was still struggling to come to terms with the past, but his trusted team would be his anchor.

Batten had a look at his phone, a text message from the senior fiscal Archie Walker. *Re Anderson. Any news?* Batten texted back *Nope*. He had just pressed send when the door of the café opened. The silence dropped like a stone. They were all disappointed when the small dapper figure of the fiscal himself strolled in.

Batten held up his phone, an eyebrow raised. 'You just texted me?'

'Sorry I realized I was passing just after I had sent it. So no word yet?'

'No,' Costello flashed him a tense smile.

Batten had not seen either of them for a few months, but recognized that they had held each other's gaze for a moment too long to be professional. None of his business. Walker's home life was difficult, Costello's private life was non-existent. As it was his intention to babysit – he corrected himself, to *monitor* – Anderson, and make sure that his decision-making was sound and that he had curbed his hypervigilance, it might well work to his advantage if Costello was close to the fiscal. Ideally, Batten wanted DI Costello in an active role and Anderson safe in the office, behind a desk. He smiled to himself as he watched Walker try to extricate Costello from the group, keen to have a private word with her. She blanked him, looking at the menu, commenting that they should wait before they ordered, wait to see if Anderson appeared and what his news was. Mulholland said that they might be better ordering now. It would be cheaper.

And he could really murder a bacon roll.

They were all keeping it light.

And then the door opened.

Again they all looked.

All conversation stopped mid-flow. The figure was outlined in the doorway; a tall, thin man, gaunt-faced, his suit jacket hanging off him loosely.

DCI Colin Anderson smiled, a worried smile that didn't reach his sunken, red-rimmed eyes. The stressed lines on his face creased up.

'Looks like I am back.'

There was a fair bit of backslapping and a small discordant chorus of 'Congratulations' as they rearranged the seating. Costello gave Anderson a hug.

'Now, Colin, let's have something to eat. I am bloody hungry and there is a case I want to get you up to speed on. Fine?' Walker looked around at the rest of them, 'Great. Now let's order.'

'And he's paying,' said Costello, pointing at the fiscal.

'Actually,' said Anderson, 'I'll pay.'

'Oh, Christ, he really has been unwell!' Costello leaned over to feel Anderson's forehead with the back of her hand. They laughed, and this time it had a genuine ring to it, deep, relaxed and happy.

Batten watched the interplay closely. After the coffee and the rolls came, Walker and Anderson slid closer together and their conversation drifted to the flooding and the never-ending rain.

It was Costello who asked, 'So what is the case? And is it for him? Or is it for us?'

Walker ripped a bite off his roll, and then dabbed the napkin round his lips. 'You plural.'

'Good,' said Costello. 'Please make it something good, my life is hell trying to stay awake during these performance meetings.' She tackled a slice of elusive bacon with her tongue to prevent further escape. 'So I get taken off that crap and put back on MIT with Colin?'

'Not exactly.' Walker put his own roll down, folded the paper napkin and dusted one hand against the other.

'What do you mean "not exactly"?'

'It's a case that is not a case.' Walker pre-empted their questions. 'I, we, are waiting for some info back from Pitt Street, but there is something I want looked into – for reasons that might not be obvious at the moment – and, as you lot are devoid of any real working brief, I have suggested that we, as a team, investigate it.'

'A team that includes a fiscal?' asked Batten.

'Why?'

'Probably thinks we can't cope,' said Costello, the words out her mouth before she could stop them. There was a resounding silence.

Then Anderson said, his voice slightly shaky, 'Well, I am not convinced that I *can* cope, so any help is good for me.' He raised a cup to toast them. 'But why should you be dragged away from your nice dry office, Archie? It's us who report to you, not vice versa.'

'My office might be involved,' said the fiscal, 'at a later stage, but I want to be in the loop from the start. This will be it.' Walker's phone went and he slid out from the booth to answer it.

They watched him pull various faces as he took the call, none of them disagreeable. 'No, I don't think he'll have an issue with that. I was going to suggest it. We have a car here, yes?' A few impatient nods, 'What now?' He flicked a look at his watch. 'Yes, OK, I think it might be more prudent for us to have two sets of wet-weather gear.' Another nod, a look back at his colleagues sitting round the table. 'Oh right, that will be great. Yip, bye.' He slid back into the seat. 'From here on in, DCI Anderson, you are behind a desk until you find your feet. Except for the next couple of hours, as we are now going to look at something of interest.'

'That's sensible, Colin. Ease you back into the saddle,' said Batten. 'And Costello can do all the running about.' He raised an eyebrow to the DI with comic exaggeration.

'Same old, same old,' she shrugged.

Batten watched Anderson bite his lip, just before he remembered to laugh. He caught the watchful glance of his friend's blue eyes. He didn't quite trust them. Or himself. Not yet, not now.

'So what has happened that's so interesting a fiscal is going to get off his bureaucratic backside and look at a crime scene?' Costello stirred her tea, knocking the teaspoon off the side of the cup with every rotation. Knowing it irritated Walker, so was worth doing.

'DI Costello, you can follow us once you go back and put in a request for all documentation on the Melrose case. Just the written stuff – no evidential material. Yet.'

'The Melrose case?' asked Costello, confirming that she had heard right. 'The one from the early Nineties?'

'Indeed. Vik? We want you as the DS on the team, but we need clearance and it is not through yet.' Walker glanced at his watch, lifting up the immaculate cuff of his shirtsleeve.

'So I am not on the case?'

'Not yet. And so far, it is not a case. And I hope it does not become one.'

Batten noticed that Costello didn't look like moving. Anderson, on the other hand, the most senior person present, had stood up, ready to follow Walker's lead.

'So if it is not a case, then what is it?' asked Costello.

Walker thought for a moment, then said slowly, 'It's a hole in the ground and we want somebody to look into it.'

Archie Walker, the chief fiscal of Glasgow, was sitting in his spotless Merc, out of the rain. As soon as Anderson pulled up behind, the fiscal got out of the car and, springing the boot open, he lifted out a Barbour coat and a pair of green Hunter wellies. He indicated to Anderson that he should join him, and pulled out another pair of boots.

Anderson stayed in his own car, gauging his feelings. Nervous? Sick? Wary? All of the above. There was a film reel of something else playing in the back of his head, something hard to ignore. A soundtrack of darkness and fire and flames, the crack of burning wood in his ears, the taste of charred flesh on his lips.

Full sensory flashbacks.

This was not real.

The rain battering on the windscreen was real. He concentrated on that. There was nothing dangerous lying in wait. There was nobody out there.

This was a test.

He realized he had closed his eyes. When he opened them, the rain was still falling. Walker was still there, one foot up on the rear bumper. It was his first day back in the job.

This was it.

This was now.

He got out of the car, pulling his collar up round his neck. The rain that rattled so hard against his face caused a hard, consistent drumming on the shoulders of his jacket.

Midsummer. Glasgow.

Walker handed him a pair of wellies, saying that he presumed Anderson wouldn't have his own with him. Nobody had expected him to be operational on his first day, but this needed a gentle and experienced hand.

'For a hole in the ground?' Anderson fished, prising the shoe off one foot with the toe of the other, his hand on the rim of the boot to help him balance. He caught sight of the wood to his right: ominous dark trees, growling at him, bending and leaning in the wind, effortlessly brushing off the rain that weighed everything down.

There could be anything in there.

'You OK Colin?'

Walker's voice floated over, but he could not take his eyes off the waving treetops. Then he realized he was fixed like a statue standing on one leg. 'Yeah, I'm OK,' he replied, holding on to the top of his boot, caressing it, taking deep, regular breaths and thinking it through logically. He knew the techniques to deal with this. Be logical. He turned to face the road, feeling the rain on his face, which was real, and trying to block out the smell of burning wood and the taste of acrid smoke which were not real.

The monster was not here.

Helena wasn't here. She had lain in a pool of blood under a bright moonlit sky. Claire wasn't in there, hiding behind a tree, terrified out of her mind. She was going back to school.

He gave a slow count to twenty. And breathed deep while he made a show of struggling with his boot.

'You OK?' asked Walker again.

'Yip, it's been a long time since I had to put wellies on.'

Walker paused for a moment to reflect, rainwater coursing down his face. 'Anyway, how are you feeling? Now that you are out and about?'

'I'm fine.' Anderson was keen to move on. 'So what are we doing here? Up in the Kilpatricks, for a sinkhole? A DCI for a sinkhole? Do you think I can't cope with anything more complicated?' he joked, zipping up his anorak, which looked four sizes too big for him.

'Did you use the postcode to get here? You might not have noticed that up there is Altmore Road. Over there is Altmore Wood. You didn't flinch when I mentioned the Melrose case.'

'I did,' Anderson lied, a little chill running through him. He felt sick. 'But didn't want to—'

'We all should feel revulsion in times like these,' Walker said, kindly, 'but come on, we are going up there. We need a quiet word with Jim Mitchell, hopefully where nobody else will notice us. And somewhere out of this bloody rain.'

'So all this rain has caused the sinkhole. Why the fuss?'

Walker smiled and banged the boot shut and set off at a brisk pace, head down, his short legs striding out past a media van, and a few soaked photographers.

They showed their ID to a constable, who was guarding a tape while hiding under a borrowed umbrella. Walker still taking the lead as they walked up the slight hill towards Altmore Road itself. Bored, the constable watched them go past. The insignificant, impeccably dressed man with his hat over his salt and pepper hair and, behind him, taller, in an ill-fitting suit and thin rain jacket, walking as if he was wearing somebody else's boots, was DCI Colin Anderson. So the rumours were true. He pulled out his mobile – this was news.

Walker had not noticed. 'Nobody knows you are here, Anderson, and I want it to stay that way.'

'If I am such a liability, then why did you ask me?'

'Don't be touchy, you are the best man for the job. Simple as that.'

DCI Anderson stood in the rain, watching the scene in Altmore Road, deep in thought. He was slow on the uptake these days. Even if he recognized the nuance, it took a wee while for his conscious mind to bring the bigger picture into focus. Connections took their time. Words first uttered, floated past him. He was learning to reach out and catch them, revisit the meaning and the association of what was being said. Ideas forming and reforming.

Altmore Wood.

He had recognized the words 'The Melrose case' when he had heard them, but it was only Costello's response that flagged up that this should mean something.

Altmore Road. Altmore Wood. Where Andrew Gyle had murdered Susan Melrose and her two children.

'That's right. Two boys,' said Walker, shocking Anderson with the realization that he had spoken out loud. 'Two wee boys killed—'

'By an axe,' added Anderson, feeling his stomach evolve into a gripping, tortuous pit. He had made that association quickly enough. Or his unconscious mind had.

Walker stopped in his tracks. 'Sorry, but that was the kind of fact I didn't think you'd want to ruminate on.'

'I am either back on the job or not. Can't cherry-pick.'

A man in high-vis waterproofs strode down the tarmac

towards them. Anderson could see the fire appliance parked across the road. A flatbed recovery vehicle with a Range Rover on board reversed with much shouting and waving.

There were a lot of people standing around getting very wet.

'Jim, this is DCI Anderson.'

'A DCI, so what the f . . . Oh yeah, the history of the place. I never thought of that. Do you think there is a connection?'

'Can we have a look?' asked Walker, ignoring the question.

'Right over there. We don't know how secure the edges are, so please harness up before you cross that line. Two guys have found something interesting down there to look at already.'

An older man, the name Greene on his jacket, climbed out of a van with two harnesses, like those that abseilers and climbers would use. He held one out to Anderson, one to Walker, then Greene helped them into the various loops and straps.

Walker talked to Anderson all the time. 'Your team has garnered an excellent reputation for this kind of case.'

'What kind of case?'

'Well, this sinkhole needs investigating in the light of what happened in the woods over there in 1992. Don't forget that Andrew Gyle has always protested his innocence. We need to investigate this sinkhole and we need this investigation to be transparent. If it's another nail in Gyle's coffin then so be it, but if it in any way lends weight to an argument that he might be innocent, then we need to know everything there is to know about it. His defence team have exhausted every appeal and every case-review process they can. It has been twenty-odd years, but it is still in the public eye and somebody is bankrolling Gyle's . . .' he searched for the word.

'Delusions?' offered Anderson.

'"Cause", I was going to say. But you might be more accurate. His supporters will get very agitated as soon as they hear about this. So tread carefully.'

'Tread carefully on what?'

'On this bloody concrete would be my first suggestion. Can we have a look now?' Walker tested his harness.

'You can. Then you can view the film from the safety of the van.'

'The film?' asked Anderson.

'It'll all become clear.' Walker turned to Greene, 'Somebody was stuck down the hole?'

'Dirk-Huntley? He's away to hospital, shoulder injury. He was jumping around so much, yelling to his lawyer, he nearly caused another bloody sinkhole. The value of his house has fallen through the floor, if you pardon the pun.'

Walker turned away from the rain, talking quietly to Anderson. 'The Dirk-Huntleys now live in the house that both the Gyles and Melroses lived in. The two cottages have been knocked into one. The sinkhole is in the garden of the house both murderer and victim lived in.'

'OK, so I can see why that is important.' Anderson looked around, not seeing it at all, not trusting himself.

'The Range Rover got badly crunched. And somebody got bitten by the dog when it was pulled out the hole. The guy it bit nearly chucked the bugger back down.'

Anderson walked slowly towards the giant cauldron in the tarmac. The terrible sucking and slavering from the water below sounded like a dragon trying to get out. He was aware of the tall man dressed in head-to-toe high-vis waterproofs. The figure next to him was much smaller and slightly rounder, a female also dressed in full-length waterproofs.

Familiarity nibbled at the back of Anderson's mind. Jack O'Hare, the forensic pathologist, turned round and said, 'Hello, DCI Anderson, nice to have you back. You remember Olive?'

Anderson didn't, but nodded and hoped the confusion did not show on his face.

'Olive Darvel, the anthropologist from the university,' added O'Hare helpfully.

Anderson recognized her but still had no idea where from. Deep breaths. 'So what do you have for me?'

'Look down there.'

Anderson looked down into the angry, bubbling water. The sinkhole was about twenty, thirty feet wide, if not more. The jagged edges of the concrete crust jutted out, the earth underneath still being eaten away by the water. Two pipes were clearly visible, a few rocks, layers of colour variations in formation underneath.

'Is it getting worse?' asked Anderson.

'We are not hanging around to see. Look down there, if you watch you will see . . . see there, that there.' O'Hare pointed. 'Right there.'

Anderson saw a flash of white, there and gone, coming back into view a few feet further on, then sliding under to disappear. At first he thought it was some fish, caught in the shallows, darting out and in the water before he could see them. 'What are they?' He leaned forward a little to see better. O'Hare put out a restraining hand.

'Bones.'

SEVEN

'Hi, I was told you wanted another body so you weren't on your own. Standing in the cold. Getting pissing wet.'

'I asked for a constable,' muttered Anderson.

'Tough, you have me. I didn't even get to finish my bacon roll, so this had better be good.' Costello zipped up her bright red jacket and looked over at the woods, turning her back to the hole. 'OK, so what are we doing? Scene of one of the most horrific murders in history over there and a hole in the ground here.' She walked round the recovery vehicle that blocked the end of Altmore Road, feeling like a late arrival to a good party.

'They will get the Range Rover back to the garage, then the street will be clear.' Anderson followed her eye line, looking up the street: four houses on one side, the forest on the other.

'I asked what are we doing here, not what are they doing here?'

'Getting some background stuff. O'Hare and Darvel are dealing with some bones. Bones at the bottom of the hole.'

Costello gave him her slow head-turn. 'Bones?'

'Old bones probably. Walker is watching on the camera feed.'

'From the dry warmth of the van. God, he has a tough job.' She walked after Anderson, who was now striding on, up the middle of the deserted road, a man in charge.

'Prof Darvel? The forensic archaeologist?'

'Anthropologist, you were nearly right.'

'Oh, she's great. Remember her giving Mulholland a flask of coffee and a custard doughnut at that crime scene on Chancellor Street, four in the morning, minus ten?'

'I wasn't there.'

'Lucky you,' Costello continued. 'Soaking wet, freezing cold, I thought Mulholland was going to ask her to marry him.' She stopped walking. 'I wonder if that was the start of it.'

'Start of what?'

'Start of Vik joining the human race. Do you know who he is seeing now? "Seeing", as in a "staying overnight and sharing a toothbrush" kind of way?'

'No. Who?' Anderson was distracted.

'Lucrezia Borgia,' said Costello.

'Good,' said Anderson, standing stock still in the rain in the middle of the road, looking up at the big dark house at the top of the road. The dark, uninviting windows and the ivy-clad walls gave it the appearance of a living, breathing thing. If left to their own devices, the trees would swallow up that house, the forest devour it. The road they were standing on must have been the old driveway to the house, back in the day when the land and the wood were all owned by the same person. Anderson looked at the trees and turned away, feeling the panic rising. 'Anything could happen in there and we'd never know.' He looked from the woods to Costello. 'This has been going on for five hours now. The water level in the hole must drop soon. The bones are being stranded and from the top they look human. The views from the camera confirm that. O'Hare is sending somebody to collect them once it is safe to go down the hole. Until there is a logical reason for those bones to be where they are, then we are in charge.'

Costello wondered in charge of what exactly. 'So what do you want me to do? A house-to-house? A mis-per search?' And did not add, *And when does a DI and a DCI go on a house-to-house?* Doing background stuff. In the pissing rain. And why is a DCI here anyway; if this was anybody's job, it was hers. He should be confined to the office like Walker said he should be.

Anderson, his hand sheltering his eyes from the rain, suddenly turned round to face her, as if aware of her unspoken question. 'I need to be here, to see this. I need to prove that I can still do the job. So we are going to do what we would usually do.'

She smiled at him, getting soaked, feeling the water run down the back of her neck. 'Of course you can still do the bloody job.'

'I'm touched you have such faith in me,' he said, smiling. The skin round his eyes looked dry and reptilian. Those cold eyes used to crackle with fun and wit and intelligence. There was still something very, very wrong.

'Not really. Any stupid git can do this job,' Costello said, and strode onward.

'Let's start with number 10. Greene said that they didn't come out to the sinkhole.' Anderson started on his way over to the two-storey house, with badly painted window frames and grass two feet high in the front garden. Cheap IKEA blinds hung in the small windows. The date 1875 was carved from the gentle sandstone in an arc over the front door.

'Weird street, isn't it? Like a microcosm of the city. All this really old stuff becoming fashionable, boho chic and the dreadful middle classes bringing their coffee shops and couscous with them. The guy in the recovery vehicle said the shop that used to unlock mobile phones on the parade is now an organic grocer. The Chelsea tractors are alive and well and ploughing up the working classes. Ten years ago this street was full of folk whose grannies could walk round to babysit. It would have been lovely.'

'Crap,' said Costello. 'Ten years ago this street was still reeling from the Melrose murders. People visited the woods to see where it all happened. Gyle's defence counsel have even consulted psychics to see if the spirits of the dead will pop back and tell us all who did it.'

'That would put an end to Legal Aid,' muttered Anderson.

'The result of it all on this mortal plane is that house prices plummeted. And there is increasing talk of getting rid of the wood, developing the area to be rid of the memory. Building a whole load of luxury flats. You can see how much they'd be worth. Twenty minutes from the airport, twenty minutes from the town centre. Yet so isolated, so secluded.'

'Changing the street name would remove the association with the murders.'

'Doesn't make the property developers a lot of money though, does it?' She punched him lightly on the shoulder. 'You didn't associate it, did you?'

So she had noticed. 'Not at first. How could I have forgotten that?' Anderson turned and looked at the wood on the far side of the road. That little connection had been lost. It was not at the front of his mind the way it should be.

'Been off your work too long, you've started thinking like a normal person. Come on.' Costello walked up the path. 'I wonder how many kids in this street go to the local school now. Tojo and Squiffy definitely don't. Big posh school for them.'

'Tabitha and Sorrell,' corrected Anderson, a brief look at his watch. Claire would be at school now.

'Whatever.' She knocked on the badly painted door, flaking and swollen from the onslaught of rain. As she waited, she looked round at the front garden, an overgrown patchwork of water and rainfall. It was sodden wet like everywhere else. 'Is this rain ever going to stop?'

'Wet weather warnings are out for the West of Scotland. Floods, be prepared and all that.'

'So that will be a no then.' She knocked again.

No answer. She leaned over, balancing on the top of the step to look in the window. 'There's a book on the arm of the chair; looks like they have gone out, except nobody saw them. They might have pulled an all-nighter and are still snoring it off.'

They were turning away when the front door of number 8 opened. A small woman stood behind, wrapped in a stained housecoat that had been white once. Dark brown hair, unbrushed and messy, was piled on top of her head, dark creases circled her eyes. She leaned against the open door, as if too tired to hold herself up.

'Did we interrupt you?' They held up their warrant cards as they walked down the weedy path of number 10 and then up the cracked slabs of number 8.

She looked at them, her big brown eyes opened even further.

She glanced down the street to where the fire appliance was now reversing to let the recovery vehicle out. 'Is it about that?' she asked, jerking her head towards the commotion at the bottom of the road.

'In a manner of speaking, please can we come in?'

Costello looked at the sky. 'Yeah, it's pissing wet out here.'

Jennifer opened the door wider, ashamed of the smell, of the state of the house. She grasped the collar of her housecoat closed, and pulled the belt tighter, then kicked the baby's pram and harness out from behind the door. Costello noticed that she was bare legged but wore outdoor leather slip-on shoes. They entered the living room, a dim room with dark brown walls. The cream-coloured wallpaper on the fireplace wall was stained with damp circles and fungus ferns. The décor was much older than this young woman, the dubious taste of the previous owners, no doubt. The house had an appearance of one where nothing fitted, nothing matched and nobody cared.

Two small children were asleep in the middle of the floor in front of an electric fire, one bar sending an orange glow over their restful faces. The slight heat it generated high-lighted how cold and damp the air was. It might not be drier outside, but it was warmer. Anderson stepped over to the baby, folded up in a Pooh Bear duvet. He noticed tiny marks on his face.

'They have been asleep for about two minutes,' the woman said, wary of the policeman so near her child. She was wondering what plain-clothes officers were doing here. There had been a few uniformed ones at the bottom of the road, but she thought plain clothes were more like detectives, serious stuff. Maybe somebody got hurt, one of the double-barrelleds from number 2. The man was looking closely at Gordy, inspecting him. She bit her lip. Her kids were well cared for, although they might not look it.

'You look like you have your hands full. I didn't catch your name?'

'Jennifer. Jennifer Lawson.' Had she done something wrong? Had anything happened to Douglas?

'What age are they?' He was rubbing his little finger along

Gordy's cheek now; her baby woke with a good-humoured giggle. It was more than he ever did to her.

Jennifer looked from one to the other. The blond man was happy to kneel on her dirty carpet, leaning over the baby, having a peering competition. The female officer with the sharp face stayed in the corner, arms folded, watching her. She knew that's what cops did. One asked the questions as the other one watched for telltale signs of deceit, but would the cop mistake deceit for the simple inability to think straight after three sleepless nights?

'How old?'

'Six months and two. Two and a bit.'

The blond man stood up. He smiled at her, pretending to be charming. She hadn't caught their names, but she had seen enough episodes of *Taggart* to know that they weren't normal police, and it would be normal police who attended sinkholes. This lot were definitely here about something else.

'Do you live alone?' the small female asked, her eyes wandering over the clothes rack, strewn with Babygros, a pair of her jeans, a couple of T-shirts. There was more on the top of the radiator. The laundry all said single mother not coping with young children. Her narrow eyes clocked the pile of dirty clothes at the door and the sofa so full of junk that nobody could sit down. She had ignored the boys totally. She pulled her wet, short hair behind her ears, making her face look skeletal, and revealing a lightning-shaped scar above one eyebrow while she flashed Jennifer a quick half-smile. She reminded Jennifer of a P6 teacher she had hated.

'Am I in any trouble?'

'Not at all. Do you mind if we sit down?'

Oh no, they meant to stay. 'Why?'

'We've been standing out there for ages,' lied Anderson. 'And you needed to get out the street? Are you OK?'

And they expected her to believe that? 'They told me to stay in. I couldn't come out with the boys, could I? I have been trying to get them to sleep all night – just as they go over, all that screeching starts at the bottom of the road. Why are you here?' she asked again, but pointed to the sofa. 'Either end, don't sit in the middle, he's peed on that.' She swivelled her fingertip at the small pool in the dip of the leather sofa cushion.

'You trying to potty-train him?'

'Yeah – not very well, though. He prefers to pee on the sofa.'

'So how long have you lived here?' asked Anderson.

'Two years . . . seems like a life sentence.'

'Have a seat, Jennifer, we need to ask you a few background questions.'

'Why? It's just a hole in the road,' said Jennifer, staying where she was.

'I asked the same question,' said Costello, looking out the window.

'We were told to make sure that everybody was accounted for. You'd think we didn't have enough to do,' he lied, beaming Jennifer a smile, a shrug of the shoulders. *Bosses? What can you do?*

Jennifer slid on to the arm of the chair, pulling her housecoat around her, tighter. 'OK. What do you want to know?'

'Do you stay here on your own, with the kids?'

'No, my husband lives here, Douglas Lawson.'

'Is he here at the moment?'

Jennifer was about to answer when Gordy started coughing. She went to the child, kneeling down beside him, loosening off the Babygro button at his neck. 'He's at work.'

Costello made a face; this was like pulling teeth.

'He's always at work,' continued Jennifer, rubbing the baby's tummy as it coughed and wheezed, legs kicking in the air. 'We have a flat in Edinburgh, he stays there a lot during the week.'

'What does he do?'

'He's a banker, an investment banker. Some folk would call him a criminal.' She smiled at her little joke.

'How old are you, Jennifer?'

'Twenty-two. Has something happened to Douglas?' Panic spread across her face for a moment, giving her face a flush of youth.

'No, nothing. It does leave you with a lot to do, though. Do you have any support round here?'

'No, I manage,' she pulled herself straight. 'So how can I help you?'

'Not much, if you have only been here a year,' said Costello, noting how Jennifer's eyes flicked out the window to the wood beyond. Something connected. 'Do you know your neighbours well?'

Jennifer shook her head.

'Not any of them? Surely you have wee chats over the garden fence while hanging out the washing? A hello while you bring the shopping in from the car?'

But Jennifer shook her head with a wry smile. 'No, but the street has its own Peeping Tom. The old guy from Altmore House, Castle Grayskull more like. Never peeps at me, though.'

Costello made a note. 'But neighbours? Friends?'

'No, they go to work. They go out in the morning, they come back at night. I was thinking this morning, when the woman from number twelve – Laura? – went out running with her poodle. I did wave at her but she didn't see me.'

'But you lived here when the wee guy was born. Didn't they come around and say hello or bring you presents? When my oldest was born, the house turned into some kind of café.'

Costello, still at the door, folded her arms and sighed.

Jennifer shook her head.

'How old is Douglas?' Costello indicated the photograph on the mantelpiece, 'Is that him?'

'Yes. He's thirty-four. He's very busy at work.'

'Did you know anything about the area – you know, before you bought it?' Costello asked, looking at the mould on the wall.

'Oh yes,' her face relaxed. 'I knew about the murders across the road. And because of that we got the house under the market value. Douglas knew about that and he was right, because with the new development going on over the hill, this land is going to be really valuable. They need the access road. I mean a thirty-five – maybe forty per cent – mark-up. So this is the investment and the real house is the Edinburgh flat. It's a really nice flat.' Her rapid flow of words made it sound as though she had said this a lot, if only to herself.

'But you and the kids stay here, so this is the proper home, and it should be warmer than this, Jennifer.'

'I know, but the boiler is a pain in the bum. There's no point in fixing it, though, not when the house is going to get pulled down.'

'Will they get planning permission for that?' Costello asked, her voice doubtful.

'Why – have you heard anything?' Jennifer wondered why they were asking her, 'I heard it was all going through.'

'The sinkhole might put a stop to it.'

'Oh God, don't say that I am going to be stuck here.' Her deflation was almost comical.

'It would be a lovely house if it was done up. Look what the Dirk-Huntleys have done with theirs,' said Anderson.

'A lot of money and a lot of work.'

Gordy started coughing again.

'I gave up and bought brand new,' said Costello, joining in the useless chitchat as Anderson made no sign of leaving.

'The Edinburgh flat is a new build. I've only been at it twice.'

Gordy started to splutter, going red in the face, his body writhing, back arching. Jennifer leaned forward to pick him up. She dug around in her housecoat pocket for a tissue and began to dab him round his nostrils and his streaming eyes. A hand presented her with another tissue; it was Anderson, now kneeling beside her. The coughing went on and on. Gordy started to go blue.

'Jennifer, have you had him to the doctor?'

'I was going to go today, but I need the double pram to get down to the bus stop and it is a long walk down to the parade. Then the sinkhole happened and I sort of lost track of time.' She hung her head and shook some sense into her fuzzy brain. 'Are you going to tell social services?'

'No. Don't you have a car Jennifer? You need one to live here; there's nothing close by.'

She shook her head again.

Costello smirked as she asked, 'I bet your husband does a big mileage?'

'Yes, and he needs a good car, he needs to go to Edinburgh.'

Costello mouthed the word *wanker* in the direction of Douglas's photograph, a handsome, Beckham-esque, metrosexual face.

The coughing continued.

'There are trains to Edinburgh, I believe,' said Costello, but her sarcasm was lost in Jennifer's submissive shrug. 'You need a car.'

'Jennifer, I don't like the marks on him, we need to get him checked out. Do you want to have a shower?'

'There's no water, now . . .' said Jennifer, her voice weak by the onslaught of life that was blowing in her face.

'Oh, so . . . and you wouldn't think about going to a neighbour?'

'Like I said, I don't know any of them. I might try the tap again; it turned off. Maybe all the water is in the sinkhole. The pipes were making noises earlier.'

Anderson lifted Gordy up from the floor.

'Be careful, he will pee on you.'

'He's had two kids, he's used to it,' said Costello, making herself comfy, leaning on the window ledge. It was nice to be out and about, however bizarre the day was turning out.

Jennifer trundled into the kitchen, turned on the tap, which gurgled and spluttered. She hoped they would get bored and go away if she hid in here for long enough. She could hear them talk on the other side of the door that refused to close. Muttering, talking about her and her sick children and her terrible house with its awful smell. The tap suddenly spurted into life; a fountain of ice-cold water hit her arm. She tried to turn it off but the tap handle turned, and turned, and then came off in her hand. The water spouted like a geyser. She stepped back; there was water running all over the floor, a small wave pushing over the cracked lino, creating a pattern of rivers and islands, carrying dirt and grime with it.

Then the man appeared in the doorway, still holding Gordy in his arms.

She must have cried out loud or sworn as his first question was, *'What's wrong?'*

She started to cry, so he handed her the baby, then asked her where there was a hammer or a set of pliers.

'Under the stairs, I think; there's a tool box there but I don't know what's in it,' she sobbed.

She stood aside as the tall policeman got to work, his strong hands gripping the pliers on the broken tap, those same hands then tapping it gently with the hammer. He reminded Jennifer of her dad. He swore a few times, muttering something about the pressure being too high.

'It wasn't like that before,' Jennifer sniffed, 'it was only a trickle.'

Anderson looked up at the ceiling, then to the mildew in the far corner of the floor.

The coughing started again. Costello was now standing in the doorway, looking at the baby. 'Jennifer, I think you really need to get the wee chap to the hospital – he is going blue round the mouth.'

'Yes, God, what am I doing, I need to get ready and get the pram out, I need to . . . but I can't get a taxi. They won't get through.'

'Jennifer, we are the police, we can get the boys to blue-light it, so go and get dressed.'

She looked at them. 'What?'

'Just go and get dressed, bring down stuff for the kids.'

She nodded and walked upstairs, her shoes leaving wet footprints on the dusty carpet.

EIGHT

Trying to overcome the pain, Lynda attempted to get up again, but her knee snapped sideways. The pain ceased. But now it wouldn't move at all. It was not fit for purpose. That was something her daughter had said to her, the stupid wee shit. Babs had turned round after a spectacularly horrific argument, stood at the door and told her they were leaving the country so she would never see her grandchildren again. Never be allowed to give them presents at Christmas or their birthday kisses. All because she enjoyed a drink or two. All because she was not 'fit for purpose'. Well, fuck them.

She had no idea where Babs was. No idea where Babs' dad was either. Well, that was men for you.

She tried again to get herself up on her elbow, keeping her eyes screwed up, her mouth closed to keep the flies out, but one arm was stuck underneath her like she was trying to waltz with the carpet. She found that funny. Still not lost the sense of humour then.

She lay back down resting. She would gather her strength and do some more shouting. She could hear the front door of number 8 opening and closing, so somebody was about.

Lynda closed her eyes, and drifted off.

'So what are we investigating exactly?' Costello asked, pulling on her boot after inspecting her sore foot. 'Anderson is driving Little Miss Daisy to hospital? I mean, why? As far as I am aware it is not against the law to be an obnoxious wanker. Or nearly drown the family dog in a sinkhole. A few bones swirling round in water is hardly news. Especially when the water is running off a hill where there is an old graveyard. Or do you think there is a crime but you are not telling us? Or do you *know?*' She looked at Walker closely, but there was no response in his hazel eyes. 'It is crazy if you are getting us to investigate something without us knowing what it is. How much is that going to mess with Anderson's head? You have tried to treat us like your own little investigative team before, and look what happened.'

'I want you to do a house-to-house. I want to confirm without any possibility of doubt that this was investigated in full and found not to be connected to the Melrose case in anyway. Make sure that everybody from this area is accounted for. No exculpatory evidence for Gyle; Police Scotland's reputation is in the gutter right now. As you well know.'

'But Sue Melrose's body was discovered within minutes of her murder, so no bones went walkabout. Gyle is serving life without parole for killing her and the boys. So why are we even doing a house-to-house?' Costello, having anticipated a day in the office in flat shoes, was now very wet, her blister complaining bitterly in the walking boots. 'Do we not have low-paid types in a uniform to do that job?'

'It's a street of four buildings, Costello – just do it. You are more experienced and quicker. And will get the gist. Just find out how long people have lived here, then get Wyngate to cross-check the records. OK?' Walker sighed, the sigh of a patient teacher trying to instil the obvious into a particularly thick pupil.

She stayed put.

'Costello, I am not going to stand here in the pissing rain and argue with you. Somebody has to write a report and Anderson is away with Mrs Lawson.'

'I hope the kid pukes all over him,' Costello said. She was wet through now, her hair sticking to her head. Her jacket was waterproof but the zip was not. She was soaked down the middle, which was even more uncomfortable than being soaked all over. And her foot was now warm, and she bet that was blood-loss from her blister.

She trudged across the road, avoiding the pipes and the hoses. The fireman hung around in the rain drinking tea and coffee. Somebody, rumoured to be the owner of the big house that looked like Castle Grayskull, had even brought out ginger biscuits. That would be the Peeping Tom, if Jennifer was to be believed. She saw another new face standing, taking the sight in, forties, good suit under a golfing umbrella. A lawyer or a civil engineer. Nobody was talking to him.

The mood had lifted, even if the weather had not. She caught a few bits of gossip as she passed. There had been a round of applause as the dog had been brought up out of the hole, but nothing when Howard had. He was 'an arse'. Esther was already away, described by Greene as 'that torn-faced woman from number two'. Costello knew the type; Esther would make her own bread and claim her kids suffered from all kinds of extraordinary allergies.

Costello walked to the gossip huddle. The fire service was still trying to pump the sinkhole empty of water as the rain was filling it back up again. The flatbed was ready with the plastic cover, crisscrossed and anti-slip. Lots of men in high-vis gear were standing around chatting about the state of the Range Rover, getting very wet while debating how much it cost and then feeling rather smug.

'Who's the dude in the good suit?' she asked.

Greene looked up, shook his head. 'Search me.'

Costello looked round to see him walk towards a white four-by-four, private plate MGH 3211. She could have run after him, but her foot was too sore, so she turned round and limped back up the street, where the old man was carrying a tray of empty mugs, walking with a stiffness of the limbs that suggested he had arthritis. An old collie tootled at his heels with a similarly rolling style. The Peeping Tom. He was still strong looking, tall and broad. Maybe Walker was right to have her snoop around, now they had a reason.

He stopped at his gate, taking his time to balance the tray on his arm as he fiddled with the latch, then he turned and looked down the street, giving Costello a hard stare from eyes the colour of washed-out denim. She continued to watch him. He walked past his own front door and disappeared round the back.

Altmore House was a large rambling place over three floors, with views over all it once owned. It had all gone full circle; now he was in poverty and the nouveau riche were moving in at the bottom of Altmore Road.

Or was that the problem? The first cottage, the Dirk-Huntleys, had their mono-blocked front drive swallowed up by the ground. Had they been renovating and disturbed something? An old mine? A culvert? The gossip said a civil engineer had unearthed a report saying there were a few disused drains within a hundred meters. It could just be the weight of the recent rainwater. A further survey with penetrating radar was being instructed to ensure the rest of the road was safe, but that would need to wait until the weather had improved.

The panic was over. It was 'one of those things'.

Still, it was impossible to buy a house these days without getting land searches and home reports. If this subsidence trouble was extensive, then some lawyer somewhere was in trouble.

The thought cheered her up as she walked past the rubbish tip of a garden at number 6 to number 4, the bright house, painted white, as neat as a new pin. It had a neat postage stamp for a front garden. Cheapo mono-block and planters from Lidl. It was a B&M type of house. There were houses like that in suburban estates all over the city. The original charm of the property had been smoothed over with white paint; it looked like a new crown in a row of old teeth. This was the home of Michael Broadfoot, his wife, Rachel, plus a teenage daughter, Cadena, if her notes from Wyngate were correct.

And he was never wrong.

A large man opened the door, wearing an X-Men vest and jogging bottoms, a leather pendant hanging loosely round his flabby neck. Even standing four feet away, she could smell the heady mix of last night's whisky and rank BO. He had his long wavy hair pulled back into an unconvincing ponytail.

But he was the one who had put himself at risk to pull the boy clear.

'Oh right hen,' he sniffed, 'in you come. Do you know when the road is going to be open? This is a blind end, you know. Canny have the road shut too long.'

'It's a rather unusual event you must admit.' Costello showed her warrant card but he was already waddling down his hall to the kitchen. She followed to get out of the rain.

'Ah'm supposed to be at the docs at three, no gonny make that, am ah?'

She stood inside their front door, noticing that this house had the wall between the hall and the living room taken down, making the ground floor open plan. There was the teenager from the sinkhole, built like her dad, dyed black hair and power eyebrows, wrapped in a pink fluffy onesie. That would be Cadena. She looked over at Costello with mild interest, smiled and waved a puffy hand, and then went back to her music video, the sound pulsing through her earphones.

'Then you will probably have to get the bus from the bottom of the parade. They can't open the road up until the engineers give the all-clear,' said Costello, positioning herself so she was dripping on the mat rather than on the very well-polished laminate floor.

Broadfoot leaned back to look at her through the archway to the kitchen, 'Aye, and pigs fly, Ah'll just gie the appointment a miss.'

'So you were the hero of the hour, pulling the boy out.'

He shrugged.

'Do you know your neighbours well?' she asked, half shouting down the hall.

'Well, Ah wouldnae have pulled his da out the car, stupid fucker. Nope, they are a couple of stuck-up tossers. I wish that sinkhole had swallowed the whole bloody lot of them, as well as their fucking dog. Anything else?' He reappeared through the archway and walked back past Costello, his socked feet padding their way on the hard floor, a full laundry basket tucked under his elbow.

'So not close friends then?' Costello asked.

'Jumped-up arses. The both of them; the bloody kids are even worse.'

'And you live here with Rachel?'

'Aye? Cannae get rid of her, the silly mare.'

'We are making sure that everybody is accounted for. Anybody else live here?'

'That lazy trollop in there,' he pointed at the girl in the living room.

Costello wiped her feet and ventured further into the hall, moving out of the way as Broadfoot passed with the laundry basket. He opened the door into the cupboard under the stairs, pulled out an iron. He slammed the door closed; it bounced and immediately sprung open again.

'Those bloody neighbours are just arseholes.' He shook his head, as if that explained everything.

'And the other neighbour?' She flicked her head in the direction of the adjoining house.

Broadfoot paused and sighed, like Costello had asked a really stupid question. 'That was the McMutrie girl's house. She's in Spain now, running away from you lot and living high on her man's ill-gotten gains.'

'Oh,' smiled Costello nicely, 'Nobody ever tells me anything. Have you seen or heard from her since she left?'

'Nope. Neither has her mum. She's still two doors up.'

'Ah, we knocked at number ten.'

'She'll be pissed.' He flicked a look at his superhero watch. 'And then there's the wee lassie with the two bairns and the wanker of a husband.'

'Jennifer?' confirmed Costello.

'There's another couple of wankers at the top. He drives the big motor and works at Goodbodies gym in town. Rumour is, he owns it.'

'Oh, I have heard of that,' said Costello, sensing that Cadena was listening now. 'Don't mean to be rude, but if they have that kind of money . . .'

'Why are they living in this shithole?' Broadfoot grinned. 'Oh, well, if the developer gets planning permission for the through road, then we are all quids-in. Nice flats here, knock down all these wee stupid houses. Can't stop progress hen, can you? It'll be like winning the bloody lottery.'

'Yes, I heard that.'

'Five years we have been waiting, and now that bloody sinkhole appears. But Ah've just phoned a mate and he says it might be good, you know. If they need to strengthen the road anyway, they may as well make it a through-road.'

'To the development over the hill?' Costello asked.

'Aye, the planning has been knocking about for years. But as soon as the road goes through we'll be in the money. Space-wise, we should have moved long ago.'

'But the house at the top? It's in the way, surely?'

'That monstrosity? That needs to go.'

'Is he up for selling it, the old guy?'

'Fuck no, stupid old bugger. He won't sell, but he's old. Sorry to be a hard-arse, but he's dodged his coffin for too long that one. We are in the money, sure as death and taxes.' Broadfoot winked. His mobile went and he dug around in his pocket, swiped at the screen and said, 'Yip Petal, aye, Ah know. Ah've got the police here about the hole, hang on.' He turned to Costello. 'It's the missus.'

She moved towards the front door. 'I'll let you get on with it.'

'Look hen, you can go out the back way if you are inter-ested. You can see what we have to put up with from the hyphenateds.'

Costello made her way along the hall, ignoring the mess in the kitchen in front of her, a cooker full of oily pans and something that was on a permanent rolling boil, while listening to the one-way diatribe against the fucking idiots next door and that bloody smell was still minging the house out. Costello could smell it from there – a real animal-yard stink of manure and urine, like old socks and month-old goat's cheese. The landing of the basement stairs was full of all the usual stuff: boxes, DVDs, a couple of suitcases. A dehu-midifier hummed away, so Jennifer wasn't the only one with dampness problems.

She walked through the kitchen to the back door, still listening to Broadfoot talking down the phone, leaning casually on the wall, 'Yeah well, Ah don't know, they had to pull it out the water and then the cops appeared and they are here now, he's away to the hospital . . .' He waved his arm at Costello, who was trying to open the back door, telling her to bump the door with her hip. It was still pouring down outside.

'Yes, Ah know you were late for work . . . aye she's still here, lying on the sofa . . . No, she's done bugger all.'

The conversation was that of a usual family, bound by love but who sounded as though they couldn't stand the sight of each other. Costello bet Anderson yearned for that type of conversation these days. She opened the back door by the key that was stuck in the lock, gave it a good dunt with her hip, pulled her hood up and slid into the back garden. Three steps down.

To the north, there was an overgrown back garden of a house that used to have children, a broken trampoline and some kind of hut thing that looked like three sides of a permanent Wendy house. To the south, the fence was more like the Berlin Wall at the height of the Cold War. The bottom boundary of the garden was a thick hawthorn hedge that ran the full length of the cottages. The ground was sodden and slippy under her feet, grass flattened by the endless rain. Or footprints, or a fox maybe, running along the grass at the bottom of the fence, looking for a way in to the chickens next door. Even with her eye right up at the wood of the fence, she couldn't see through it. So she went back to stand at the top of the three steps, pulling herself up on the handrail to see over the fence.

The smell was different here. The air had a nasty tang: rotting vegetation, scorched hair and fresh manure. She could hear sound of something crunching. The garden next door looked like a scene from the Somme. Mud, mud, and more mud. There was a chicken coop, raised up off the ground. The goat, a black and white creature, was standing at the back of a pen, near the door but still under the shelter of the roof. Beside the goat was a filthy golden retriever that regarded her with sad eyes. She was feeling very sorry for herself. The rest of the garden was mapped out in neat rows for veg and plastic tunnels for fruit, with two big greenhouses at the back. All waterlogged.

The smell was unbelievable. The Broadfoots' garden would get no sun because of the height of the partition. Looking across the grass, Costello thought she could detect the faint imprint of flattened grass down to the hawthorn, where there was a gap. Somebody used the path at the bottom of the gardens? The Peeping Tom?

Her phone went. Archie. She walked back through the house, passing Broadfoot.

'I need to take this call,' she said.

Broadfoot nodded out the window. 'Can you do something about them next door, all that noise and stink? It mings like a Greek wrestler's arse.'

'Better hope that you can move soon then, eh?' said Costello, and left through the front door before she got involved in any neighbourhood disputes.

Colin Anderson made a point of going home at five thirty. His first day had been OK, apart from the bolt to the hospital, which he knew was an escape, but he had needed it. He had steeled himself to return to the station, but all was normal, just a different normal. He had spent an hour drinking coffee and reading a background report on the behaviour of some previous residents of Altmore Road.

Costello had already flagged up to the team the disappearing act of Barbara McMutrie, and at the moment her mother was none too visible either.

Most of the reports were about Iain McFettridge McPherson, a name like a bad Scrabble hand. He had lived at number 6 with his two young kids and his girlfriend, the elusive Barbara. From the reports, Barbara had been trouble since the day she was born. From vandalism to housebreaking, then a wee bit of dealing to a big bit of dealing, and then Barbara and Iain had got themselves in trouble with one of the big boys. Though who that might be in that part of town these days was anybody's guess. It might have some bearing on the bones, if they were recent, and the result of a violent death.

He wondered how Claire had got on at school today, her first day back. She should be in class with her old friends, but after a year out she was now adrift educationally. It would be too much stress for her to catch up, but equally too stressful to sit in a class of people she didn't know. And why was he putting her through that? They were rich, Claire didn't need to work. But that would be too easy for her. She needed normality with her peers right now.

What would happen when they found out about the inheritance was anybody's guess. He couldn't bear to think about that.

So at half five he'd picked up his car keys and walked out, not remembering how he normally said goodbye. He settled for a wave. Wyngate and Mulholland, deep in an argument about Scottish independence, ignored him. But he saw the photographs from the file they were reviewing. The body of Sue Melrose, her head against the Clachan Stone of the Doon. In the foreground was a blood-splattered sunflower hat. To the side, a small blue bear lay next to an axe. Anderson averted his eyes and walked.

When he got home they were laughing. It stopped the minute he walked into the living room. He said hello, kissed Brenda, who was tackling a huge pile of ironing. The source of their humour was the awful Seventies sitcom on ITV3, where a Cockney bus driver had sat on a fish supper.

He went to ruffle his daughter's hair but didn't, stopping himself in time.

Brenda gave him a look, *Don't push it.* 'Peter is in his room, as usual,' she said, stomping the iron on to a crumpled shirt. She had stopped work early to collect Claire from school, in case there had been a wobble. 'Lots of jokes on the radio today about holes in the road.'

'It's a police matter,' he said.

Brenda almost laughed; even Claire turned her head away from the bus driver, now standing in comedy long johns.

'Yip. Long story.' He thought about kissing her cheek, giving her a cuddle.

'Was it OK?' she asked, vaguely.

'I am glad to be back.' And he felt the sweat on his lip as he asked the question. 'So, Claire. How did you two get on today?'

Brenda answered, 'As well as could be expected. Your dinner

is in the oven. We've already had ours, it's only macaroni cheese.' He turned round to take a shirt from Brenda and slid it on to a hanger to hang on the sconce on the wall. And that was all it took for Claire to leave the room, slipping out silently like a ghost. Then she whispered, 'She coped well today. It's been a big step. So how was your day, really?'

'Difficult, a few wobbles. Do you want a coffee?'

'I'll finish this first.'

He walked into the kitchen; the oven was purring gently. He took out the dish of macaroni, the cheesy skin already browning. He opened the cupboards to look for the brown sauce. Peter put it in the fridge, Brenda kept it in the cupboard. Claire didn't like it and put it in the bin. He looked in the fridge, there was a bottle of tomato ketchup. He took it out and turned it upside down, splattering the contents on the side of the plate.

The red liquid splattered. He no longer saw the cheese and the pasta. He saw a little sunflower hat, splattered with blood.

He made it to the sink before he was violently sick.

NINE

Saturday 22 August 2015

Lynda McMutrie was lying in the basement of number 10, drifting in and out of unconsciousness. Time had passed. She was hungry and really needed to empty her bladder. She couldn't get up on her feet. Her knee was sore; it was better to sleep to let it pass. Except each time she woke up, the pain was still there. Every time she moved, the agony in her knee was like a blunt saw going through the bone.

She shouted for help. She called. She was ignored.

God, she needed a drink.

She drifted off, the pain fading and the daydreams drifting to warm fantasies of the man in the photograph. Her face felt peculiar – prickly, but nicely prickly, as if something warm and furry was rubbing at the soft skin of her neck, like her lover when she was young. Her lover's stubble stroking her cheek, his fingertips dancing across her eyelids. She would get up and leave the cottage, walk into the wood to meet him at the Doon and snog his face off on the Clachan Stone – in the early days, that was. Later, there would be a lot more than snogging on that stone. Her heart still gave a little flutter when she thought of the way he was then. To be truthful, her heart still did when she bumped into him now. Not that she was often out of the house these days; drink lasts a long time in the cupboard.

She thought of that poem 'Maud Muller', where he was the judge and she was the maid. And that last line, she couldn't recall. Not any of it. She sailed off on a sea of sleep as she reminisced, reliving the way he nibbled at her ears, making her laugh. Lying in the grass with her good-for-nothing lover, that beautiful handsome man, and how her parents had disapproved. And how that had appealed to her rebellious nature! Oh, his fair hair, that chiselled square jaw and that wicked gleam in his eyes. He could always make her laugh. She had climbed out of her window and he would be at the bottom of the parade on his old motorbike. Which was too knackered to go anywhere, so they just sneaked into the wood instead.

Life would have been good.

It would have been so different if . . .

How did that bloody poem go again? Something about the saddest words being 'If only . . .'

If only her parents hadn't split them up. If only she had been strong enough to stand up to them.

He had never married. He had never left. He was still here, in front of her, constantly reminding her of a life she could have enjoyed. It was the constant regret that made her drink, but she'd never confessed that to him, the big-headed bastard.

Recalling those days, those days spent with him, deep in these woods having picnics, drinking cheap wine and smoking French cigarettes. His dog, what was it called? A wee black dog that would take biscuits out of her mouth; the dog's little teeth nibbled her lips gently. It had tickled then and it was tickling now. What had made her remember that all of a sudden? It was a good ratter, that wee dog.

*   *   *

On Saturday morning, Jock climbed the opposite way, going round the north end of cottages to get on to the hills before cutting back to his own house. He wanted to see what the new development was doing.

Down on the street he could see the line of official cars at the side of the wood. So the police were still interested in something. He looked down into the Steeles' back garden as he went past. Their plastic grass was very green but unconvincing.

The drunken bitch at number 10 hadn't been seen for a few days, so she would be on a bender. At number 4, the Broadfoots' garden was almost under water. Next door, the scarfed harpy had taken the kids and the cleaned-up dog to the summer cottage for the weekend. Dad was in hospital, so it was left to the Polish nanny to pop in and feed the goat and the chickens.

The wee lassie at number 8 hadn't been seen since they went off in a police car yesterday.

All food for thought. The husband certainly wasn't back for the weekend.

His curiosity salved, he went on his way. Betty following him so close he could feel her body on the side of his leg. They walked round the back of his own house, up the path to the old graveyard. He had seen the cops on the hill looking for disturbance. There was nothing obvious on the surface, but Jock knew what he was looking for, what the cops would miss. They needed to know the land. The grass undulated under his steps, where the lairs had dropped down, the soil eaten away. Some of the movement had been slow; that was usual in an untended graveyard like this one, and the grass had time to adapt and grow longer in the nitrogen-rich burial site, and hid the depressions in the ground. So the seemingly flat surface was a trap to unwary walkers and hikers taking a short-cut. It was being eaten away from underneath in a slow, ongoing process of decay. Just like what was happening in the street below.

Jock was looking for something more recent, a dropping of the ground level, a precursor of a sinkhole. Eight feet long, three feet wide, and he found them exactly where he thought he would. He felt his heart weary. They were not in the contour line of the hill, but at the bottom, a gentle curve. Three of them, probably only visible from this elevated viewpoint. It was recent

enough for fresh earth to show; earth as fresh as that on the
side of the sinkhole outside the wanker's house.

He found a depression under his toe and felt around, four
inches deep for most of its six-feet length. He wondered if it
had contained any of his family. Prodding with his stick told
him that the soil was soft but not overly so. It was wet with
the constant rainfall of the last month. They had endured rain
like that here before, of course. The snow and ice drifts eventually melted and ran off the hills to cause problems, but not like
this. He walked on, past the remains of the old church. Betty,
keen on the newly exposed soil, trotted around, nose to the
ground, exploring then sniffing then sneezing. On he walked,
up the slow rise of the hill that began at the back of his house.
It took him forty minutes to get to the top; this hill, Saircoch,
was an old extension of the Kilpatricks, the run-off here was
down to the Clyde eventually.

Eventually.

The land in the woods was dry and it shouldn't be. Over the
years he had installed a drainage system that was now wet, but
not flooded, not overwhelmed the way they should be in this
weather.

Jock Aird was an old man who knew the course of the rivers
before the intervention of Scottish Water, before the row of
cottages had been built, before the new development at the back
of the hill was begun.

At the moment the north side of the Clyde had more water
than they knew what to do with. The overground rivers were
obvious, the underground rivers were secretive. A few folk knew
about the Molendinar, the river that ran under Glasgow. It was
a tributary to the Clyde, little more than a stream or a trickle
at times. And the Dorcha, the obscure river, that was probably
running somewhere under his feet right now.

He finally got to the top of the hill and took a deep breath.
Betty made her way up slowly behind him, sitting down beside
his leg and panting, her tongue lolling, getting her breath back.
Jock knew how she felt.

He didn't want to look down but he did. The building
work was well under way. That bastard Gregor had put in a
lot of work. The plots pegged out, grass disrupted in a central

channel. Beyond lay a field of detritus, that looked suspiciously like landfill, illegal landfill. They had already started work on the perimeter wall of what was going to be a gated development. If they got planning permission. They must be confident of success, then, to go ahead with the expense of building the wall.

Jock felt his heartbeat give a little dance, a sharp pain flitted across his chest. He took a few deep breaths and decided to stand there a little longer until the fire in his legs subsided.

He needed to get back down the hill, but before he left the summit, he took one final look. Underground rivers were like icebergs. It was the unseen that was dangerous. By the time it made itself known, it was too late.

Costello had found it difficult to sleep, the blister on her foot constantly nipping, a doubt nagging at the back of her mind, a doubt about Colin. Something she didn't feel she could tell anybody about. Not without feeling disloyal.

She had taken a copy disc of the crime-scene photographs home with her last night. It had kept her up until the small hours. Anderson hadn't asked to look at it, although Mulholland had the relevant images printed out ready.

She had phoned into the office before driving out to the site, leaving a message to say she wanted a better sense of where this had all happened, and asked Wyngate if anything had been actioned. He got back to her as she was turning into Altmore Road, just before eight a.m.

His text was succinct. *No.*

Once she had parked her Fiat behind the pathologist's Vectra, she called Wyngate back and asked him to look into the background of all the players involved in 1992. All of them. Professors O'Hare and Darvel were at the sinkhole, supervising the sifting of the water from the churning depths. They walked around in their plastic suits, each with a dark blue anorak on top, discussing the contents of small trays that emerged like magic from out of the hole. As she approached they were in deep discussion over something small and brown which was lifted with a delicate gloved hand; their touch was reverent. So Costello didn't need to ask if the bones were human.

'This is the sixth time I've got wet in two days,' she said to the pathologist.

'Eighth for me. You should be used to it,' replied O'Hare.

'I've never actually dried out,' added Darvel, holding a small white fragment to her eye.

'We have nothing to report, not yet. When we do report the nothing that we have to report, do we report to you or Colin?'

Costello was used to the double-talk. 'To me, if you want anything done with it.'

'Not good then?'

Darvel sidled away, showing a respect for other people's privacy that struck Costello as remarkable. She herself would have leaned in closer, so she didn't miss a word.

'Under par, not on the ball. Not at all.'

'Good God, the man has been off on the sick for over a year. He's back for less than an hour when he's thrown into this. Give him a chance to get his hand in, at least.'

'You should have seen him with that Jennifer woman; he was desperate to get in there and help wipe bottoms and stuff. Doing his *Driving Miss Daisy* routine to take her to hospital.'

O'Hare raised a grey caterpillar of an eyebrow.

'He got that daft misty look in his eyes as soon as he saw her, all lonely with those two wee snotty-nosed ankle-biters. Him and his knight-in-shining-armour complex.'

'I'm sure Prof Batten will have a name for it – post-traumatic hyper-empathy, or something. It will be a condition. Or a syndrome. Names for bloody everything. If you're not on a spectrum, you don't exist nowadays.'

Costello dusted the raindrops from her hood. 'He's a bloody soft touch. She is not a single parent. She has a husband who should get his arse booted and dragged back to base to look after his own fricking kids.'

'And who else do you know who works all the hours God sends and leaves his wife alone with two children? Anderson spent his whole career doing that, he's probably looking at that relationship in the light of his own experience and trying to make it right.'

'Or he was skiving. He's not doing so good.' She nodded to

the tray of brown-pitted bones lying on the tray, covered with a Perspex lid. 'And what about him?'

'He's not doing so good either.'

Knowing that was all she was going to get, she said, 'Speak to you later then.' She walked away, checking her phone. As soon as there was confirmation of human bones in this street, the press liaison office would be in touch. Andrew Gyle's solicitor – somebody Rossi, she recalled from the file – would be vocal, twitching his nose for a right to appeal. Same song, different tune.

Walker had instructed that the brief was to show there was no exculpatory evidence for Gyle here. They needed it to be clear; all had been considered and accounted for. She walked on up Altmore Road, wondering who was watching from behind the curtains. The street was quiet compared to the circus of the day before, but the skies were still heavy, damp, with dark, threatening clouds. Costello wiped the rainwater from the end of her nose. Her hood seemed to be a special type that funnelled the raindrops into her eyes. Rossi, Gyle's lawyer, was being bankrolled by somebody. He seemed to have a never-ending supply of money to spend on defending Gyle. Wherever he was getting the funds from, it wouldn't be from the sale of the property on this crummy wee street. Why was Gyle still protesting his innocence? He had still been at the scene, covered in blood, when the first officer appeared.

Costello was now paused at the gap in the rhoddies, the way into the wood. The mud footprints showed the path was well used but not overly so, the grass had not worn bare. Twenty-three years ago, Sue had walked through here with the boys. She had met Gyle, her argumentative next-door neighbour, by chance. Something was said. Gyle lost the plot. He attacked them. The weapon only had his DNA.

Nobody ever claimed it was premeditated, but any argument of innocence was a load of bollocks.

Walker would have been a young fiscal in those days. Was he harbouring any doubts? Or was this a PR exercise? Costello had seen mistakes in cases like this before. Even in the Shadowman case, people got carried away in the horror of it. They wanted it closed. Gyle was there, cut and dried. Maybe the SIO signed off on a ground search that was little more than a quick look around. Maybe the forensics were restricted to supporting evidence. Twenty-three years later they had a sink-hole with some bones in it, which Costello hoped were entirely unconnected.

Most folk didn't give a shit if Andrew Gyle rotted in that cell. She picked up her phone again. 'Wyngate? Gyle had a daughter, didn't he?'

'Yip.' She heard a slurp, Wyngate was enjoying a morning coffee. 'Lorna Gyle. Wrote *Friday's Child*, her biog. It was a bestseller.'

'I recognize the title.'

'Batten has dropped in a copy. He's read it.'

'Ta, I'll call him.' She redialled.

'Hi. This book, *Friday's Child*? What's it about? Can't be arsed reading it.'

'Good morning to you.' He went into a fit of coughing. 'This bloody weather.'

'Not the forty-a-day then.'

He ignored her. 'It is a very unsensational book. Quite fascinating. A simple family, Mum, Dad and a wee girl. Fate threw a lot at that family, stuff that everybody could relate to. Gyle was the everyman murderer just as much as Sue was the every-woman victim. Society pretty much lined itself up on those two lines. Gyle was a good man who snapped. That was his Lorna's opinion. It's a touching tale, Costello. But Gyle himself has refused to join any media circus, he just reiterates his innocence. He believes the person or persons who carried out the triple murder is still out there.'

'I am at the woods. There is nothing here to mark the site, nothing. Is that odd?'

'It was five years before Diana's death – we didn't go around leaving flower shrines all over the place in those days. The bodies were cremated; there is nothing to become an attraction for the morbid tourist.'

'I think it's odd.'

'Can you visit your brother's grave?' asked Batten.

'No,' Costello ended the call. Batten was too good at his job sometimes.

She turned her head to the sky and pulled down her hood, letting the rain cool her face and soak her hair. She thought for a few minutes, enjoying the silence. Without looking she phoned Wyngate back. 'Specifically, trace Lorna Gyle for me?' Then added, 'And Steven Melrose.'

TEN

Jennifer watched the figure walk past the house. She had recognized the red anorak when they had walked up the street earlier. It was the same one who had been in with Colin yesterday, the nippy one who had looked at her washing and scowled. The figure stopped, pulled the hood from their head so they could look up. It was her. She was very wet, and holding a phone. Then she turned round and looked straight into Jennifer's front room, and raised her hand – a slight wave, some form of recognition anyway. Excited, Jennifer waved back, thinking what it must be like to be out there in the big wild world. To go to work and be able to nip out for a cuppa. The freedom of eating breakfast when you want to eat breakfast, rather than having to stuff a slice of cold toast into your mouth when there is a break in the merry-go-round of childcare: eating and drinking and being sick and filling nappies.

And Colin had been nice yesterday, all the way to Queen Elizabeth University Hospital. As they were driving along, his car filling with the smell of her children, he had said, 'Call me Colin.' She hadn't dared.

She had walked into the massive atrium of the hospital, so high and airy she wished she could fly. It was quite beautiful. She had walked around, the baby in her arms. The policeman took Robbie. He was good with children. The children liked him. The greeters in their red T-shirts thought they were a couple, a proper family.

Jennifer still had her hand in the air when she realized the female cop was walking up the broken slabs. Jennifer had time to nip into the kitchen and put the kettle on. She could say that she was in the middle of a cup of tea and she'd offer her a cuppa. Then tell her to take her jacket off to let it dry a bit. But it wouldn't, the house was too cold. Jennifer stepped over Gordy to turn the fire on . . .

Then came the knock at the door.

Jennifer went to the door and opened it wide, swinging her arm open 'oh do come in', while hoping she sounded mildly surprised at the visitor.

'Hi, just checking up to see how you are.' She stepped in, not into the house so much as just out of the rain. 'How did you get on at the hospital, the wee guy?'

'Oh, they took some bloods and gave him some antibiotics. He had a better night last night. Can you thank Colin for me? He arranged for us to have a run home and everything.'

Colin? 'All part of the service,' muttered Costello. 'And is Douglas coming back, or is he still in Edinburgh? It is Saturday.'

Jennifer caught the accusation in her tone. 'Oh no, he is coming back. He said that as soon as he heard about Gordy. We have to go back to the hospital but Douglas will take us.'

'So he is coming home today?' The grey eyes looked deep into hers, probing. 'Well, if he doesn't, you make sure you give him what for.' She looked beyond her, into the hall. 'Have you had the dampness in this house looked at? It can't be good for the children, you know. Did the hospital say anything?'

Jennifer hadn't said a word. Gordy was young. They get everything at that age. They wanted to look at his rash but Jennifer wanted to go home. They were getting suspicious and she had wanted to get away. 'I know, but it's not here all the time.' She felt pushed to explain more at Costello's quizzical glance. 'It was terrible last night, I could hear water pouring everywhere. Strange noises, like somebody crying. I didn't get a wink of sleep.' The woman gave her a strange look; she had said too much. 'It's the dampness.'

'That will account for the way the wood is warping, you can't even shut that door properly now.'

Jennifer felt tears prick her eyes; somebody else had noticed, it wasn't her going mad. 'Will I put the kettle on?'

'I don't really have time. I'm actually looking for Lynda McMutrie.'

'Oh, next door. Number ten. I have coffee as well, it's a bit of a story.'

'I'm kind of short of time, do you know her?'

'OK, she drinks. A lot. I don't see her. But then I am never out this house.'

'So you haven't seen her recently?'

'Weeks can pass and I don't see her.' She shook her head. 'Is it true her daughter had to run away to Spain? I mean, I don't know, but that's what I have heard.'

'What have you heard?' asked Costello conspiratorially.

The usual nonspecific story of somewhere in Spain followed. 'When we moved in at first, last year, their kids were always running in and out of other people's gardens, but they left soon after that.' She looked out the back of the hall, through to the kitchen and the back door beyond that. 'I've seen that Laura go in to see Lynda. I think she takes her drink.'

Costello made a mental note, but was more concerned with the wariness that creased Jennifer's eyes. 'Does anybody else come into your garden Jennifer, at the back . . .?'

'I don't really think so.'

'Well, I think you do think so.'

'Douglas says it's my imagination.'

'Douglas is not here, so he doesn't really know what you see. You might not be the only one, Jennifer.'

The words came out as a torrent. 'Well, I think it's that old guy from the Big House. He walks down that path behind the houses. I mean, there is no path, he is in our back garden and Douglas said that it was trespass and the old guy told us to check our title deeds. So Douglas went to our lawyer and the old guy's lawyer did something and . . . Well, I don't know what happened there but Douglas was told off by you lot for abusing the old man verbally. But he didn't say anything; he was worried about me being here on my own with Gordy and Robbie. And there is a rumour that he used to own all these cottages and that he thinks he still does. And that he might be going a wee bit mental and senile and try to come in the house and maybe do something to me so I have to keep out the way and keep the kids out the way. Have you met him? He's gaga.'

'I still have that pleasure to come,' said Costello. This was the man who gave Andrew Gyle his alibi for the Melrose murders. 'But Douglas must have believed you if he went to all that trouble.'

'I suppose so,' said Jennifer, slightly confused. 'I think he doesn't want me to worry. I don't think the old git really knows what he is doing, living in the old days, thinking that he's walking round his land. He goes through the field every day, up through the forest, him and that skanky dog of his. We have young children and that dog might come through the garden. Douglas shouted at it once and it growled at him. It even showed its teeth.'

'Jennifer, if Mr Aird alarms you, then I will have a word with him. He won't know that it was you who complained about him.'

'He found out the last time,' Jennifer shrugged. 'But no, thanks. I don't think he is dangerous, just a little odd.' She smiled a little. 'It's a lonely place here, this wee row of houses. He's stuck up at the top. I'm stuck down here. Everybody else gets out. So if walking around helps him cope – well, who am I to stop him?'

'Sounds like you feel sorry for the old goat?'

'Walk a mile in his shoes.' Jennifer smiled, her dark hair fell forward on her face.

'Well, if you have any issues, you know you can phone the station. I'll leave you my card.'

'No thanks, I have Colin's.' Jennifer smiled.

'Of course you do.' Costello walked away, looking up to the house at the top of the road. It was early morning but dark clouds were rolling in. The house itself looked foreboding with the grey sky tumbling over its roof. The house's face had closed eyes, the mouth shut in a grin. The big double doors looked as though they had not been open for many a year.

Maybe Jennifer was not the only one feeling abandoned in Altmore Road.

Anderson was in his own office in the police station. He sat down and tried to control the shaking in his hands. He pressed a sertraline and a lorazepam out from their tinfoil bubbles. He

exhaled, deeply, then pressed out another lorazepam. He swallowed the lot with a mouthful of tap water.

He had managed to get about an hour's sleep last night. Peter
was playing his computer game in his room, Anderson could
hear it through the wall – the click of the joystick against the
desk and the occasional utterance of a good shot or a good kill
or whatever. Of course once his brain had tuned into it, he
couldn't ignore it. It went through his head like an ice pick.
And he had got angry. He needed sleep. His son was keeping
him awake. Anderson had barged open Peter's bedroom door,
ready for . . . what? He knew it was part of his condition. So
he had gone downstairs until the anger wore off.

Peter had just shrugged.

He had then fallen asleep on the sofa, only to wake up when
he saw the flames creep out from the corner of the room. Helena
and Claire were behind him, expecting him to save them. To
do something. He couldn't. The vomit rose in his throat, the
urge to empty his bowel was overpowering. After ten minutes
in the toilet he went into the kitchen to make a cup of tea. Don't
force sleep, they had said; distract yourself and sleep will come
when ready. While waiting for the kettle to boil he heard steps
upstairs, Claire was midnight-walking with her own demons.
All of them living in this same house; all leading independent
lives with the same nightmares.

So today he was tired but anxious to get on. Batten was right,
his mind needed a problem to work on, something to distract
him. Mulholland took some pleasure in telling him that
Costello had already tasked Wyngate to trace Gyle's daughter
and Sue's husband, as well as copy a disc of the crime-scene
photographs. Did he want another copy?

It sounded like a challenge. Are you up for looking at those
pictures: two children hacked to pieces, a young woman
dismembered? Anderson said he would be fine with the files
just now, to which Mulholland had agreed and added that
Costello should have waited until they heard from O'Hare. She
was costing the service a fortune.

It wasn't a case, it was a subtle review. But the files were
sitting on his desk, dangerous but inviting. He removed his

jacket, squared up the pile, noting the psychologist's report sitting slightly askew. He pulled it out, opening the folder, intending to clip it back in properly. But of course, he started reading it. Profiling in the early Nineties? How convinced they had all been, how seduced by it. It was all *Silence of the Lambs* and unidentified subjects. God knows how many classifications of serial killers they'd had in the end. Nowadays, in the enlightened 2010s, it was still common sense that held tight and true. Good parenting led to good children growing up as well-balanced adults. Psychopaths were born not made, but they were made dangerous by being denied a moral compass to guide them through life. He started to read despite himself. A Dr Scott had done the report, a complete review of the psychology of Andrew Taylor Gyle. It might have been a power rape had he not been disturbed. Batten had noted there was no rationale for this by today's criteria. He classified it as a typical rage killing.

Sue Melrose had walked into Andrew Gyle. The fact she was pretty was neither here nor there. Gyle was a man with a sick wife. There had been complaints from the Gyle house to the Melrose house about her sunbathing in the garden. There had been complaints to the Gyle house from the Melrose house about Andrew Gyle looking at Sue Melrose while she was in the garden. The Gyles complained at the noise of the Melrose boys. Sue Melrose complained about Gyle's Johnny Cash collection. Tit-for-tat complaints over the two years before the killings, but no real suggestion of anything.

Gyle had erupted. And Anderson could empathize.

Gyle might have gone on to take his own life if it had not been for the approach of PC David Griffin, who had been in the vicinity, on his route as a community cop. It was usual for him to walk the outskirts of the park, looking for young boys who might be drinking a bit too much booze, getting high and a little badly behaved. Griffin had 'heard something' and gone deeper into the wood, thinking he was going to find some kids messing around. What Griffin had actually heard was the murders. Gyle had taken his victims by surprise. Somebody had cried out. An axe is a silent weapon when it falls.

Nowadays they put more trust in geographical profiling, local knowledge. The killer knew the woods well. Gyle knew the woods better than anybody.

This disenfranchised, bitter man had felt a surge of power when he saw Sue alone with her little children. For once, after years of baiting, he was the powerful one and she was as weak as a female could be. The impotent had become potent, the sexual power was unspoken. Dr Scott went a little further. Susan Melrose was pretty, married, healthy, well read, well spoken, with a nice husband who worked hard to provide for his wife and his family. Gyle was not so bright, not so well read. His family were struggling. The dynamic of the street was changing. As the Melroses flourished, so Gyle's inadequacies shone through. At the time of the murders he was fraught, looking after his own wife and daughter.

Something in his psyche had let rip. He found the axe in his hand.

A normal family man pushed too far.

Anderson got up and walked out to the little kitchen that had been installed at the side of the office since he had been here last. By kitchen, he meant a kettle and a microwave, a small fridge, and what Claire would call a 'cookie jar'. There was a Post-it note on the tea caddy, written in Costello's loopy hand-writing, 'Get your hands off, you caffeinated gits.' On the wall was a quick breakdown of the status of the coffee and tea kittys. The Hobnob kitty was devoid of cash.

He placed his hand on top of the cookie jar; the tremor was still there. He so wanted to be back in this. But he was scared; terrified that he might not be up to the job, of letting himself down. Again. He wanted to join the Hobnob kitty. That would be a sign that he was back. But they hadn't asked him.

Maybe they thought he wasn't up to it.

Who was he to argue?

He was mooching for the switch to put the kettle on when the door banged open. It was Costello, dripping on the carpet.

'I'd make you a cup of tea, if I could find the button.'

'It's turned off at the wall.' She leaned over him and flicked a switch, somehow managing to drip on him.

'Still raining out there?'

'Just a tad,' she wiped her nose. 'I was down at Altmore

Road, trying to finish the house-to-house. The Steeles are not answering their phones. Or their door; the gym says they might be away for the weekend. Lynda McMutrie is drunk somewhere. I looked in the window again.'

'Can you try again this evening?' asked Anderson, slipping his hand in the cookie jar.

'Yes, if I dry out first. That'll be a pound for the Hobnob committee.'

He smiled, it was good to be back.

He didn't have any money on him.

ELEVEN

B y eleven o'clock, after he had been fleeced for the Koffee Klub and the Hobnob Honchos, Anderson was settled in his office with Costello; they had a hot mug each and a huge pile of paperwork between them.

'So, Altmore Road, what do you think?' She stuffed a Hobnob into her mouth and banged her feet up on the desk, letting them rest there. She had taken off her wet boots and socks; the skin on the soles of her feet was white and crinkled, like dead flesh. She had wound a few pieces of toilet paper round her foot to absorb the blood from the blister from hell.

'Do you know, the Doon, where they were found, is where the Devil lost a claw? God chased him out of the Pulpit. It all happens in Altmore Wood, eh?'

'It was too wet to go in. It's very overgrown now. But O'Hare was still there; get the feeling he has something to tell me.'

'Us,' corrected Anderson.

'Indeed. What are those two doing?'

'Wyngate is doing whatever you tell him, seemingly, then having a quick look through McMutrie Junior associations. It's minor stuff. A posh car fell down a sinkhole, that's all. Andy Levern was in charge of the Gyle case in '92. He would have done a good job, so why are we doing this?'

'Because we did so well on the Shadowman case? Because

we have to be seen to explore the bones and discount them once we know what they are. Because these murders,' she tapped the file, 'are beyond the belief of most mortal men. And we are being forced into this investigation because it will be all over social media and, if we don't, there will be claims of a cover-up. We are governed by tweets.' Costello took a sip of her tea, slowly. 'Or twits. Or twonks.'

'It was a horrific crime; it's deep in our psyche. The kids were three and one. Andrew Gyle murdered them all. He nearly decapitated the dog. Another reason for the horror to cut so deep.'

'But Andrew Gyle has always protested his innocence. To the point of refusing counselling, therapy, because they all had the proviso that he should show remorse. And he won't do that. And nobody really knows why he did it.'

Anderson looked uncomfortable. 'Maybe he does not know himself.'

'There was huge ill-feeling between the families; they lived in close proximity,' Costello reminded him, giving him some wriggle room. 'Rossi has already been on to the fiscal's office, by the way.'

'So we leave this until we hear from O'Hare, officially.' Anderson was not for moving. 'Do you think those two wee kids at number eight are at risk? Is there anything we can do to get that husband to stand up to his responsibility?'

Costello was glad she was looking at her foot. This disconnected logic was a new Anderson. She kept to her own chain of thought. 'I asked Wyngate to trace Lorna Gyle and Stuart Melrose. What about David Griffin?'

'Who's David Griffin? Remind me.'

'The one who found the bodies, the young constable. He lost the plot after that, went a bit loopy,' Costello said pointedly.

'Nothing wrong with that, Costello,' Anderson flashed her a wry smile. 'But we are here as a public service, Jennifer needs help with those two wee kids. Her husband should be held accountable.'

'But he didn't attack anybody with an axe, Colin, you need to get some focus here. When we find Griffin, why don't you have a chat with him? From the case files, he was involved in the case, up close and personal. He knew the families. It might give you a better view. Will I find out how Wyngate is doing?' She lifted the phone.

'We don't need focus, Costello. We have a twenty-three-year-old case that was solved and the perpetrator is serving life without parole. And we have a hole in a road. At one end of that road, up a hill, is a five hundred-year-old cemetery. And we have bones after heavy rainfall. It is not a case. Unless there is a case for having a chat with that property developer? The one who is working on the other side of the hill. Some heavy plant machinery might have disrupted something that caused the sinkhole. The phone log is full of nutters suggesting that. Other nutters are going on about the movement of rainwater.'

'It goes downwards,' said Costello, helpfully.

'We could be reporting in a lawsuit later on if someone is accountable. Somebody could have been hurt.'

'The property value is a common theme between them, the Lawsons and the Broadfoots. It's why most of the folk living in those cottages are at each other's throats. No bugger wants to be there. So if you are thinking of preventing further crime and acting as a police service, then maybe that is an area you might want to look at.'

'Why?'

'By their nature, property developers are opportunists. They will be ready to pounce if that McMutrie house comes up for sale. There is already huge tension between the Broadfoots and the Dirk-Dastardlys next door.'

'What are you suggesting?'

'That they might be predatory. How could they develop that land by the back of the hill, by the old church? I wonder if there is something cooking in the council, something underhand and nasty.'

'I think you are sneaking around looking for a reason to keep an investigation going. And I am not having it, Costello. I want you to go round and finish the house-to-house on Altmore Road, type up a few words, conclude nothing, keep the boys upstairs happy and then we can all get on with something that has not been solved. I want these files off my desk now, until we have real evidence of criminality and foul play to act on. Real evidence.'

To make his point he lifted the file and popped it on top of the stack of others. 'You can take your feet off my desk and put all these outside in the office. I'm only having active cases in here.'

Costello opened her mouth to argue.

'If I am back at work, I think I should have something better to do than this non-event. And I have spoken to DI Levern; he recalls the case well. There was no doubt about Gyle's guilt. No doubt at all.'

Costello took the offered files, got up and limped out the office. She was still sitting, picking at her blister, when she heard the phone ring in Anderson's office. She refused to appear interested, rolling up her sock again, teasing out the wet laces of her shoes, ready to put them back on, ignoring Anderson, until she realized that he was gesturing for her to rejoin him in the office.

She walked back, ungainly. One shoe on, one shoe off.

Anderson was leaning forward at the desk, one finger on the phone; he didn't look happy. 'Just hang on a minute, Prof, I am going to put you on speakerphone.'

The educated tones of the forensic pathologist floated round the small room. 'Oh, hello, just to let you know I'm soaked through and pissed off. How are you?'

'I'm fine, Jack. Please tell me you want to talk bones. Old bones. Very old bones that mean we have nothing more to do with Altmore Road.'

'Yes, I can do that.'

Anderson shot a look of victory at Costello.

She sighed, 'Oh, I thought you were getting excited about something that was floating down that hole.'

'Yes, I was.'

Costello shot a look back at Anderson, and then folded her arms for effect.

'Bones,' said the disconnected voice. 'Other bones that have not been submerged for long, neither have they been exposed to fresh air.'

'Meaning?' snapped Anderson.

There was a reproachful pause before the pathologist spoke. 'Well, most of the bones are a hundred years plus, and that is fitting with the graves up at Altmore Cemetery. It's an old place, so there is no point in talking to the parks and rec, but if you do I think you will find there is some movement in the land and that can—'

'The bones, Jack,' pressed Anderson.

'We have nine bones of a foot. We are missing cuneiform and a cuboid. And they are recent. Much younger than any of the others. We will go back down the hole once the rain has stopped; it keeps filling up so we are looking for small pebbles at the bottom of a large pond. But that was how they caught Haigh, by finding a gallstone on a gravel path. So it is not all in vain. But in the meantime we will press on with processing what we have. The bones have been photographed and the lab have them now. Interesting points for you are: One, it has not degenerated so it has been protected in some way and in a dry environment. Two, we have a lower end of the fibula fragment and the upper surface of that is clean-cut and striated. The periosteal bone has not yet had time to fracture. Three. The cut is straight, so it was chopped off. It has not yet had time to flake so—'

'Chopped? As in an axe?' asked Costello, her eyes burning into her boss's.

'Don't jump to conclusions, Costello. That would be very dangerous in a case like this.'

'That's what I have been trying to tell her,' said Anderson.

'Is it a female foot?' asked Costello, not to be put off her track.

'It would appear so. And there are stress lines in the bones, which suggests that it was a young, hardworking foot. Like a dancer, and by that I mean a young woman who danced a lot. If you look at this foot under a microscope, there should be no periosteum left. Bones that are old, hundreds of years old, have lost their periosteal covering. It fractures slightly, then flakes off. We can age the bone roughly by the degree of flaking of the periosteum that is still present. And this bone has minor flaking of the periosteum, so it is not that old and then—'

'What do you mean by "not that old"? Not how old?' asked Anderson.

'Well, not hundreds of years.'

'About twenty-three years?' Costello's voice was insistent.

There was a silence; a faint burr came down the line.

'It's an opinion, an educated opinion, but I'd doubt twenty years. I think that this young dancer died within the last ten years. I am telling you two, and I am telling Archie Walker and ACC Mitchum. What you tell the press is up to you. The bones need to be broken down and tests done to extract any DNA present and that is going to take time. Matilda needs to drill a section, boil it, treat it, powder it and soak it in solution to get the DNA out and then—'

'How long?'

'Days.'

'If the bloody rain lets the hole drain, we may find other bones to strengthen or weaken the theory.' There was silence in the room again.

'Can you tell us anything?' Costello picked up a note pad, scribbled 'Andrew Gyle' and double underlined it.

'Unofficially? Female. Slight build. Five foot five or thereabouts. Narrow foot. Size five. No gross malformations so she wore good shoes. In the sense that she didn't spend a lot of her time in four-inch heels. But her feet worked hard.'

'On her feet all day, you mean?'

'Like I said, more like a dancer or an athlete, something like that. Where the muscles are attached there are little rough bits. In a normal person who walks about and then sits at a desk, that would be completely smooth, so the muscles in her foot were used a lot. And the foot bones were protected, above ground.' He paused; they could hear Mulholland and Wyngate chatting outside the glass. 'But you need to be ready for the media storm. You are investigating another suspicious death on Altmore Road.'

'Another murder by an axe? So Gyle did another one. That is another rope we can hang him with,' Anderson put his hands behind his head.

Costello looked at the phone. 'If I understood you right, Jack, you said less than twenty years.'

'More like ten. At the time of the Melrose murders, this lady was still growing, walking around and breathing, probably still dancing. So he was incarcerated when this happened.'

'So it is unconnected, Gyle was in jail,' said Anderson.

'Or it is connected and Gyle is innocent,' countered Costello. 'Gyle's lawyers will have a field day with this.'

'Not enough to grant leave to appeal. I'm going to the loo.' Anderson stood up and left the office, leaving her sitting on the desk where she had been all the way through the conversation.

She felt vaguely sick. Gyle sharply divided public opinion. It was the duty of Walker and the fiscal's office to decide when to tell Gyle's defence team, the laws of disclosure being what they were.

Anderson's desktop phone went again, and as she reached over she saw the sweat marks on the arm of Anderson's chair. He was really stressing over this. She answered the phone; it was McColl downstairs looking for Anderson. She took a brief message, smiled to herself and sat back up on the desk, amusing herself by picking at her sore foot again.

'You know that cop I was asking Wyngate to trace? David Griffin?' she asked him as he opened the door.

'The first on the scene?'

'Well, there is no point in Wyngate going any further. He's found us. He wants you to call him.'

Anderson had indicated he wanted Costello to lead, so she took her place at the whiteboard, a black marker in her hand. Mulholland and Wyngate ignored her, too engaged in a debate about independence. It looked as if it was about to get nasty. Mulholland was fired up with self-governing righteousness, Wyngate was sarcastically showing Mulholland what a calculator was as he obviously couldn't add up. He was embarking on a diatribe of Norwegian oil revenues when Anderson coughed pointedly.

'And as for that fat . . .' Wyngate continued his debate.

'Shut the f up, you two,' said Costello, her left forefinger tapping the board. 'We have work to do once you are finished sorting out the problems of the nation.'

'Nations,' corrected Mulholland.

They both murmured apologies while looking at each other in a way that promised it was not over.

'This has just come through.' She pointed to a photograph on the wall, a small collection of pebbles and chess pieces.

'What are they?' asked Mulholland, putting his glasses on to see well.

'A navicular, a calcaneus, a few metatarsals . . . two cuneiforms. Is that the distal end of a fibula?' asked Wyngate.

Costello was impressed. 'Yes foot bones. How do you know that?'

'He's had the benefit of a wonderful education under a Scottish Government. But doesn't appreciate it,' said Mulholland.

'I read the report that came with the photograph. We unionists do our homework properly.'

'So you think—'

'Shut it,' said Costello with deadly mildness. The room was immediately quiet. 'Bones found at the sinkhole. They have been washed there probably out from a culvert further up the street. It's too dangerous to go down until Health and Safety can make the rain stop. We are waiting for a precise date on the bones, but the sheer edge suggests unnatural death. To simplify, if these bones are older than twenty-three years then we must consider that Sue, Bobby and George were not the first victims of Andrew Gyle. The owner of the bones might be. If the bones are less than twenty-three years, then they died while Gyle was incarcerated and have nothing to do with him. The third theory is that Gyle . . .'

'Is innocent,' added Batten, who had slipped in the door unseen. 'And the body count is four against an unidentified subject. The "unsubs", as the FBI calls them.'

'I think a fourth theory, that somebody killed Foot Woman in a copycat style so, at a later date, they could argue that all four victims were killed by the same person and as Gyle was incarcerated at the time, then he is wrongly incarcerated, can be excluded, as the body has been hidden too well,' said Costello. 'Walker wants an open book on this.'

Costello looked at Batten, who was standing in the corner stirring coffee. Black coffee with no sugar in it, which made the act of stirring it a bit pointless. Costello wondered at what point a shrink needed a shrink.

'There is a problem of guilt here. And a bigger problem of innocence,' said Batten.

'How many years in university did it take you to work that one out?' snapped Costello.

'*Friday's Child*, the book Lorna Gyle wrote,' said Batten as Wyngate held up a well-read hardback copy. 'The ghostwriter was very good. She wrote it in 2009 when Lorna was twenty-one. I am sure it was commissioned as a story of growing up with a monster and all the horror and the abuse but, famously, it's not like that at all. It's the story of a normal family who went on picnics and to the supermarket and built castles on the beach. The sheer mundanity of the text is charming, very Anne Frank. Little story after little story,' said Batten.

'And then the dad slaughtered a woman and her wee boys. One barely more than a baby. He nearly took its head off. So no, not so normal,' Anderson said.

'I'm not reading it. Batten and I are going to visit him tomorrow. I don't want any kind of prep. I need to take him as I find him with no preconceived ideas.' Costello made a panto-mime of covering her ears as Wyngate dug out a photograph of the young Lorna, sitting on a deckchair, all blonde curls and toothless smiles, a small lace shawl round her shoulders.

'Lorna believes he is guilty because the jury found him guilty. She thinks the evidence against him was overwhelming; there was no other explanation for what went on in the woods that day. So she accepted it but finds it hard to believe. Then, as the book goes on, she works it through, seeing it through an adult's eyes. Gyle was stressed out of his box when he killed the Melroses, and it was the Melroses who were causing him all the stress. It's bad enough being stressed, but much worse to have the triggers of that stress shoved under your nose every two minutes – every time he opened the front door, every time he went out into his back garden.'

Costello looked at the picture of Gyle, slightly balding, crinkly hair round the side of his head. He looked like the wee guy from the *Carry On* team, the one with the sniggery laugh whose name she could never remember. 'I'm sure his daughter would try to rationalize it somehow. It is difficult to see your parents in any light other than as your parents. Even though you know the most awful things about them. I know that more than most.'

Batten waited until somebody went past the door outside,

hesitating until the footsteps had halted and a door slammed. 'But, Costello, imagine Gyle is innocent. His daughter believes that he is guilty. Imagine that as a barrier between them. Notwithstanding the fact that he is incarcerated for something that he didn't do, imagine the impact of him knowing that she believes that he did it. She is the only person he has in the world. And she believes that he is capable of that. Imagine that for a moment all of you, your own kid believing you are a murderer.' He stopped, sipping his coffee for dramatic effect. For a moment the room was silent, just the never-ending patter of the rain.

'But he is guilty. He did it,' said Anderson.

'You don't know that for certain. You weren't there. He has not admitted it or let something slip in any of his interviews that pointed to the guilt being his,' pointed out Wyngate.

'He was found guilty by his peers. And only his DNA was on the axe, so that kind of confirms he did it.' Mulholland sat down, swung his feet up on the desk, put his hands around the back of his head.

'I agree that he was caught up in some psychological rage. In another time, another place, it would never have happened,' said Anderson. 'But he did do it.'

'Let's have a look at the evidence and see where it goes. Let's see his reaction when I confront him with the reality of his situation, his incarceration and the fact that his daughter does not want to know him,' suggested Costello.

'I think he knows what his daughter thinks about him. She doesn't visit him; she has disowned him, even as a wee kid. I know our social services believe that even murderers have a right to see their own children, but I hope they would draw a line at letting a five-year-old back into the life of a man who had killed a three-year-old and his wee brother.'

'She hasn't visited her dad since she was sixteen. Her adoptive mother's details are in the file. I've had a good look at the visiting log and Andrew Gyle only has one regular visitor, a chap called Jock Aird,' Wyngate read out from his notebook.

'Who lives in Altmore House at the top of Altmore Road? He gave him his alibi, his false alibi. I am starting to have my own thoughts about Mr Aird. I'd like to sit down and talk to you about how power corrupts,' said Costello.

'The love of power corrupts but not power itself.' Batten looked back at Costello over the top of his coffee, but she was looking at the ceiling, already thinking about something else. 'But his daughter has stayed clear since, until she could legally say, *I don't want anything more to do with him*. That must hurt.'

'So she saw sense and realized that her dad was a total psycho and broke all contact.'

Batten said, 'Lorna was taken into foster care, then adopted, changed her name legally then got married. She got away from him and made a new life for herself. She'd be in her late twenties now.'

'I am finding it difficult to trace her,' admitted Wyngate. 'Oh, Costello, better luck with Sue's husband, last seen at the Findhorn Community.'

'Good, so he ran away as well,' Costello nodded.

'Lorna might take some persuasion to make herself known. She is behind an invisible wall. She believes he did what he did because of the stress he was under. It was very out of character for him. Both sides at the trial agreed for him to have brain scans because they thought the rage might be organic, some growth or something that made him snap. And that's why Costello is to do the talking to Gyle, see how he responds to a female.'

'Christ, he put an axe through the last one,' said Mulholland.

'Typical violent reaction of the nationalist,' muttered Wyngate.

'Seriously though,' Batten turned to address Costello directly. 'He has waived his right to have his solicitor present, so keep it light, make out that you are on his side. That you are pressing for the new evidence to be analysed as it might have some bearing on his conviction. Enough to go in front of the review board. He will have seen the sinkhole on the news this morning and he is not stupid enough to think that forensic pathologists turn out because a sinkhole appears with some swirly water in it. We are better taking it to him, rather than his legal team bringing it to us. Just play the "in the interest of justice" card, like you are just doing your job.'

'And forget that he is a wee slime bag who killed three people, and a dog with an axe,' said Mulholland.

'Yeah. It would be good if you could push that to the back of your mind a little,' Batten said.

'Well, once we turn up, he's bound to know something is afoot,' Costello smiled at her joke and Batten threw a crumpled piece of paper at her. It missed.

TWELVE

Sunday 23 August 2015

She collapsed again, hitting her face on the carpet. This was bloody embarrassing.

She looked into the darkness of her own eyelids, more relaxed this time. Through the feathered gap of her own eyelashes, she saw the black fur dashing into her vision then turning on its own length and disappearing back into the shadows.

It made noises with its feet, noises that were suddenly loud, scurrying. Its keen beady eyes flashing, claws rattling on the wall, squeaking. Then there was another, then another.

She was having a nightmare, a nightmare of rats. So she tried to wake up.

But she couldn't.

Now, she couldn't tell what was real and what was not. She thought she was young but now she was old. She thought she was calling out for help but she had been asleep. She thought she was sober but she wasn't so sure about that one. And now she was lying on the floor, on a carpet and she could see rats.

She had thought she was safe; maybe not so sure about that one either.

Jock Aird dislodged his large golfing umbrella from the stand behind his front door and clipped Betty on to her lead. Then he left Altmore House by the back door. He had not used the front door since the late Eighties but he couldn't recall why.

In the back porch, a ramshackle half-glass half-wood construction, he pulled on his old boots. He thought about his wellies, but he kept them for going through the wood, through the long grass, and they were leaking despite him doing yet another repair. He must have got really soaked the last time he was out; they were still wet now. He was planning to walk up to Partickhill; it would take about an hour. More if he walked round the botanics, but he would enjoy it. He might be old but he was very fit.

And he planned on staying that way.

He slipped on his Barbour, and set off out into the torrential rain.

He was wet and sweating heavily by the time he got to the reception of the police station. The door was closed as usual, so he pressed the buzzer and waited, making use of his time by shaking the excess rain from his umbrella. He climbed the two stairs carefully, and opened the door as the buzzer sounded. Another door opened, the glass shutter slid to one side and a friendly young desk sergeant looked out at him.

'Hi sir, how can I help you?'

Aird told the dog to sit. She didn't. He swept his long grey fringe over a high, intelligent forehead; faded blue eyes looked directly at the desk sergeant.

The desk sergeant didn't dare to tell him to tie the dog up outside in case he got a lecture about young people today. Aird looked the sort.

'Hello, you are?' he asked imperiously.

The young cop decided to humour the coffin dodger. 'PC Kevin McColl, I'm on the desk today.'

'Yes, I can see that.'

'So how can I help you?' McColl pulled a note pad close to him, ready to look interested. It would be a neighbour watching *The X Factor* before nine at night with the sound up too loud, or next door parking their car outside his house, spoiling the view out of his front window. Or somebody feeding the pigeons. Yes, some little old lady next door feeding the pigeons. He looked the type who would want to bring back the death penalty for that.

When he spoke, the voice was strong, with a rather querulous tone that was used to having a good argument and winning.

'I'd like to talk to whoever is in charge of the incident at Altmore Road.'

'Oh, the sinkhole?' McColl pulled the pad closer.

'And the rest of it, I want to speak to whoever is in charge.'

'And your name is?'

'Jock Aird. I have lived in the street all my life. I know what is causing all the problems. It's the water.' He shook an annoying droplet from his hair.

'You don't say.' McColl pushed the pad away again. 'If you leave me your name and number, I'll pass it on, and I'm sure they will get back to you.'

Aird continued to flick his hair around, and then flick the raindrops from the shoulder cape of his coat. 'I have taken the time and trouble to walk down here, in this terrible weather, because I have information that I believe will be of some interest, and I think it would be both polite and useful if somebody listened to me.'

'I am listening to you,' smiled McColl, pen in hand, wondering how rude he was going to have to be to get rid of the old bugger.

'Let me make myself clear; if somebody *in charge* listened to me,' clarified Aird.

'I'm in charge of the desk.'

'And you write with a biro. On a chain, so I don't think they trust you with a pen, so I am hardly going to trust you with my important information. So can you please get somebody in charge to come down and speak to me?' To prove a point, Betty sat down and sighed.

Now McColl was the subject of disapproving looks from both man and beast.

'Are you sure? It might take some time. You might be better to phone in, it can be quicker.'

'I have already phoned in twice; now I want to talk to somebody in charge.'

'Well, if you have already phoned in and left your information, then we would have got back to you if the intelligence, the information, was of high relevance. Once it slips from priority, then it can take a little longer. That's how we work; that's how things get done.'

'Well, that relies on you knowing the significance of what

you are being told. And I'm sure even you, PC McColl, can
see the flaw in that argument.'

'But it is about a sinkhole,' asked McColl, getting rattled
now.

'It's historic information; it's our history that makes us what
we are today. How well do you know the rivers in Glasgow?'
he asked.

'The Clyde, the Kelvin, I used to fish.'

'Do you know the Molendinar, Glasgow's underground river?
And there are three rivers in the hills above Hardgate: the
Humphrey, the Cochno and the Dorcha. And do you know
what's strange about the Dorcha?'

'No, but I am about to find out,' said McColl.

'You can't see it.'

'Good! Look, I'll get the phone and see if there is anybody
available,' he smiled at the old man standing in front of him,
with the damp dog, stinking out the reception office.

'I think you should find out *who* is available, not *if.* I am
very old, I can't hang around for ever. Chop chop.'

McColl closed the glass and lifted the phone.

Costello was sitting at the back of the investigation room,
drawing out the plan of Altmore Road on a bit of A4 paper and
double-checking who was where at the time of the murders in
1992. The houses then were numbered evenly from 2 to 14,
now it was 2 to 12 as the Steeles' house is 12 and 14 knocked
together. The Melroses and Gyles lived in 2A and 2B respec-
tively. That building was now knocked into one, and was home
to the Dirk-Huntleys, their goat and a sinkhole. The Broadfoots
were at number 4, and they seemed to have purchased it from
the estate of Phyllis Carlisle who had been there for sixty years.
So, no lead to follow up there. Miss McMutrie junior and her
family had disappeared off to Spain, their house – number 6
– had been empty for months. And had been empty at the time
of the Melrose murder, according to the electoral roll. The
Lawson house – number 8 – had been rented out for eight years
before they bought it, the previous owner having died, another
elderly woman. Lynda McMutrie was in 10 on her own. Then
there were the Steeles at what is now number 12, who should

be back from their weekend in Oslo tomorrow morning. That property too had been unoccupied at the time of the Melrose murders.

A new set of crime-scene photographs of that Thursday 27 August 1992 was being sifted by Mulholland and his selection was being placed on the wall. It was unlikely, the initial investigation concluded, that a stranger had killed the family. So that left the very inhabitants of Altmore Road or somebody that Sue Melrose had gone out to meet. Except Gyle, and maybe Aird, the residents had all been cleared from any involvement in the case. And the original investigation had pulled apart Sue's private life, as had Gyle's defence team, and both had found nothing other than what she appeared to be: a slightly lonely woman in her house with two young children. She had moved from the trendy, vibrant west end of Glasgow, with its Guardian reading, coffee-house culture, to Altmore Road, only seven miles away, but culturally she might as well have been living on the moon.

Costello had the Google map open on her computer, trying to drop the wee yellow figure into the street, but he wouldn't go. He dangled in mid-air, his legs swinging like a condemned man on the gallows. She was not going to wait for the DNA to come through; they couldn't afford the time. This was Anderson's big comeback case; he couldn't be allowed to fail. She wasn't being altruistic. If he failed it would be a stain on all of them. If he was seen to be struggling, which he was, then she would shine if she brought the case home with good investigative logic. If he rose to the challenge, then her contribution to the case would also be acknowledged. In reality, he seemed to have his mind set on Gyle's guilt, and he was probably right. The one thing she could not afford was Anderson being blinkered by that. So she was keeping an eye on him, keeping her own notes.

She reasoned that, as O'Hare had a few bones from a single left foot, she had better get on with that rather than talk with Colin, who was content to whinge on about Jennifer Lawson, what a good mother she was, the state of dampness in that house and what on earth was her bloody husband thinking.

Costello was more interested in the fact that somebody had chopped up a young woman and put her in the ground. She wondered if there was a borehole or a culvert near the end of the driveway. The Dirk-Dastardlys had only moved in four years before. They had purchased the property five years ago and set about taking out the conversion that had divided up the old single house and turning the huge corner plot of land beyond into a smallholding. At any point, a body could have been put somewhere in a drain, and now it had been dislodged by the recent downpour. She had requested Wyngate to compile a list of all missing women in Scotland over ten and under fifty who had gone missing in the period from 1995–2005. She had no idea if the parameters were any use, but she had to start somewhere. When not pinning things on the wall and fighting with Mulholland, Wyngate was doing a fine job on the database trawl. Lorna Gyle had become Laura Reid when she'd been adopted, and that was as far as she had got. He was working through a list of follow-up addresses.

Joining the photographs of Gyle and the foot bones was the crime-scene photograph of Sue lying in Altmore Wood, 'the sunflower picture', as it had become known.

Costello needed a stiff cup of tea. The kettle had been set to boil in the wee kitchen for the last ten minutes, and then she realized that Anderson had unplugged it. She was there when the door opened to reveal ACC Mitchum and Archie Walker. Mitchum was in uniform, hidden under his raincoat, which he was sliding from his shoulder and shaking dry all over their nice lino floor. Walker's jacket was a chiaroscuro of damp and dry.

Five minutes later they were all seated around the table. ACC Mitchum had a large file in front of him, a small electronic device sitting on top of that. Walker was thin-lipped and serious, Wyngate was sitting at the adjacent table, at his beloved computer, ready to come up with any data they might ask for. Mulholland was sitting still, rubbing his ankle. Costello thought he was going to start moaning about how he could tell it was raining because his fracture site was starting to play up. He had turned into an old man overnight. She wondered if it was the influence of the humourless Miss McCulloch;

something had certainly knocked the most annoying character traits off him.

Anderson was sitting at the top of the table, his hands clasped in front of him. Knuckles white, fingers grasped tightly together. It was not warm in the room, the heating being off as it was supposedly summer, but distinct streams of sweat were working their way down his forehead. Costello, being in situ, had been forced to make the tea and open up the digestives. They had all said thank you, except Walker, who had taken the mug from her hand without any acknowledgement, because he was explaining to ACC Mitchum about the photographs on the wall and where they were taken. It was a useless way to move the situation forward, but it served to concentrate their minds as to why they were here.

The ACC's face was grim. 'We don't want any embarrassing situations. Gyle is guilty of these murders. We don't want any aspect of that verdict being brought into question, no smart lawyers seeing it as an excuse to start an appeal process.'

Anderson nodded, 'Indeed.'

'Do you have any forensics back on this foot? I'm hearing all kinds of rumours that I don't like.'

'Nothing definite yet. An athletic young woman. O'Hare thinks the bones have been protected from the environment – kept wrapped up, maybe. The cut is clean and sharp, made with a blade. Time since their death? Maybe ten years or so, judging by appearance. Confirmation will be another couple of days yet.'

'So there were two killers working in the same street?'

'Or somebody just used Altmore Road as a deposition site,' said Mulholland.

'How are we doing on missing persons? Don't answer that: it is a huge undertaking, I know.'

'Six matches, two of them have turned up safe and well and nobody thought to tell us. Of the four,' he placed four colour prints on the table, 'Elaine O'Shaunessy, Pauline Rigby, Pamela Squire and Tamara McMaster. All under forty, between five feet two and five feet five. Tamara was the only one who could be described as a dancer. Of the pole variety. She has a criminal record as long as the wall of Dubrovnik. Wyngate and I are doing the groundwork. Better to wait now until we get the DNA.'

The ACC nodded, then continued, determined to make his point. 'Andrew Gyle, everybody is agreed, is not a multiple killer.'

Batten agreed. 'One incident, one kill. Nothing led up to it, nothing since. If O'Hare is right, then he was inside at the time of the other murder, so somebody else must have done that.'

Or the other person did them all, Costello thought.

'So, DCI Anderson, you are in control of the investigation – now might be a good time to call your team to heel and get them to behave. We want no dubiety about the Gyle murders, nothing at all. Find out who that foot belongs to and leave it there. Understand me, Gyle killed Sue Melrose and her kids. End of. Clear?' Mitchum's gaze fixed on Anderson.

'Perfectly,' said Anderson, but Walker caught Costello's eye and held her gaze.

'And keep it from the press. Where are you now?'

'As Wyngate said, we are waiting for O'Hare's report, and he needs the rain to go off so they can investigate the hole for the rest of the bones and where they came from. Three residents of Altmore Road are proving elusive. Costello and Batten are going to talk to Andrew Gyle.'

ACC Mitchum looked around. 'Good thinking, getting Costello to go. If he has a problem with women, she will provoke it.'

Walker smirked and nodded discreetly.

'Wyngate is tracking down Steven Melrose. He has been at the Findhorn community and is now at some Carron commune. And I am interviewing David Griffin.'

'You seem to be spending a fair bit of time on the Melrose case,' said Mitchum, 'when I thought I had just said not to.'

'Making sure there is nothing exculpatory for Gyle – you know what Rossi can be like,' said Walker. 'You recall Griffin?'

'Oh Davy, yes I do. Good man Davy. Drives an old Morris Minor. Beautiful car. Pass on my regards to him. It was a loss to the force when he didn't make it back.' Mitchum seemed to look at Anderson before standing up and walking out. They watched the door close behind him; it seemed to take a very long time.

'He always had a soft spot for Griffin, I think he knew his dad or something,' explained Walker. 'So we run the two investigations side by side. I am not having the fiscal's office accused of not doing our duty properly. We look at Andrew Gyle's conviction. OK?'

'Were you listening to what Mitchum just said?' asked Anderson.

'Yes, but it's not him who has Rossi on the phone, asking questions. The door is already open, we have to be transparent here. There is the investigation and then there is the law.' Walker looked Anderson straight in the eye. 'Colin? Have you looked at that file? Have you seen how little was done in that investigation? They got Gyle at the scene and Levern got complacent. I don't blame them, but it doesn't mean that it's right.'

'If you investigate it further, then all you will do is put the tin lid on it, I am sure,' said Batten.

'Are you aware that anything you uncover needs to be shown to the defence? His lawyer is going to lap this up – do you really want that?' argued Anderson.

'Colin? You need to; if this goes tits up they have you as a fall guy. You need to reinvestigate, and if it does stand you *need* to say so. Mitchum was not here to see how you were feeling.' The words spat from Costello's mouth, her finger pointed at her boss's face.

Then Walker's quiet voice cut through the tension. 'In fact it has to be shown to the fiscal's office and we will make the decision as to who sees what.'

'It is our duty to investigate,' said Batten, adding, 'he had a daughter you know. That wee five-year-old grew up thinking that her dad took an axe to those two wee boys.'

'But he did do that awful thing,' argued Anderson. Mulholland nodded vigorously.

'But what if he didn't? I am saying that the events of that night had a lot of terrible consequences. That woman is now twenty-eight, and still thinking that her dad did that,' said Costello.

'She got a bloody fortune for writing that book. Bit of a

bummer if you prove her dad's now innocent,' Batten smiled, but nobody laughed.

'But then she would get even more dosh for the revised version. And his version. Probably get a film deal out of it. He can do chat shows. She'll be on *Celebrity Big Brother*,' Mulholland mused.

Batten pointed to the photograph of the small bones. 'Alternatively, you can ignore Gyle's guilt or innocence. And find *that* killer.'

THIRTEEN

It took Batten and Costello over twenty minutes to get through the security in the prison, the scanning machines, various bits of clothing on and off, the phones, the clanging of locks and doors, swipe after swipe of ID card. On the short drive to Barlinnie, Batten had instructed Costello to act the hard-nosed cow, and resisted the temptation to add that she shouldn't find that too difficult.

Eventually they were taken through to the meeting area. Apart from his hideous crime, Gyle was considered a non-violent prisoner. He worked in the machine shop, mostly on his own. He preferred everything to be on his own.

A prison officer came to meet them. He looked at his watch, commenting that it would be a few more minutes yet. He unlocked the doors of the office and invited them in, offering them a cup of tea or coffee, which they both declined.

Costello wasn't keen to let him, a useful source of information, go. 'So do you work with Gyle then?'

Alex Knight, the prison officer, said, 'Yes. I've been on his wing for a few months. They rotate us so we don't get too friendly – not that you'd get friendly with a man like him.'

Batten stood up and shook Knight by the hand. 'Professor Mick Batten. You must have a lot of experience of lifers?'

'I'm old, you mean.' Knight relaxed and perched his backside on the desk with the accompaniment of the jangle of keys.

'And what do you think of Gyle – a bastard or a beguiler?'

Knight crossed his legs, relaxing at the psychology shorthand. He tapped his fingertips on the desktop and looked as if he was considering the question with some seriousness. 'He seems a straight kind of bloke, not many of them in here. But most of our clientele are career criminals. Gyle is not that type of animal. I think in his early days he tried to engage with the staff, trying to distance himself from the rest of the inmates. A lot of them do that at first. It doesn't work. It's one of the tactics of those who protest their innocence. He's still doing it.'

'And you don't think he is? Innocent, I mean,' asked Costello.

Knight turned to Batten. 'Where did you get her, a lucky bag? He's as guilty as a fat kid in a chip shop. He's an animal. Never forget what he did. He's not allowed to forget it. He's been attacked a few times, so we keep him out the way. And he likes being on his own anyway.' Knight paused. 'That sinkhole? You guys were prodding around in it. Said on the news that you found some bones. You think he's guilty of more than . . .' His voice trailed off.

'We are going to say something like new evidence has come to light and we are exploring the possibility that it might have a bearing on his case,' said Costello, with the air of one bored already.

'Are you joshing me? You telling me that he might be innocent, is that what this is about?' Knight laughed. 'Are you two on drugs?'

'I said that was what we were telling him, not that was what we believed,' said Costello, slyly. 'But he will buy the story that we are thinking like defence counsel. Does he have any pals in here?'

'Nope, he's a loner. He has the occasional professional prison visitor and they are always Christians.' Knight said it as if they were carriers of the plague. 'And yes, there is one visitor—'

'Aird,' added Batten. The psychologist rubbed his chin. 'Has Gyle ever shown an outburst, like the one that caused him to kill the Melrose family?'

'Only once, he went for somebody's throat.'

'And what provoked that attack?'

'Somebody said something about his daughter.'

'And was that immediate? Not a knife in the shower three days later?'

'It was there and then. You don't turn your back on many of them, but you can walk past Gyle without your hands on your keys.'

'So why do you think he keeps protesting his innocence?' asked Batten.

'Who knows what games they play to get what they want? It keeps him in the news with no effort whatsoever; there's always some do-gooder about, sending him messages of support. He should admit to it and get on an anger management programme, which would get him somewhere. Moaning to that old bloke who visits him, whingeing on about his innocence, does him no bloody good.'

'So he moans to Aird?' asked Costello, knowing the answer.

'Yeah, they seem to have a lot in common. I think they lived in the same street for many years.'

'That will be the street the bones were found in.'

Andrew Gyle, the monster, was a small balding man with a bad limp and a worse cough. The usual prison deadness behind the eyes. The grey skin underneath fell into translucent folds like old flowers that had never seen the light of day. He greeted the two visitors with a curt nod, not giving anything away. He was wearing jeans and trainers. His white shirt had been washed, ironed, but still looked grubby.

Batten introduced himself and Costello.

Gyle looked from one to the other, wary. 'I thought it was a police visit. I didn't think it was a doctor coming to see me.' His accent was rough, working-class Glasgow.

'Why, you had enough of that?' Batten allowed his voice to lift a little.

He got a sarcastic smile back. 'I've had a few. So why are you here? Is the bloody sinkhole my fault as well?'

'No, we'd like you to go through it again, the events of that day, twenty-three years ago,' said Costello.

Gyle blinked slowly. Tiredness? Frustration? He sighed, 'Why?'

'You have always insisted on your innocence.' Costello gave

him an earnest smile. 'If any other evidence, anything at all, comes to light, then we have a legal and moral duty to investigate it. But if you don't want to, that's fine. There's nothing we can do about that and it saves us any bother.'

The three of them sat in silence in the big white room with the pale blue chairs on their metal frames and were assaulted by a brief burst of 'Bohemian Rhapsody' as somebody put the radio on.

Gyle folded his arms. 'It was you bastards that put me in here in the first place.'

'It was the jury who put you in here. And the person who killed Sue, Bobby and George Melrose. And if you and he are one and the same, then all is well in my world.'

'I didn't do it.' The words fell off his tongue. Like they were a habit.

'But, like I say, if you don't want to talk to us, there's nothing we can do about that.' Costello held her ground.

Batten appeared bored, looking from one to the other, reminded of that quote about the irresistible force and the immovable object.

Under the glare of those grey eyes, Gyle supplicated. He leaned forward and clasped his hands on the table in front of them. The skin of his knuckles was grey and calloused. 'So the bones found at my old house? Down the sinkhole? I presume this is something to do with them?' He spoke quietly, very aware of the prison officer sitting within earshot.

'You have been asked if you want to have some legal representation. You said no, do you want to reconsider?'

Gyle's eyes moved from one to the other. Batten was watching him closely. Gyle was getting anxious now, daring to hope that something might come of this.

He shook his head. 'So what do you want to know?'

'We would like to know what happened when you saw Sue in the woods that evening.'

'I freaked out. She was lying there, like she was in some horror film. Blood everywhere, deep cuts, black. A colour that you don't expect to see. Then I saw the two wee kids and . . . Well, I think I saw the sunflower hat, but I've been told that was a memory I picked up later.' He shook his head. Either he

was being truthful or he was a good actor. 'Then Griffin appeared
and punched my lamps out.'

'I meant the first time you saw them.'

'That was the first time I saw them in the woods, but they
were my bloody next-door neighbours. I saw them earlier in
the day. But in the woods, it was when I got back from helping
Jock. I was going back to where I left my stuff. I saw her and
kneeled down to see if there was a pulse. I got covered in her
blood. That was what did it for me. If I had gone for help and
left them, I wouldn't be here. But it is a natural instinct to try
to help, when you see somebody in that state. No matter what
you think of them.' He shook his head at the unpleasant memory
of the scene – or the memory of getting caught. 'God, I was
sick. Never want to see anything like that ever again.'

'What had happened to Mr Aird?'

'He had slipped at the Pulpit. I helped him back to the
house, sat him down, had a quick cuppa with him and left.
More than half an hour, more like forty-five minutes. Then I
went back.'

Costello waited for him to continue. He was recalling it
clearly.

'You know, earlier that day, the wee guy, the kid was out on
his swing in their back garden, screaming at the top of his voice
and his mum just let him do it. May was sitting in the . . .' He
closed his eyes, playing back the scene.

Costello threw a look at Batten to find out if Gyle was acting
this out, trying to recall an earlier lie, but Gyle lifted his fist to
his face and wiped a tear from his cheek. When he started
talking again, his eyes were red-rimmed. Costello had read this
part of the story and knew what was coming.

'May was sitting at the French windows. I had pulled the
seat over to give her a bit of sun; she'd been asleep all day. We
got her to eat something, she had her leg up.'

'Was she not well?'

'No, not at all. Not then, and we didn't realize just how ill
she was. Well, I didn't.' Gyle's voice hardened. 'Lorna was
playing in the garden quietly, she knew not to wake her mum
up, then the racket started from next door. I mean, it wasn't
just a kid enjoying itself. It was that full-blown screaming,

shouting and bawling. The sort that makes your ears hurt. All I asked her to do was keep her kid a bit quieter. She told me to fuck off.'

'What was she wearing?' asked Costello.

'What?' The question seemed to pull Gyle back from his memories.

'What was she wearing? Sue.'

'Her?' Gyle thought for a moment. 'Jeans I think, nothing special. Nothing different. Just normal kind of stuff.'

'And later, when you saw her in the woods?'

'It was red, she was a mass of blood, black and red. I know now it was white, a dress or something, wee floppy shoes. Not her usual trainers or anything.'

Costello slid a picture of a long white dress across the table, keeping her finger on it. The prison officer lifted his head up, to see what she was passing over.

'I don't recall anything as fancy as that. But I've seen that picture before.' Gyle gave a slightly sarcastic smile, looking closer at Costello, as if he was seeing her as a woman for the first time. 'You two know something, don't you? Look, I didn't do that crime, I never harmed that woman or her kids.' His voice broke slightly. 'Whatever it is, you have to . . .'

'You know you could get out if you pleaded guilty and took the courses on anger management. They would consider parole on your life licence. It's not ideal, there would be restrictions, but you would feel the sun on your back, you could eat when you wanted, get out of bed when you wanted.' Batten leaned back a little. 'You could hook up with your daughter. You would cease to be a celebrity.'

'But I have to show remorse. And I can't feel remorse for something I did not do. Why should I? But if I ever do get out, I'll find the bastard who did it and I will bloody kill him. I think I should be allowed that at least.'

'Understandable. Do you have anybody in mind, a suspect, a suspicion, a vague feeling? Is there anybody who you thought . . .?'

Gyle shook his head. 'I have thought about it and thought about it. I know that there must be something, something that everybody missed and that little thing will set me free. But I

don't know what it is. What is it? Somebody came across her
and the boys, something happened. They used my axe, I admit
I left it there. I had done that a few times before, but it was
hidden behind a tree, not somewhere obvious. So were they
watching me? I heard Jock shout and I went. I came back half
an hour later, they were dead.'

'There was only your DNA on the axe, no sign that anybody
else had touched it,' said Costello. 'That is pretty hard to explain
away.'

'And I can't explain it.' Gyle shrugged. 'I don't understand
that, and I don't understand the crime – why do that to somebody but not bring their own weapon with them?'

'Kind of arguing yourself into a corner there. The killer did
bring the weapon with them, and it was you.' Batten nodded,
folding his arms, as if he was one professional talking to another.
'You had that rage. You had the weapon. A more organized
killer would not go out hunting without the means to engage
his prey. Whereas this hunter, supposedly, turned up and hoped
that a weapon would appear. This guy got into a rage and picked
up the one weapon at hand. The weapon is incidental in this
type of crime; it's the rage that is important.'

'And?' asked Gyle.

'So what did she do that enraged you so much? There were
a few wee things over the years, but what was the big one that
broke you? The pretty dress? Her smile? Her lovely life?' asked
Costello.

'I did not kill them.'

'Well, I think you did, you were the one with the weapon,'
said Costello, closing the file as if she was now really bored
with it all. She had pushed Gyle as far as she was happy to.
He had been consistent.

'And they said the killer knew her – how did they put it . . .?'
Gyle frowned.

'Somebody who'd had a previous relationship with the
victims,' added Batten.

'And that would be you then,' said Costello, 'again. They
said there was something sexual in it, all that cutting and cleaving
of young flesh, a nice woman in a beautiful white dress walking
through the woods, it's all a bit . . . porny.'

'Freudian?' offered Batten.

'Yeah, at the trial they said that I fancied her skinny middle-class arse.'

'And you didn't?'

Gyle grumped. 'No thanks.'

'No?'

'No mate, I didn't.'

'Your wife was sick.'

'And I had a five-year-old daughter.'

'You have not seen your daughter, have you?'

'No, Lorna doesn't come to visit me. I wish that she could, but it's better for her that she doesn't. She did try . . .' His hand drifted to his stomach. 'I understand that.'

'Have you read the book?'

'I got to read it before it was published. *Friday's Child*. Named because that was the day her life changed, the day she was told what I was accused of.'

'And how did that make you feel?'

'If I was in her shoes, I'd probably think the same. Lorna accepts my guilt.'

'But you say you are innocent.'

'I know that, but she doesn't.'

'Do you recall anybody else hanging around Sue Melrose at that time?'

'Do you mean a lover? No, I never saw anybody. Neither did my wife, and she was in the house all day.' He folded his arms and gazed somewhere into the middle distance.

'Mr Gyle, are you sure you saw nobody else in the woods?'

'I didn't see anybody, but it was summer, the leaves were dense. They could have been hiding anywhere. There must have been someone else. There must have been.'

'And you went off when you heard Jock scream?'

Gyle perked up, he was on solid ground here. 'He didn't scream, he shouted, and no, I didn't see anybody else. It was sunny but the woods are dark, it doesn't mean there wasn't anybody there. Just that I did not see them. I didn't see her or the kids before I heard the shout. I only saw them afterwards.' The blue eyes looked across at the both of them. 'But somebody was there.'

'It must be hard to live with those memories, of those bodies lying there.'

Gyle shrugged, 'No more difficult for me than it was for any of the other ones who saw it. I didn't put them there so my conscience is clear. It's not that that stops me sleeping at night, it's the fact that my wife died thinking I was capable of killing that woman next door.'

'Sue,' said Costello. 'Her name was Sue.'

FOURTEEN

Wyngate was trying to get the girl from Central Records off the phone. At some point in the recent past, he must have mentioned to her that his son, Artie, was on to solids, and she had never forgotten it and resumed baby talk at every opportunity. The yellow light was flashing to say there was another caller on the line, and he looked out through the window into the hall, where a tall man stood, dressed smart-casual in jeans, a dark blue long-sleeved jumper and an anorak dripping over his shoulder. Wyngate took the opportunity to hang up and from the safety of the inner office, Anderson watched him welcome the visitor, David Griffin, the first officer on the scene.

The ex-police officer was now a counsellor with his own practice in Edinburgh, a kind-faced man, an expression that invited confidence. Kind hazel eyes, short grey-flecked hair, a trusting smile and a hint of a beard. He was the kind of man you would want to appear at your house after a terrible incident: capable without being overbearing, self-assured without being arrogant. He was confident in his own skin.

He shook Colin Anderson warmly by the hand and introduced himself, although everybody in the room knew exactly who he was. 'DCI Anderson, we meet again.'

'We have met before?' asked Anderson. 'Sorry, I don't recall.'

'No, you probably wouldn't, we were both quite drunk at the time.' He turned to smile at the rest of the room. 'And it was a very long time ago. DI Costello I recognize. DS Mulholland, Vik is it?' He nodded, then said to Wyngate. 'I hope this lot treat you better than my team did when I was a DC.'

'Doubt it,' said Wyngate, 'I'm the coffee boy.'

'Mine's white with two sugars, ta very much.' Griffin clapped his hands together in delight. 'Works every time.'

Wyngate pulled a face and sloped off to put the kettle on.

'So, have a seat. I need to get up to speed on this one, David. We could do with an account of what happened that evening,' said Anderson.

Griffin coughed slightly, a nervous swipe of his hand through his hair. He sat down, and took a deep breath. 'Not something I like to revisit. It remains one of the most awful crime scenes I have ever come across.'

'What made you go into the woods in the first place?'

He shook his head. 'It was a noise. I don't know what I heard, some kind of scream I presume, but I know at the time I did not think, oh my God somebody is being hurt. I walked up to the corner and heard something, saw something that wasn't right. I think later it was the noise of the dog, maybe of one of the kids. I don't know. But I know that I ran down that path. It was an early summer evening. Sue, I knew. I knew her husband from way back – we went to the same school. I was used to walking that beat, and I never expected any trouble. Not from the street, but the woods themselves were on our detail of places to patrol, teenage drinkers and the like, trying to have a bonfire and setting themselves alight. The odd junkie, nothing much.'

'But on that night I must have known something was wrong, I ran until I was right on top of them. At the Doon, I found Sue. I thought she was sleeping, then I saw the red, and him standing, covered in her blood.' He shook his head, the memory was painful. 'I still thought she was sleeping. In that frock of white and red. I remember stopping a few feet away from him, I nearly ran into him. I was sick, then I screamed. At first I thought there had been a terrible accident. Then I saw Bobby.' He swallowed hard. The room was silent. They had seen the photographs of what had happened to the wee boy.

Anderson wondered how much of that was his true memory, or how much of it had been altered with every retelling. It would be sanitized in Griffin's mind by now. Many things would have been dropped from the story: the sheer brutality, the spilled blood, the clefts of flesh, the smell of it all, the blood and the shit and the piss – the fact that people in death are ugly and twisted; they do not lie nicely as if they are sleeping. They look as though they have fought, struggled and been terrified until the very last breath in their body has been squeezed out of them.

'The evidence against Gyle stacks up.'

'It does. There was some evidence he had been pestering her. He was older, she was pretty. His wife was ill and Steve was away a lot. Sue was very lovely, genuinely nobody had a bad word to say about her. She loved her kids, she loved her husband, sweet person. Steve was working that night, she had been in all day, so went out for a stroll with the boys at tea time. Gyle was out cutting wood. What happened next is anybody's guess. But I finished it. I knocked him down then punched him.' He shrugged, seemed to drift off. His eyes stared into the middle distance, his face drained white, his fingers went up to his lips. The room was silent apart from the hum of the computers. Anderson caught Wyngate's eye, the young detective was near to tears. He had a son that age. 'Sorry, I can't stay here. I can't look at those photographs.' He wiped his face with the palms of his hands. 'It's exactly as they say, that the most terrifying images you have ever seen in your life are on the back of your eyelids. And they are there for an eternity. Sorry mate, no can do. I'm not up to this, not here.' He glanced at the photograph of the scene at the Doon, and the bloodstained sunflower hat, then looked at his watch. 'Say I'll meet you in the pub later, Horseshoe Bar? Sorry.' The door closed.

'We should have taken them down before he came in,' said Anderson.

'Why? It's going to be all over the news tomorrow.'

'I am going for a sniff-about. There is something not right about this, but nobody wants to know. First thing, could Gyle hear Aird from the Doon? It's a long way through dense trees. The initial investigation said no.' Costello was on the phone to O'Hare, feet up on the desk, slowly turning the top of the Hobnob packet, twisting it round and round so nobody else could get in – well, not without making a noise. 'So I was thinking about Gyle's story. He took Aird from the Devil's Pulpit to the house, going in the back door as Aird never ever used the front one. When he was asked what they did there, he said that he made Aird comfortable, there was a wee argument. Aird didn't want to go to A and E, Gyle wanted to drive him there.'

'I do have a job you know,' said O'Hare with dry sarcasm.

Costello said, 'Wheesht, in the original statement he uses the phrase, *I made him a cup of tea* or *I put the kettle on for him* – something like that when asked a direct question. But when we were talking to him in the Bar L, he said that he stayed for a cuppa. Then he said he was sick at the scene.'

'Please don't ask what—'

'I was thinking if there was any of Gyle's stomach contents in frozen storage that might prove that he had drunk some tea, thereby proving he had been at Aird's house.'

'Is that all? Would you like me to prove the existence of God in my lunchtime and solve Fermat's Last Theorem before coffee break?'

'Is that a no then?'

'I'm afraid so. Costello, we are talking years ago and, well, it doesn't really mean anything in the context of what happened that night.'

'It lends weight to their story.'

'And how did that go? He was called away by Aird, he leaves his axe, he comes back, he sees bodies everywhere, he gets down to see if he can help Sue, he gets covered in her blood, then he gets rugby-tackled by a young police officer who had heard the scuffle. They both got covered in blood as Griffin wrestled Gyle to the ground. And punched him. I remember the case at the time.'

'But the dog bark. Gyle never said he heard the dog bark.'

'Well that proves he is lying, doesn't it?'

'I think they both might be right and there was someone else there.'

'Don't be so brave, Costello. This was an open-and-shut case. Gyle was sent down, people do not want this dragged up again. What do you think you are doing?'

She snorted. 'Not sure that I know. But Griffin said he vomited at the scene. Gyle said that he did too.'

'There was only one sample of stomach contents collected, Griffin's.'

She could hear him flick bits of paper over. 'But not Gyle's? Why not?'

'Costello, it was over twenty years ago,'

'But there would be a lab report. Do you not DNA-test ginger biscuits – you test every other bloody thing these days?'

O'Hare ignored her jibe. 'Not in a witness, Costello. And nobody was saying Gyle was poisoned or had ingested magic mushrooms, so it would not have been analysed. It was Griffin's vomit we collected. And that was only because it was there.'

'Why not Gyle's?' she repeated.

'He wasn't sick, not according to this.'

'He said he was.'

'Maybe he said it made him sick, as in, it made him feel sick. But then, if you can't stand the sight of blood, don't go chopping people up. But to be clear, there were no samples of Gyle's vomit collected at the scene.'

Costello could hear O'Hare's fingers on a keyboard.

Then she had an idea. 'What about the top of his boots? In case any vomit got caught there, as he spewed his guts up.'

'Long shot.'

'Come on, he's been in the jail for over twenty years, you have the correct permissions. It would take Matilda ten minutes to check.'

'It would take a lot longer than that, as you well know, and it would lend absolutely nothing to your timeline. And it would cost money.'

'So?'

'And it would lead to awkward questions, wouldn't it? So sorry, no can do. Not without opening up a huge can of worms. It could, and would, sound like you knew that the prosecution had withheld evidence of not collecting a sample from the scene, or concealing the results of the analysis of that sample, and that could lend weight to Gyle's argument of a miscarriage of justice. If that comes out there will be trouble – no smoke without fire on police cover-up. You only have one comment from Gyle that he ejected his stomach contents at the scene, and God knows he has had twenty years' worth of dark and lonely nights to think that one up.'

'So if you look and find nothing, then at least every stone has been turned. I think that's what we have been told to do here. Or maybe I misheard?' She tried to smile down the phone, but something in his tone told her it would be a step too far.

'I have to answer to my bosses as well, Costello, so sorry: no can do this time.'

Colin Anderson and David Griffin were sitting at a corner table in the Horseshoe pub, an orange juice in front of both of them. Two forty-something women at the bar turned round to look at them appraisingly. They were impressed. Anderson looked away but Griffin lifted his glass to toast them.

'God knows what they think of us, sitting here with bloody orange juice.'

'Well, they will either think that we are light on our loafers, or that we are not drinking because we have our Maseratis outside.' Griffin leaned back on the chair and smiled, taking it all in. He seemed very at home in a pub, very keen to be friendly to everybody. 'Not that I have a Maserati; I have a Morris Minor and a Hillman Imp that I spend money on. And a boring Ford Focus I drive about in. So here's to us, the last of the big drinkers, eh? Cheers.' They clinked glasses. 'Tinkering with old cars was how I got through it, you know. Being on my own, distracted doing something physical that was of no use to anybody. Just a tip for the future. Drink does not help.'

'But getting out my house does,' said Anderson. 'I feel it's like a pressure cooker in there.'

They sat in silence, following the overloud conversation of the redhead who was getting a new bathroom.

'So what are you thinking?' asked Griffin. 'While it's nice to be in touch, I can't say I enjoy revisiting that day. Thursday the twenty-seventh, 1992.'

'To tell you the truth, I need to get a bit of emotional background on it all. It looks awful written down in black and white.'

'It was awful.' Griffin nodded, holding on to a mouthful of orange juice before swallowing it. He lifted his glass to his mouth again then put it back down. 'It's been twenty-three years but it's still the first thing I think about every morning. Or I wake up, the sun is shining, and I think, oh it's going to be a lovely day, and then it flashes into my mind, for like, no reason at all. There's . . . well, it's difficult to understand.'

'Maybe not so difficult. I think the Shadowman will taint everything I do in life from here on in.'

Griffin eyes widened. 'God, well you do know then. You are one of the few people who do.' He shook his head before downing half a pint of orange juice.

'How well did you know them? Sue and Steven?'

'Steve. He was always called Steve. But yeah, as the community officer I knew them as a couple. And I knew Steve from school vaguely. He was a couple of years above me. They were a lovely couple, two nice wee kids. They had moved into that house two years before and were really trying to make it through those tough years, you know when the kids are really small and you walk around exhausted all the time. The mortgage stretched them and Steve was working all the hours in the garage. I think money was a bit tight. But in my role as community officer I had been called out a few times when Sue accused Gyle of this and Gyle accused Sue of that. It's all in the file. It escalated quickly over that long, hot summer. I was too young, too inexperienced to deal with horrific crime. That's why I ran out of Altmore Wood that evening screaming and crying like a baby.'

Anderson was content to let Griffin talk, realizing it might be easier to creep subtly up on the terrible memories of that day twenty-three years before. 'So you have kids?'

'Me, no. Not after that. Well, it was a result of that. My marriage broke up and that was one of the reasons. I fell to pieces after it; I was a bloody mess. No use to man nor beast. Just really shook my faith in human nature. For that to happen somewhere I knew well.'

'Oh, I never knew you were a local lad.'

'Yes, I was a banky, Clydebank born and bred. Only been

in the job for a couple of years when it happened. Never got back to my work afterwards, not really.'

'Was there a lot of trouble in the woods?'

'They wanted no Hardgate neds to get up to their mischief. The lower part of the wood was more accessible from the road in those days. So on a warm balmy evening like that, we'd walk up the path and make sure nobody was lighting a bonfire or getting way too drunk, look out for syringes – this was 1992 remember.' Griffin's bright blue eyes seemed to cloud over. 'I keep wanting to say that I heard a scream, but it wasn't a scream. It was a noise.' He lifted his glass again, draining the little juice that was left. 'A terrible, spine-chilling noise.'

'Was that Sue, or one of the . . .' Anderson found he couldn't ask the question.

'The dog, I think it was the dog. It sounded as though he was tearing its guts out.' Griffin rubbed his arms, cupping his hands round them, comforting himself. As the cuff of his shirt lifted slightly, Anderson saw some old scars on his arm. Had Griffin been driven to self-harm? He felt a knot at his own stomach – twenty-three years later and Griffin was still suffering.

'I think Sue and the boys were already dead by then,' he said quietly, eyes welling up. Then he pulled some strength from somewhere. 'I ran over to them; I ran over and launched myself at them. I knocked him flying and there was a fight that I don't recall anything about.'

'You punched him in the face.'

'I might have done. I have no memory. I do remember seeing that Sue was lying with her head against the wall, like a doll. Her head was at an angle. There were these cuts to her skin, like streaks of blood with black and white insides, it was the worst thing I . . . I picked her head up. She was dead; it was obvious she was dead but my brain just—'

'Wouldn't accept it. I get that totally.'

'Afterwards, in counselling, they said that my brain was protecting itself from what it was seeing, by not believing it. You can read the file for what happened after that. I really don't want to go through all that again. Fancy another drink?'

'I'll get them.' Anderson got up and walked towards the bar, his hands shaking. It could have been Claire, Helena, Peter, any of them. All vulnerable. Somebody bumped his arm gently, one of the women, too old for her thick power brows, smiled at him invitingly, hoping he was going to buy them a drink and invite them for a seat. He smiled back and walked up the bar a little way, to where there was a clear gap, hoping that his action would be seen as a gentleman not wanting to disturb them. In reality he wanted time for his nerves to steady. And what had Costello always told him to do? Mutter that the cops were about to raid for sex workers plying their trade so they had better leave. By the time the designer-bearded barman asked what he wanted, he had totally forgotten why he was there and who with.

FIFTEEN

Monday 24 August 2015

Lynda McMutrie woke from her sleep, her eyes sticky with tears and dirt. She was breathing in the moisture from the dirty carpet and it stunk of faeces. She lay with her head down trying to protect herself from the onslaught. Her ears were red raw, the skin of her nose was burning as if it was being peeled from her, layer upon layer. Her left foot was heavy, throbbing and hot. She could no longer feel her right leg. She nuzzled the floor, thinking that the pillow was hard, a little damp. Then she recalled she was on the carpet in her basement, any other memory was fuzzy round the edges. So she wasn't at the Doon, and a great many vodkas had gone down her throat since she split up from her handsome beau in the photographs.

She looked round when she heard the gentle scuttling of the claws, the flashes of sleek black and brown, moving so fast she didn't think she actually saw them at all. But she knew when the first of the blowflies arrived. They landed on her face so she closed her eyes and tried to ignore their hairy feet and the drone of their wings in her ears. She shook her head to keep them off, but when they returned there were more of them, clustering and feeding, humming and droning.

She began to recite the poem, recalling the odd line here and there. The saddest words, it might have been.

She spoke out loud but all that filled her ears was the roar of the blowflies. Then she realized the top of her forehead was getting wet, a gentle lapping from ice-cold water. It crept along to her face, moving like fingers through her scalp. It was working its way in small wave form across the floor, soaking the carpet and coming towards the underside of her ear, the side of her face, then her shoulder, along the side of her chest. By the time it was touching the top of her thigh she realized the water was deeper. She had to lift her head up as it was covering one eye now. Even holding her head against the strain of her neck, the water was then slipping round the bottom of her nostril. She kept trying to lift her head clear.

Thinking more clearly than she had done for years, she realized that she would drown. If she opened her eyes she could see the water deepen, an inch, and inch and a half, ever deeper. She tried again to get on her feet but failed, trying to get some leverage with the arm that was locked underneath her now. Five minutes later, all she could hear was her ears roaring with the pressure and the noises of the flies and the rats and the water itself as it spun into all the nooks and crannies on the floor, the eddies and vacuums of the incoming tide as it swept towards her, enveloping her. Then she heard a footstep on the stairs. Somebody was coming to rescue her.

She heard them moving towards her, stepping over her to get to her head. They tried to lift her up. She opened her eyes to see the bottom of the old Hunters, with the small white strip; she knew them. She closed her eyes and praised the Lord.

She heard her own voice saying, bubbling through the water, 'Help me, please. Help.'

He bent over and pulled her arm out. Then he seemed to stand back up, as if he was thinking about what to do with her. Then she felt the weight on her back, the gentle pressure that increased steadily, forcing her head down.

She tried for one last lungful of air but got a mouthful of water instead.

Wyngate put the phone down. He had been on the line for over forty minutes to various people who considered it their duty to be obstructive. His ear was hurting. He examined the piece of paper in front of him, lined and pockmarked, crumbled and crisscrossed here and there, names written and crossed out. It had made some kind of sense when he was scribbling it down. Through the middle was a wavy line that was the ancient route of an underground river called the Dorcha, a river that might not be so ancient after all. Was it now nibbling its way back where it belonged, taking the foundation of the driveway at number 2 Altmore Road with it?

He logged on to Goggle maps and found the Greenside Reservoir. The old nutter had been talking about that when he had been in yesterday, wittering on about the good old days when he owned all the land, and the wood, and most of the Kilpatricks and, according to him, most of the west coast of Scotland. He had managed the wood and the grass and, again according to him, the wind and the water. Wyngate had nodded, pretended to take notes, and wondered how much his two-year-old's birthday party was going to cost him. Why did Artie need a new outfit anyway? All he was going to do was cover it in jelly.

The old guy had droned on and on about what was built in the old Dorcha basin. Then there was the bit that Wyngate now, with the benefit of hindsight, wished he had listened really carefully to. Something about the woods should be flooding with all this weather, but they were not. The floor of the Pulpit was dry-ish. Wyngate understood what the old man was saying. The water was going somewhere else.

The civil engineer's report said the water was coming into the sinkhole via some kind of culvert. The weight of rainwater had burst through an old drain to make a connection. Wyngate suspected the foot bones had been in the drain. The older bones could have been kicking around down there for a century or more. The engineers had packed their tools away and left with a recommendation that the Dirk-Huntleys should get in touch with their lawyer as the land search when they first purchased the house had been insufficient. The end result, one sinkhole had devalued number 2 Altmore Road by 70 per cent.

Wyngate was not an imaginative or an intuitive cop. He worked with facts and information. There was something prickling at the back of his mind, something that he had seen twice and not connected. He was on an internet trail that would take him somewhere, but he had no idea where he needed to be.

It would have something to do with the task that Anderson had set them: to track the ownership of the Dirk-Huntley house, and the other properties on Altmore Road and match that with the lists at the Land Registry. Who might have had access to the drain? Who might have had access to put the foot bones there, only for them to be washed twenty feet to the sinkhole?

The old guy had been talking about excess rain and how overflow gates come into use to protect the surrounding land, preventing too much stress on the walls of the reservoir, about the building site on the other side of the hill and the geographical pressure of landfill. The overspill of water would try to get back to the Clyde, down the old route of the rivers from before the days of the dam. They still worked fine.

Then Wyngate's attention had wavered as his visitor had started ranting about green belt, the new build, and the way that might change the course of the river again. Not all of it, but too much water for the new watercourse to deal with, so the rainwater had traversed to its ancient route, the Dorcha. He looked again at the Google map of the area. He pulled his glasses from his forehead down on to his eyes and peered closely at the screen, reading the smallest, faintest words on the map. High on the hill, the notations of the burns and rivers that veined the land.

Cochno. The Humphrey. The Dorcha was not there, it was underground.

But that could have nothing to do with a single old drain filling up in a street down the hills, close to the river. That was a rain issue. Not a river issue. Water from above caused one problem, water coming up from below caused others.

He turned the thought over in his mind a few times, then scaled the map out. There was a river, a narrow ribbon that twisted and wound round the Kirkpatrick hills, on the verge of Hardgate, to come out at the Clyde; it travelled in a huge loop. And it must do that for a reason. The ground in the middle was too high, so the river went round it.

Not as the old guy had hinted, under it.

Wyngate looked out through the window into the rain, the endless downpour. The gutter above that window was over-flowing and the water formed a silver curtain. Would that volume of water be enough to change the course of the river, the excess running down and round, cutting a straight path down to the river, if something else had tipped the balance? He looked back at the map on the wall, trying to find Altmore Road, nothing more than a tiny spur in low-lying land on a map of this scale. A few houses and a cross to mark the site of the ancient church.

He looked up the planning applications for the area. It took him another half an hour, but he found it in the end, a planning application from McGregor Homes for the development of twenty luxury homes to the north of Hardgate: rejected. Rejected due to lack of an adequate access road to the north. New plans were pending re the acquisition of more land so the road could come up from the south. And the obvious choice was Altmore Road, which at the moment was a dead end. All they had to do was knock down the Big House. And he couldn't see Jock Aird agreeing to that, but it did give the old guy a reason to be on the doorstep of their station shouting the odds.

The old guy had said that something might have diverted the river, somebody who knows nothing about water and their ancient paths. Water might go up, down, round and about, but it would always go in the direction it wanted to; in this case, the shortest way to the river. He looked back at the map, wondering if some building work had already gone ahead. He could see no permissions for the landfill site his visitor had mentioned. It was too much of a coincidence that all this was happening at the same time.

A quick search into the Melrose file threw up the background check on Aird that had been carried out at the time. John 'Jock' McKenzie Aird, born in North Uist, had come south as a teen-ager to work on the land round Altmore, which was owned by his family. He had never married. He had no family. He had

stayed with his relatives in Altmore House and inherited it on
their death. Wealthy, gentleman farmer. There was a recent entry
that he had threatened Esther Dirk-Huntley with a knife, but
no further action had been taken. He had a licence for a shotgun.
Wyngate requested permission to access his bank records. He
was a good friend of Gyle, and his landlord. Was he still bankrolling his friend's defence?

Altmore House, Road, Wood. The something that had been
irritating the back of his mind jumped to the front, something
he thought he recognized. Altmore. Alt more. Allt mohr.

He typed the word into Google translate, from Gaelic to
English.

Big river.

Anderson was wondering what Wyngate was doing in the outer
office. He had been on the phone for a long time, which is what
Anderson would have expected, but then he started typing at
speed, his glasses down then scribbling like a demon, looking
up at the map and more scribbling. He was very interested in
history all of a sudden.

Anderson left him to it and called up the report Costello had
written for him. A brief history on Thomas Andrew Gyle, a
man jailed for a murder so vicious that the first officer on the
scene had been unable to continue in the job, despite all sorts
of psychological support. Yet Gyle had not shown any violence
at all while incarcerated. Except the one incident Costello had
highlighted as he scrolled down; somebody had insulted Gyle's
daughter.

Anderson let his eyes scan over the words, most of the facts
he knew. He was looking for any other nuance as to why Gyle
had fallen so far, so quickly.

Some weird fascination in case he felt himself going the
same way. Gyle was a vile and vicious murderer, killing wee
boys. Anderson could see the axe raining down on them, cleaving
their flesh again and again and . . . he stopped thinking about
that, digging his nails into the palms of his hands until they
bled. This was not good, not good for him, not good for anybody.
He had to get this into perspective. They had found some bones.
That was all, nothing to do with Gyle. He didn't have to look

at Gyle's documentation, he didn't have to, not until some link was proven.

But he just couldn't help himself.

Andrew Taylor Gyle. A quiet-living, family man. Anderson had always thought of himself as a happily married, loving father. Maybe they were both wrong.

Anderson reached and picked up Costello's notes, swirls of biro highlighting the bits she thought he should read. Gyle had been a security guard, well trusted but not very well paid. His hours had been cut, his wife was off work on the sick. There were copies of the bank statements for the year running up to the killing of the Melrose family. Costello had done her home-work well, she had annotated the odd payment here and there. One to the Nuffield to see a private specialist about May's leg. When they had barely enough money to pay the rent, the land-lord waived it so they could pay a private orthopaedic consultant to review the treatment. She had also ringed a payment of five grand, which paid off their overdraft and put them on the straight and narrow. There was no note about where the money had come from. Five grand in debt was nothing to a lot of people, but Andrew Gyle was old school. He didn't have a credit card. If he couldn't pay, he didn't get. It would have worried him, kept him awake at night, fretting. It might have been the start of the slide that had ended in the brutal slaughter of the Melrose family. From a quiet family man to a man who could lift an axe and put the blade through the body of a baby. Costello suggested putting Mulholland on the trail of the money.

The meeting with Griffin had been interesting and Anderson had enjoyed his company. There was a vague arrangement to meet up again when Griffin was back in the west. He had worked in the area around Altmore Wood at the time of the murders. There was a deeper well there to tap, especially the tension between the two houses. The house had been one dwelling at one point, as it was again now. The Gyle family lived in the smaller portion – Andrew, May and their daughter Lorna. The Melrose family next door, in the larger part of the conversion with the corner plot of the garden. The two couples were very different. Andrew and May were in their forties by the time their daughter arrived. May was a quiet woman who had suffered from bad health. Andrew enjoyed his garden, the woods and his Johnny Cash records. A normal family.

Costello had highlighted part of Griffin's background statement. The story of May Gyle summed up the story of Andrew's fall to notoriety. One incident started a chain of events that ended in three brutal murders. May had forgotten her purse. She had been going to work in the café in Debenhams. It was a long walk down Altmore Road to the bus stop on the parade. Anderson thought that this was the same walk that Jennifer Lawson had been faced with that morning in the teeming rain. When May realized she had forgotten her purse, she turned back, rushing so she would not miss the bus. She tripped up on the stone step of her front door and lacerated the skin on the front of her shin. The skin ripped badly, folded back almost to the bone.

Gyle had been at work so Aird had driven May to the hospital. And that had been the start of it – from there to a cellulitis, a septicaemia, and more and more housebound. It had ended up a lonely death by multiple organ failure in Gartnavel Hospital, just months after her husband had been sentenced to life and her daughter had been removed from her.

For all of that long hot summer, Gyle was overworking; stressed and underpaid. Looking after their five-year-old daughter, running back and forward to the hospital, struggling to keep his job. According to the statement, Gyle was devoted to his wife and considered his neighbours noisy and inconsiderate. May had started to come home from hospital on weekends then gradually increased her time at home to see how she coped. The Thursday of the incident was the first Thursday she was home for many weeks. Gyle had taken the day off work. He was going to chop logs, worried about the expense of heating the house during the long winter. May was going to have a lovely quiet day home in the sun. There was a shepherd's pie ready to go in the oven. Gyle had made it before he went out to the wood.

May was dead, but her statement spoke for her. She knew Sue was waiting in for a roofer. The kids were stuck in the small back garden, but as Steven had banned them from playing where he kept his cars, the kids were playing right outside the French window where May was relaxing, trying to get some fresh air after being in hospital for weeks on end. She had asked Sue if she could keep the noise down.

And that was the nail in the coffin. Somebody had put in brackets that May was too distraught to continue her statement. After that, her opinion was considered so unimportant that nobody had bothered to follow it up.

Anderson went back to the file. Wyngate had collected – and Costello had collated – witness statements and supporting evidence. Taken singly they were meaningless, but they were greater than the sum of their parts. Tiny waves that formed a tsunami. Sue was always the one who called the police. May kept out of the way. Andrew shouted over the garden fence. Steven poured oil on troubled water. It was Steven who spoke about the wee chats over the car engine, the odd shared beer. Anderson turned the page, Costello's biro, triple underlined. 'Gyle was a nice bloke,' Steven was quoted as saying. About the man who had killed his wife and sons. Anderson turned back, double checking. Melrose was always 'Steven', Griffin must have been a good friend to call him 'Steve', probably a habit from childhood, although if his memory served him right, they had only known each other vaguely at school. He made a mental note and read on.

That afternoon, Gyle had taken his axe to go and chop some wood deep in the forest. Sue Melrose and the boys had gone out for a walk deep in the woods.

Something terrible had happened.

But the mystery was about human nature.

Not about who had wielded the weapon.

He was still thinking about Gyle when his mobile rang.

SIXTEEN

I t was all going wrong for Jennifer. Douglas had his phone switched off and was out of the office, so Jennifer was leaving messages all over the place to tell him that Gordy was back in hospital hooked up on an antibiotic drip. Doctors kept looking at the cuts on her son then looking at her. At one point they tried to take Robbie into another room to examine him, but the wee lad had stuck resolutely to the sleeve of her anorak. So she watched them as they weighed, measured, bent and flexed her eldest son, waggling all his joints about. They kept asking her questions. They were polite, very polite, listening closely to every answer and analysing her own questions, often answering one of her questions with one of theirs. Where did the boys sleep? What did they eat? How long had Jennifer been on the mainland? Where was her accent from? They seemed to ask all about her, nothing about Douglas and where the hell he was.

Then they stopped and a nurse dressed Robbie so Jennifer could go down to the café for a cup of tea and a sandwich. As she waited to pay, she scrolled through her phone, trying to hold back the tears. They were waiting for somebody to come and have a word with her. Then, and only then, could she go and sit with Gordy, and even then, only if Robbie didn't cause any disruption. Was there nobody who could come and take him off her hands?

No.

How bad did that sound? She had no family here. She didn't know any of her neighbours. She wished she had waved to the jogger and the dog, got them in for a cup of coffee. Then they might have come to help. Her mum was no good, still out on the island, not really talking to the daughter who had dared to get out and tried to make a life for herself, away from the smell of the sea and fish. Glasgow too always smelled of fish, with top notes of salt and vinegar. It was a very different kind of imprisonment. She got to the end of her contacts on her phone. It was a very short list.

She pulled Colin Anderson's card out of her pocket. They came from Partick somewhere. That wasn't a million miles away. Dared she phone him again? He answered on the third ring, half talking to somebody else as he did, 'DCI Anderson.'

'Hi,' she said, not thinking what else to say.

'Jennifer? Is that you? Is the wee guy OK?'

'Yes, yes,' she assured him, and what was she going to say now? She blurted it out. 'I had to bring him back to hospital and

I can't get hold of Douglas. He's in an important meeting and the switchboard kept saying he was unavailable. But this is an emergency and they don't believe me.'

'Leave it with me.'

Seven minutes later, Douglas phoned, almost beside himself with anxiety. He was coming back over to the west; he'd be at the hospital in an hour. She was to sit tight. And he had been in a meeting, it wasn't that he was messing about and avoiding her. She heard a male voice ask if everything was OK, and reassure him it was fine for him to leave.

Two hours later, as she was sitting by Gordy's cot, holding the dressing that covered his pinkie, the door had opened and Douglas had appeared and given her a hug. The baby had woken up and given him a big smile. The icy nurses had melted and been lovely to Douglas – not that they had been horrid to her, but they were so pleasant to the lovely, handsome man who was so concerned about his wife and his child. Robbie was not so thrilled to see his dad and stuck to his mum like a limpet with separation anxiety.

Before they left, one of the senior nurses had taken Douglas off to a side room, or maybe Douglas had taken the nurse off to a side room. They were joined by a woman who had the words 'Child protection social worker' written all over her. She looked worried when she went in, but relaxed and happy when she came out. She didn't look at Jennifer, but did look at Robbie and gave him a smile. He burst out crying.

Douglas came out of the room and took Robbie, still crying, from her arms. Then he carried him outside and handed him back to Jennifer and said he was going off to get the car. He wasn't even two steps away when he got his phone out and she heard the words, *Hi, how are you?* Whoever it was, Douglas was pleased to talk to them.

As soon as they were all in the car, Jennifer had fallen asleep, cuddling into the big warm seat, the gentle noise of the wee one sleeping in the back and the hypnotic swipe of the windscreen wipers.

But they had left the baby at the hospital, her sleep would not let her forget that, and as she woke and tried to look out through the front window, she couldn't tell if it was the rain or the tears that were blurring her vision. As they drove up Altmore Road to do a U-turn, she looked at the scary big house, in darkness. The Steeles, with the pink Fiat parked half-on half-off the pavement. The drunk's house had a light on in the hall. Cadena was staring out of the upstairs window of her parents' house, watchful. Jennifer looked in to the garden of the abandoned house at number 6 with its cracked sinks and bits of car engine. She had seen a rat in there once, but Douglas had told her it was her imagination. Rats liked to live near water, not in front gardens.

As usual, her own house was on its best behaviour because Douglas had turned up. The smell had gone, the closed doors stayed closed, the open ones stayed open.

The heating went on and the radiators warmed up a little; the rain had even eased off. He turned on the water, there was pressure. He suggested she have a bath, put on a nice dress. He would take her out. As she lay in the bath looking at the bad plasterwork on the ceiling, wondering if she could ask him to take them back to Edinburgh tomorrow, she heard him on the phone and held still in the water so she could make out what he was saying. He was booking a table in a restaurant so she wouldn't have to cook anything. Maybe he had looked in the kitchen cupboards and realized there was not only nothing to eat, but nothing clean to eat it off.

She climbed out of the bath and got dressed slowly, then packed a little overnight bag. Pulling her old coat out of the wardrobe, she realized it was covered in mildew.

So she put on her older, everyday coat, knowing Douglas would frown at it. He had left his jacket hanging in the hall. A thought struck her. He had been lying to her, so why should she be the good wife? She slipped her hand into the pocket and took out his mobile. She retreated back up the stairs and redialled the last number. It went straight to voicemail. It thanked her for calling. It was a counselling service. Douglas was having counselling? She felt guilty, guilty about looking, guilty about what he was going through, something he could not tell her about. She was not a good wife. She put her best smile on as she went down the stairs. Douglas was sitting in front of the fire, his long legs bent in front of him, reading a classic car magazine.

'I've booked a table at Frito's, the best Italian in Glasgow.'

'We need to see Gordy first,' she said, quietly, aware of his scrutiny of her coat.

He looked at her. His face turned to thunder. Then Robbie, sensing trouble, was sick.

SEVENTEEN

Anderson and Costello were just about to leave the station, standing at the bottom of the stairs, pulling up their hoods and collars before facing the onslaught of rain. Costello had been trying to engage him in conversation about Wyngate's difficulties in tracking down Lorna Gyle. Anderson had looked at her as if she was asking to play a round of golf with Kim Kardashian, then shook his head.

'She was five years old, she can't add anything to the case.'

He was right, of course. It was all over the news. If the woman wanted to be found, she would have come forward, but she had chosen to slip away from her previous life.

Costello tried to point out that Lorna couldn't play games like that. Nobody could choose who they were related to. No matter where she was, Costello wanted to ferret her out. She had the right to know that her father's case was being, however superficially, reviewed, but if she pushed the point, Anderson could issue clear instructions that Lorna was to be left alone. How much of that was a reflection of how he felt about his own daughter, Claire? No dad would want to drag his daughter through that. She had a bit of respect for Gyle now. Anderson's instructions were to identify then explain the presence of the bones. With an alternative explanation of them, there was no exculpatory evidence for Gyle. It would be another nail in his coffin of guilt and his supporters might be silent for once.

It was one of those blanket statements so untypical of Anderson. The old Anderson would see that – regardless of the outcome of the bones – there was still the suggestion that the initial investigation had been 'hurried'.

Lack of sleep, lack of concentration, an inability to think in a linear fashion. The case was jumping all over the place. She wondered about how things were going at home. Not well, she presumed, but when asked, Anderson had clammed up, telling her nothing. Which she thought was unfair, as she had been the one who had endured Brenda's early morning visit. And Anderson's phone rarely bleeped these days. He never glanced at it, smiled and slid it back into his pocket, the way he normally did. It was the absence of what he said, an absence of chitchat. No kids texting him, wanting a fiver for this or a pick-up here or a drop-off there.

Nothing.

As they walked to the corner of Hyndland Road, Costello had the feeling, maybe wrongly, that Anderson was lonely at home. Was he still being subtly punished? Fourteen months on and still being punished. The boss wasn't eating; he drifted away during conversations, and he looked awful, tired and worn.

Whatever was going down, it wasn't good. And he was going to have to face the media soon. That needed heading off at the pass. A garage door banged open as they passed. Anderson jumped and grabbed on to Costello's arm.

'Christ!'

She carefully unwound his fingers, but kept walking, pulling him along. 'It's somebody putting a wheelie bin out, Colin, get a grip.'

'I hate loud noises these days, they . . . I don't know . . . they hurt . . .'

'Oh, calm down. Look, there's somebody waiting to see you,' said Costello, nodding at the Focus, parked on a double yellow. 'They were thinking about getting out until they saw me.'

'Really?'

Really. So polite. Old Anderson would have said something like, *Well, you do have that effect on men.* Costello stood in front of him; he seemed at a loss about what to do next. 'Do you know who that is?'

'I think it might be David.' He lifted his hand to shield his eyes from the rain.

'David Griffin?'

'Yes,' snapped Anderson, as if Costello should know.

'I thought you saw him last night.'

'I did.'

'So what is he doing here now?'

'Costello, will you give it a rest? Now bugger off and leave me alone.' And off he walked in the direction of Griffin's car.

Go to hell, she thought. She had an invite from Walker to go out for a curry, and she felt like accepting it, but out of habit she clocked the plate of the dark red Focus. The figure behind the driving seat got out of the car and raised a hand to her in greeting before walking towards Anderson, greeting him with a smile and handshake, almost a hug. There was a short conversation. Griffin scratched his beard as if he had thought of something. Anderson pointed, obviously saying that his own car was over there. Griffin was pointing up and down the street, the coffee shop, the pub. They were going for something to eat.

Feeling hungry, Costello watched the play and filled in the dialogue, while getting very wet. Anderson was smiling, Griffin was laughing as they walked away.

Well, at least some bugger was happy. If Costello didn't know differently, it looked like Anderson was being picked up by some guy who had had his eye on him for ages. As she watched, Anderson looked at the dark sky as he put his hand in his pocket and pulled out his mobile phone. So that will be him phoning Brenda to make sure she is OK, to make sure that Claire is OK. Rather than going home to find out for himself.

Whatever way it was, Costello was glad that it was not her problem. Her entire childhood had been spent tiptoeing round somebody else's problems and emotions. In the end it was a game of control.

The way to win was not to play.

Brenda and Colin were dancing around each other, using Claire as the pole in the middle, round and round but never actually talking.

If push came to shove she would gladly bang their heads together.

And if push really came to shove, what was an ex-police officer doing having an off-the-record chat with the SIO on another related case? One informal chat was enough to garner an opinion. If Griffin had something concrete to add to his official statement at the time, he should be in the station, dictating a bloody statement about it. Her phone went. Archie Walker. Her stomach rumbled.

'Oh hi.'

'I'll have to call off. Pippa's very bad at the moment, I can't get her to settle. I think it might be all this rain. Something is affecting her and, well, that's the only thing I can think of.'

'No problem,' said Costello, still watching the two retreating figures, two middle-aged blokes hurrying along the street in the raindrops, chatting, laughing in each other's company.

'You're not upset, are you?'

'No, why should I be?'

'You sound distracted.'

'I am standing outside work. I think I'm going to go back in again. I've just seen Griffin and Anderson go off together like Wallace and Gromit.'

'Batten thought that might happen.'

'Why?'

'Counselling. Griffin is a counsellor for carers. He has suffered from PTSD after the Melrose incident – well, you have seen the pictures; nobody walked away from that with their soul intact.'

'And he's counselling Colin?'

'Pretty much a foregone conclusion. We can talk to these people until the cows come home, Costello, and it will have no real resonance, but when a copper with PTSD meets another who is suffering the same thing, of course there is going to be a degree of empathy there. It will do him good.'

Costello sniffed.

'Or are you jealous that he is not talking to you? Do you need to be the important one in Anderson's life? You are not. He needs male friends to go out down the pub with. He has belonged to his work for too long.'

'You really have been talking to Batten,' Costello snapped, instantly dismissing the last conversation.

'But you agree? Do you see? It takes another police officer to see what you go through in your work, and to understand it. If he is talking to Griffin, then good luck to him.'

'They are not meeting in the station,' said Costello defensively.

'Then it is not about bloody police business, is it? Can that poor guy not have a chat with a mate without you scrutinizing it? It's great that he is talking to somebody who is not going to write up a report on him.' Walker sounded almost envious. What strain was he feeling – these days of 120 per cent commitment to the job while coping with a wife like Pippa. 'Are you hanging about on street corners watching him like he is some vulnerable adult in need of a minder?' At that point, Walker's wife shouted at him; a sharp, needy voice, like a child's, calling across the park, wanting him to come over and push the swing higher. 'Look, I need to go.'

'Yeah, don't you always?' Costello turned round and headed back into the station to speak to McColl. 'I'll go back into the office.'

'Why?'

'I have nothing better to do,' she answered with a modicum of honesty, then changed her mind as she saw another call come through. Men are like buses – none, then two at once. She told O'Hare she'd call him back when she was somewhere dry.

By half past eight Jennifer was sitting in the back of the Audi with a special fish supper, dipping the chips into curry sauce. Robbie was helping himself to any that had not been covered in vinegar. He didn't like that. He was squishing the rest of the chips into the back seat and Jennifer let him. They had barely stayed twenty minutes at the hospital. Robbie being sick on his dad's suit just as they were leaving the house had soured his mood as well as the air. He was not pleased. Jennifer had explained that kids did stuff like that, but Douglas had been annoyed. It really struck her, for the first time, how hopeless he was with the boys. The nice detective would have known what to do, having had two kids of his own.

They were late to the restaurant to then be told that they didn't allow children of any description. Jennifer turned to leave; Douglas stopped her. She thought he was going to make a scene and insist that his exhausted wife and sick child get a seat in a corner somewhere and something to eat. But he gave her the car keys, some money, and told her there was a chippy up the street and she could take the food back to the car and eat it.

He was bringing a client here next week, he really needed to test the menu.

She had looked at him as if she had never seen him before, not really believing what he was saying. So he expected her and Robbie to eat chips in the back of the car. She thought that through, her heart pounding, and determined not to cry in a posh restaurant with her make-up on. So she walked out.

And was now sitting in the car, calm and greasy fingered.

It was after nine when he joined her, immediately complaining about the smell, and then moaning that they had better not have made a mess. He drove off, jarring the car into gear, saying that all he needed was a bit of space in his head; he had important meetings this week and paperwork to do. He dropped her back at the hospital, but not before phoning and turning on his charm to ask if Robbie could stay there with his mum, otherwise he would really pine for her.

Jennifer sat in the back, feeling used. Before he got out of the car she rubbed the remains of her chips under the seat, wiping her curried hands on the cover. That would serve him bloody right.

At the hospital she snuggled into the chair, Robbie curled up beside her. She had looked at her phone. One voicemail. That would be from Douglas, apologizing. It was from Colin Anderson, asking her how the baby was.

EIGHTEEN

'You had something to say about our chat yesterday, something to add?'

'I'm not sure.' Griffin coughed slightly, picked up another onion bhaji and had a bite. 'Do you know Harry Easdale has died?'

'Yes, he died of cancer a few weeks after he retired. Well, I think it was medical retirement, I didn't know him well.'

'He was the SIO on the case.'

'I thought it was Levern; it was Levern I spoke to.'

'On paper it was Levern, on the field it was Easdale, and he had to close that case and close it fast.'

'Understandable.'

'The case was investigated properly but—'

'There are a few buts. We have got that far, David. All leads were followed but it was cursory at best.'

'Easdale allowed me on the team but I should not have been there. I should have gone back to my duties as a beat bobby in the community and never been allowed near a case where I was a material witness. Where I knew the locals well, all their little traits and issues.'

'Like the McMutries?' Anderson's phone went. It was O'Hare; no doubt it was about the bones. He thought about accepting it. The peshwari naan arrived on the table, and for the first time in over a year he felt hungry. He rejected the call.

'Oh, they were dreadful, a real problem family. But they were not involved; they were small-time. They were housebreakers and vandals, then they started dealing and messed about the wrong people.'

'Yeah, well, I think McPherson had to go abroad, for the good of his kneecaps.'

'Barbara's man?' guessed Griffin. 'No surprise there.'

'Sounds like you keep up with things?'

'People don't change.' He sipped his Kingfisher. 'I'm good at people. I have a good practice, do a fair bit of PTSD work, "stress at work" type of counselling. Everything from people going through horrific surgery to people who get sick at the thought of going to work. We do a lot of work for banks and multinationals. We are so busy we are thinking of opening an office here in Glasgow. I mean, workers now get a BlackBerry so they can be contacted twenty-four/seven, then I get paid to talk them through the stress of being contacted twenty-four/seven.' He looked at Anderson, a concerned smile. 'How are you feeling now? How is this case affecting you? I can see the signs. I spent some time googling you, I hope you don't mind. But if you need a chat, outwith this environment, I can put you in touch with good people.'

Anderson sat back, relaxing. He didn't mind being here with tasty pakora and no nightmares, away from his wife and his daughter and the madness that seemed to invade his every thought. 'I'd like to get into the head of Andrew Gyle.'

'No, DCI Anderson, I think that is the last thing you want to do.' Griffin talked quietly, although there was nobody in earshot. 'There is something that has always bothered me.' He put his hand out, fingers splayed, as if stopping any runaway thoughts Anderson might have. 'Now this was going round at the time. It was looked at, but maybe not as closely as it should have been. Altmore Road has always been a strange place. There were rumours about Jock Aird, the guy that owned it all at one point . . . enjoyed . . .'

'Enjoyed?'

'Enjoyed the power. The women. The McMutrie woman, when her man left her, he kind of stepped in and . . . Used her, like a slave for . . . well, living in the house, rent free.'

'What kind of slave, a bit of housekeeping?'

'A bit more than that.' Griffin's eyes were fixed and deadly serious, an unspoken message.

'What?' Anderson nearly burst out laughing.

'I'm telling you what the rumour was at the time. Not with the wife, she was a drunken old slapper, but with the daughter; she was young at the time. But Easdale would not investigate. The path at the back of the cottages, I presume it is still there?'

'It runs along beyond the back fences – yes, it is still there.'

'And if it looks used, then why does it look used? There is no reason for anybody to use it. There's a bloody great road and pavement in front of the house that serves the job better. It always puzzled Easdale, that did. Who was going where unseen?'

'Foxes.'

'Bloody tall foxes. Branches at head height were snapped in that way something doesn't bother growing when it's constantly being disrupted. If there are any young girls in that street, teenagers? You know – you should keep an eye out. I have no proof but I felt I needed to say something.'

Anderson recalled wee Jennifer Lawson saying something about feeling watched. Peeping Tom? Was he still at it, twenty years later? He let his mind tick over. 'There was no support to Gyle's alibi other than Aird. Lorna was five at the time, she no longer speaks to her father.' He was about to say something, he heard Costello's voice in the back of his mind; there was a connection that he had not made. He waited, picking at a bhaji. 'Somebody paid five grand into Gyle's account to help with bills, his landlord waived the rent. Aird?' He put his bhaji down, his appetite gone. 'Would you recognize her now, the Gyle girl?'

'Lorna? Doubt it, twenty years on. I don't have enough memory of her to see the adult that the five-year-old would grow into. I read her book when it came out but all the pictures in it had been redacted. I'm bloody sure she would not want anybody to know who her dad was and what he was capable of.'

Anderson, thinking about Aird, asked carefully, 'So you do believe, beyond all reasonable doubt, that it was Gyle?'

'Yes.' He put his beer down. 'Yes, I do. But as you say, Aird had power. Gyle had no life. Where did that five grand come from? The free rent? Aird was the landlord. Gyle had one thing of value. His daughter.'

Anderson slipped his jacket from his shoulders and tried to stop the nausea welling up. He couldn't, so he made his excuses and walked swiftly, following the sign for the toilets.

O'Hare's opening gambit had been *You don't have your problems to seek.*

At first Costello thought he meant about the foot, about the case then realized he was talking about Anderson.

O'Hare explained he had already phoned the DCI and he had – O'Hare picked his words carefully – 'been busy'. As O'Hare had pulled strings to get the bones processed as quickly as possible, he was more than a little pissed off.

Costello could hardly believe it – well, she could. Anderson was so disconnected to the case but had attached to Griffin like an old friend. So, with nothing else to do, she offered to drive round to the morgue. It was on her way home anyway. Sort of.

O'Hare had only got as far as pulling out the trays of bone fragments when his pager had gone, leaving her alone in one of the labs off the side of the mortuary. It was cold. An assistant was moving aluminium dishes around, clattering them about. The noise echoed and bounced off every hard surface.

She had said to him, 'Could you possibly do that any louder?' And he had obliged.

So she walked away, over to the arrangement of bones: light brown, dark brown, pitted and broken. These bones had been collected, roughly dated, and reported to be of no interest to the investigation as they had been washed down from the old graveyard on the top of the hill, beyond old Jock's house. She thought back to what Wyngate had been researching – the geography, the sinkhole, the volume of water, the bones at the bottom. Jock Aird had known where all this was coming from. He might be older than Noah's granddad, but he knew his stuff, he knew the land.

Somewhere up there was another body. Not one a hundred, two hundred years old, but one much more recent, and bits of it had ended up swirling around in the bottom of the sinkhole. They had to find the rest. And then the rain started again.

She looked at the little bones – 'pebbles and chessmen', somebody had said. She peered closely at them. O'Hare said they fitted together; their facets and age were all consistent to this set of pale cream bones. She wondered what other stories they had to tell. She walked round being nosey, looking at this and that. She saw a pile of paper, computerized bar codes. She recognized them as the markers that go over the evidence productions as they go through forensics. Everybody had their label, everybody was traceable. All evidence trackable. She flicked through; the number of the Melrose case was committed totally to her memory. And there it was. Swabs taken from a pair of size ten workman's boots, from the superior/anterior toe area.

So the old goat had checked it after all. A wee word to Matilda to have a look, see if any organic matter was present. If it was present, then it would look bad if they had not tested it. But he had pressed her to look in the first place. The great thing about pathologists was that they didn't care how unpopular they were.

NINETEEN

Tuesday 25 August 2015

L ynda McMutrie was lying in the basement, bloating
and starting to darken. Her white nightgown floated and
bubbled on the stinking water, forming islands of bluebells
on the surface.

She was not resting in peace. It was very noisy with the blowflies swarming around the parts of her body above the waterline,
and the rats dipping and diving like kids in a play pool. They
emerged from murk to rest on her shoulder blades and perch on
the roundness of her buttocks. They washed their pointy faces,
running their paws over their chubby cheeks full of the human
flesh they had nibbled and torn off with their razor-sharp teeth.
They sat and groomed the water from behind their ears with
lightning-fast movements of their front paws, claws out, little
hands pulling through their hair, drying off excess water.

Then they would slide back into the water for another gnaw on
an exposed bone, another chew on some soft tissue. Their half-
inch-long incisors worked with supreme mechanical efficiency,
biting and pecking all the way. Occasionally their claws got caught
up in the heavy sodden knitted wool of the cardigan, and they
stopped to pull and stomp their front legs, struggling to get free.

The water poured into the basement, gurgling its freedom
from the disused culvert. The river rabbled around, searching
out the corners, seeking out the walls to slap against so it could
tumble back on itself. When the movement of the water coin-
cided to form a wave, it tried to give Lynda a gentle shove. A
bluebell island lifted, a red slipper drifted, but Lynda herself
remained still.

It was nearly eight o'clock when Costello got to the station.
She slumped in her seat, not knowing if she was suffering more
from fatigue or frustration.

Professor Batten put a cup of tea down in front of her. And pulled over a chair. He had made himself some toast which he chomped at noisily. He stank of stale fags.

For a few minutes they sat in silence. Then Costello growled. 'I'm going out to that bloody place again.'

'What bloody place?'

'Altmore Wood, Walker wants me to go out and . . . check stuff.'

Batten ignored her, examining a burnt crust. 'Has it struck you? The similarities between Jennifer Lawson and Sue Melrose?'

'Nope. I am too busy dealing with a foot that nobody wants to know about.'

'Socially I mean.'

'Nope.'

'I was thinking.'

'Don't you start . . .'

'Are they so different? Sue had come over from the West End, Jennifer from Tiree, both a type of refugee, if I can be culturally ironic. They both have families that are a little estranged from them. Marrying Douglas was Jennifer's rebellion, leaving the island. Sue rebelled in reverse, away from the trendy west end to rough it out in Altmore Road. They both suffered a lack of family support. No respite from the washing, the ironing, the cleaning; neither had much support from the school or the preschool. Both had been stuck in this street, Jennifer in the rain, Sue in that long hot summer. Sue had seen the forest as a respite, a refuge, and Jennifer sees it as a jailer. It separates the street from the rest of the city. It's no distance at all, but it could be on the other side of the world if you can't get to it. How am I doing?'

'Sounds good so far.'

'Without the trees they might even have had a good view. But in Altmore Road they live on top of each other. Fine in the anonymity of the city, but not fine in a wee row of houses like that.'

'We have looked at most of that,' said Costello wearily.

'Both women in trouble, both husbands not helping out, both husbands distracted by career or . . .' He let the argument lie, taking a sip of tea.

'No sign that Sue was having an affair, or Steven. That reminds me, I've to go and see him. If I don't do it, no bugger will.'

'But if you prove Andrew Gyle is innocent, then it is a wee tad obvious that the killer is still out there. Maybe still hanging around? Maybe we should look at it like that? And then I was thinking . . .' He noticed Costello was looking back to her list of missing women: Elaine, Pauline, Pamela, Tamara.

'Are you saying anything of importance, because I have to call up the DNA samples of these four for comparison, so we are ready to go as soon as O'Hare has the results. Do either of them strike you as an athletic dancer type? Mulholland and Wyngate have a sweepstake, you know.'

'Sad bastards.' Batten put his hand on top of hers, preventing her from lifting the phone. 'Think about those women. The killer coming back, showing an interest in Jennifer, then maybe whatever it was about Sue, whatever triggered the rage, might also be present in Jennifer. What do you think about that?'

'Crap. There has been twenty-three years in between. If it is somebody else, they are probably dead; probably pushing up trees, never mind daisies.' She swung round on her seat. 'Where did I put that bloody phone number? I need to get hold of Steven Melrose.'

'He lost his two sons. I don't think he will thank you for that.'

'Yeah well, there's a lot of people pussyfooting around this investigation and I'm getting a bit hacked off with it. You know how you talk about offender profiling versus victim profiling, so before you start wittering on about Jennifer, you should be having a look at Sue.'

'She was looked at really closely at the time, Costello. She was a bored housewife, she had no lovers under the bed, nothing illegal going on. It was a rage killing, the spark of flame. Look at the psychology—'

'Oh God, do we really have to?'

'You need to understand. Rage is a reactive aggression. There is a desire to harm others with impulsive thinking and no planning, exactly what Gyle did. Then consider Gyle as the small man with no pride, no dignity. It was a psycho-pathological issue if you widen the predisposing factors to include low self-esteem, and the trauma Gyle had suffered in the previous year. He kept going with that axe until his victims were dead. Once it is over, the small man is back. It's textbook.'

'It would be more helpful if you looked a bit closer at Sue and I'll look a bit closer at Steven.' She found the slip of paper. 'No phone number, but he was last known at the Carron Bridge Community. He was at Findhorn before that. And that is, what, an hour from here? Do you think I can get up there and back before twelve? We are going out to test a theory about how far you can hear a shout in those woods.'

'OK, that sounds like two good "getting soaked" things to do, with a nice wee hour in a car in between to dry out.'

Costello took a large slurp of tea. 'You know, there is somebody who is paying Jennifer Lawson far too much attention.'

'Who?'

'Anderson.'

Batten rolled his eyes. 'Concentrate. Let's take human kindness. Apart from the murder, let's look at the events in Altmore Road. I think we both agree that nothing substantive is going on, so we are looking for something subtle, some small pattern of behaviour that appears very normal. It's all superficial to us. Say, Jennifer had accepted a lift here and there. A wee lunch in town, a wee coffee. All this is from person X who is being kind but then gets drawn in. Say they are a loner who has never lived that kind of domestic life and they are fascinated by it, or once had the chance of that life and something sabotaged it. They are drawn to Jennifer.'

'Now, transfer that to Sue walking in the woods. He wants to go for a walk with her. She is looking for some quiet time with the boys; she says *no thanks*. Maybe she is a bit pissed off at the way the guy jumps out of nowhere as if he was watching her front door, waiting for her to appear.'

Costello spun in her seat and pointed at the whiteboard. 'So, in reality, this is an isolated community. The person who did that would have been in residence on the road all those years ago. And wasn't. Unless . . .'

'And your candidate is . . .?'

'Aird? Would he have been strong enough to do it then? How old was he?'

'He had an axe, he didn't need youth on his side.'

'But he alibied Andrew Gyle.'

'Or Gyle wittingly or unwittingly alibied him.'

'It's easy to insist on somebody's innocence when you know damn well they are. Maybe that's why he bankrolls Gyle's campaign, because he himself is guilty.'

'So if Aird is at large, are we watching Lawson? For her safety, we could really put the cat amongst the pigeons by sending her to Edinburgh to stay with her bloody husband. We can't fund anything on a whim of a speculation of an idea.'

'Did anybody look back into the history of Jock Aird?'

'Wyngate. A wee bit. He waggled a knife in Esther Dirk-Huntley's face once.'

'Get him to dig deeper – a broken romance he never got over, something like that. There's generally a woman behind it somewhere.'

Refuelled with more tea, Costello swung on Wyngate's chair, staring at the wall. She looked as though she was doing nothing, but in fact she was multitasking, staring at the picture of Jock Aird, at the faded blue eyes, the strong mouth, thin lipped but grounded by a fine, elegant chin. He would have been a handsome man in his youth, she had no doubt of that. Tall, even in his seventies with a slight curve of his spine, he was still a fine man.

Costello was wondering if the initial investigation had been seduced by the man. Costello had seen him out with the coffee and the biscuits when the sinkhole happened. He was a rich man, a landowner, a boss. Many people in that position were, on the surface, benevolent. Aird seemed to be on hand to run the ailing women of Altmore Road to hospital. He was on hand to give the Gyles money when they were in debt. He had given Gyle his alibi when he needed one, and that alibi had not shifted one iota. Aird was the one person who had stood beside Gyle during the trial and while he was in prison. He had also paid for the funeral of May Gyle when she passed away.

All-round nice fellow. Or . . .

Costello had her doubts. Jennifer Lawson had said something about him sneaking around. It was a story as old as man, the power of the strong over the vulnerable.

Lawson was a young woman, a vulnerable young woman. May was a sick woman with a wee daughter. Sue was an attractive woman but was daggers drawn to Aird, because she was not weak or vulnerable and was going to call him out for the old creepy perv he actually was. And McMutrie, living rent free, but so pissed she never opened her front door. Her daughter left the street as soon as she could. Gyle was poor, in trouble. He had a young daughter.

Laura Steele from number 12 was still playing telephone tag from the evidence of the log. She needed somebody to talk to Esther Dirk-Huntley and Michael Broadfoot. But how to do that without giving rise to suspicion?

How far it went was anybody's guess, but Costello was sure Aird belonged on some list somewhere and should be watched. Age was no get-out-of-jail card. She'd get the bastard.

Anderson was sitting in the office, pretending to be reading reports but really trying to pluck up strength to go out and face the team. They all seemed focused on the case in hand when he had no idea what he was supposed to be doing. Was it all about Jock Aird? Had they stumbled on to the same suspicion Griffin had all those years ago?

He needed to apologize to O'Hare and ask him about the foot bones.

His phone went. Internal call. He looked up and saw Mulholland gesturing to him with the phone. He picked it up, aware his hands were sweating. Scared of this being something that he couldn't cope with. 'Vik? What can I do for you?'

Even to his own ears, it did not sound convincing,

'I have Brian Steele on the line . . . at last . . .'

Anderson had no idea who Brian Steele was, but knew from Vik's tone that he damn well should know. He heard Costello snap something to Vik, then wrestle the phone from him.

'Colin, the wee shit is refusing to talk to me. He wants to

talk to the man in charge, so that is you. We have left messages for him at number twelve, at the gym, on his moby, on the landline, at his bloody hotel, and he has at last decided to get back to us after taking advice from his solicitor, would you believe? So can you arrest him for something? Anything? Here he is.'

There was a quiet click on the line; something was switched over.

'Hi.' The voice was friendly enough.

'DCI Anderson here. We have been trying to track you down.'

'I heard you were in the street making enquiries about the sinkhole.'

'Yes, we were.'

'And what does that have to do with me or Laura?'

'Probably nothing, just wanted to check that you were OK and have a wee chat on a related matter.'

'What kind of related matter?'

'A missing person's enquiry.'

'We don't know anything about that.'

'We do need to get a statement from you.'

'I'm giving you a bloody statement, am I not?' Steele was getting a little rattled, Anderson gave him time to calm down. 'I'm sorry, I am a wee bit stressed. Look, we don't know anything about any missing people. My wife and I are accounted for.'

Anderson waited, then said, 'We can't take your word for that on the phone. You could be anybody.'

Steele was quiet.

'When did you move into Altmore Road?'

'Two years and a wee bit more. Number twelve.'

Upriver, as Wyngate had started to say. 'Did you do a lot of work to it?'

'Why do you ask? Oh the sinkhole?' Steele's voice relaxed. 'Nothing to do with us, mate. Our property was knocked through in the sixties, it used to be twelve and fourteen. The only thing we did was get the basement lined – cheap job, nothing structural, as we don't expect to be here for very long, but being the first house at the bottom of the hill the basement really was in a state. The damp was tracking up the exterior walls. They did a good job, though. So we didn't do anything that disrupted the road or the concrete, nothing that could have affected the foundations of anything. I'm not responsible.'

'That was all I wanted to talk to you about. Did you really need to see a lawyer for that?'

The voice on the end of the line toughened up again.

Anderson waited.

'That was the missus. She gets really nervous around cops. She had a bad experience – not with the police but with, well, you know. It was a matter that the police had to attend to. And she was worried that it was all going to be brought up again, maybe even get into the papers.'

Anderson felt that fog in his head again. He really didn't want to cause this woman any more pain. His own was bad enough. If they were about to dig up memories of a rape or an assault, then who the hell were they? 'We need to speak to her.'

'No, I don't think you do.'

'We do and we will. But if you want I can do it myself. You make the arrangements and I will be there. If it is not relevant to the investigation then it will remain between the two of us. I need to tick that box, and then we can all forget about it.' He saw Costello out the glass front of his office, badgering Wyngate for something, that persistent, insistent look on her face. 'And that box will have to be ticked. It is routine and we won't stop until it has been done. I want you to believe me when I say that she's much better off with me than she will be with some other members of my team who are a little more focussed, or belligerent, than I am.'

Steele gave a little laugh, 'And I bet you are talking about one of the fairer sex, aren't you? No, don't answer that, there is a law against it. I'll talk to Laura, she'll be in touch. Just be mindful that she's still on her tranquillizers and I don't want her upset.'

'Tell her not to worry. We can meet in a café, somewhere neutral, if that makes her more relaxed.'

'Sure, give her a cake and she'll talk to anybody. Leave it with me. Please go easy on her, she's not as tough as she looks.'

Anderson put the phone down and looked at his watch. It was the MeisterSinger watch that Helena had bought him for his birthday. She had sought Claire's opinion on what watch he would like. Claire would have gone to school today. He should go home early tonight to face the music. The subtle accusations in Brenda's eyes as she danced silently around him, getting upset on Claire's behalf but making it impossible for him to connect back to either of them. Brenda had built a shell round Claire, a protective carapace and it was becoming a wall between them.

He looked out at Andrew Gyle's wizened face, as he was now. Then at the man he was when the murders had happened. What had happened to his daughter, the blonde five-year-old? He hoped Lorna Gyle had gone to Australia, got as far away as she could get. Laura Steele had had a difficult past. Jennifer Lawson was facing a difficult future.

And then there was Claire.

TWENTY

Anderson found himself looking at an extremely attractive woman dressed in her well-fitting gym gear. Her long blonde hair had worked its way loose from its elastic grip, falling over her forehead. She was pretty, slim, her make-up disguised any natural imperfections. She sported light brown tattooed eyebrows, with lips either naturally full or slightly enhanced. She didn't look as if she had gone for the full, *I've been smacked in the mouth by a dead kipper* look yet, but she might succumb in a few years.

'So how can I help you?' he asked, but he thought he knew the answer to the question.

'I haven't told anybody that I am here, but I guessed that Brian had phoned you. He was trying to tell you to leave me alone, wasn't he?'

'Yes. He is very protective of you.'

She looked up and down the street. It would have been comical if she wasn't so obviously distressed.

'Danny's Coffee is still open,' he suggested. 'Neutral territory. Laura.'

They settled in, both of them uncomfortable. They ordered. She took a black coffee, having a look at the Fitbit on her wrist.

'Does that help? Surely you are not watching your weight?' He realized it was a crass thing to say. 'I mean, with you being an owner of a gym and everything, I thought you would not need those.'

'I have a very sweet tooth I need to watch.' A shy smile. She had no idea how pretty she was.

The coffees came. She folded her arms, sat head down looking at her cup. 'I need to tell you something and I would like you to promise that it will not go any further.'

He was about to say yes, then reconsidered. He was a DCI. 'I can't promise that, not if it has a bearing on the case. If not, it can stay off the record.'

'What is the case?'

'We have a missing person.'

'Oh well, I am not missing.'

'But your husband did not seem keen that it became public knowledge who you were.'

'Where I am,' she corrected, shifting uneasily in her seat. 'It's that the street, by association, is infamous. It might get into the media, and once it is out there, it is really out there.' She looked down, picked at a manicured nail, asking a question she did not want answered. 'Does any of this have anything to do with the Melrose murders? It said in the paper that the case was being reopened.'

'I can assure you that's not true.'

There was something in the way she said it, a wariness about her eyes, that made Anderson lean forward. A sheet of long blonde hair tripped over her face; she pulled it back, her left arm moving over her forehead to clasp it back, fingers moving deftly. He saw a bad scar on the top of her shoulder.

'Did Andrew Gyle do it?' she asked.

'All the evidence points that way. At the risk of repeating myself, why do you want to know?'

She picked up a napkin with her fine manicured fingers, folded it carefully and wiped a tear from under her eye. 'I'm sorry, I'm not used to talking about it.'

'It's OK, just take your time.'

'I was married two years ago. Before that I was Reid, Laura Reid. I changed my name aged eight when I was legally adopted by a lovely woman called Vivienne Reid. But I'd changed my name before, much younger than that.'

'And what was your name?' he asked, looking into her dark blue eyes and knowing the answer.

A tear filled the corner of her eye. 'Lorna. Lorna Gyle.'

They ordered another coffee. She had relaxed now that the difficult part of the conversation was over.

'I am sorry to ask this, but do you recall anything of that day?'

'No,' Laura shook her head. 'I had all kinds of things done to me.'

'Why?' he asked, vaguely thinking of Jock Aird.

'To help me remember. But I have only vague memories. My dad went away. On the Friday my mum told me he might not be coming back. We went to a hotel but then my mum was taken to hospital. I was taken to stay with a foster mother. She was nice, but that was only for a couple of days. I know that Jock came to see me, he took me out for cream soda. Every time I see that on a menu, I think of him, yet mum didn't like him coming round the house. I never noticed.'

Anderson couldn't bring himself to ask the obvious question. What exactly was the adult in front of him telling him about the child she had been?

'Then I went to live with Vivienne and Nick; they were very good to me. My memory seems to restart at that point.'

Anderson remembered Batten saying that if a personality resists a memory, it will simply invent a new set of memories.

'It was my mum who really left. My dad killed these people and is effectively dead to me. He was there, then he was gone, but it took my mother a long time to die and I watched her suffer. My memory cuts off at the point she died. November the sixth, 1992. Another Friday. I know this will sound hard but I am not that person. I have returned there and faced my demons.'

'You are not scared of Jock any more?'

Her bright eyes sparkled, a look of fear then gratitude as she realized they were on the same wavelength. 'I have a new life with Brian. I am not that victim. We have a good professional reputation. So you can see why I don't want any of that getting out. I don't want them knowing who I am. Especially Jock Aird.' Her words were hard, rattled out like bullets.

'Has he not recognized you?' asked Anderson.

'He's an old guy with bad eyes. But I don't care if he does. I am not that victim any more,' she repeated.

Anderson wondered if that was a therapeutic mantra for her.

'So why move back to Altmore Road?'

'Lorna wouldn't have, but Laura is made of stronger stuff. Strong as Steele,' she laughed. She had a nice laugh.

'But to the same road? Why?'

'Money. You will know from talking to the neighbours about McGregor Homes' development on the other side of the hill?'

Anderson nodded.

'So we're sitting on a gold mine; most of us are waiting. That's why the silly cow in number eight stays in the damp house that is killing her children. That's why the McMutries moved but didn't sell.'

'But the Dirk-Huntleys are holding out.'

'And now they've got a sinkhole, so go figure. The development will happen anyway, as Altmore Road will have to be re-engineered.'

'Aird's house stands in the way,' pointed out Anderson.

'And I want to be there when it falls.'

'Hi, Jennifer Lawson?'

She walked into the room, Robbie holding tightly on to her hand. The wee guy was scared and so was she. The doctor was there, the nice one with the beautiful head with his roots in North Africa somewhere. A nurse was messing about with the sink at the corner of the room, and then there was the woman who had been talking to Douglas. She was sitting with her legs crossed, funny-coloured tights under her boots. She looked as though she should be knitting lamb's wool in a yurt somewhere. She had an iPad in front of her, there had obviously been some discussion going on before she came in the room, and Gordy's file was on the top of the pile.

'Hi, Jennifer, come on and let's have a look at Gordon. Have you seen him today?'

'Yes, of course I have. I was told to come through here and speak to you. And we call him Gordy, he knows himself as Gordy.'

'Of course, Jennifer this is Yvonne. Yvonne, this is Jennifer, Gordy's mum.'

'And this wee man must be Robert.'

'And we call him Robbie.'

They spoke between them back and forward, including her in what they were saying but not actually talking directly to her.

At the cot side, Gordy was lying asleep in his plastic womb. He had a drip attached to his arm now.

'He has an infection. And his condition is mild but his temperature is high. He's vomiting, he's not eating. You can see the redness around his eyes. He has a slight rash and the reason you brought him in was the cough. We do need to keep him here. In ninety per cent of cases, it will be fine. We need to treat him, hydrate him, and hopefully he will make a full recovery.'

Jennifer trembled, her hand gripped Robbie a little tighter.

'Well, in young children such infection can lead to meningism. He had a seizure yesterday evening, while you were out, as you know.'

'No, I didn't know.'

'We told your husband, I'm sure he mentioned it to you.'

Jennifer shook her head, noticing the look that passed between them. They were thinking of her as a bad mother, thinking that she could not cope, that she could not remember.

'Your baby is ill, Jennifer.'

'Yes, I get that. Can you make him better?' She leaned over the cot, stroking the baby's cheek.

'We are from social services, we believe wee Gordy here isn't doing too well. Would you mind if we came to have a look at the house?' asked Yvonne, polite but insistent.

'Why would you want to do that?'

'Because Gordy's medical team have raised some concerns about him, about his welfare and where he came into contact with the rat. We need to get the house sorted before you take him home, you can see the sense of that.'

'The rat?'

'Yes.'

'They said it was an infection,' she turned to the doctor. 'You said it was an infection, didn't you? The rash? The skin?'

'We just want to check that your house is suitable for the child.'

'I have another child, he's fine.'

They looked at each other again. 'Robbie is three, and still in nappies? So he is not in nursery, he's not meeting other children. He's not developing as he should. If Gordy needs looking after, then it follows that we might have some concern about Robbie, if he is in the same house.'

Jennifer felt the ground beneath her feet shift; she took a step back. 'I'm sorry, I don't understand.'

'It has been reported to us that the house is unsuitable for the children. Because of the rats.'

'I don't have rats. If you need to come and look at it, for the kids, and make sure it is fine, that's OK. But it is damp and the doors don't close and there is a smell.'

'And Gordy had a chest infection. Robbie has been coughing,' said the doctor. 'So I think the boys should stay here overnight, and tomorrow we will come out and see the house.'

'Gordy can stay, I'm taking Robbie home. You will need a lawyer or something. I will tell my husband and he will get it all sorted.' She finished with a note of triumph, holding herself back from adding, *So there!*

'Jennifer, it was your husband who spoke to us. He is the one concerned.'

The drive up to the Carron Bridge Community took an hour and a half, mostly due to the terrible rain. She had heard of the community; there were a few such places dotted around Scotland, full of crystal healers, vegans, people who smelled of garlic, alternative therapists, chakra-balancing, gong-baths and past-life regressionists.

The whole place stank of shit. Bullshit.

There was a café in the middle. The alternative community

was an attraction of sorts, and the citizens were not above making a few bob out of the constant influx of nosey tourists who sauntered through the carless streets, looking at the ecological lodges and the wooden pods.

Steven Melrose was easy to spot. Costello recognized him from the photographs even twenty-odd years further on. The residents of Carron Bridge were allowed to have cars, old cars, the sort that could be fixed by taking them apart and putting them back together again. Steve Melrose was an old-fashioned car mechanic, so he was a perfect fit. She stopped to read a sign that said how big the carbon footprint of new car manufacture was compared to running an old one, and beyond that was Melrose leaning over an open bonnet of a 2CV, a baldy, chubby man with a wee ponytail at the back, a goatee beard at the front.

She put her warrant card flat on the wing of the car and slid it under his nose. 'DI Costello, Police Scotland. Can I have a word? It is Steven Melrose, isn't it? You are not an easy man to find.'

After twenty minutes he joined her in the café, apologizing, saying that one of the rules they had here was no Swarfega. The Ecover handwash left a lot to be desired. She pushed a cranberry juice and a carob cake in front of him, and tried to make herself comfy. Her seat had no back, was carved straight from a tree, and the carpenter had left most of the splinters in. She had folded her wet jacket underneath her so was now getting a wet arse as well. Steven slipped off his own wet woollen jacket that was starting to smell worse than the puce vegan mash bubbling in a cauldron at the till. Her mind suddenly thought about how the testing on the vomit sample on the toe of Gyle's boot was doing.

The bell on the door tinged as a man came in. Costello guessed he was in his mid-thirties. His long hair and serious face gave him the look of Neil Young in his Harvest years. The girl behind the counter with the horn in her ear smiled at him, and he sat down in the corner. But Costello did not miss the slight look of panic he cast in their direction, small-community prejudice to a stranger.

'So what is this about? I've heard there has been some activity back at the old street.'

'I'll give it to you straight, seeing as you guys seem to believe in love and peace and truth.'

'You won't say anything that I haven't heard before. But I would appreciate it if you wouldn't spread the word about where I am, please.' He looked at her in earnest.

'Of course not, we only found you because we employ a computer genius and because you have a car registered to your person. An old VW Beetle.'

He nodded, as if to say fair dos. 'So, how can I help you?'

'To put it bluntly, was Sue as lovely as everybody makes out? She seems to have become angelic, a woman who could do no wrong. Time and tragedy tends to twist our perception of people. There are very few folk who seem to have known her still alive, you were the obvious one to track down. Her mother has passed on. Her father has got Alzheimer's and has no reliable memory. So it is down to you. It's difficult to find an enemy when all we are told is how lovely somebody is. Everybody annoys somebody.'

'Old Eddie has dementia? I am sorry to hear that. But yeah, Sue was OK, she didn't deserve what happened to her.'

'Nobody deserved that, but that is not what I am asking.'

'We were not getting on.' He flashed a look over to Neil Young, who seemed to be trying to pay attention to the conversation. 'We were not a happy couple.' He put his hands down on the table, rattling his fingertips against it.

'We have a statement from her mother, taken at the time, that said something like you got on well but you weren't really what she wanted. And that the marriage would not have lasted. Is that accurate?'

He nodded. 'I was looking for something, she was looking for something. They were not the same things. I liked going out with the dog and the fresh air, she liked loud music and shopping. But I miss my boys so much.' He stopped, the sorrow still strong. 'I got away.'

'Did she do anything to wind up the neighbours?'

'She did everything she could to wind up Andrew. It got beyond a joke. It became a bit of an obsession. She was bored.

She was bored that day; she wanted to go out or something. We had no money,' he rubbed the side of his face as if he was massaging the memory. 'We were finding trouble paying the mortgage. I was working late, grabbing all the overtime I could get. She took a drink sometimes; I hated that when she was alone with the boys.' He gave another small sideways glance over to Neil Young, who was now sipping something that looked like steamed mud. Melrose blurted, 'I was the one who persuaded her to go out for a walk that evening.'

'I don't think I read that anywhere.'

'I've never told anybody, but it was me.'

'You weren't to know.' Costello nibbled her dairy-free chocolate cake. It had the texture of a brick and tasted of bitter cocoa. 'Was there any reason she changed her clothes?'

Steven shook his head, 'None at all.'

None that you know of. 'From the outside, it seems people in that street acted . . . well, strange. Why?'

'It's the crowding, you know. Altmore Road is short but isolated.'

Costello narrowed her eyes.

'I mean, look at this place. We have time to breathe and get away from it all. Sue was caught in that street with neighbours she hated, all older than her, stuck with Bobby and George. Every time she looked out that window, all she ever saw was that wood.'

'I thought she liked it.'

'She did on a good day. I'm sure you like trees, but don't like to be near them when it's blowing a gale and they are creaking and groaning. It can be very intimidating. They move and breathe you know, trees.'

'I suppose you hug them here.'

'Yes we do,' he said without a trace of irony. 'But Sue did what she wanted to do and didn't give a shit what anybody else thought.'

'Was she having an affair?'

Melrose thought for a long time before he answered; he swirled his cranberry juice round in the thick glass. It looked like blood. He put it down on top of the table and watched it settle. 'Doubt it. She would have rubbed my face in it. She wouldn't have been so bored. She was flirtatious and fun but not everybody's cup of tea. Sorry if I can't be any more help.'

'Do you think Gyle did it?'

'Nothing that Sue did warranted what he did. There's irrefutable evidence. The axe.' His eyes clouded. 'You could get that DNA-tested again. New techniques, but the result will be the same. And his story did not add up. The police checked if sound carried that far, from the Pulpit to the Doon. And it does not.'

Costello was about to say, well, that remains to be seen, but Melrose was pulling out his wallet.

'Do you want to see a picture of them, as they were, at the time?' He sniffed; it still hurt. 'When they were alive and . . . well, this is how they reign in my heart.' He opened the wallet, folded it back on itself, not wanting Costello to see the photograph on the other side, the photograph of the fresh-faced man who bore a resemblance to Neil Young, his long brown hair caressing his face. She concentrated on the picture of the two wee boys opposite, one of them wearing a sunflower hat. 'He'd be twenty-four now, making his own way in the world.'

'Do you have any other children?'

'What, to replace them?' snapped Melrose.

'No, just wondered if you had family now.'

He went to stand up, she grasped his hand.

'No, please don't go. No, not yet. I think your sons deserve a wee bit more of your time.'

TWENTY-ONE.

All Jennifer could answer was: *The house seemed fine to us.*

She ought to know, she bloody lived there. She was about to explain about trying to keep the heating on, although the boiler was old and next to useless. She was going to explain about ironing the clothes so they were warm when the boys had to get dressed. But she didn't get that far; the woman with the thin lips had cut in with, *So can you tell us what caused the marks on Gordon's hands and feet?*

His name is Gordy. And it was his fingers and toes; tips of fingers, tops of toes. But she had no idea, of course. She thought his skin had just cracked open. That's why she had wanted an appointment with the GP, but Colin had brought her to the hospital. Gordy was getting worse and now they had reluctantly sent her home with Robbie and she was to expect a visit.

And seemingly, before he went back to the flat, Douglas had shown them the house on his iPad and making out it wasn't too bad. Implying it was her. She was very angry.

She held on to Robbie as the bus crawled round another corner. It was taking ages, Glasgow was snarled up with the bad weather. Everybody on the bus was wet, coughing and spluttering. As she pulled Robbie's hood up so the collar could cover his nose and mouth, she wondered if there was a paper-hanky shortage. Somebody sneezed down the back of her neck. She wiped Robbie's face; he was such a dribbly boy, always something coming from one end or the other or, she suspected, sniffing the air around them, both ends. But at least he kept his germs to himself.

A young man in a sodden hoodie got on, thought about sliding into the empty seat next to her, then had a sniff and went to sit elsewhere.

It took her over three hours to get home; the rain hadn't let up at all. As she got off the bus and settled Robbie on her hip for the long walk, it seemed to come on harder to spite her. Robbie moaned a little and snuggled deep into her jacket, going limp and heavy, falling asleep at the rhythm of her stride in the seclusion of the path. Maybe the constant drip-drip of rain was hypnotic when you were warm and cosy and only two and didn't have to worry about rising damp or the roof letting in. She could recall that from a camping holiday, the mildest of showers on the bright orange canvas had sounded like a down-pour in a rainforest as they had lain in their sleeping bags, snug and comfy, like Robbie was now. She couldn't recall the girl she'd gone camping with, not a Scooby. Her dad had owned a chippy, though, and stank of vinegar – she could remember that.

Once in the house, she put some logs on the fire and coaxed it to flame with a firelighter and an old car magazine of Douglas's. She slid Robbie from his wet suit and laid him on the sofa, where he snored gently, the leather of the cushions cold and damp like frogspawn under him. She got the Pooh Bear duvet and dropped it over him.

Without taking off her own anorak, she went upstairs to the wardrobe and started rummaging around, wondering how much of her husband's stuff was actually still here. He had been taking it away under her nose, always going out with enough stuff for his few days in Edinburgh and never bringing any of it back. How had she not noticed that he was moving out right under her nose?

All his gym gear was gone.

Had she not cared? Did she care now? Well, she might care a wee bit more if he had paid any attention to what was going on with Gordy. But he might have a lot on his mind as well. Her calls to his mobile were again being met with voicemail. She sat on the bed, the duvet cover feeling damp through her jeans, and picked her mobile from her pocket. She dialled, this time he answered. She was on the verge of saying something when she caught the soft background music and the gentle clunk of cutlery. She could hear somebody say something, not enough to make out the words.

Jennifer pressed end call and waited until he had phoned her back – four minutes later and from somewhere with a dull echo to his consonants. No background music. The door at his end banged. He had called her from the toilet.

'Keep me informed' was all he said as he refuted what the hospital had said. He was concerned for Jennifer, not about her ability to look after the boys. She was trying not to cry when she thought about the words, too difficult to say in the light of his betrayal. So she did not say the words, 'Rats have been eating our baby.'

She didn't say them.

She didn't want to hear it.

Archie, being Archie, had all the gear. Jackets that were folded neatly, a belt with wee bits that you could hang things off. He had waxed leather boots with socks that rolled up over the top. He looked at Costello's anorak as if to say, *no wonder you get wet.* He asked her to synchronize her watch to his before they set off, entering the wood by the narrow path, the path that ran up alongside the hedge on one side of Altmore Road. Anybody looking out of their front windows would see them. Well, they would see Costello in her bright anorak, but Archie was well camouflaged, like he had some inner desire to be a soldier on a top-secret mission. A thought that was reinforced by the plasticized map he had brought with him. Wyngate had given her a laminated folder of photographs that she tucked under her arm as they followed the narrow, overgrown path for half an hour or so until they reached the Doon. This was where it had happened, and they could tell by the atmosphere, long before they saw the dry-stone dyke with the Clachan Stone standing in the middle.

It was strangely cold in here. Was that because it had been a long hard walk, or because there really was a chill in the air, a stillness born of tragic events?

This was a definite area of seclusion. The air charged with memories.

It was darker, the leaf canopy above closed over their heads and the raindrops that dropped on them were larger, joining together, waiting until they got heavy enough to fall. Costello felt as though they were raining on somebody's grave.

Now it was silent. The stones looked cold. The grass dying due to the lack of light. Walker took her by the hand, neither of them spoke, just absorbing, thinking back to that day twenty-three years before.

It was an empty stage.

Costello had to look and check that Susan Melrose was not still lying against the Clachan Stone as if she was sleeping, and that George was not forever slumped, facing the sky, his stumpy wee arm up. He had died trying to defend himself.

Costello flicked to the first of the photographs, which showed the baby lying near his mother, his body covered in daisies. The next photograph was the sunflower hat image that had made all the newspapers, leaked by a cop at the scene. They never found out who. The little hat, the stains of violence, told their own poignant story.

Walker lifted up his camera and took some photographs to capture the essence of the Doon now as Costello tried to orient herself.

Her pictures suggested Sue had been holding Bobby and turned when Gyle approached. There had been some interaction, then Gyle had felt the axe in his hand, and used it.

It wasn't a large area, one explosion of pent-up rage in a confined space. There would have been no escape.

'Where was the dog?' asked Costello, aligning herself with the Clachan Stone. 'It had gone into attack first, well, defence I suppose. He nearly cut its head off. So,' she looked about her, 'Gyle came up this path if the dog rushed out to get him.' She turned her back to the stone and pointed to her right. 'But said he was at the Pulpit, and was on his way back, so he would have come up this path.'

Walker checked the map. 'But the dog was found down here,' he pointed to the lower left corner of the Doon. 'So the evidence suggests he came up here, from the path we've just taken, from the road. He probably heard her coming and that was that. What kind of rage lay in the heart of that man?'

Costello stood in the middle of the ancient building, the outline of a church was quite clear once she knew where to look. The boys had been playing, probably climbing over the stones, playing king of the castle, or climbing up things that were now fit for no purpose other than to be climbed on.

'So Sue was found lying against this stone, facing the path that goes to the road.' She pointed. 'And Gyle said he came down here, from the Pulpit.' She pointed up the slight hill.

'Well, as I read it, she kind of stumbled into him. He was here and she walked into him, he was chopping the wood . . . He turned round when he heard her approach.'

'What wood? In here.'

'Not in this clearing, he would have been in there somewhere, but this area here, this has good vision, and she would have seen him. He might not have seen her. Not at first.'

'So we don't really know what happened, Costello. Three of them died, four including the dog. He says that he was up there on the Devil's Pulpit and came back down here and his axe was missing and they were lying dead. He tried to help.

Nice story, can't disprove it, can't prove it. All it needed was
for him to see the Melroses coming. He was having a break,
sitting in the clearing, in the sun and heard them coming. She
didn't hear him, too busy with her boys. She sees him, a fight
starts, and he loses the plot.'

'So there would be no noise of him chopping wood. If she
had heard that, she would have turned round and headed back.
Why carry on, was she going somewhere? Maybe to meet
somebody?'

'Where was the wheelbarrow?'

'Here, in the clearing.'

'So she would have seen that. Maybe Gyle wasn't here,
maybe he was in the Pulpit and did come back by this path.'

'So why did the dog die over there?' Walker took the photographs. 'Griffin says he was down there on the parade, so he
must have come the way we came.'

'So he must have seen the dead dog first?' Costello started
turning, aligning her body with the photographs. 'But then he
was not a detective. He was used to helping get cats out of
trees and old ladies out of baths. Maniacs with axes were a bit
of a new thing to him.'

'Is that how you see Gyle, an axe-wielding maniac?'

'I did struggle with that, but then folk struggled with Christie,
so that's no judge.'

'Agatha?'

'No, John Reginald Halliday.'

'So Griffin comes through here, after hearing – did he say
the screams? One scream, I think, but the dog was going mental.
He heard a commotion, anyway, the order of it all was actually
in the notes. He bounces through the woods, comes into this
clearing and sees the carnage, blood everywhere. He sees the
dead dog, it had nearly been decapitated, right in front of him.'
Costello pointed, trying to think it through. 'And that's not
right.'

'What do you mean?' Walker was interested.

'The dog would attack first surely? Be killed first, so why is
the dog in one corner and Gyle in the other?'

'Maybe, depends on the dog.'

'But even if the dog was beside Sue, the body would be in

here, in the Doon. But it is not; it is at the top of the path. So the killer came up the path.'

'That's a stretch, Costello.'

'We need more info on the nature of the dog. Sue was here, still breathing, and Gyle is leaning over her. Griffin appears, radios in, they fight, Griffin punches him. Griffin tries to do CPR, he gets covered in blood. She dies right in front of him, he . . . well, he loses the plot really and has never been the same man again.'

'So who decapitates the dog?'

They stood in silence, listening to the sounds of the trees and the leaves, the gentle wind in the grass and the rain on their jackets.

'So we are not taking their word for the ability of this forest to carry sound. It's quiet today, there's no huge wind, and there was no wind at all on that evening. You stay here and I'll get to the Pulpit and shout back. I'll come back in fifteen minutes, anyway, so if you hear nothing, don't you leave here.'

'Why? Are we going to check on the Steeles and the McMutrie woman?'

'We are. And I need a run home.'

TWENTY-TWO

Anderson sat in his front room, with no idea where Brenda or Claire were. He was flicking over pages of *Friday's Child*, looking at the pictures and thinking about Lorna, taking control of her own life. After her mother's death, there being no other family, she was taken in to foster care and looked after by a lovely family, who had guided her through the funeral of her mother and the trial of her father. Lorna had grown up with good memories of them. Her next 'parents' had ended up adopting her. And they too had been kind people, just not her real parents.

He read her words: clear and calm, and utterly compelling. It would seem that she was OK with the idea of her father's guilt. Vivienne, her adoptive mother, had not thought the book was a good idea, but the money was tempting and so Lorna took the cash and got out. The tabloids had been on her tail anyway so she thought publishing the book would draw the fire away from her, as she had put it. She had simply removed the bait and gone public on her own terms. She had even hired a tabloid journalist to ghost-write the book, and that journalist had never actually met Lorna, which only added to the mystique.

Anderson couldn't imagine what it would have been like to grow up like that, always knowing in the back of her mind that she was different. Her father was the notorious killer of the two wee boys she had seen play next door, and their mother, a woman she had very clear memories of.

Anderson studied the photographs in the middle. Her face was redacted, fuzzy, but a burn on her upper arm was clear to see. She had light brown hair in the picture, now she had dyed her hair blonde. She had not put on weight as such, but had firmed up; she looked stronger and more mature, Anderson noted. More herself. She couldn't live a life where all everyone saw was 'Andrew Gyle's daughter'.

On the way back to the car, Anderson had noticed how much more relaxed she was as she talked about becoming Laura. She had moved out of the family home and into a flat by herself. Vivienne had even given her money to get her nose remodelled. Just to change a little. She had married Brian Steele, another name change, another move on, another degree of separation. Brian had known all along. She thought that he might have walked away, but he was in it for the long haul. It all made no difference to him. As they walked, Anderson noticed that she rubbed her upper arm as she had said it. He knew now that she was rubbing the burn scar, the scar that was hidden by the shawl in the photograph. The book said she had been injured as a wee girl, dragging a pan of boiling water over herself. Her dad had pulled her free and the water had only caught her shoulder and her upper arm. Over the years, there had been many appointments to get it grafted. But she was either grieving or growing, it was never the right time, and now she felt rather protective over the red marks streaming down her upper arm.

So she decided to hold on to them. She had had enough false identities.

He read on, the words more chilling as he could now hear them in her voice.

> One afternoon my dad went out, and left me and my mum in the kitchen. I was painting, Mum was putting Dad's shepherd's pie in the oven. The door was open into the garden. We heard some noises, a few car doors banging. There were a lot of people about.
>
> I never saw my dad again, not in normal clothes. I saw him in the newspaper, a wee clip of a photograph taken in the garden. They cut me out of it, and I remember being annoyed at that. He was my dad. There was another photograph, my dad, but he looked very stern and strange, not really the man I knew at all. Then I saw him in the newspaper in a suit that I had never seen him in before. I went to see him in prison, I think maybe twice, but that was all.
>
> He was a kind man, the best at giving me coaly backs and we'd race round the garden, me riding high on his shoulders. That summer was endless and stifling, tempers were frayed. My mother was very unwell. We were very short of money and Dad was working all hours. He had a lot on his plate. I don't blame him, but I don't want to know him. My adoptive mother told me that he was happy for me to drift off, that it could do me no good to be associated with him. It was the one big kindness he could do for me, so he did it and I am grateful that he did. This is my life that I am living, not a life in his shadow.

Anderson read that again, thinking about Claire. Would she feel the same about him? Deep down, his own daughter blamed him for the death of her friend. Would their lives be easier if he, too, let them go; if he walked away and didn't look back? Once the money came through that was a possibility.

He flicked through a few more pages, a section catching his eye.

*I often wonder what happened to their dad, Mr Melrose.
The forgotten victim. He lost his wife and his two children.
I hope he has found another life. It was hard for him – the
other victim, if you like – but he is still alive. His name
has slipped from our memory; his face is one that few
recall. We all know the famous picture of Sue with the two
boys, but nobody remembers him.*

*I hope he is well, he is content and he has rebuilt his
life.*

*He lost his wife and two sons. My father was their killer.
I hope we have both made it out the other side. Many
years have passed. We both are victims. I hope he does
not hate my father. That would mean a lot to me.*

Anderson closed the book, looking at the picture on the back
page. Lorna as a wee girl, with her mum and dad, holding her
teddy in her left hand. Andrew Gyle was standing, both his
arms lying round his daughter's neck; she had a straw hat on.
They were all smiling, eyes slightly narrowed at the sun, holding
teddy close.

They looked a nice family. Andrew looked a protective dad.

Lorna had asked him to keep her secret, and he would.

Nobody would hear it from him.

Costello set off through the woods, following the rise in the
land. It didn't look it, but it was a thigh-testing walk. Her legs
ached, and she was short of breath as the incline increased. She
was scrambling up the side, holding on to low branches, getting
hit in the head by them as they escaped from her grasp and
sprang back.

She nearly toppled into the Pulpit, unable to right herself
from the momentum she had gathered up. She looked down the
steep sides. It was a drop of about seventy feet. There was a
lip at the part she stood at. There was no way she was going
down there; she might never get out. She needed to go back
and make her way round the rim, to the opposite side where
she could see through the trees on that side to the greenbelt
farmland beyond. That would be the fields beyond Altmore
House. She reversed away from the edge, stopping once she

felt safe to look at her watch to check the time. She would be late getting back to Archie. He would have to wait.

She clambered her way round the rim, stooping when trees got in the way, climbing when the branches were too low to let her get under them. She was crawling along at some points, on her hands and knees, through the wet grass and last year's dead leaves, which had begun to ferment in the warm rain. Then she found herself on something that could be called a path. From here it was easy going up to the top of the Pulpit, a breathtakingly steep walk, but clear access. She stopped at the top and looked down; it was less steep here but very deep.

She started at a rustle of leaves behind her. It was that old collie. And Aird. She stood to the side, automatically putting her hand on her mobile phone, just in case. She could take the old guy in a fight, and the dog didn't look in the first flush of youth either. She wondered if it had any teeth left. But there was a steep drop behind her, and it could snap her neck if she took one step back too far.

'Oh, I swear to God that this hill gets steeper every bloody time I come up here.'

'Hello Mr Aird.'

'Have we met?' he enquired.

'I'm a cop.'

'Oh,' was all he said, with mild surprise. 'I am a pluviophile. One who sees the beauty in rain.'

'Well, there's a lot of it about. You like it up here then?' She stepped away from the side, dropping about three feet in height. He went up past her, keen to get somewhere, a stone ledge on the top, where he sat down, confident enough to let his legs dangle over the side.

He took a few deep breaths. 'I've been coming up here since I was a boy. I am not going to stop now. So why are you here?'

'I'm testing out a theory.'

'You are testing my alibi.' He might be old but he was sharp.

'Yes, you said you were here and you fell, you screamed.'

'I shouted. I didn't scream.'

'Then Gyle heard you and he came. He got you out and walked you back to your house, and all that time you didn't hear the attack?'

'We heard nothing; there was nothing to hear. I know you have all your fancy ways of timing this and re-enacting that, but if we had been here and they were killed over there, I think we would have heard the commotion, don't you?'

'Does that not disprove your story? He might have killed them and come over here, then gone back and played at trying to revive them when he heard the approach of Griffin.'

'He wouldn't have had time. And he was his usual self. He wasn't upset or flustered. Andy was a shit liar – I'd know if he had done that. Takes some nerve to do that and walk away.'

Costello realized that he had a point. And he had given it some thought, playing other theories through in his mind, which might suggest that his story was true.

'Somebody else was there, saw him put the axe down and took their chance, a very unusual crime, unplanned, opportunistic.' He sighed, thinking deep. 'Three young lives snuffed out like that,' he snapped his fingers, strong and loud. Betty pricked her ears and turned round.

'Does she bite?'

'All dogs bite if you annoy them enough.'

'What about Heidi, the Lab? Did you know her?'

'Typical family dog. Sue's dog.' He coughed a little, then stopped and looked straight at Costello. 'If you are asking if Heidi would have protected those children, then yes. Any dog would – any female dogs, any road. They get in front of their pack, they defend. It's in their nature.'

She nodded, thinking about the paths. The dead dog was in the wrong place. 'Gyle?'

'Andy? Yes?' He looked at her imperiously, he was enjoying this.

'You were friends with him?'

'I still am.'

'Doesn't make you popular.'

'Don't give a sugary shite.'

'They tested the alibi, you know. You can't hear somebody shout from down there.' She pointed to the bottom of the Pulpit. 'Not from where the bodies were found, from where he says he was chopping the wood.'

'I wasn't allowed to be there. Otherwise I would have told

them that I wasn't down there, I was here.' He tapped the ground with his stick.

'I thought you fell? They put a uniform cop all the way down there.' She pointed to the bottom of the dip – sixty, seventy feet below. 'You did fall? Or is this all a fabrication? To help your pal?'

'I fell, but I fell off here. To there.' He reached out his stick and tapped the ground. 'About two feet and twisted my ankle.'

'Just your ankle?'

'Yip, you can ask my doctor.'

Costello felt that thrill of another piece of a jigsaw going in, or being taken out. 'So Gyle helped you back to the house, then what?'

'He made a cup of tea, I had a painkiller. He left.'

'Did he have anything?'

Aird's answer fell out his mouth, 'Aye he had a wee cuppa, standing in the kitchen, a couple of ginger biscuits. But he was in for less than ten minutes.'

'So you fell, from the lip to two feet off the lip?'

'Right there. Bloody hell, did they think I tumbled down there and got away with a sore ankle? Pish.'

She walked on to the rim where she was, about six feet away from him, out of his reach. Betty had disappeared off somewhere. Costello tested the ground with the toe of her boot, soft, slippery but not too bad.

'Can you shout to my colleague? See if he hears you. Shout "Archie".'

He did.

They heard it echo round the trees, bouncing back and forth. The trees came alive, then came Archie's answering call, before Aird's echo had finished, and the two sounds swirled round her head like their voices had been stolen by the lost souls of the wood and were captured here for eternity.

Archie was right; somebody had ballsed up big time.

Costello and Walker had to make their way back out to Altmore Road before she could get a signal on her phone. She had left Aird at the Pulpit; he was content to sit there with his dog. She phoned Wyngate, who was glad to hear from her, as Mulholland had spent the day doing nothing but moan about Anderson who was now back in his office, reading a book.

'Good,' said Costello, 'Walker and I are on Altmore Road, so we are going to visit the Steeles and McMutrie. Can you find—'

'Don't,' said Wyngate, 'not the Steeles. They have been interviewed and no further action to be taken.'

'Who says?'

'The boss.'

'OK, so do we still do McMutrie?'

'Yes.'

'And can you trace David Griffin's ex-wife?'

'Why?'

'Can you just do it?' He agreed and she closed the phone. 'Just a theory about him and Sue Melrose,' she said to Walker's enquiring look.

All she needed was a statement from Lynda McMutrie – that would be a box ticked. Costello went on to house number 10, with its overgrown garden and front door that had been battered by the elements. It was a sad house, it had given up. It looked as though it would have gladly jumped in the sinkhole of its own free will. She knocked on the blackened brass knocker. No answer, so she walked round the side, but the cheap IKEA blinds were closed. Walker stayed a few paces behind her. The side of the house had a simple wooden door, hanging off its hinges, and beyond that the little back garden. It was fully green; the few flowers left had been battered by the weather. In the corner covered by ivy was an old rusty swing. There must have been kids in this garden at some point. She pulled up her collar and knocked on the back door: no response. She tried to listen to the wood, but the noise of the rain was too much. She went down the single step and trod over the small dark path of earth, lying in clumps and fighting off an invasion of weeds. She reached up to look into the window. These curtains were still closed, but she did see the flies; blowflies, dead flies, live flies. She turned and shouted to Walker: this was a job for a man with his socks tucked into his boots. Walker kicked the back door in; it gave way at the hinges rather than at the lock.

'You first.' He stood back to let her in.

Costello gave him a snarky smile and handed him the torch and two shoe covers. Then she pulled out gloves from her own pocket and shouted into the house, asking if there was anybody home.

No answer. The house was dark and empty; cold and dampness hung in the air. It felt as though the house itself had died. She walked into the kitchen – reasonably modern, looked after. Looking in the fridge, she saw it was nearly empty; a jug of something that had overgrown, something that looked as if it used to be a block of cheese. She opened the cupboards. Empty. She stood on the pedal of the bin; full of Rachmaninoff vodka bottles.

The kitchen told its own story. Costello shone the torch into the hall, a pile of mail behind the front door. She saw the old pink carpet, a dirty middle track showing the way up the stairs. She opened the living-room door. The blowflies buzzed around her head, looking for a new target – *looking for fresh meat* was the phrase that ran through her head. These flies hadn't been here yesterday.

'How old was this dame?' asked Walker, wafting his hand in front of his face.

'Old enough to have a daughter of thirty-two. What age do you think from this?'

'About a hundred and four?'

She stepped into the living room, a pale green carpet badly stained, and a three-piece suit in brown velour. The flies were worse in here. Costello put a hand over her mouth, nodding gratefully when Walker handed her a paper handkerchief. The smell of expensive aftershave nearly choked her.

'Is this a showroom for nicked Capodimonte? Few photographs there, a book, vodka bottle. Empty glass. Christ, where is she?' She spoke through the paper of the tissue, scared that if she took it away, the flies would attack her mouth.

'There is going to be something very unpleasant somewhere. Upstairs?' suggested Walker.

'We go together, we do it by the book. Come on.' Costello followed Walker back out into the hall, into darkness. She shone the torch up the stairway, all panelled in the fake wood that was all the rage in the Seventies.

Costello paused at the bottom of the stairs, swinging her torch from side to side, looking round the top landing window. 'The flies are not so busy up there.' She flashed the torch back to the door of the cupboard under the stairs. 'This house is higher up the hill, it might have a—' She opened the door and a cloud of flies swarmed out. They both recoiled, hands over their eyes and noses. They waited. 'Basement. I think we have found her.'

She was on her own. Walker's nerve had failed, he stayed on the stairs and made the phone calls as Costello stepped into the under-stair space, on to another small landing and saw the wooden, narrow stairs going down. She took her time; the stairs felt slippery, as if covered in something slimy. The air smelled like week-old soup: flies, fetid air, human waste, and dampness, something wet like plaster. Costello moved the hanky up a little to cover her nose and mouth; she closed her eyes as much as she could. So far, she had not seen a light switch. She turned her head, and the torch, to check the wall. The tissue came away from her lips and a bluebottle flew into her mouth. She spat it out and fought them away from her hair, hitting the back of her head against the wall.

Counting to ten then swearing, she stepped down. One step at a time, gingerly. Her toe touching first to the slightly slimy wood underfoot. She could feel the moisture on the sole of her shoe covers. One step at a time, one foot down, the other playing catch-up, and all the time the flies buzzed about her head, dive-bombing her with their annoyance at being disturbed. The smell was getting stronger, a sickly sweet smell, a smell of rotting flesh and decomposition.

She knew what she was going to find down there.

She reached the bottom of the stairs, right at the wall and at the lowest part of the house. Taking a deep breath, she shone the torch into the basement. The search beam created a bright corridor of light and gave the swarm of flies centre stage. They buzzed around her, thrummed around her head, aware of the fresh air coming down the stairs from the open door above, scenting it and gathering to fly up together, some collective intelligence working. The beam of the torch caught the figure lying on the

floor of the basement, looking like an old rolled-up carpet, covered
with black sleek bodies, writhing and feasting.

She nearly dropped the torch, unaware that she had squealed.

'I presume you have found something,' called Walker from
his place of safety at the top of the stairs.

She shouted back, 'Get O'Hare.'

TWENTY-THREE

Anderson put the phone down and dropped his head into
his hands, a slow breath out, counting to ten then
counting backwards again. Costello was on the warpath.
That was bad enough, but knowing that Walker was with her,
witnessing it all, made it so much worse. But he couldn't, no
matter how much he tried, he couldn't motivate himself. It
wasn't that he didn't care Lynda McMutrie had been found
dead. Or that Costello was ranting about Gyle's version of
events possibly being true.

He took a lorazepam and closed his eyes, listening to the
voices of Wyngate and Mulholland outside; they sounded as
though they were down a dark tunnel.

He sat up, finished his glass of water and scrolled through
his phone, finding two voicemails, one from David Griffin and
one from Brenda. His wife was asking when he was coming
home, and did he remember that he was only supposed to work
nine to five these days? Claire had lasted a whole day at school
and had seemed bright and chatty. They had already had their
tea and were now settling down to watch a film, so could he
text her when he was ready to come home.

And that was exactly what it said. Anderson read the subtext.
He knew the minute he walked in the door, Claire would find
an excuse to go upstairs and avoid him. That didn't seem fair
on anybody and maybe it was better that his daughter had some
quality time with her mother. He was walking into the main
office, looking at the wall chart. He had a pile of reports and
notes in Costello's loopy handwriting that he was supposed to

sift through to action or non-action. She was in charge down at the McMutrie scene, so he was kind of redundant here. He looked out to the board, looking at Sue Melrose and her two wee boys. Was the man who killed them familiar with them as a family? Did he know what made Sue tick? Griffin might know, he had been a close friend of Steven as well as the first officer to stumble on the tragedy that had taken place at the Doon. That might have been years ago but it definitely had its roots in the dynamics of Altmore Road, so he phoned Griffin back while walking into his office.

'Hi, how are you doing?'

'Hi, it's that I'll be staying overnight in town and I'm at a bit of a loose end. I had an idea to go out for a curry and wondered if you wanted to join me, have a few beers and a good bitch about life in the force?'

Anderson heard the words 'yes, that'll be great' come out of his mouth before he had even thought about it. For God's sake, he had tried everything else, so he might as well try getting pissed and falling over and see if that made him feel any better.

It was a sad truth that Lynda McMutrie's death created more interest in Altmore Road than her life ever had. Costello sat in Walker's car, listening to him on the phone but not hearing what he was saying. She was looking out of the window, watching the black van, two police cars, O'Hare's car. The crime scene manager was there already. There was normally a babble of people – lookers-on, nosey parkers, the bored and disenfranchised – who would be hanging around outside waiting to catch a glimpse of something gossip-worthy. Here there were just the outcasts of Altmore Road, peeping out from under their stones. There was nothing here, just a drunk woman had taken a slip on the stairs, it happened every day. Shame on the neighbours for not noticing she was not around. Shame on her for not gaining entry sooner, Lynda might have been saved.

Everything had such clarity with hindsight.

She spent half an hour watching Jock Aird watching the scene, a hawk of a figure in a dark waxed coat, the dog visible at the window. Cadena Broadfoot, her hair pulled back into a large doughnut on the back of her head, filming unobtrusively on her mobile. Costello only knew it was her because the wind kept blowing down her hood. The big car came past, bouncing up the pavement, being stopped by a uniform, a quick conversation, voices raised through the pitter-patter of the rain. The car drove up the driveway of number 12.

'Brian Steele?' Costello said out loud, watching the tall slim man with a number-one haircut step out and be caught in the rain. As he walked towards the gaggle, Michael Broadfoot came out of number 4 to drag Cadena away. The girl tried to shrug off his hold. Then a blonde came out of number 12 and remonstrated with Brian. This would be Laura, who had already been interviewed by Anderson.

With all that going on, the passing of Lynda McMutrie into the black van went quietly unnoticed. Costello saw Jennifer Lawson, red eyed, standing at the door of number 8, a female officer standing with her, keeping each other company, keeping out of the rain. She looked in her wing mirror to the big house behind her. Everything about it was oppressive and dark, except for the single candle burning behind a window on the upper floor.

It took a long time to get everything done; the rain impeded their progress. Costello had made a big decision. It looked like another accidental death, but there had been some criminality going on in the street before and she couldn't lose their one chance to collect evidence – that was the sort of decision that came back to bite people on the bum. She insisted it was treated as a crime scene. Anderson would go ape-shit over the budget, but he wasn't here. She made arrangements to pop into the lab the following day; the house was too unpleasant with its flies and the stink of decaying flesh and rat faeces. By half nine at night, she had everything covered. She needed to get back to her own car, then buy some heavy-duty hand wash. The stink of the McMutrie basement had covered her like a blanket and she had been glad to stand in the rain to help wash off the stench that clung to her anorak.

She was trying not to dwell on the scene she had witnessed. It seemed a very sad death, drunk, alone, unsteady on her feet and heading down to the basement for some mundane reason they might never know, and falling, a slow bleed, death. They had found two photographs trapped under the body. They had asked Costello if she had wanted a look, but she declined. She'd see them later.

She had more of an urge to see what the Broadfoot girl had been filming – not that the young needed any excuse these days. She had a brief word with Walker, with O'Hare, then she hitched a ride back to her own Fiat by a police car.

She collapsed behind the wheel. It was the back of ten o'clock, the light was failing badly. She realized how tired she was. Her whole leg was hurting now; maybe she was walking awkwardly because her foot was so sore with the blister from hell. It was black in the middle now, red round the edges. She checked her phone. Wyngate had a lead on Griffin's ex-wife; instead of walking the fifty feet into the station she phoned him, making brief notes on what he was saying and looking at the clock on the car, watching her life tick by. God, she needed sleep. If she got her act together she could move on this now, and she really needed to buy some hand wash and disinfectant.

She was now on the track of Griffin's ex-wife. She needed to know what sort of man he was, and bloody Anderson thought the sun shone out his arse. Anderson had not sanctioned the search but Costello was intrigued to find out what the man had been like in his pre- and post-traumatic stress days. How was that memory of the crime scene? She was still sitting in her car when the man himself walked across the road in front of her, a little unsteady on his feet. It was twenty past ten and he had come from the car park at the back of the station. She put her phone in her handbag, stuck her bag under her arm as she locked the car and then made her way to the car park. Anderson was leaning against the door of his own car, flicking through his keys trying to find the right one. He was swaying slightly and stank of pakora and whisky. She put her hand out. He looked up.

'Hi Costello! How the hell are you? What are you doing here this time of night?' He was looking at her through half-closed, unfocused eyes. She took the keys off him and phoned a taxi, not trusting herself to speak.

TWENTY-FOUR

Wednesday 26 August 2015

In the lab, Matilda McQueen, forensic scientist, sat like an astronaut looking for the space station. She was a small woman who usually had to show her ID to buy a drink. The protective lilac suit bulged around her unflatteringly as she checked labels on the pile of evidence bags stacked up on the table in front of her.

Costello was sitting on a stool in the corner and had been told not to move.

'You are not popular. Can you stop finding things that would rather remain unfound?' said Matilda, not looking up.

'Sorry, I thought you were bored.'

'Last night's looks straightforward. Usual clothes for somebody who spends more money on drink than shower gel. And these?' She passed over two plastic folders, each containing a dried-out photograph of the same handsome young man, his face crazed with folds and wear of the paper.

Costello looked closely at them, examining the features, looking for a resemblance to somebody.

'And these are from twenty-three years ago. Not so straightforward.' Matilda placed her hand on a second pile of plastic sleeves.

'Are these the actual clothes? Gyle's clothes?' Costello looked at the jumble on the worktop, trying to imagine the skelf of a man in the Bar-L wearing a heavy metal T-shirt.

'Yes indeed. We have,' she pointed with her pen, 'Iron Maiden T-shirt, working denims, black underpants, woolly socks and leather work boots.' She was going through a big list on an A4 sheet. 'But there are a few things I want to look at more closely. One is the blood spatter on his chest.' She handed a photograph to Costello. 'Look at that blood. That's all transfer blood. With a wee bit of exhalation spray. That's what I would suggest if that was placed in front of me now. We will get an expert on it.'

'So not cast off from the axe?'

'No, more saturation from contact, i.e. he was close. Either he was helping her or trying to strangle her or rape her or something. And a wee bit of spray from out her nose, so again close – either helping or . . . not helping. What *is* absent is any cast-off from the axe down his back. Would we expect to find that, in the open air, with a big weapon, and a man of Gyle's height? Maybe not, but I would think we would see something. But we will ask an expert, the photos are already away.'

Costello rubbed her face with her hands, trying to make sense of it.

'What I am saying is, the microscopic evidence on the front of the clothes might lean towards Gyle's story.'

'OK,' said Costello slowly.

'And one other thing. Heidi, the dog, had blood in her mouth, in between her teeth, and some white linen? Cotton?'

'From Sue's dress?'

'No idea. It was noted but not retained. I have no idea why, but it is here in the notes.'

'So she bit Sue? Or somebody? She was at the top of the path?'

'So, if Andrew Gyle has got no dog bites on his body, then . . .' she shrugged. 'Again not conclusive but . . .'

Costello felt vaguely sick. She could hardly bear to ask the next question. She didn't need to.

'Gyle's boot was interesting, sent a few samples over for further examination. I am hopeful.' She smiled.

Costello didn't know what she was hopeful of.

Wyngate had been on the phone to Barbara McMutrie and was now drinking a cup of hot milky tea to calm down before he typed the report of the call into the intelligence log. She had, to put it mildly, not been happy to be contacted. He started giving Mulholland the edited highlights, and Mulholland, who was bored, starting typing. Wyngate flicked through his notes.

'Lynda was difficult to live with before she started drinking and impossible afterwards. She was not part of my life, why

don't you ask that bastarding brother of mine? Why are you even talking to me? What is happening with the house? Do I inherit it? Has that bastard Aird got anything to do with this? He's a right old perv.'

'Unspecified pervert?' asked Mulholland.

'She didn't elaborate. Also unspecified brother; I don't have any notes on a brother. Must be much older, otherwise you would know. Phone her back?'

'Piss off.' He wrote it down on his notebook to check on a brother. And went back to his dictation. 'Where was I, Oh yes, *Nobody had better be taking ma mum for a ride* – I think that was in relation to the house. *Weird place Altmore Road, better pulling it all down.* She both did and did not know Andrew Gyle, calling him a wee sad bastard. There were no infestations in the house at the time. She asked if there was anything worth selling.'

'Lovely kid, eh?'

'But she was happy for Aird the pervert to ID the body.'

'Lovely!'

Anderson was watching them. He could smell Mulholland's coffee and, although he had already drunk two, he badly needed more. He sat very still in his chair, trying not to let it swivel. Brenda was definitely not talking to him now and he had no idea where his car keys were. He had a vague memory of Costello waving him goodbye, but didn't dare ask her. She was being nippy as well. 'So, we have a hole in the ground. The bones of a single female foot. A dead body that nobody noticed. And an underground river, maybe.' He looked out at the white-board, but his eyes could not focus that far.

'The Steeles? How did you get on with the Steeles?' asked Costello.

'Oh, it's OK, I have spoken to them, just not written it up yet. Sorry. What do we know about Lynda?'

'Well I'm not going to the PM. Are you?'

'Are you kidding?'

'She seems a very private person with a life in a slow down-ward trajectory. She drank too much, she smoked too much. She never went out. She existed. But read a lot. Her house is kind of empty, as if she was rubbing herself out? But she didn't take her own life, did she?'

'Not in a rat-filled cellar. No, Costello, people do not kill themselves like that. She fell and died. There's a son Wyngate is trying to trace. They had not spoken in years.

'I am going to interview Vivienne Reid and Griffin's ex-wife.' She stood up.

'Why?'

'Why not? Both were close to the Gyle situation, by proxy if nothing else. And we still have no ID on the foot. We need to be careful, Colin, if these crimes are linked. Where is Lorna Gyle?'

'Why do you need to know?'

'I'd just be happier knowing Lorna was OK.'

'She is OK, she just does not want to be found. Good God, imagine the field day the press would have with her with all this going on? She is loved and cared for, she has a new life. I have told you that. I think you should leave it,' said Anderson.

'I think it's worth talking to Vivienne Reid; she knew Lorna better than anyone. We need to know what has happened to her in the last nineteen years.'

'I don't think you should.'

'And you taught me the rule about never talking to the person to get at the truth; you talk to the people round the person.'

'Leave Lorna alone.'

'You look really tired, I think you should go home.'

The house was a large sandstone property, circa 1929. It was a fine residence, if a little tattered round the edges. The Fiat undulated on the big camber on the road outside as Costello parked. The path up to the double storm doors was twisted and covered in dandelions, the door itself was painted in dark blue gloss that contrasted with the polished red tiles on the floor in the hall. The stained-glass panel was original and intricate.

The door surrounds were being stripped back to the wood so they were obviously on a renovation project. She walked up the front path and found the bell on the stonework.

She pressed; a deep burr rang out from inside the house somewhere. A single woof of a large dog coming towards her – the intruder. That's what dogs did. She was sure that is what Heidi had done. The sound of an internal door opening; a female

figure came along the hall, closing the inner door, talking to
the dog that was now being barricaded inside the front room.

The door opened to reveal a woman in her mid-thirties,
dressed in workman dungarees, covered in spots and splashes
of dark red paint. 'Hi?'

Costello held out her warrant card. The face of the young
woman fell immediately. 'There's nothing wrong,' assured
Costello. 'I was wondering how long you have lived in this
house.'

'Two years, not quite two years.'

'And who lived in it before you?'

The young woman closed her lips, and nodded. 'Yes. I think
you should come in. Mind, the hall floor is full of buckets. You
don't mind dogs, do you?'

Ten minutes later, Costello was sitting on a stool in a half-
built kitchen, with a cup of hot tea and a plate full of digestive
biscuits at her elbow. Nancy McIver was at the sink, washing
a paintbrush, filling a jar with thinner, sticking it in a row with
many others on the window ledge. She peeled off the straps of
her dungarees so they swung round her waist. The house, though
in a state of major refurb, was spotlessly clean. The dog, which
looked to Costello like a long-haired Labrador, was now curled
up on her basket, eyeing the digestives and considering who
would be the best person to beg from.

'You are looking for Lorna, aren't you? You are not the only
one; the odd reporter has called by. I have no idea where she
is. I was told that she had got married and moved away, leaving
her past behind her. Poor girl. All that will really follow her
round, but she's not responsible for anything.'

'So you don't know where she is now, Lorna Gyle?'

'Lorna Reid, I think. The house was owned by Vivienne Reid.
We bought it from her estate. If Lorna inherited all that, she'll
be a wealthy young lady.'

'Was she here when you bought the house?'

'No,' Nancy sat down on the stool at the end of the worktop
that would soon be a breakfast bar. 'It's so sad. Vivienne was
killed by a hit-and-run driver, just before Christmas a couple
of years back. She was just out walking the dog. You never
know, do you.' Nancy turned round to look at her own dog as

she did so. 'They didn't find the driver or the car. And Lorna did not come back here; the house sale and everything was all done through the solicitor. Mayweather, Glasgow. In town.'

Costello noted the name. 'Personal effects, did she come back for anything out the house?'

'No, nothing I think. You can ask the lawyer. Lorna was the only beneficiary. The neighbours might know more than me, but I think that Lorna had moved out in her late teens. Vivienne wasn't her mother, you know, I think she had passed away. And her dad was in jail. Shame that somebody, well, you know, adopting a child, then ending up like that, killed in an accident. You'd think that God would give them a break.'

Costello slunk down the inside of the door, landing her bum on the carpet, then looked surprised that the floor was so close. 'I don't think I can work with him any more. He was so drunk last night. He's bloody impossible. He's holding out on me about Lorna Gyle, who has – I have discovered – the finance to do a very nice disappearing act, thank you very much. *Lorna is OK*. What the hell is that supposed to mean? Why is she still up on that wall? *Lorna is OK, the Steeles are OK*. Well, Lynda McMutrie was not OK, and Vivienne Reid was thumped by a car at half past nine on the night of the fourth of December 2013 and her head bounced off the bonnet of a car that has never been traced, so no, it's not OK.'

'Well, you have always been impossible, but you don't hear us yabbering on about it all the time,' muttered Mulholland. 'I presume you are talking about your boss.'

'Our boss.'

Batten looked up and nodded his head in the direction of Anderson's empty office, 'Do you want to have a word?'

She looked confused momentarily. 'Yeah OK, but is it not locked?'

'He doesn't lock it any more.' Batten stood up and opened the door, ignoring the faces Mulholland was pulling.

'You've got work to do,' said Costello. 'Find the accident report on Vivienne Reid. Please.' She pointed at his keyboard on her way past, limping a little; she had found it difficult to get up from the floor, using one foot to keep her weight off her blister. She was sure it was infected now. Far too much running around after a year of sitting in boring meetings. She went into the room and sat down, taking the chair on one side of the desk as Batten pulled the other chair out from the wall. They left Anderson's own chair vacant. It stayed behind his empty desk.

'You know, Costello, maybe you shouldn't be saying that in front of his team.'

'Saying what?' she snapped.

'That you can't work with him.'

Costello narrowed her eyes, the small scar flared white. 'Is this a "many a true word spoken in jest" conversation?'

'Was it spoken in jest?'

'If I didn't think I could work with him, I would have asked to be transferred back to . . .' but she twisted round on her seat. 'He's not that bad, is he? I mean, I was only joking.'

'No, I don't think you were. How much did he drink last night?'

'Too much, I still have his car keys. He has never, ever been irresponsible like that.'

'He's getting side-tracked – you know it and I know it. This lassie, the wee one with the long dark hair, it reflects on him and his relationship with Claire. That is why he is going out of his way to protect her. Maybe this Lorna, too. She is a damsel in distress and he loves playing the knight in shining armour. He did it with Helena. In their early days, I bet he did it with Brenda, but now she is dominant in that relationship. She has corralled the family for their own safety. He is surplus to require-ments and has been cut off. He has transferred to this Jennifer; he thinks if he can save this one, then maybe he can save his own daughter.'

'From who?'

'From herself.'

'I'm glad I'm thick, because I don't really understand how driving a stranger to the hospital but not being at home to see his daughter after her return to school, a difficult return to school, is going to help. Then going out on the piss with a man he hardly knows but is suddenly his best pal? I mean, I really don't get that,' she said.

'Well, it's because his own daughter does not want her dad

to be there. So he's transferred that paternal role on to somebody else and, like I said, he has no mates. This bromance with Griffin might do him the world of good. Although drinking on that medication will not.'

'And he disregards stuff about the enquiry. Sue Melrose didn't deserve to die the way she did. Nobody deserves to die like that, but equally she does not deserve the angelic mother tag that she has been labelled with since the day she was—'

'Brutally murdered with a hatchet in front of her own two wee boys . . . That's why she has that tag on her, Costello. I think we should at least give her that in death. She was a pretty young brunette.' He opened his arms in supplication. 'Come on, Costello?'

'That's not what I mean. We have evidence that says her boys annoyed the neighbours, that she annoyed the neighbours.'

'And it was the neighbour who put a hatchet through her head, so I think you might be arguing yourself into a corner there.'

'But does that fit, psychologically? It wasn't the nasty neighbour complaining about the lovely girl next door. OK, look at it this way. She never asked to help them, never offered to take their kid, Lorna, to school, although she was walking the same way with her dog.'

'Antagonism runs deep. Folk do enjoy their enemy's misfortunes.'

'Was that why Sue didn't just get on with her own life? What was in that life that we might not have come across?'

'You seem very down on the victim – she was a human being. She had a right to her life.'

'Why did she get changed?' Costello pondered. 'And Andrew Gyle has a right to liberty if he is innocent. What do you think? That it wasn't about Sue? What if it was about her husband? The crime resulted in Sue and the kids being removed from the situation. All this Sue being angelic and Gyle being a demon might have nothing to do with it. This situation is not as black and white as it looks.'

Batten nodded, his fingertips at his lips. 'Yes, I will go along with that.'

She leaned forward. 'And Gyle is not as black as he is painted.'

'He was found guilty of killing a woman, a child and a baby with an axe.'

'I'm not sure that the investigation looked at anybody else too deeply. Gyle was already painted as the devil in the press. How much effort does it take to keep insisting you are innocent? He's been stabbed twice in the nick – in 1997 and Christmas 2013. He could be up for parole by now if he had admitted his guilt and shown his remorse.' She tapped her fingers on Anderson's desk, looking out of the window. 'And he says he can't show remorse for something that—'

'He did not do. God, if I had a pound for every time I have heard that . . .' Batten shook his head. 'But, seriously, why are you thinking along these lines?'

'Gyle's persistence. Anderson is waiting for the DNA to solve the ownership of the bones issue and ignores the huge question mark. There is something wrong with that investigation into the Melrose case. Every time I put a bit of evidence in front of him, he ignores it, so what is the point?'

'Why do you think Andrew Gyle is innocent?'

'Mick, the evidence is starting to point that way. It's not just that the evidence might tell a different story, it's that the evidence might be, just might be, backing up what Gyle has argued was the truth all along. He found them, he went to help. The person who gave him the alibi still stands by his statement. And is still paying for his defence. It makes you think.'

'You have changed your tune. But have you heard the theory that Jock was a pervert, he was messing around with the girls on the street? Maybe Gyle's daughter? Maybe that is the tie that binds them? There are no other witnesses, Costello. Lorna isn't hanging around standing up for her Dad, is she?'

'That's why I want to talk to her, but Colin won't let me.'

'No other witnesses, Costello, not one. Evidence after twenty-three years? Come on. Not a hope.'

Costello sighed, her shoulders slumped. 'Would you go for female intuition?' His phone beeped. 'Oh God, a call from Brenda Anderson.'

'Say you're busy.'

TWENTY-FIVE

R at bites. Jennifer Lawson was angry. The rats had been breeding and growing in the front garden of number 6 and had been all over Lynda's body in number 10. She was the rat sandwich of number 8. She decided she would bloody well find the rats herself and then she could get Gordy back.

She rummaged around in the wardrobe for her wellies, her old wellies from way last winter. From the previous house, in fact. She pulled them on and rolled up an old pair of socks, stuffing them round the top and ramming them in tight so it made her calf hurt when she walked. Then she made her way downstairs, and found a hammer, a torch, one oven glove and one leather glove. She felt invincible. She swapped hands and swung the hammer about a few times. Then she took a deep breath to calm her racing heart and started down the basement stairs. A little slide, a slippery feeling underfoot, probably just the wellies on the wooden steps. The wood seemed slimy, dry and raised looking. She put her hand against the wall for support, feeling the plaster soft and crumbling under the quilt of the glove. At the bottom of the stairs she switched the light on. There was no sense of movement, no sense of anything scurrying away. No living thing had heard she was coming and vanished before she got here.

It looked the same as it always did. Plastic storage boxes piled up. Stuff she hadn't got round to unpacking. An old exercise bike, a bookcase that needed fixing, or demolishing. An old office chair that was to go with the desk, once she had got round to building the desk for the laptop.

That had no Wi-Fi yet.

All those things she was supposed to do.

She walked into the middle of the basement, took a good look round. She knew the house at the top of the road, the double-barrelleds, had converted this room to a sitting room.

The previous owners had got as far as putting down a carpet and somebody, maybe the owners before that, had Artexed the walls, roughly; too rough to use this room as a playroom for the wee ones without stripping it off or covering it. And then somebody had painted it all green. Army green.

She tapped her way round, climbing over boxes and cases, looking for gaps in the skirting board where rats might get through. There were bits where the Artex was coming away. She wondered if there were any holes behind it, and if the rats might be slithering between the layers as she stood here. She knew they could get into tiny places. She sniffed. The air was cool and fresh. The bad smell had vanished, as usual. It was never there when she needed it. Maybe it was all her imagination. But the little bleeding marks on Gordy's fingertips and toes, the scrapes on his face were not in her imagination; they were real enough. His disease was real.

She swung the hammer at the top, as far as she could reach. Little bits of flaked green Artex rained down on her. She tapped a little lower into the corner. It sounded fine. She got brave and started tapping it with her knuckle, the way builders did before telling her it was best to do the job properly and it was going to cost but he would try to do it for a good price. In the middle of the wall, lower down and behind an old TV set she wasn't even sure was theirs, the wall sounded hollow. She stopped, thinking that it might be better to get a builder now, in case she brought the whole wall down. Maybe even the whole house. But that would involve phoning Douglas and trying to get some money from him. He didn't need to add to his worries. But then, if she made a mess of it, he would have to stump up for a professional. She carried on tapping and then prodding with her forefinger. The plaster gave slightly, as if the whole wall was paper thin. She felt along the bottom, along the top of the skirting board, feeling for a patch that gave a little more.

She tapped it hard with the hammer. It flaked – green then dirty white, then wee lumps of wood. Then a hole big enough to get her fingers through. But she couldn't see what was on the opposite side and she wasn't taking any chances. She got up, feeling her jeans slightly damp where she had been kneeling, swinging the hammer again until it stuck, then pulling back so the claws ripped through the Artex and the thin wet plasterboard behind. She hooked the claws in deep and it came away easily. No mass of rats leapt out. Just a faint gust of air from somewhere. The hole was dark, very dark, and very wet at the bottom. She was looking at a wall of different colours of mud, layer upon layer; some black, some almost red. She made the hole a bit bigger, more confident now. She pulled the torch from her anorak pocket and shone it around, her nose catching the smell of something that was unpleasant, something sweet and rotten.

Keeping well back she pointed the light beam around, taking in the gap, the bricks of an old wall that had crumpled, the small amount of water seeping through it. The overhead light blinked on and off, then on again. She waited; it went off and stayed off. As she knew it would. That would be the water seeping into the electrics. That was a bad mix.

She got up, her torch beam moving as she did so, casting its light vaguely round, here and there, and, in passing, highlighted a face behind the wall. A face that looked back at her with big laughing eyes and a smile the width of the Grand Canyon.

Jennifer screamed and fell backwards over the old TV she didn't even think was theirs and landed flat on her back on the basement floor. The torch fell with her, hitting the carpet somewhere above her head and she knew no more.

Costello followed the woman down to the checkout, feeling a little elated, feeling like a spy. So many of her colleagues were doing things 'off the record', there was no reason why she should be acting any differently.

Life moved in small circles sometimes. Wyngate knew somebody who worked at the school where the geography teacher had once been married to the man who had been first on the scene in the Altmore Wood murder case. A quick check of records proved that it was correct. Costello could imagine how such gossip would delight the pupils.

A call to the school told her that she had missed Mrs Prentice, but that she would be in Asda wearing a white trenchcoat, and gave her a mobile number. Costello did not bother ringing her; she went to Asda and watched. She had found her straight away. Catherine White, as she had been born. Kate Prentice, as she was now. Cathy Griffin, as she had been when married to David. She had married again, with two kids, eight and ten. She looked as though she had popped into the supermarket for a pint of milk and a loaf, and ended up with half a trolley full.

Costello waited until Kate was through the checkouts and on her way to the car park, then stopped her near the queue for the kiosk.

'Kate? Kate Prentice?'

The petite woman looked uncertainly at her, a nervous flick of fingers through short dark hair. 'What do you want? I am not buying anything.'

Costello tried to smile at her, trying to engage her. 'Would you mind if we had a cup of tea?' She pulled her warrant card from her pocket and flashed it at her, covering it with her palm. 'You are not in any trouble.'

'It's about David, isn't it?' Kate was on the ball, already suspicious of why the detective was here.

Costello nodded, looking about her, making sure nobody was overhearing.

'Are you on a murder case? Sue Melrose? Helen McNealy?'

'Helen?' asked Costello.

'Just somebody, it's fine.' She glanced at her watch – nothing evasive, just checking the time. 'I have twenty minutes, half an hour, before I need to go and get the kids. Will that do you?'

In the end, Kate had phoned her mum to go and get the boys from the football training they attended after school. She seemed glad to talk, a black coffee and a Bakewell tart in front of her. Her first question was interesting to Costello's trained ear. 'He can't trace me through you, can he?'

'No, not at all. But I found you easily enough. Was it a bad divorce?'

'He divorced me, broke my heart. So why do you want to talk to me?'

Costello started the conversation with the party line on the case of David Griffin and the Melrose murders. *It was a terrible thing for a young police officer to stumble across.*

Kate agreed that it was. Griffin was not the same man after that, and she was sorry the marriage had fallen apart. Some marriages can't stand that sort of challenge.

Costello agreed, 'Perfectly normal personalities get caught up in something that human psychology cannot cope with. The mind crumples; the emotional state goes into some kind of high alert. It becomes difficult to live a normal life after that. Normal things don't seem important any more.' She realized she was talking about Anderson, but she thought it might hit home and get Kate to open up.

'Oh, he was a bastard before I married him. He was a bullshitter; he'd never amount to anything. He talks a good game, that's all. I know that now, but back then I loved him. What can I say?'

'Really?' Costello was surprised. So David Griffin, a rising star of the force, was a dirtbag, in his wife's opinion. Had the legend become bigger than the man? He had left the force, so what evidence was there that he was going to reach the dizzy heights? Had Anderson been beguiled by that as well?

She sighed; there was a strange friendship in there, between the two of them, and she was going to have to tread lightly. She needed to know more about David Griffin, the sensitive young policeman who bravely tried to save the life of a young woman who had had her chest cleaved open with an axe.

And why would his ex-wife mention a specific name in conjunction with Griffin and the word 'murder'? Kate was not a stupid woman; she had made a connection in the back of her mind somewhere.

'Do you ever get the feeling at work that the place has too many chiefs that never tell the ground troops anything?'

'I'm a teacher, it goes with the territory.'

'Nobody has told me anything about Helen McNealy?'

'Oh . . .' Kate Prentice tried to smile, then it folded. 'I don't think I should be saying this.'

'Saying what?'

'The big stress for David, I think. Was keeping quiet about Steven?'

'Steven?'

'Yes, it only came clear in hindsight, when I read about Helen McNealy.'

'Do you want another coffee?'

TWENTY-SIX

C ostello had fallen asleep in the chair in the office, ending up slumped over a keyboard, and woken up with the imprints of the individual keys on her cheeks, as if somebody was making a mosaic.

A system search for Helen McNealy had come up with an unexpected result. As soon as Costello had seen the words 'car mechanic', she had got that chill that she was on to something. Steven Melrose was a mechanic, and women who got involved with him ended up dead. Her phone was ringing, vibrating its way across her desk like some demented little dictator. It was Brenda Anderson again. This was the third time: she couldn't ignore it any longer. Costello steeled herself and sang a few lines of 'Private Life'.

No, she had no idea where Anderson had been that night, but she did know it was a male colleague. No, she wasn't his keeper. He was a grown man. Brenda went into a stress-fuelled rant. This was all over and he didn't care about them or his daughter. He was out drinking.

Letting off steam was all Costello could say.

'Well, I'm sending you the picture. Is this the man?'

Why don't you ask him yourself? It was a selfie, which in itself spoke volumes about how drunk he must have been. Anderson grinning over a pint and pakora. Griffin with his arm raised. Costello looked closer at the picture, trying to increase the size on her phone. She couldn't so she sent it to her email and opened it there on the computer and sat for a few minutes looking closely at Griffin's rolled-up shirt cuffs and the skin of his forearm.

She didn't know if she was elated or devastated. Or mistaken.

She texted Brenda a heartfelt thanks, and she was forwarding the picture to Matilda McQueen when the door opened. Wyngate was rubbing his eyes, tired of being in the office. Tired of the rain. Tired of being tired.

'God I am wet.'

'Do you want a cuppa?'

'Oh, yes please.'

'Good, get me one while you are at it.'

Wyngate sighed, that was twice. 'I'll just drip all the way from here to there.'

In the end she put the kettle on as he spoke; he was reading and drying his face with a paper towel at the same time. 'We have a dead body of a mother, one daughter abroad who doesn't give a shit. And a son called Gregor McMutrie, he'll be forty-four. So I got back to the sister who said, Quote: *If we are that bloody interested, then we should effin try to effin find him ourselves.'*

'Charming!'

'He's the director of McGregor Homes.' Vik Mulholland didn't look away from his screen.

'I've heard that name before,' said Costello.

'He's the builder on the far side of the hill.'

'You found that very quickly.'

'I've known all along, I put it on Anderson's desk yesterday. I thought the son might know where his mum was.'

'For God's sake, Vik. We've been looking—'

'Well you should have asked me.'

Wyngate kept talking, wishing the floor would open up; he did not want to get caught in the crossfire.

'They don't speak.'

'Neither does anybody in here, seemingly. So Walker is going out to the post, we are too busy here. O'Hare is not ruling out natural causes, he's not finished his tests. The rats have eaten some bits but the cartilage on her nose was disrupted. It had been snapped, pressed hard against something. Like the floor, probably when she fell. God knows my mum went down like a sack of spuds when pissed.' She walked back to Anderson's desk. 'I think I have fin rot, my feet have been underwater so often.'

'I've not finished,' said Wyngate. 'Matilda from forensic services was on the phone when you were out. There was some organic matter on the toe of the boot – lots of big words and then the word vomit. And she spelled this out for me: Z I N G I B E R A C E A E. Do you know what that is?'

'I bet it's ginger something. So she found traces of that?'

'She said to tell you. Is it important?'

'Very, OK, I am off to the B-L.'

'You are going to see Gyle again?'

'I am indeed. I have survived the gong-bath tea, I can survive anything.'

'Were you looking for a FAI on somebody called Helen McNealy?' asked Wyngate. 'It's here now.'

Costello nodded and Wyngate began to scroll, his fingertip pointing out the highlights. 'Died, age twenty-nine, nurse, fatal accident, killed outright. 1972 MG Roadster . . . nice car that. It hit a wall, out East Kilbride way. The twelfth of May 1996. She was a member of the Braveheart Bangers.'

'The who?'

'I think they are a Scottish classic car club.'

'OK, OK, google them. Has Steven Melrose ever been a member?'

Wyngate got to work as Costello thought out loud.

'Steven Melrose was an old-fashioned car mechanic, which is why he fitted so well into the Carron Bridge Community. OK, loads of people like old cars, but how many of them end up with dead female friends?'

'Yes, he was a member from 1988 to 1998.' Wyngate sat back, pleased with himself. 'But he has an alibi for the death of his wife and kids. He was at work.'

'At a garage? Under a car, the radio on? We believe he was at work.' She went back into Anderson's office. Steven had sat opposite her, his hands still red raw from the vigorous hand washing. Was that a sign of guilt? No, it was a sign of not wanting to eat with hands covered in oil and engine dirt. She started flicking through the crime-scene photographs, looking for something, but she did not know what.

She googled the Braveheart Bangers herself, a group of Scottish classic car enthusiasts. They looked like a right bunch of anoraks. They sold bits and bobs for huge sums of money, including really old car badges – old AA badges, RAC badges, the metal kind that clipped on to the grille of a car. Their own badge was a car, maybe a Hillman Imp, in front of a St Andrews cross with jaggy edges. She thought about that and something that had been mentioned on the very brief PM report she had found on Lorna Reid's adoptive mother, Vivienne Reid. A distinct mark on her leg at the point of impact, where the car had hit the side of the knee. So she sent Matilda the reference to that as well.

The poor girl would be sick of hearing from her.

Watching her time, she opened up her emails, scrolling through to anything that might be relevant. Matilda McQueen from the lab. She had retested the skin samples that had been taken from the wooden handle of the axe. They were all Gyle's. The report on the blade from 1992 showed all kinds of matter – brain tissue, blood, muscles, skin, fat. Plus some canine tissue and hair from Heidi the family dog. Costello could take or leave dogs, but the death of that animal was emotive. Something about the way the dog completed the perfect family picture. That bloody dog at Inchgarten had peed on her. Then she remembered Nesbit, before Anderson rescued him, biting Mulholland, back in the old days, in the room next door. She flicked through the files for the PM report on Gyle. There was no mention of any dog bites on his body at all. Gyle had been wearing a black T-shirt. Sue had worn the white dress. She wondered what Steven had been wearing.

'*I was the one who persuaded her to go out for a walk that evening.*'

She went back to the pictures. Looking at their hands, the blood, Gyle's hands covered, his T-shirt covered, the spray that forensics had pointed out. It had been a warm night. She could see the covered feet of three men. She flicked over, looking up for a wider-angle image. It was Griffin talking to two detectives, one of whom she recognized a little. He had his jersey on, the white collar of the old uniform visible underneath.

He was talking, his hands out explaining something. She flicked through, looking at the hands, hands here and there covered in blood. Both men had bloodied hands. She dialled Anderson but put the phone down; that was the wrong person to ask. She dialled Archie – not unusual for her to call him at home, but she needed to know. She asked her question and he said he had no idea – maybe try O'Hare, he might know.

He might know about the state of AIDS and HIV and hepatitis in the early 1990s.

He might know about the perceived infection risk of a community police officer from disused needles in an old park.

Jennifer moaned slightly and tried to turn over in bed, except she wasn't in bed, she was lying in the dark on something so cold it was damp and the dampness had seeped through her jeans and through her jumper. She was cold, unbelievably cold. There was a noise of somebody or something above, walking about upstairs. Douglas had come back. If so, why was she lying on the floor? She tried to get up, on her elbows, ignoring the spinning in her head. There was something she was supposed to be panicking about, but could not recall what. She was wearing an oven glove. She wiped her face, blood everywhere, her nose and cheeks felt as though she had been out in the wind. And she had a terrible headache.

She had come down to the basement to look for something; she had wellies on. She couldn't recall why. The floorboards creaked upstairs. She had fallen down on the damp again, slipped into some kind of semi-sleep, the way she did when she was trying to ignore the alarm and was refusing to get up, in those days when she had a job. Nursing; she used to be a student nurse. Then she'd met Douglas – he was lovely and they had the family, so where were the kids now? Why was there a claw hammer next to her foot?

A weird creeping feeling came over her; something bad had happened. Her head was sore. She was bleeding. She sat up slowly, her head swimming, the room swirling in front of her eyes. She got on to all fours and crawled towards the wall. At the stairs, she tried to climb up. There should be a banister. Why not? That was her next job. There were a few things she was supposed to do but could not remember, so she climbed the stairs on all fours, like a dog. Her head pounded at each pull up, every time she used her knees. Her head thumped, she was so tired. She stopped as she drew level with the old worn carpet of the hall. Nearly there. She needed to stand up and turn right, and suddenly that seemed a very complicated thing to do. So she rested back on her knees, sitting down on the back of her thighs. She heard somebody walking about. She kept her head low, crouching in the old hall cupboard, listening and watching. Soft feet were walking back and forward. She knew it wasn't Douglas; he wouldn't have left her in the basement. This was a man in leather brogues, old leather brogues and thick tan cord trousers, old man's trousers. The man had her son. He was walking around her house. He was wrapping Robbie in a blanket and the back door was open.

He was going to take him away.

And she remembered. She was lying in the basement because somebody had turned the lights off. She'd seen somebody's face so they had hit her on the head and she had fallen. Now he was here, taking her child.

She crept on to her feet, leaning against the wall, still in the recess of the cupboard. She stood for a wee moment, getting her breath. Then she leapt forward, reaching into the kitchen and picking up her frying pan. Turning quickly, she battered him across the face as hard as she could, catching him off balance and sending him flying.

She picked up her son and ran out into the rain.

TWENTY-SEVEN

Thursday 27 August 2015

Professor Jack O'Hare pushed the warm water up between his fingers, ground the soap and then the sterilizing agent into the gap, and then up under his fingernails and into the folds behind his knuckles; one of his little rituals to start the day off for him. Like the way the younger generation stopped to buy expensive coffee in a cheap paper cup on their way to work.

The dubious pleasure of being the first recipient of O'Hare's attentions this morning went to Lynda McMutrie. And he would not be alone. O'Hare had a new companion in the mortuary. Dr Paul Rees was good, young and enthusiastic, but there was more than that to being a good forensic pathologist. The untrained talent was being an awkward bugger, never accepting the obvious, and aspiring to be a right royal pain in the bum, independent of what side of the judicial fence was paying the bill. O'Hare looked at his lined face in the mirror as he dabbed antiseptic and antibiotic liquid round the end of his nostrils. He had a simple way of thinking about his cases, the bodies that lay in front of him every day. Never take it for granted, always let them surprise you. And know nothing beforehand.

It was impossible for the human brain to 'unknow' something. And it was very tempting to take the easy way out. In these days of cuts and shortcuts, there was a temptation – a dangerous temptation – to read up on the case beforehand.

It would never happen to him, he thought as he wiped his hands on a sterile paper towel. He would never let it. Early in his career, a senior had been embarrassed by the result of a second tox screen on a body that had suffered a gunshot wound to the head. There had been a self-administered accidental fatal overdose hours before the bullet entered the brain tissue. The cause of death was as wrong as it could have been.

Always look beyond the obvious, just in case.

He was getting gowned up when the door bumped open, the mechanism giving an irritated hiss at the alteration of the air pressure.

'Prof? How are you?' The young man bounded in, full of energy and enthusiasm. O'Hare doubted he himself had ever been that keen. They nodded at each other; there was no shaking hands, no touching of flesh when it breached infection control.

'I am very well. We have a busy day ahead.' He pulled on his boots and the younger man pushed the tap with his elbow and got to work quickly on his own hands. O'Hare was relieved to see it. Their patients might not be at risk from infection, but they themselves were right on the front line.

'Who is first up? The old guy that fell down the stairs? The substance abuser from Easterhouse or the chronic alcoholic they found in Altmore Road?'

'The latter,' said O'Hare, quietly disapproving of the short-hand speak. Assumptions had already been made. And that could lead to sloppy thinking. *But not on my shift* – a line from a film floated back to him.

They went into the PM room, saying hello to Barry the technician, and the photographer who was fiddling with his digital camera. The body had already been brought through; the bag was sitting folded up on a trolley, in case it was needed for examination of cast-off evidence. The body had been washed, the trolley still showed the odd spot of water on the stainless steel. The runoff water would be filtered as they worked. It would be logged and labelled, waiting to go over to the university if further analysis was needed. For now, it was just evidence.

'I must be getting popular.'

'Infamous more like, Mr Gyle. I don't like being here.'

'Neither do I. And you can get out.'

'Well, I find you endlessly fascinating, Mr Gyle,' said Batten, sitting in the plastic chair, putting one foot up on his other thigh. Like he was sitting in the pub, relaxing for a nice pint and a chat. 'You ever been bitten by a dog?'

'Nope.' Quick, automatic. Gyle nodded at them, his lips moving nervously. 'Is this about the sinkhole? Have you found something? It said in the paper that you found bones.'

'Should we have found anything?' asked Costello.

'Oh Jesus Christ! I am in here for a crime I didn't do, and suddenly you two are here. Then here again. And it can't be about the crime I'm doing my time for, because for you guys that case is cut and dried. So there is something else going on.'

He looked at Costello whose bony face did not flicker, but when he looked at Batten he got a smile of confidence, encouraging him to talk.

Gyle's demeanour changed, his eyes furrowed. 'So why are you here? What's this about dog bites? If you haven't found anything?' He held his hands in his head. 'I have come to terms with it. I am fed up with telling folk that I did not kill that woman and her children.'

Batten said slowly, 'Her name is Sue. I have told you, her name is Sue and she was twenty-seven years old. You killed her with an axe. And the fact that you cannot bear to say her name means that you still want to dissociate yourself from your act. If you didn't do it, you would still be thinking of her as Sue the annoying neighbour. So you are condemning yourself; your subconscious mind is condemning you all on its own.'

Costello pointed to the professor. 'As you know, he is a doctor, and he said that's what guilty people do, so if you want you can cut the crap and confess that you did it.'

'I didn't do it.'

'So why are we here?' Costello asked Batten. 'He is too stupid to even realize that all he needs to do is confess and repent and get counselling and parole and then—'

'I hated her.' Gyle's voice was loud but calm. 'I hated her.'

Costello and Batten both sat back. 'Hated her enough to kill her?' asked Costello.

'No. Her own life was shit, so why should I cut it short?' His mouth pursed into a narrow line.

'What did you call her in the house?'

'My wife and I called her The Slut Womble.'

Costello burst out laughing. 'Slut Womble.'

Gyle was smiling at the memory, 'Lorna liked Wombles, so we started calling her that. It was a joke, but we could say it in front of the wee one. Instead of me swearing.'

'So she was a slut?' Costello tried not to look at Batten. This was something new.

'No, she wasn't. Really. She wasn't.'

'So why did you call her that?'

Gyle rubbed his face with his hands. 'It was the way she pandered to her man; it was weird. It was same way Lorna pawed her Womble. But Steven was married to her. They could do what they liked to each other as long as they kept it away from my girl.'

'So what did you think of Steven?'

'He was OK, like I say. He was a bit embarrassed by her, I think. We shared a beer.' Gyle shrugged. 'He would have let Lorna play with the boys but not her. Oh no!' Gyle gave a little laugh, 'No we were too working class for Susan Melrose to ever, ever let her boys anywhere near our daughter. She was a huge snob. And she is largely irrelevant. I did not kill her. The person who killed her is still out there. So my interest is in him, not her. And that interest is growing now that you are here.

I've been here for twenty-odd years. When I thought there was no chance of me getting out, I resigned myself to always walking that tightrope of protesting my innocence. It keeps me going. But now, I seem to have some hope. I want Lorna to know that I did not do this.' His eyes reddened, Costello looked away. 'Sorry. That's why I am talking to you without my solicitor. They can hold things up, trying to get a deal, and don't tell them this and don't tell them that. I have nothing to lose and everything to gain by telling you everything I know. I want out of here with my name cleared. Completely cleared. I want you to find who killed her and her kids, then I can get my daughter back.'

'That's exactly what I would expect you to say,' said Costello, sticking to her guns. Goading Gyle was one way through to the truth about Sue and maybe Steven. Batten looked at her: *Don't back down; push him as hard as you can.* 'And what if your daughter does not want you back?'

'Once she knows that I am not guilty, she will be back.'

Costello leaned forward, talking conversationally. 'If I asked you what you thought of Steven Melrose as a person, what would you say?' Then she added. 'Honestly.'

Gyle hesitated. 'Steven? Quiet. She gave him a miserable life.'

'He was under her thumb?'

Gyle gave a wee smile. 'He always tried to calm things down between her and me. I had a beer with him, a few times, at the bottom of the garden, when the Slut Womble was out. He was an OK guy, Steven. When she parked her car across our driveway just to bug me, he would move it if he saw it first. We could hear her screaming at him through the wall. He would tell her to sober up and she would laugh in his face. She took out the trees that separated the back gardens, so Steven gave us the money, you know, to cover expenses, and we bought some small fir trees to put on our side of the fence. A week later they had been pulled out as well. So yeah, she called the police to us. I shouted at her.' He shrugged. 'But they gave her a talking-to. Steven was embarrassed by it all, I think he wanted a quiet life. Well he has it now, doesn't he?' Gyle crossed his arms, that little smile played on his lips. 'I don't know who or why, but something gave me the impression that he had another woman somewhere. I hope so.'

Rees was doing the post. O'Hare was observing and recording. It was a proud part of Scots law that there had to be two of them present, true corroboration of any findings. O'Hare, who had done a bit of teaching in his time, often found it difficult to keep polite in the face of untidy cuts, rushed procedures and sloppy workmanship, as they had no place in the mortuary. They were the pedants of pedantry. There were very few absolutes at a post mortem. It was all a balance of probability, and the cause of death that made its way into the final report was the one the pathologist felt was the most likely, given the information lying in front of them on the table.

The most likely.

The weight of a professional opinion.

The body lay between them, and they were her satellite people. All here, just for her. She was a small, rather overweight woman. Sixty-three at the time of her death. She lay on her back, her open eyes staring into the recording equipment above the stainless-steel slab. Her face showed some compression trauma that suggested she had been lying on her front. The skewbald pattern of white and purple showed the body had been resting on the front shortly after death and had remained in that position for a few hours. The fact that she had been found in that position lent weight to the supposition that she had died where she lay. But it proved nothing. She had been found with her arms above her head, her face down, against a hard surface, probably the floor of the basement where she had been found. And her body showed the biting of the rats, frayed flesh that was now black, hard round the edges. The maggots from the blowflies had been washed through and would be caught in the sieve. Rees was chatting about the political news of the day as the mortuary assistant pulled over a trolley of stainless-steel saw blades and instruments of various sizes. The door opened and a small, impeccably dressed man, grey short hair and a red tie fixed by a gold tiepin, walked behind the glass screen, up to the microphone and wished them a good morning.

'Have you met the Glasgow fiscal, Archie Walker?' O'Hare asked Rees.

'In passing,' said Rees dismissively, running his gloved fingers round the hairline of the body.

The senior pathologist exchanged glances with the senior fiscal.

'I believe you are to be congratulated re your expertise on old footwear.'

'Matilda's, not mine.'

'Will that stand up in court? Twenty-three-year-old vomit?'

'I think it would be vulnerable to a vigorous defence,' replied O'Hare. 'And she, Matilda, has some interesting findings from the stairs to the basement. The wood is covered in slime; you can get a good shoe-mark print out of slime mould, when the wearer stands to the side of the step and the footmark remains untouched by other foot traffic. Size eleven Hunter wellies with a repaired patch under the right hallux, big toe.'

'But this is natural causes?' said Rees.

'Bumps on the head?' O'Hare pulled a face. 'Never keen on calling any bump on the head natural until we know what bumped it.'

'So are we ready to get going?' asked Rees, not enjoying listening to a conversation that he wasn't part of.

'Of course,' replied O'Hare, and Rees started dictating the overall impressions of the body, following the usual script. *The body is that of a sixty-three-year-old female Caucasian.* O'Hare listened vaguely as the photographer bounced around the room, taking images by standard practice, and of anything the pathologist indicated might be of interest: the location of the rat bites, the moles, scars, tattoos, lacerations. O'Hare continued to listen to Rees, but followed the photographer around with a small set of plastic rules, placing them beside the cuts and bruises to give a scale as the camera focused in or panned out.

Rees seemed happy to let O'Hare get on with that as he provided the running commentary to the preliminary visual examination of the external body.

Lynda was lying on her back, her skin nacreous, her hair swept back off her face. The black dashes that crisscrossed her body showed where the rats had torn flesh from flesh. Her eyes

were red bloodied slits; the rest of her face looked like she
had been used as a punchbag. Rees was following O'Hare's
lead now. All pathologists had their own way of working, it
was bad to switch mid-exam. That's how something might slip
through the method net. O'Hare started by making the obvious
observations of the lacerations made by the rats. He started at
the top and worked down the anterior aspect of the right side
of the body, the face, the neck, the underarm. He was looking
for any disruption of the structure of the veins, the condition
of the subcutaneous lymph nodes, the condition of the structures
in the cubital fossa, the forearm, the fingers, the webs of skin
between the fingers. They were all favourite injection sites,
self-harm sites, sites with evidence of long-term trauma,
defence wounds. They all told their story.

He pointed at the suspicious hairline laceration to the head,
a typical finding when somebody bumps their head or has their
head bumped. Had she been drunk at the time? Her habitual
drinking, as reported by the neighbours, would suggest that she
had been. The empty bottle of vodka lying beside the fireplace
in the living room also told its story. But the tox screen would
tell them for definite.

Rees was still dictating in the background, flicking through
a file, talking about her nutrition, her usual medication, stating
when the body was found and that they were going to take liver
temperatures, etc. but the state of decomposition was in keeping
with the theory that she had died a day or so before the body
was found.

Rees switched off the recorder and picked up the temperature
probe, regaling them with a story of a body he had worked on
the previous summer. As Rees talked, O'Hare carried on working
his way down the right arm, noting the bruise marks on the
ventral aspect of the forearm. He looked across the torso to
the other arm. Out of the corner of his eye, O'Hare could see
Walker move up close to the screen.

'Is there a similar contusion there?'

'Less pronounced, but there is a minor abrasion here.' He held
the arm, turning it slightly and placing the scale rule beside it.

The photographer snapped a few shots and nodded that he
had caught it in large and small scale.

'It looks like she fell forwards,' said O'Hare.

'She was found face down, that with the bad blow to the head on the hairline, so she landed heavily on her front. There's the bruises on the knees as well. The left patella is dislocated; that might have contributed to her inability to get up . . .'

'Did she fall forward or was she pushed?' asked Walker from behind the screen.

'Pushed or pished?' joked Rees.

The fiscal smiled and got a warning look from O'Hare.

The examination continued, with O'Hare looking closely at the abrasions on each knee, the left more apparent than the right. As Rees kept the commentary going and the mortuary lab assistant took scrapings from under the filthy fingernails, O'Hare was examining the lower part of the rib cage, prodding the ribs, and then he asked for a brighter light.

'Do you think there is some bruising there?' asked Rees.

'If she died quickly, it would not have had time to form, so we need to look microscopically at the subcutaneous tissues. We will get to that when we take her skin off.'

'So what do you think?' asked the fiscal.

'Pretty obvious to me,' said Rees. 'She was drunk; she came down the stairs to the basement, bumped her head and fell forward. Her knee injury meant she couldn't get up. She would have bad motor skills with her drinking, made worse by her age. We will find a bleed in the brain or something in her throat that shows she choked on her own vomit.'

'Unlikely if she was prone,' muttered O'Hare.

'She was a drunk,' stated Rees, 'it's what they do.'

Archie Walker looked at O'Hare, who simply raised his eyebrows, warning him not to be so sure. The post continued, the two men talking between themselves, not always about the body in front of them, sometimes about a related matter, an interesting piece of research, but she was always the centre of their attention.

Then the body was turned over, sliding on her side, then falling on to her front with a quiet slap.

Rees took a look, skimming his eyes over the pale freckled skin of the back of the chest, 'Nothing much to see here; all the insult was to the front of the body. As we would expect.'

But O'Hare was bending down, running his eyes across the top of the skin. 'What do you think about that?' He pointed a gloved finger to the spinous process of the mid-thoracic spine.

Rees regarded his older colleague. 'Well, it's bra strap irritation. The constant movement of material on the skin at that level tends to leave a roughening that produces that slight discolouring,' he explained to Walker behind his screen.

Walker nodded at this useless information, but stopped when he saw O'Hare's face.

'There is slight swelling there in the soft tissue, a slight touch of ecchymosis. So there was a trauma here, a bruising before death – and *just* before death. We need to see how far that spread, the pressure and the scope of that injury.'

'But there is no damage to the cutaneous structure.'

'But there is to the subcutaneous structures. Deep pressure,' he explained to Walker. 'Slow, strong pressure at the back of the ribcage as she was lying on her front.'

'She could have been struck and fell forward, Jack. We have this down as an alcoholic having an accident in her basement, falling over and goodnight Vienna,' said Walker across the sound system.

There was a short silence interrupted by the hiss of the air pressurizer.

'And I might have it as a woman under the influence being held down on her front, her arms up above her head, as if she was trying to get herself up.' He put his hands up as if in surrender, to demonstrate. Then he pointed at the almost invisible patch of discolouration on the back of the chest. 'So maybe the reason she could not get herself up was that somebody had their foot or their knee firmly in her back. I think she might have been drowned.'

'Drowned?' repeated Walker, thinking he had not heard right.

'Drowned?' Rees could not keep the disbelief from his voice.

'Yes, is there an echo in here?' snapped O'Hare.

'Drowned, in a dry basement?' asked Rees.

'Well, in a basement certainly. Safe to say that it wasn't dry. Not at the time,' added O'Hare. 'Obviously. And it's always good to have wellies to walk through water. Somebody was on those stairs with patched Hunter wellies. I know what my next move would be.'

TWENTY-EIGHT

Anderson stood at the bottom of Altmore Road, watching the comings and goings, looking at the big house, knowing that Aird was probably watching him. He was hoping to see Jennifer, but all he saw was a young girl with thick black hair go for a wander up the road, and back again.

Anderson was there so long that in the end Aird came out and asked him in, Betty wagging her tail at some newfound friend that smelled of dog.

The kitchen was big, bright – much brighter than the entire rest of the street, which had suffered from eternal gloom ever since Anderson had arrived. It had nearly stopped raining. It wasn't that the sun had actually come out, but there was a brightness in the air shadowing down from the glass in the old conservatory. The back of the house was almost cut off from the road and the wood. It backed on to the hill, which rose, effectively blocking the wood and the road from the building site going on at the far side and beyond.

The dog subjected Anderson to some investigatory sniffing. Anderson found himself telling Aird about Nesbit; the old man replied that dogs were grand things and Betty was the best of the best. Betty showed what she thought of this idea by walking away and slumping down in her basket in front of the Aga.

'Have you found out who owns the foot yet?' He fingered a bad cut on his face. It looked recent, probably the whiplash of a twig while walking in the woods.

'We have some DNA that we are trying to trace,' said Anderson, taking his chance to study the old man. He himself was sitting at the fireplace on an old armchair, an armchair that felt loved and sat-upon. A pair of old wellies were drying out by the fire; much loved, much repaired. A pair of hard-core socks hung over the mantelpiece. The man with his back to him was tall; even with the slight stoop he would have been six feet tall. Casual trousers, a cashmere jumper that had been well worn but still looked expensive, the Tattersall shirt underneath. He still sported a long lock of grey hair that fell across his face; a broad, tanned hand sent it back over his forehead. He was a handsome man. The shoulders were a little hollow, the natural wasting of age, but he would have been a powerful man in every sense in his day, and in this street he still owned the wood, the street, some of the property. Anderson was sure of that and that the Dirk-Huntleys would legally pursue anybody remotely liable for the sinkhole, and pursue them through every court in the land. The new money coming in, people who thought the street was cute and wanted to re-gentrify it, ignoring the fact that at the top of the hill there lived an elderly gent who might want to live in his past.

'Have you ever married, Mr Aird?'

'Me? No.' The answer was short and simple. A pot of tea was placed on the big oak table, a cup and a plate of biscuits pushed towards the easy chair where Anderson was sitting.

'Never been tempted?' asked Anderson, trying to sound casual.

'I'm sure you didn't come all this way to check on my romantic history, Mr Anderson. What do you want to know?'

'How well do you know Jennifer Lawson?'

'Jennifer? Oh, at number eight. She gave me this.' He fingered the cut gently. 'I'll go over later and explain myself. I have no feelings for her except pity. Why, what about you? How well do you know her?'

Anderson had to check that he was not joking. 'A little, professionally.'

'But I think we are both concerned about her. That child is not well. In hospital now, I believe.'

'Yes.'

'People buy property here without thinking the matter through.' He chuckled as if the thought of causing trouble amused him.

'So to be blunt, who does it go to when you pass on? Do you have—'

'I have a son, but he will not be an heir, not by any means.

To the contrary, I have done everything in my power to make sure the wee shit gets nothing.'

'And who is his mother?'

Jock moved slightly along the counter, moving his weight a little, as if more than the thought was uncomfortable. 'There was a woman once, a beautiful woman. But God she was a handful, much younger than me.'

'How much younger?'

'She was in her early twenties, I think I was in my late thirties. But her family thought I was not good enough for her, even with all this.' He looked out of the kitchen window, a lonely man. Betty, sensing his disquiet, got up and nuzzled his hand.

'We had all this but we were cash poor. And she would end up just as skint if it went any further. She had money, her dad was some kind of stockbroker or something, in the days when that was an honourable professional, so she threw me over. I don't think she was happy about it; she was forced into it, I am sure of that, and later she came back.' He played with the dog's ears. 'Her family fortunes had taken a turn for the worse and mine had taken a huge turn for the better. I had a good job and I turned the fortune of the Altmore estate, if you want to call it that, round. She saw the writing on the wall and tried to come back to me. I wasn't having any of it, but we had a fling. I think I did it to get back at her, and our son was the result of that fling. Then she took up with a terrible man, a drunk and a wife-beater.'

'And you didn't take her back?'

'Did I take her back?' He contemplated the question. 'Did I take her back? Did I hell. But I kept an eye on her. Not close enough though. It's all very sad. It was Lynda, Lynda McMutrie.'

Aird had seen the activity outside number 10 the previous day, but talking to Anderson about Lynda's death seemed to take the wind out of him. The old man settled into a chair, Betty beside him.

'I know this is inconvenient, but I'd like to ask you about Lorna Gyle,' said Anderson, aware that time was passing.

'Wee Lorna? Not seen her since she was five or so. She ran in and out my house like it was her own in those days.'

'What kind of relationship did you have with her?'

'Relationship? We built tractors with Lego.' Aird reacted like one who didn't understand the subtext of the question.

'What about the Melrose boys, did you know them?'

'Not really, their mum was about. Andrew was struggling with May being ill, remember, so yeah, Lorna used to pop into my house, play with the Lego, sit and watch the TV.'

'Have you seen her recently?'

'Wee Lorna? No. Why should I have? Has she been to see her father?'

Anderson shook his head, 'No.'

'I know she tried to see him the Christmas before last but couldn't; he had just been stabbed, so Andy's not seen her since she was a teenager.'

'Does Lorna have any features that you might recognize her by?'

'Why? Has something happened to the lassie?'

'No, not at all, we are just checking somebody's identity and want to be sure. We don't want to upset her dad by asking him.'

That lie fell flat. The old man's eyes narrowed. 'He's serving life for a crime he didn't do. I think you'd have to go some to upset him any more than that. So you have a female in mind and you are not sure if she's Lorna or not?'

'Something like that.'

The old man clucked his teeth together, rattling them, then got up and swore at the pain on his hip. He slowly made his way over to the bookshelves. There were books everywhere; it all looked an absolute mess, but whatever he was looking for he was able to find it very quickly. A makeshift folder made from two pieces of card and a few strips of Sellotape. He squeezed it until it opened up and wiggled it slightly so that a few photographs slid out.

'I've seen some of these in the book.' Anderson shuffled them back and forth, stopping at the one of her with her parents, the one with the straw hat on. 'Did you read it?'

'No, load of piss: "*my dad the mass murderer*". She should have written, "My Dad is Innocent."' He shook his head. 'She didn't know him, though, did she? She was five when you cops started putting pictures of that murder scene in front of her

and saying, "*Look, your dad did that.*" Then her mother died.'
He tutted. 'I mean, what was the wean supposed to grow up
thinking?'

'You make a good point,' conceded Anderson.

'But Lorna did suffer a burn, hot water from a pan when
May was boiling the spuds or something. I took her in the car
to the hospital. The wee one all wrapped up in a blanket, May
holding her like she was a bunch of flowers. That's her.'

He passed the picture to Anderson, who looked at the fair-
haired girl sitting on a blanket in the grass, an upturned bucket
beside her. A black dog walking away, looking back, showing
the small kiddy's spade it had between its teeth. There was an
older boy in the background, stooped forward, hands down,
obviously calling the dog. Anderson could tell it was Aird's
back garden back in the days when he could mow the lawn.
The burn on her upper right arm was visible, from the shoulder
to the elbow, long and slim, following the track of the water.
That wouldn't be fixed by a graft without leaving a scar.

And he had seen that scar himself. 'And who is that then?'

'That, that was Penn, she was a great dog.'

'No, the boy. I mean who was the boy?'

'Oh him, that's my son Gregor.' And that subject was closed.

'Mr Aird, what would you do if you met Lorna now?'

He thought for a moment, 'I'd slap her spoiled little arse and
tell her to get campaigning for her dad's release.'

Anderson set off down Altmore Road. It was still raining but
a little more lightly now. It was too much to say that the sun
was coming out, but there was a lightness in the air; the breeze
was pleasant rather than vicious. He should go back to the office
when really he wanted to go home and take the dog out.
Everybody else would be at school or at work or somewhere.
And the meeting with Aird had just put him in mind for some
quality time with Nesbit; somebody who would not judge or
talk back, just somebody to listen.

He heard a rat-tat-tat.

He looked behind him – nothing – then saw a frantic waving
at the upstairs window of number 8. It was Jennifer, her face
pale, holding wee Robbie up at the window, and he was not a

light child. Anderson crossed the road, wondering what eyes
were watching him, past the overgrown front grass of Lynda
McMutrie's house. Its ownership would now pass back to . . .?
Who was going to inherit? Flashes of connections going past
his head about ownership and inheritance.

The connection was there and gone.

No doubt bloody Costello would have logged it on her iPad
and printed out the answer by now.

He should not be drinking with these tablets.

He walked up the cracked path of number 8, the door opened
before he got there.

'So you thumped Mr Aird?' he said in jest.

'Oh my God. Am I being arrested?' Jennifer eyes widened.

'You really have a good imagination. No, he knows he gave
you a fright, he was in your house, was he not?'

'Oh, I saw you go up there. I thought he was going to
complain and get me arrested for assault or something.' She
stood there, big T-shirt over her jeans. Robbie was now back
on the leather settee, covered in the Pooh Bear duvet.

'You can sit there, he has not peed.'

And she told him the story of going down the stairs to the
basement and seeing Jock's head behind the wall and then he
hit her on the head and knocked her out. 'But I know that is
not right. But I did see something. I know I did.' She started
to cry. 'So I went back down to look, and there is nothing there.
I thought I might have seen something – a doll, or . . . something. Am I losing my mind?' The sobbing was now that of
extreme despair, depression, blackness. 'They will take my
children off me.'

'No they won't.'

'But they said at the hospital. And Douglas thinks I can't
cope.'

'Well, he is not here to help you, is he? So let's have a look.'
Anderson got up and walked downstairs to the basement.
Jennifer followed, as he walked round the boxes, the old
computer monitor, smelling the dampness and the wet plaster.
He saw the irregular hole in the wall, plasterboard chipped off
and pulled away, earth and brick behind.

'You didn't imagine breaking the plaster, did you?'

'No, I did that with a hammer. I was looking for rats.'

She missed the quizzical look Anderson gave her but he looked through the hole, down on his knees, his trousers getting wet as he braced his arms against the damp plasterboard to lean forward and see through the gap in the basement wall.

'There's nothing there, Jennifer.'

'But there was. I did see him. Now I think I'm really bonkers.'

'Hand me that torch.'

She handed it to him. It had been lying on the floor since she'd dropped it. Anderson turned it on, and leaned back in, shining the torch right round, deep on to the cavity against the wall to his right. He could hear the gentle gurgle of running water. The beam caught a flash of light green polythene. He held the torch steady, picking out two starting eyes, teeth, a flattened nose, a swarm of hair working round the feature – they were flatten and distorted by the plastic bag over them, but they were still recognizably human. Recognizably female.

'Can you see anything in there?' Jennifer's voice was infantile in its enthusiasm.

'Yes,' he said quietly. 'I think we should both go upstairs. Now.'

TWENTY-NINE

Wyngate was typing up a report, logging it into the system because of the location. Douglas Lawson had reported an assault on his wife by Mr Jock Aird. Wyngate typed on, wondering why he was so angry when both his wife and Mr Aird had been quite happy once the situation had come clear. Jennifer Lawson had fallen and knocked herself out and when she woke up was confused and attacked the man she saw in her front room. One smart hit from a strong young woman right into the side of the head of a seventy-seven-year-old man. With a frying pan.

Wyngate was trying to explain that only one person had gone to the hospital: Jock. He had been on the premises because he had gone out with the dog and saw Robbie lying on the couch crying. He was returning over an hour later and the child was now on the floor and crying. He admitted entering the premises; the back door was unlocked. There had been no answer to his call. He had picked up the child, made sure it was OK. Then he was looking around for Jennifer. And got hit in the head.

Jennifer then ran into the street with Robbie, where Michael Broadfoot saw her in a hysterical state. The police arrived.

And Douglas Lawson wanted Jock prosecuted. But Wyngate got the feeling Lawson was subtly pushing, trying to get his wife into trouble.

Now Anderson had phoned in requesting a forensic team.

He had found a human head in Jennifer's basement. Female.

Mulholland looked over, rubbing his thumb and forefinger together, humming 'Money Money Money'. 'I bet you it's Tamara McMaster. She went missing Christmas 2013. She was a pole dancer. It will be her. You owe me fifty quid,' Mulholland gloated.

'Well, somebody's dreams of a happy ending are going to be shattered. But you might be right. I'll look out Tamara's misper file. If Douglas Lawson phones again, tell him I've left for a fortnight's holiday.'

O'Hare was off on one of his long explanations. 'You see, when a body is sealed, like this head has been sealed, the gases of decomposition cannot escape, and it becomes a bit like a floatation device. Now if it is well buried in stable ground, no matter how much gas is trapped in the bag then the head will stay put. But, if—'

'I am trying to eat some toast,' said Costello.

The pathologist carried on regardless. 'There is some movement in the land, then the head might became loose and slowly it will work its way up. By movement, I mean a lot of rain. The movement will be infinitesimal at first, but it does happen. The laws of nature state that the gas will lift the head to the surface, and of course, sooner or later, over time the head might become visible. And then it would end up where the path of least resistance takes it.'

'To Jennifer's basement?'

'Obviously.'

'Washed there by an underground river that can appear and disappear at the drop of a hat.'

'At the drop of a rain cloud might be more appropriate, but it wouldn't surprise me.'

Costello put her toast down on Wyngate's beautifully typed report. 'So when she thought she saw somebody in her basement with large staring eyes and a wide smile—'

'The soft tissue round the eyes has gone, the tightening of muscle round the mouth would cause that rictus grin. It makes sense.'

'Wyngate is looking at the path of the Dorcha burn, the old river that goes right under Castle Grayskull?'

There was a snort at the end of the line.

'I mean the big house at the top of Altmore Road. Do we know how long the head has been there, rolling around in the burn?'

'Two years, a year. The virtuous humour in the eye, easy. Much easier than trying to date the bones. All we can say about them is approximately ten years.'

'Oh, so we can get going on the identification?'

'No need, I know exactly who it is. I checked her dental records, and I even knew what dentist to go to.'

'OK, we have a bet on in here. It's Tamara McMaster, isn't it? She's the right height, age and was a pole dancer. The hard-working feet?'

He frowned, 'I really don't want to make your day any worse, but it's Lorna Gyle.'

'Kindly, don't talk to me like that.' The phone went dead.

Costello swore under her breath, seriously worried about Anderson now. OK, he had been annoyed about his car keys being at the bottom of Costello's handbag, and about Brenda not giving him a spare set – but did that not mean his own wife thought he should not be driving.

And she, his DI, had just called him an irresponsible bastard.

What she couldn't fathom was his total belief that Lorna Gyle was alive and well. He had still been in the taxi, going up to see Jock Aird when she had told him that they had identified who the foot and the head belonged to.

His answer was a bark of incredulous laughter and a raising the stakes of the fifty pounds bet that the dental records were wrong. He said it was an investment and switched his phone off.

Costello put down the phone and put her head in her hands. Then had another look at the log, amusing herself with the Aird/Jennifer story. She was a tough girl that one, deserved better. She made a cup of tea and walked, in her socked feet, over to the wall, looking at them. Lorna? Lynda? Sue? Helen McNealy? Vivienne Reid? What connected them? She made alterations to the wall, drawing things in, and was still rubbing out lines when the phone went again.

It was O'Hare. Anderson had been on the phone asking him what he was playing at. 'So we worked backwards from the head. We have the remains of the foot under a slide; the head is sitting in a box all cleaned up. The body has been cleaved with an axe.'

'Clean edges?'

'Indeed. And Matilda had checked the DNA on the Y chromosome. So both head and foot have Andrew Gyle as a father. And the same dentist. She had died as an adult and in the last couple of years. You can tell Anderson that when he calms down.'

Laura Steele opened the door, dressed as she always was in running gear. She looked as though she had just come out of the shower; she was super-clean and shiny.

Anderson felt old just listening to her. 'I've been down at Jennifer's house for the last wee while, I'm sorry to bother you.'

'In you come. I saw the police car, is she OK? The baby?'

'Fine. But God that house is damp. Laura, this might seem a bit cheeky, but they think they have identified the missing person.'

'Oh,' said Laura. 'Is it somebody I know?' She frowned. Then flashed the briefest of smiles.

'It's supposed to be you. You don't have a twin sister, do you?'

'No. It's supposed to be me? It can't be. I mean, if they have old material from 1992 kicking about that lab, then it's obvious they have got their samples mixed up. What is it you call it?'

'Cross-contamination, that'll be it. Could you give us another sample? I don't have my kit with me so you'd have to come to the station.'

Laura looked around for a minute 'I have a lot on just now. On the telly, they always ask for a hairbrush or toothbrush or something. What one do you fancy?'

'What one can you spare?'

'I'll give you my old hairbrush then. I have just treated myself to a new one, which is supposed to massage the cells of my brain as I brush my hair. I should be a genius in three weeks. Not noticed any difference yet.'

'Let me know if you do,' said Anderson, 'and I'll buy a box.'

She appeared down the stairs with a hairbrush. Anderson put it in an evidence bag with a seal on it and called the courier on his mobile phone. It would be at the lab in half an hour, and if Matilda rushed it through, the DNA would be back within two hours. He thought about calling Costello, but instead sent her a text saying that Lorna Gyle was alive and well and a sample of her DNA was on its way by courier. And he left her to make what she could of that, stroppy wee bitch. That would serve her right.

'I wanted to thank you for being so supportive through all this, I hope I didn't get you into any trouble.' She flashed him a troubled smile, 'I could do with a coffee. Shall we try my new fancy machine?'

He looked at his watch, the present from Helena. And he wanted all of this to go away. He put his mobile down on the coffee table, glass-topped on an aluminium frame. 'Yeah, why not?' If nothing else, it would help with the three-day hangover.

Anderson passed the time by pressing buttons on a futuristic espresso machine until he got the blend he wanted, while nibbling Italian biscuits. Laura was happy to chat away in the big chair, Anderson's anorak drying out on the back of the settee.

'That is all so weird. I mean, you know I am me.' She rubbed the scar subconsciously. 'There have been times during all this that the only thing that kept me focused was my scar. It's the one thing that does remind me who I am – I have changed my name three times. Do you know how difficult it was growing up like that?'

'I have a teenage daughter, she has issues.'

'So you will be familiar with it. I was striking out as a teen to find myself and I had a whole load of selves to choose from.' She stood up and went to the window as a motorbike pulled up outside. 'Courier,' she said.

When Anderson came back, her attitude had changed. The enormity of her situation had sunk in. 'Are you OK?' he asked.

'Don't know.'

And he had the second woman in tears in front of him that day. He sipped his coffee, watching her right arm come up, her loose-neck T-shirt swing round her throat, showing a long slim brown neck and the start of the ugly red scar on her upper shoulder, flat and outlined in brown. He shook his head, feeling slightly dizzy – a bit woozy after all the nights of no sleep and early starts; too many old films at three in the morning and strong black coffee to get him jump-started. Then the bucketful of drink he had had recently.

'Is Brian at work? Maybe you should call him.'

'That will lead to an argument. We argue all the time now, I think somebody is going to find me out. It makes me tetchy.' She pointed to the case at the side of the sofa.

'You going somewhere warm?'

'I wish. I'm putting stuff out for the charity shop. Or am I?' She looked round the room, rather wistful. 'How old was she, the dead girl?'

'Late teens, early twenties. She was a dancer.'

'A dancer.' A tear drifted down her cheek. 'We are leaving here. I have no choice.' Laura started to weep again as her eyes swept round the living room.

'Not necessarily.'

'Oh yes, I need to go.' She wiped the tears from her cheek with her cuff. 'They will come after me, like a pack of wolves. Dad will be granted a retrial. The whole media circus will start again.'

'But your dad—'

'It's not enough, unless you convict the man who did it. My dad will always be guilty in the eyes of the public. And you are never going to convict anybody, not now. This time last week, I had told myself he was guilty. I understood why he did it – now look? People are going to find out who I am. For Christ's sake, you have just been at HIS house. I am an innocent victim too.' She collapsed into tears.

'Nobody is disputing that, Lorna.' Anderson knew this was a damaged woman he was talking to and, at the moment, he was not the one she should be confiding in.

'Laura,' she corrected. 'So we are going to move, I need to speak to Brian. He thinks I shouldn't let Aird drive me out of my house.'

'He's right. You should get counselling, get some help.'

She stood up, the strong young woman again. 'So, do you want anything else from me?'

'No, not really. I need to be able to tell them who you are, then we can follow the correct lead. Not get bogged down in things that are not relevant. When you left your adoptive mother, you really covered your tracks well. I can't let them waste time and resources when I know where you are.'

'Of course, but you must see that means I have to move on.' She picked up Anderson's cup, the bracelet on her right hand jangling, and took it through into the kitchen. 'You are pally with the wee Lawson woman, aren't you? You were down in her basement where this river thing goes – well, you tell her this is what she needs. Those wee kids shouldn't be living like that. Come, I'll show you.' She got up and walked into the hall. 'You have heard about the dampness and the rats?'

'Yes.'

'Bloody awful, well, we got a membrane put in. You should send Jennifer up to see it.' She opened the cupboard under the stairs, switched on a light to a bright stairway. He could smell recent plaster. A gentle heat wafted up. 'Sometimes you need this to get the door open,' she picked up a hammer from a toolbox, 'but I'm getting a dab hand at it, it's more technique than brute strength. The air is drying out and so is the old wood.'

He followed her down the stairs, watching the back of the brown, lightly tanned neck and the wave and fold of the fabric as it fell. He could see the top of her scar from here; the contour lines of it looked flat, not puckered like a normal scar – more like a tattoo. He wondered if she had ever attempted to get it covered.

She was standing in front of a wooden door, half sanded, waiting for a base coat of paint. She hit the area above the handle with the hammer – a gentle tap, nothing more – then she turned the knob and the door opened. The room beyond was warm; she turned the light switch and the single low-energy bulb, swinging from a wire in the middle of the ceiling, took its time to illuminate the room.

Laura was walking around like an estate agent, 'All this is membrane sealed right up to the cornice. It makes a good finish. You can feel there is no moisture anywhere in here. Touch that, it's bone dry.' She knelt down; her tanned, slim fingers felt along the skirting board.

'It looks really good,' he said, kneeling down beside her, aware of the closeness of her, her scent, her vitality.

Then he felt the blow on his temple. He thought that it hurt and then he thought that he would bag his trousers falling down on to his knees like that. Then he was wondering why he was lying down on his front. He didn't think it was time to go to sleep. But he went to sleep anyway.

THIRTY

Friday 28 August 2015

Anderson woke. The pain in his head was unbelievable. He had Nesbit nestling in beside him, the small hairy body of the Staffie curling into the small of his back, wriggling around, snuggling up into his neck and over his hair, along the back of his hands, trying to get his wet nose up the sleeves of his shirt, up the legs of his trousers. Nesbit was everywhere. His little claws daintily jagging him as the dog ran around. So many feet for such a little dog.

Colin reasoned he must have got up and made his way to the bathroom as he washed his face – that's why he was wet, and now the water was running into his mouth and up his nose. He straightened himself up, expecting to see his own reflection.

He jolted at the high-pitched squeals that sounded off, sharp little pains in his hands as something small and pincery took nips of flesh and ran off with it. He opened his eyes to see the brackish, dirty water lapping towards him. Sleek black bodies ran away from him, over him, under him, trying to get in him. There were rats everywhere. His brain tried to recall where he was. Where had he been? He had been walking through the forest and there was the fire behind him and the smoke in front of him. The head burning at the soles of his feet and at the palms of his hands. That's why he was lying in the water; he was floating in the loch away from the horrors that were ashore: the screaming, the pain and the blood.

The blood.

All the blood.

The blood he could taste at the side of his mouth, the blood congealing into a sticky mess in the hollow of his cheek, the blood swilling in the water. He couldn't see it, but he could taste and smell it.

Somewhere in his deep subconscious he heard Claire's voice saying, *Get up Daddy, get up*, but it is difficult to get up from floating when everything around you is water, nothing to stand on.

But he thought he should give it a try for Claire.

But then what had Claire done for him recently? Not once had she said, *Are you OK, Dad?* Not once.

The fabric of his shirt clamped down on to the skin of his back as he tried to raise his head. Blood poured down his face. Horrible, dark, stinking water. His vision cleared like a curtain, lifting on his own stage of horror. He saw the rats. Everywhere. They were surfing on the wave of water that was pouring in through the wall, jagged splinters of wood being flattened smooth and washed away by the torrent. Sharp edges of bright blue fabric flapping at him like flags waving goodbye. The carpet was awash with water one, two, three inches deep, four and five. More and more water gushed into the hole, tearing it wider.

He was in the basement with Laura. He turned round to make sure she was OK, but she was gone. The door was closed. The water was building up against it. There was something in a bag floating, the water lifting it, nudging it slightly. Something about the way it moved disturbed him. The ties on the plastic bag were not secured. He watched, transfixed, as the mouth of the bag floated open, the handles unwound from each other and a small nose was unveiled, sodden white wool, closed eyes. A small blue-pink tongue trapped between the teeth.

The dead dog.

Dead dog.

He tried to think past his confusion and the pain in his head. So somebody had attacked him and taken Lorna. That same person who had killed Sue all those years ago?

Right now, he needed to get out. The membrane's filaments of fabric were splitting with the water pressure. He was in a sealed box with a tsunami coming in. It didn't look like slowing down.

Something Wyngate had said, about the rain and the underground river . . .

He needed help. He searched his pockets for his phone. It might be wet; there might be no signal. Then he realized his phone was perfectly dry . . .

. . . upstairs on the table.

He had to get out and tell the team to get after Laura. It had all been about Laura. Lorna? Laura? He had to find a way out.

He crawled to the door, on his hands and knees, blinded by the blood. The dead dog floated past in its makeshift plastic coffin. Lorna's dog.

His forearms were invisible in the muddy water, now six or seven inches deep. Every inch forward was a huge effort as the volume of water moved and sucked and pulled at him, like an animal drawing him deeper into its jaws. The rats swam around him, under him, over him, perfectly at home in their subterranean submarine world.

At the door, Anderson held on to the handle and tried to pull himself up. He collapsed and fell back under the water, his forehead jammed against the wood of the door. As he pulled his hand away, he instinctively raised it to protect his face. The palm came away covered in red jelly sauce. He was losing a lot of blood. He sat upright in the water, angling his back against the door. He was facing the gap in the membrane, bigger now the water was coming in by a column of rapids, tumbling over each other to get at him, tearing the wood as it went torrent upon torrent, gallon upon gallon. Bringing more rats.

If he didn't get out of here he was going to die with the rats, drowned. Some people's idea of hell. All this water would put out the fire in his soul. The rats might be on the side of the Gods. *Come on Daddy.* It was Claire who had dragged him away. C*ome on Daddy.* The voice was becoming more insistent. He started crawling towards the hole in the foundation wall, his elbows collapsing, the water relentlessly punching him in the face. He fell on to his side and the rats jumped at his face in their persistent attack.

But he kept on going.

Jennifer was lying on the settee, Robbie in her arms, half asleep half awake. There was a knock at the door. She thought about not answering it. If it was Douglas, he'd use his key. If it was that bloody social worker she might swing for her, swing for her big time. All the forensic people had gone; they had been nice and polite but she was exhausted now. She thought it might be Colin coming back. She slid off the settee and crawled over the floor, aware of the dampness and the stickiness of the carpet that had lain there for God knows how many years, and how many occupants of the house before them. Before her. It stunk like a three-week-old nappy.

Hiding underneath the window, she put her fingertips on the sill and pulled herself up, hoping that whoever was at the front door would not see the top of her head and the unruly mop of dark hair. There was nobody there. The driveway was empty, the street was empty. The knocking was coming from the back door.

She got up and pulled her dressing gown around her again,

annoyed now. Coming to the front door was something, but coming round the back door meant they were hiding something. It wasn't easy to get to the back door of these houses. And she had a headache. She had painkillers but needed food to take them. So she was furious by the time she reached the door, yanking it open. It jammed. The rain made it swell. Most of the time nowadays, she left it unlocked. She pulled again and felt the door buckle around the handle – that was all she needed now, for the bloody door handle to come off in her hands.

'Who is it?' she shouted.

'Jock.'

She turned on her phone. She wanted Douglas to deal with him, to hear the story. She pressed Douglas's mobile number; she only had a tiny bit of charge left. It went to voicemail. She quickly scrolled down and pressed the flat number. A male voice answered, tired, woozy, sleepy. Jennifer held the phone out, saying nothing. Feeling like her guts were being strangled as she heard a voice, Douglas, sounding as though he was inches away from the phone. And horizontal. There was a phone beside the bed in that flat.

'There's nobody there,' said the husky voice.

I am a nobody. Jennifer cut the call and sank to her knees behind the door.

'Are you OK, hen?'

She was trying not to cry.

'OK, I'll leave you alone. I've brought you some doughnuts, to say sorry for giving you a fright yesterday.' He sounded genuinely sorry and the shadow moved away.

As if sensing her pain, Robbie woke up and started shouting, screaming at the top of his voice, one long vowel that reached into the middle of her ears and scratched at the nerves. *Maaaaaaaaaa . . .*

'Oh God,' she said, trying to stand up, climbing up the door.

'Is that wee one OK, the other wee laddie is still in the hospital?'

She looked at the back of the door, too tired. So what if he was a serial killer; he had doughnuts. It would be somebody to talk to, somebody to stop that bloody wean greeting all the time. She pulled the handle. 'I'm sorry, I can't get the door open.'

It bumped slightly from the outside; he had put his shoulder against it. So she would be found murdered on her dirty kitchen floor, lying on a pile of dirty nappies. Douglas wouldn't come home for weeks and nobody would find her body. Robbie would be sold to a paedophile ring. The door opened and she was still on her knees, looking at a pair of baggy brown cords, old man's thick cords.

'The door got stuck,' was all she said.

'It's swollen with the rain – has your man got a plane? I'll take a bit off it for you.' He was waggling the door back and forth, looking at the hinges and the frame, making tut-tutting noises. 'Just a wee bit taken off the side of it, that's all.'

The kitchen door was open. There was a rectangle of sunlight on the old lino, showing up the scuff marks and the dust balls rolling around in the draught.

'The sun is shining,' she said.

'Aye, it's still pissing down though.'

Anderson slowly made his way across the floor, his knee squelching in the sodden carpet, the water clutching and grabbing at his wrists and in between his fingers. He had lost a shoe somewhere. He seemed to be moving forwards for a long time, but was getting nowhere nearer the hole in the wall. Twice he fell over, crashing into the water, the freezing cold sucking, engulfing water. He couldn't feel his hands or his feet, or his kneecaps, but he knew they were sore. The throbbing in the side of his head robbed him of his vision and his balance. He only had to go about ten, twelve, fifteen, twenty feet. The more he tried, the further away the gap in the wall seemed to get.

But, surely, he was crawling through the water, up to the plasterboard that was now gaping open. The water was still flowing through steadily, bringing rats.

And bones.

And the bones.

There was something there, deep in his mind. Leave that for later; he had to get out of here.

He crawled right up to the panel and put his hand through

it, pulling away a few more bits of plaster and wall and loose bricks. This time the force of the flowing water was with him; he didn't even care about the rats that swarmed over his hands and got caught in his shirtsleeves, struggling to get free. Their warm wet fur was smooth against his skin; slippery, strong bodies struggling to get free from him.

The light went out.

The water was getting into the wires. He grasped either side of the panelling and slid through the hole, twisting slightly. The ground on the far side was much lower; he tumbled into it, submerged. His mouth open to gallons of the scummy water as the rats ran round the walls, like bats, moving at lightning speed, squeaking and squawking at their newfound freedom from the underground dam. Anderson found his feet on the rocky muddy bottom of a drain, and managed to get himself upright. The roof was low, so it was easier to stay crouched down in the water as it swirled around his neck. The blood was still pouring down the side of his face; he dreaded to think how infected that injury was going to be.

Then he noticed the noise. The rushing water had gone, to be replaced by sound more familiar – quiet but more constant rainwater, more precise raindrops hitting something hard. Everything had calmed down.

He needed to do this. He needed to get out. He took a deep breath and a moment to think. He was in some kind of culvert somewhere underneath Altmore Road. A big brick tunnel. Old Victorian; his knees were wading through a sludge of God knows what. The tunnel narrowed and widened as the bricks became stones then earth that crumpled under his fingers into sodden lumps that splashed on the way down, hitting his head, slamming into the back of his neck. So he looked up. It was dark here. His eyes adjusted to the lack of light, but he could see something, a few rays of daylight coming from somewhere ahead. There was a sense of fresh air. So he went on another few feet, standing now in a depth that seemed to go on and on. He stepped forward, waist-deep in water, then he plummeted. Nothing underfoot. He was under his full length so he was six feet down. Still dropping. His arms and legs flailing to get hold of something solid. He touched something slimy and soft yet solid. Instinctively he pulled his hand away, bumping his elbow on a solid wall at the back of him in the recoil. He turned, finding the wall, and feeling around for outcrops of the old stones he could use to pull himself up. The surface of the water had only been a few inches above his head. He took a few deep breaths and tried to calm his heart.

He knew what he had felt, the thing that brushed against his hand. Body parts. Turning to look, he saw a white torso, wrapped in clear plastic. Tape wound round the body, too white to look human. But he knew it was.

He didn't know who it was.

He had to get out.

It was logical that he was now walking along the bed of an old underground river, walking upstream. This was the old river fighting to regain its ancient course. He leaned back; his heel caught on a jutting ridge and he rested himself on it, ignoring the stones grinding into his shoulder blades, the rats running along the bricks on the opposite bank, darting dashes of silkiness in his vision, there and not there. Rats, cats, or visions created by his imagination, he didn't care. They were there and he was glad.

One foot had no shoe.

So what? He had a gap to get across. He could tell by the stillness of the water. Here it was three feet deep, between him and the daylight was a dark pool. A drain?

He had no choice. He should be able to feel around with his free leg reaching for the other side. If he could just keep his balance. He reached out, his other heel slipping off the stone, and down he went, water flooding into his ears and the roaring and the screaming of his eardrums. A rat swam past, his body silvered with air bubbles, perfect little feet spread to propel him through the water. His cheeks chubby with air, giving him a grin. Little beady eyes, keen and intelligent, wondering what he was doing down here in this dark place.

Anderson stuck his hand down, fingers feeling around, down and down until his fingertips touched plastic. He grabbed. A crisp packet, salt and vinegar.

THIRTY-ONE

'W here has bloody Anderson gone?'
'On another jolly with Griffin? Who knows? He tells us nothing these days.'

The phone went; they all looked at each other. It was Wyngate who picked it up. He was nearest. His face was devoid of expression. 'It matches. The DNA matches.'

'So the woman living at number twelve is indeed Lorna Gyle, as she said she was,' pondered Costello, confused. 'And the foot and the head also belong to Lorna Gyle.'

'Yes, so she is alive and dead. She's identical twins.'

'Or, or,' said Mulholland, proving that he was paying attention, 'two options. One: Lorna Gyle has had a foot transplant, which we presume the woman living at number twelve has not as she is a gym bunny, goes running, does all kinds of healthy shit.'

'Option two?'

'The Sherlock Holmes option. If that foot belongs to Lorna Gyle, then Lorna Gyle is dead. That must be true. We don't actually know whose hair sample that is; we don't know whose hairbrush that was.'

'OK,' said Costello. 'Say I wanted to be Lorna Gyle. What would I do? Get to know her, study her, read her book. We are similar build, similar age . . .'

'She has the advantage of already having an assumed identity.'

'Yes, good point, so I would tattoo myself with birthmarks or scars, then change my hair, my face, my weight. I am unrecognizable from who I was and would be accepted as a Lorna Gyle who needed to change.'

'And Anderson fell for it. He was played.'

'He was vulnerable.'

'And why do all that to *not be* "Lorna Gyle"? The woman at number twelve is not putting herself out there.'

'The money,' suggested Costello. 'She got paid a huge sum for that book, she got the house and . . . oh hell. A nice identity for somebody who wanted to shed their own.' She looked round the room, pointed at the wall. 'Lorna's adoptive mother died in a hit-and-run. Car never traced, weird marks on her leg that they couldn't ID.'

'Is there anybody around who can identify her? Lorna, I mean. As an adult?'

They thought.

'Her dad? Aird?'

Costello phoned Anderson again. His phone was switched off.

An hour later, Jennifer felt much better; the sun on her back, a cup of warm coffee in her hand, put there by a man who had cleaned a dirty cup without comment. The coffee was strong, and milky. He had gone away and brought back some milk from his own fridge, and a wee bit of whisky for the bairn, as he called Robbie. The fractious two-year-old was now in his car seat in the middle of the floor, having had some milk with a few drops of whisky in it. He had sucked at it hungrily, and had promptly gone off to sleep. The old man had swung him around a few times, wrapping him up tight in his blanket, binding him round his arms and legs.

'You are not supposed to do that nowadays,' said Jennifer from her seat on the step, getting some sun but staying in from the rain, looking at the dark clouds coming over.

'It works with lambs, it'll work with this wee beastie.'

Jennifer called Robbie a traitor under her breath and took another nibble out of her doughnut. It was a good one with a really tarty jammy centre. 'Where did you get these?' she asked.

'That new place on the parade. Coffee tastes like goats' piss, but the cakes are good.'

Bloody hell, he meant the patisserie; it was a bloody fortune in there. 'Thanks,' she mumbled. 'I haven't eaten today, I need to take a painkiller.' She tried to get up to the box on the worktop but he got to his feet before her. It was an easy reach for him to pass them over. He went to get them. She stayed on the step. The old collie wandered into the kitchen and looked at her with one blue eye, one brown eye. It sniffed at her, circled round and lay down behind her. Her warm body at the small of Jennifer's back. Quiet dog, quiet baby, a little sunshine, having a coffee and a doughnut with a paedophile serial killer old geezer.

There were worse ways to die.

Jock was back with her handbag which contained the pain-killers. He handed it to her.

'So what happened last night, when you went downstairs into the basement? I saw the police earlier, quite a commotion going on.'

'I got a fright when the wall came away, and there was this head. It had big eyes and a big grin, like it was wearing false teeth. It was awful. I thought it was you.' She sipped her coffee, the dihydrocodeine was kicking in. She was feeling a bit more human. 'Sorry if that sounded rude.'

But he laughed, folding his arms, making himself comfy on the wall of the back step. Not too close to her, not too far away.

'Do you ever see anybody at the end of your garden?'

'Like what? Fairies?'

'Oh, dinnae mock it. You've no idea what I've seen in the woods after I've had a wee dram or two. No, I mean, there is a path at the bottom of your garden, so somebody must use it.'

'I've never been down to the bottom of the garden,' she confessed, letting the sun relax her and warm her bones. If the rain stopped, she could put a wash on and get it out to dry. She needed to go and see Gordy in the hospital. There were a hundred and one things she needed to do.

'Never see any men creeping about?'

She opened her eyes at that. She had. She had told Colin Anderson. In fact, she had thought it was Jock, but she couldn't say that now, not now he was here making her coffee and giving her doughnuts. 'No.'

'Is your man coming home to take you to the hospital?'

'No, I'll get the bus.' She answered quickly; it was too painful to think about Douglas and her being a nobody. 'I should really get going.' She realized how long they had been sitting there – too long. It would be dark soon.

'Well, I'll let you get ready. You smell like a pigsty, hen, but I'll come back and get you, run you down to the hospital, I'll just take the dog out.'

There was a ping.

'Oh, that's my phone, it's been out of charge.' There was a text. That might be Douglas. Jock reached over the worktop and unplugged her phone, handing it to her.

It was from Colin Anderson, sent on the Wednesday night. A polite request to help in a police reconstruction – just to walk through the woods with the boy and sit at the Doon. He would meet her there. There would be police around; she was to ignore them.

She phoned him back but got his voicemail. Then she phoned the station and spoke to somebody, saying that would be fine and sorry for not getting back to him earlier, but she had only just got the message.

'He's so nice,' she said to Aird. 'I'll see Gordy later, Colin will run me over there after we've done this.'

Jock stayed at his counter in the kitchen, listening. 'Did he mention it when he was in earlier?'

'No, he got a bit of a shock. But he did come in to tell me something. He must have forgotten.'

Aird looked at his watch. No time to walk the dog; he was going back to his house to get his gun out the cabinet.

Anderson was neck-deep in water that swirled around him, angry at him. The flow of water coming from somewhere, along a culvert of some deep waterway that had jagged walls and a rough floor. He stumbled through the water, often going under. He tried to climb over rocks on the bed of the ancient river, piles of stones where the roof had collapsed. He often had to crouch under the rocks that made up the roof, where bits of concrete jutted out.

He was moving along like a monkey in a tunnel of water. The bloody rats were with him every step. The force of the water washed them towards him and he struggled on all fours against the force of the flow. One thing in his mind was that the crisp packet was recent. And he could see daylight from somewhere, playing on the black, seething water ahead. The crisp packet had washed down here from a drain or a culvert, and from there he might be able to attract attention. He was trying to ignore the thumping in his head, and the pain that was growing in his head. Something kept blinding him, pouring into his right eye so he couldn't see. He couldn't afford to panic.

He couldn't afford not to panic.

This was water – cold, freezing, dirty water with rats.

But there was no fire.

So on he went.

Stumbling in the darkness, the rocks cutting his feet, thinking about Lorna and what had brought her to this, how scared she had been. He felt himself going under for a third time.

Now he found it difficult to get up; tired, tiring, too tired . . . He swirled around underneath, clambering to get back to the surface; it was very turbulent here, and he saw why. The joining of two waterways: one looked manmade; the other natural, old. He tried to see along it.

The little ray of daylight was getting closer.

A little ray of hope.

And there was a waterfall, like a curtain of burnt umber. A grated drain cover above. High above him. He needed to climb, if he could reach it. He could call for help, shout. Anything. So he started to clamber, his bleeding, broken hands trying to grip the brick wall of the drain. His back hit something hard, narrow. An iron handle. Something to climb up. He took a deep breath and started.

'Costello, why are we here? The last time we did this I nearly ended up getting burned alive.'

'No, you didn't, you nearly ended up getting an arrow through your vital organs. If you are going to be melodramatic, at least be accurate.' She mimicked Mulholland's lazy, superior voice. '"Have you seen the phone log? Jennifer called in to confirm something, something tonight." What a tosser! And Anderson has his phone switched off . . . He is not where he should be; Lorna is not where she should be. Neither is Brian, or Steven Melrose. Thank Christ for Aird and Jennifer, otherwise I'd start to think they were all bloody in it.'

'Steven?'

'He left the Carron Bridge Community early this afternoon. I phoned him.'

'Why?'

'Just wanted to noise him up a bit. I wanted to see if he would move, who he would contact. He's in this up to his greasy little armpits. It would take him less than an hour to get here, if that is what all this is about. We have the bruising on the front of Vivienne Reid's body and the fact that Helen McNealy was a member of the Braveheart Bangers classic car club. It's a small link to make, but something is connecting all these crimes and we are not seeing it. Maybe Steven Melrose wanted his marriage to be over and she wouldn't go. Who knows what happened between him and the boys? Hard though it is to accept, he wouldn't be the first father to kill his children in anger. And somebody phoned Jennifer Lawson pretending to be Colin Anderson. And although there is no connection we can see between Jennifer and Sue, Batten thinks there may well be one in the eyes of the killer.' Wyngate and Costello sat in her Fiat, watching the night fall and the wind rise.

'So what do we do now?' asked Wyngate.

'Whatever we do, it had better be off the record, Wyngate. Colin, our DCI, was last seen with Jennifer, for God's sake! He is messing around with a witness, and by messing around, I don't mean in the sexual sense. I mean in the emotional sense, and if that gets out he, us, the whole shebang, could be jeopardized. By jeopardized, I mean totally fucked.'

'So what do we do now?' repeated Wyngate.

'Find him and belt seven barrels of sense into him.'

'Where do you think he will be?'

'What's with the questions? He was seen here, in this street. You go up to the Steeles' place. I'll go down to the Lawsons'.'

'It was a nice evening earlier.'

'Yeah, with clouds of midges hanging round street corners, waiting for us to step out so they could feast. So well done, rain. Now you won't be itching in your bed tonight and be scratching like a scratching thing with an extra reason to be itchy.'

'Thank you, Baldrick.'

'You go up and chap the door, see if you can find Anderson anywhere else. I'll go in and see if I can find Jennifer. Keep your radio with you. And hope that we don't need them.'

*   *   *

Wyngate pulled up the collar of his anorak and tried to stride against the wind. The hesitant sunshine of the late afternoon had gone, leaving the sky to darken. The power of the rain increased, stinging his face as he walked into the oncoming deluge. He had no idea what he was supposed to be looking for, and even less idea of how he was supposed to see it when he couldn't open his eyes without the rain stinging. He walked up the path of number 12 with its neat little garden and knocked on the front door. There was no response. The Chrysler was parked out on the street heading down towards the parade, and the pink Fiat was parked rather badly askew on the new slabs of the drive. There was no response at the front door, so he walked round the back, listening for any sign of life – the bump-bump of a young gym bunny listening to music, or the animated conversation of a Friday-night drama.

He could hear nothing.

Standing in the shelter of the garage, he phoned both the house number and the mobile numbers of Brian and Laura Steele. There was no answering ring from inside the house. Round the back there was no answer at the back door. He balanced himself on the planter and looked in through the kitchen window; he could see right through to the front door. The house didn't look right. Drawers slightly open, things discarded on the floor, on the worktops. Somebody had left here in a hurry. This was his chance. He had always been the geeky backroom boy, the one who stayed in the office with his searches and his databases. Now he could prove that he could be as effective as the rest of them and as unconventional. The back door was closed, but he saw through the pane of glass that the key was in the inside lock. He picked up a small plant pot and tapped the glass sufficiently until it broke and all the glass was removed out of the small frame – enough to get his hand through without cutting himself. Within a minute he was inside the house. Once his eyes had adapted to the lack of light, he looked round the kitchen. The sink had a few dirty dishes in it, the fridge was humming away. He walked over to the state-of-the-art coffee machine, he could smell fresh coffee grounds and the steamer was still warm to his touch. So somebody had been here recently.

He ignored the quickening of his heart, the nausea that squeezed deep in his stomach. There was a noise upstairs, a shuffling sound. Then it stopped. Wyngate stayed perfectly still, then crept forward as quietly as he could, closing the door to the downstairs cupboard as he passed.

He called 'Hello.'

No answer.

The noise happened again, closer. It was the weather; it was turning out to be a wet and stormy night. He looked into the living room – was somebody packing? A small suitcase sat on the carpet beside a pile of neatly folded clothes. Glasses, medication, keys gathered on the coffee table. Then he saw Colin Anderson's anorak lying on the back of the settee.

OK, so he was here somewhere. Doing what, he didn't like to think, but Costello was right. Better they found out before it became public or official.

He didn't want to put the light on, so he went upstairs, bedroom to the front, bedroom to the back, bathroom at the top of the stairs. On the top landing he paused, no noise. Nothing at all. He called out, just to make sure. Again, no answer.

He turned into the main bedroom, black wall, red bed. Lying on the bed was Brian Steele, dressed in a dark blue suit. He could have been asleep, except people don't sleep in their shoes. And the gash of dark red across his throat, another huge patch of blood at the bottom of his stomach. Wyngate turned round to get out as fast as he could, pulling his radio from his pocket, but he didn't get past the bathroom door before the spray hit him in the face.

THIRTY-TWO

Costello had walked up the overgrown path of number 8. Jennifer Lawson's house looked in the same depressed state as its owner. The rain abated a little as Costello opened the wooden door in the high wooden fence that ran the length of all the cottages, effectively making them a row of terraces. She went round into the back garden. There was no sign of any life in the front room, so she pulled herself up on the windowsill to check in the kitchen. The adjoining door was open, and from the kitchen window she could see right through to the back of the front door. It looked like one of the baby harnesses was missing. Maybe Jennifer had left it at the hospital or, more likely, she was out doing something that she'd agreed with Anderson and taken the baby with her. The most obvious thing was that Anderson had agreed to run her to the hospital.

Except he had no car keys. Surely he wasn't meeting a woman half his age for some kind of romantic tryst? Costello knew Anderson was struggling with some aspects of his mental health but, as far as she knew, he hadn't lost the plot altogether. There was the sneaking feeling that he was trying to solve this case on his own. It was Friday evening, August, darkness was dropping, and somehow she thought those facts were not insignificant. She walked quickly back round to the front of the house to see Michael Broadfoot getting into his car. He waved at her, she waved back. He called out through the open car door that he was nipping down the chippie, and wasn't this weather bloody awful?

She walked up to him. 'You've not seen anyone hanging about, have you? Anyone that shouldn't be here?'

Broadfoot narrowed his eyes. 'We've always had a Peeping Tom round here, and if Ah ever catch the wee shit, Ah'm going to batter him from here to next Tuesday.'

'Where do you see him?' asked Costello.

'Ah think he uses the path at the back and Ah'm sure he is trying to catch my Rachel in the scuddie, but don't you worry, Ah'll keep an eye out and Ah'll get him.'

'Have you ever come close to catching him?'

'No, he is too quick for me.' Costello looked at Broadfoot's eighteen-stone bulk and thought that a Galapagos tortoise was probably too quick for him.

'He's a fit guy, though,' said Broadfoot. 'Ah've seen him get over that fence, no bother.' Broadfoot pointed at the seven-foot wooden lattice and Costello felt her heart sink. It wasn't Jock Aird then. She turned back round, seeing an old Hillman Imp do a U-turn at the end of the parade, the rattle of its engine drawing her attention. She waited until she was sure it had gone away, not coming up the road, not going up to the wood.

Jennifer sat on the cold stone of the Doon. The sun had been chased away by dark, ominous clouds. The wind had got up, the trees were starting to sway and whispered in the breeze. It was all a wee bit creepy. She knew she was alone, but she couldn't shake off the feeling that somebody was watching her, unseen eyes observing her.

But she always thought that when she was in woods. She had grown up on the island, with a lack of trees. She had thought it would be good coming to study in Glasgow, the friendliest city in the world, and it had been like that at the start; as a student, the fellow nurses had made her feel welcome. The first year of her course had been a riot, then she had met Douglas and it had all seemed so wonderful. Then it had all gone wrong. Now she was trapped more than ever. She was even afraid to walk across the street and sit amongst the trees. She checked her watch; she had only been there five minutes.

Jennifer heard a noise behind her. Somebody was coming through the woods rather than up the path. She dropped Robbie's straps and held him closer, readjusting her grip. She thought about calling out, but Colin's text had said there would be police about. She had not been so excited to see anybody for a long, long time. She couldn't really recall being that excited ever to see Douglas – well, maybe a few times in the early days.

The police would be testing how and when they could see her. She was being Sue in a re-enactment. It should be very exciting. So why was she so scared?

Since the murders, a fence had gone up along the parade, so anybody coming up here now would have to come up Altmore Road, or come in from the opposite side of the wood, which was miles away – surely the police would not do that. They would be trying to trace the way the killer went.

Twenty-three years ago.

It struck her that she was the same age as the baby who had died would have been now.

She turned at the noise, closer now. Somebody *was* coming through the trees, hiding behind the trunks; now you see him, now you don't. She thought it was Anderson; it was a tall man, walking slowly with his arm out, caressing the bark as he passed each tree.

Robbie gurgled a little, she held him safe. Anderson liked wee Robbie – almost every time they had met, the detective had picked the boy up. He was a good father, much better than Douglas and his whoever girlfriend with the deep voice. Jennifer bet she had a flat stomach.

'Hello,' she called.

But he had disappeared in through the trees somewhere.

'Hello,' she tried again. The wind breathed hard on her; the leaves in the Doon raced and twirled. It was getting dark and chilly.

Instinctively, she shivered. She heard a brush in the undergrowth, she turned around. Nobody there. Just fresh air.

Or did she see something, lower down, white and moving away at speed. A deer? A rabbit?

She tightened her grip on the harness, ready to stand up, desperate to get out. Lamb to the slaughter, used as bait. The picture was clear when she had closed her eyes. The feather-white tail wagging, the waggling walk of an old collie.

Wyngate had never felt pain like it. He had once stuck his finger in his eye after chopping chillies, and this was a thousand times worse. And all over his face. It burned at his eyes, his nostrils, his mouth, and ate at his lips. He felt his tongue swell and thought he was going to choke to death.

Think. Think.

This was the kind of excitement he had craved. He needed to think his way out of this and control the panic. She had come out of the bathroom; she had been waiting in there with the pepper spray or whatever it was. And the bathroom meant water. He blindly fumbled in that direction, feeling with his hands until he got to the side of the bath. He scrabbled around for the tap and turned it on.

Nothing came out but he could hear the spray of the shower. In the end, he climbed in.

He felt along the metal scales of the shower connection hose, all the way to the spray head, and washed his face with as much cold water as he could get out the nozzle. He had no idea how long he spent, splashing water everywhere. The pain changed from burning hot to the bite of ice cold; his skin was scorched. It felt as though it had been burned off. Lorna had been in the house and he had let her get away. He searched his pockets, feeling for the radio, the phone, his wallet. All gone. He wrapped a towel that smelled of rose round his neck, protecting his nostrils and his mouth, and set off down the stairs. The towel stained with rosettes of blood, oozing from every pore. Outside, in the fresh air, the pain of raindrops on the exposed, burning skin of his forehead felt like a hundred thousand pinpricks, stabbing him harder and harder as he turned round the side of the house, through the door in the fence and then on to the main road. He was aiming, blindly, for number 8, where Costello was. His sight was failing him. He was hurrying along the pavement, glad that his back was to the driving rain, when he heard a cry. A human cry, like somebody was calling for help.

Or an animal yelping.

He turned round, the rain belting him in the face, the death of a thousand cuts.

A noise. Like a pantomime villain, he pulled his hood down, eyes smarting, his tears joining the rain that splashed on his face. He turned his back to the hedge as he looked up and down the street. He stopped, holding his hand up to protect his eyes, and focused on the two parked cars. He turned further round to face the wood, his back to the big house.

'I'm here.'

'Where? Where?' he asked; it had sounded very like Costello.

Then a hand came out from behind the hedge and grabbed him round the neck. He pulled away violently; the owner of the hand screamed, sharp nails drew across his neck.

'Oh my God, oh my God.' The screaming went on and on. 'Who the hell are you?'

'Who the hell are you? Calm down, I'm a police officer,' Wyngate muttered, voice muffled by the bloodstained towel.

The girl put her hand to her mouth in shock. 'Fuck, don't tell ma dad. Where's Brian? I thought you were Brian! Oh my God, what's up with your face?' And she screamed again.

'Who are you?' he asked, the pain eating at his lips now. He pulled the towel away.

'Cadena Broadfoot. I'm supposed to be seeing Brian. Where is he?'

'Cadena?' He had no idea what to say. 'You need to walk me back to your house. You live down here, don't you? Please, I can't see too well. You need to get me an ambulance.'

'I can hear somebody shouting,' said the teenager.

So could Wyngate, but he couldn't care. He was going blind. He pulled his jacket closed, thinking how quickly Cadena had gone from vamp to teenager, thinking that he had all that ahead of him. His two wee boys, like Sue, like Jennifer. People he might never see if his sight was gone. He held on to Cadena, stumbling with her as she stepped off the pavement into the gutter to guide him round the overgrown hedge of number 10. He withdrew his hand from his jacket; it was covered in dark, sticky blood. He had been stabbed. He heard Cadena swear. And something else – somebody calling his name. He looked down into the gutter, saw a flash of something his damaged eyes couldn't recognize. The water gurgling through the bars was calling his name; something was waving at him. A crisp packet? His eyes were deceiving him. They didn't hear the big Chrysler pull away, running on silent, lights out, but steadily gaining speed with the slope of the road. They didn't hear it at all until it hit.

THIRTY-THREE

In the dark, all Costello saw was the shadow of a car taking the turn on to the parade way too fast for a corner that tight. She looked up the street. Dark. No streetlights, just the rain glistening off the tarmac, the small river gurgling in the gutter, and something that looked like two bin bags having rolled away from the hedge at number 10. Except nothing would have been thrown out. Not from number 10. She started to jog, one hand holding her hood up. One bin bag was rolling back and forth, growing arms and legs.

There on the ground was Wyngate, conscious, eyes closed, moaning slightly. Across the pavement, face down, was another figure. A female, short skirt.

She pulled out her phone: ambulance, two please, quickly.

'Gordon, what has happened, what is wrong with your face?'

He was in the gutter, slipping from consciousness. He was suffering. His hands up over his face, groaning; the skin on his face was red, pitted with blood. There was something very wrong. He was trying to say something. *Laura, Laura?*

'Ambulance is on its way, Gordon. You will be fine.'

'Amberson?'

'Ambulance,' she corrected, reaching over, trying find a pulse on Cadena's neck. Something weak, but it was there. She was unconscious, staring at the dark sky. God. Costello loosened the jacket round her neck, trying to make her comfortable.

She could make out Wyngate saying: *Anderson . . .*

'Yes. He's an idiot.'

Then she saw Michael Broadfoot's Mazda reversing back up the street. She waved at him frantically, as if flagging down a low-flying aircraft. Broadfoot got out, abandoning the car. He started to walk, then jog. By the time he got to his daughter he was running.

'I've called the ambulance, you stay with her. She needs to know you are here.'

The big man was on his knees, incoherent, sobbing, holding on to his daughter's head. She backed off to give him some privacy. Wyngate grabbed her arm, the blood was everywhere.

'Anderson,' he said, pointing to the gutter, and Costello looked at the blood pooling from his side.

He was concussed.

'You just rest, the ambulance is on its way. You have lost a lot of blood. Tell them you've been stabbed.'

She still hadn't found Jennifer. That worried her. Call it intuition, but something was going on with that girl. Something not right. Broadfoot was phoning his wife, more help was coming. There was only one place she thought Anderson and Jennifer could be, so Costello slipped into the woods.

*   *   *

Costello pushed forward into the forest. It was wet underfoot now and she found herself recalling the case at Inchgarten which had led them all to this point, when her colleagues Samantha and Elvie had made their way round the island, in conditions as inhospitable as these. Except it had been warmer.

She thought of Elvie, slipping and sliding through the mud, and what that must have taken out of her, and still she had kept on going. What a load of crap that was. Elvie was fifteen years younger and super-fit. Costello had been dashing about all day with an infected blister. Twenty, twenty-five minutes. She kept checking her watch. The path was unfamiliar to her in the dark, and in the rain it had taken on a personality all of its own. She knew damn well that the branches had not grown since she was last here, but it seemed that way. They were reaching out and grabbing her. Whatever was going on in the Doon that night in the woods, the trees did not want her to witness it.

She had nearly stumbled right into them, just like Griffin had done all those years before.

Costello stopped just in time, and crouched down behind the old wall, so far that her face was on the grass. But with her hood up, covering her blonde hair, and her head turned sideways, she had a good view of what was going on. And the most worrying thing she could see was Jock Aird behind a tree with a shotgun and Jennifer sitting in the middle like bait. She needed her arse slapped, that girl. She stepped forward to talk to Jennifer, then heard a rustle of undergrowth from the opposite side of the Doon and she withdrew back in the shadows.

A policeman emerged from the trees.

Costello immediately straightened up, thinking this was going to be okay. It was indeed a kind of reconstruction that Anderson had planned, without telling any of them. She was already on her feet when she realized that something was terribly wrong; the uniform was wrong. It was too old. It didn't fit. It was too tight. There was no utility belt, but the thing that was wrong most of all was the last thing she saw.

The huge knife in his hand.

And he saw her, but directed his words at Jennifer.

'So, Jennifer, do you get it now?'

Jennifer said, 'Get what? Who are you?' But the sight of the blade had made her pull Robbie a bit closer to her chest.

Costello tried to take a step backwards, but David Griffin lifted the knife to arm's length and pointed it at Costello, while never taking his eyes off Jennifer. 'I'm Douglas's lover, Mrs Lawson. You are in the way.'

Jennifer burst out laughing, but Costello could see some realization on the back of those big brown eyes. Griffin smiled slightly and looked from one woman to the other. 'Don't even think about it,' he said. 'I can slit her throat and you wouldn't get a hundred yards and I'd slit yours as well.'

'So is that what you do when nobody leaves an axe lying around?' asked Costello, pieces of the jigsaw falling into place. On that night, all those years ago, they had accepted his story. He was a cop, the distressed police officer. They had taken his word for what happened that night. They all had. Her just as much as anybody else.

Jennifer looked from Costello to Griffin. 'It was you, wasn't it?'

Griffin smiled and turned the knife in his hand, twirling it like a majorette. 'Nobody stands between me and true love. I'm in the flat in Edinburgh with Douglas, Jennifer. We are the couple; we are the family. Do you think he's really interested in you? All we need is you out the picture. Leave the boys behind and we will have the ideal family. After all you have been through, you are going to have a wee accident. You are a disgrace as a mother, not seeing that your child had been eaten by rats. Leaving him to be infected. You are nothing. Just nothing, a nobody.'

'Fuck off,' said Jennifer, voice trembling, but Costello couldn't doubt her guts.

'Nothing gets in the way of true love,' repeated Griffin.

'But it wasn't, was it?' said a voice from the far side, somebody using the same overgrown path as Griffin. Costello took the opportunity to move closer to Jennifer, who was still sitting in the middle of the Doon like a foundling in the forest.

Griffin exhaled deeply. The knife was still in his hand, but his arm was now down at his side. Costello squeezed Jennifer's

shoulder, trying to tell her silently to get ready to run. They
didn't want another bloodbath here, and Jennifer, and indeed
now herself, were directly in the line of fire. Griffin was far
too close with a very sharp blade. Griffin's attention had been
totally diverted, though, his face almost dissolved into the young,
handsome policeman he had been.

'Oh my God, it's you. I never thought I'd see you again.'

Steven Melrose looked down at the knife and then looked at
Costello. He took a step back. Melrose was trying to think of
the right thing to say, but couldn't. His eyes closed slightly, his
lips twisting into a line, 'Did you kill them?'

'I killed them for you,' Griffin said.

'What do you mean, you killed them for me?'

'We were in love,' said Griffin.

'No, we weren't. We were friends, Dave.'

Costello squeezed Jennifer's shoulder again, but the young
woman had turned to stone. Out the corner of her eye, Costello
saw the plumed white tail of a collie skirting its way through
the trees that surrounded the Doon. She thought of Heidi, the
mess Griffin had made of that dog. She willed Betty to walk
away. If anything happened, it would break Jock's heart.

'Why did you kill them?' Steven Melrose's face was streaming
with tears. 'My wee boys?'

'Because, without them, you would be mine.'

Then Costello said, 'So if you kill Jennifer, do you think
Douglas will be yours?'

'Douglas *is* mine.' There was no mistaking the madness now.

'No, he fucking isn't,' said Jennifer.

Melrose put his arm out. It was a slow gesture that could be
either placatory or an instruction. 'Go on, kill her. Why don't
you just kill her?'

Under the palm of her hand, Costello felt Jennifer's body
stiffen. Griffin took a step to the right, then two steps forward.
Costello straightened her arm, pushing Jennifer and Robbie
down on to the flowered moss of the Doon.

There was a deafening bang and the middle of David Griffin's
chest exploded.

THIRTY-FOUR

Costello was dry for the first time in a week. Her neatly bobbed blonde hair was tucked back behind her ears. She was now on antibiotics for the infected blister, but she was suffering the pain to wear her good high-heeled shoes. So that she could, if she felt like it, stick her heel into the testicles of one of the most horrible men she was ever going to meet. And she had met some horrors in her time.

Dressed in her neat blue suit, a single buff envelope under her arm, she pressed the buzzer of 169 Renfield Street and pushed open the old wooden door. She walked across a pristine green carpet and started up the stairs to the offices on the third floor, with the fiscal Archie Walker two feet behind her. She opened the door of McGregor Homes – property developer, builder and fraudulent scumbag – without knocking, and nodded at the secretary who was sitting looking at her own Facebook page on the computer.

'I'm here to see him.' She gestured into the office, where the tall, tanned man she had seen at the sinkhole was sitting behind a huge desk. Car reg: MGH 3211. A grade Arsehole. Five-star bastard.

'Do you have an appointment?'

'I don't need one,' said Costello. 'I have this,' and she waggled the brown envelope. She strode into the office, Walker following.

She closed the door.

'Nice to see you're so conscientious, here at your work when your dad died last week.'

Gregor McMutrie looked confused, then said, smugly, 'I'm deeply upset at the loss of my father but, as I'm now going to inherit all the land and the wood, I have a lot of work to do. Ninety per cent of the houses on Altmore Road are now either mine or in negotiation for me to buy. I am starting to project-manage redeveloping the entire wood. By this time next year, it will all be luxury flats.' A broad grin spread across his face, like the cat that got the cream with the cherry on top.

'You're a crap liar, so don't speak, just listen. There's a copy of your dad's will. You get nothing. Not only do you get nothing, he's rescinded the rental rights of the land to the north of Altmore House. You get nothing. You have nothing. But don't worry, you will have somewhere to live as the fiscal's office, Police Scotland, two environmental agencies and Scottish Water are building a very nice legal case against you. To say nothing of harassing your half-sister so much she left the country.'

Gregor McMutrie opened his mouth, but Costello wagged her finger.

'No, no, no, no. Don't speak. You will also be charged as an accessory before the fact, attempting to pervert the course of justice, and anything else we can think of, as your manipulation of house prices in Altmore Road has caused the death of Lorna Gyle and Lynda McMutrie. You kindly offered your lawyer's services to your friends, Douglas and Brian, for a cheap rate, knowing damn well that while they might own the bricks, they would never own the land. You were just waiting for your dad to die to get that.' He was still smiling. 'You even fleeced your friends for profit. And don't think for a minute that you can put all this at Brian Steele's door, because the one thing you can never do with dishonest people is trust them. And you and Brian made the mistake of trusting someone you knew as Laura Reid, who was in fact a little psycho called Tamara McMaster. She has more brains in her pole-dancing little finger than you have in your iPad. So you can contemplate that as you hide behind your big desk. All that rubble and concrete that you refused to pay to get taken away, all that crap you dumped in your own illegal landfill, managed to damage and block a culvert and to redirect the Dorcha back to its old course. At this moment it is still eating away at the foundations of Altmore Road, and it will all come tumbling down, just like your nasty little empire. Once the criminal law courts are done with you, the civil courts will have their day, especially the Dirk-Huntleys. Because of you, his Range Rover went down a sinkhole. They are so going to crucify you. They are not wee people like the Jennifer Lawsons of this world, or the Michael Broadfoots; the D-Hs are going to hunt you through every court in the land until you don't have a pot to piss in or a Kleenex to wipe your arse with. But I don't think you'll need anywhere to live, I think you will be staying at Her Majesty's pleasure.' She put the envelope in front of him. 'There's your dad's will and testament. You might want to read it. You never had any of it – not you, not Douglas Lawson, not any of you!'

And with that, Walker made his way towards the door. Costello had placed her forefinger on the handle and had turned back to look at Gregor McMutrie, who was now a slightly paler white than the wallpaper behind him.

'Just one thing,' she added. 'I am a very good liar. Your dad is perfectly fine; he's just lying low for a while. He sends his regards.'

And with that she closed the door.

'Do you think you lot could have followed procedure for once?' Walker asked.

'We caught the bugger, didn't we? And that's all that matters.' Costello ended the phone call and turned the phone off, knowing that wasn't true. She was sitting in the large meeting room in Barlinnie. Jock was standing on the far side on his own, along with his thoughts, quiet music playing. It had all the charm of a crematorium.

She wished for a quick burst of 'Bohemian Rhapsody'.

If they got this over in time, Costello was supposed to go and visit Anderson in hospital. She was hoping the meeting overran so she didn't have to bother. She couldn't face Brenda and her accusations that somehow she, Costello, had been responsible for the mess Anderson had got himself into.

Anderson's cries had eventually been heard by one of the paramedics, and he had been pulled from the drain suffering from hypothermia, blood loss and a mild case of septicaemia. The psychological ordeal for that already fragile mind would take longer to heal, but it seemed to have done him the world of good. In any case, a wee chat from Professor Batten would be more beneficial.

Costello did not want to think what might have happened if she had made sense of Anderson's attempts to get their attention. She would not have gone into the wood to look for him. She would have asked Broadfoot to drive the car up, used it to pull the drain cover off. She wouldn't have made it to the Doon. And then?

Jennifer? Griffin? Melrose? Any combination, depending on how fast Jock could reload that shotgun. There would be another bloody enquiry now. No way Anderson could walk away from this. But then, he had inherited a fortune. He didn't need it any more.

Wyngate had stayed in hospital overnight, and was now recuperating at home, looking as though he had suffered bad sunburn. His eyesight had been affected, but not permanently, so he was keeping a low profile until, as his elder son had put it, *Daddy stopped looking like a Halloween cake.*

Cadena was still in hospital, fractured skull, broken heart. Still thinking that Brian loved her. In some ways, being stabbed by Tamara was a better fate for Brian than what Michael Broadfoot would have done to him.

Tamara had a long criminal record; no wonder she had jumped at the chance of a new identity. That case had been transferred over to another team. There was nobody from Partickhill left standing.

O'Hare and Matilda McQueen had been very helpful in tying up the loose ends of the Gyle case, and Costello was wondering how to write it up without mentioning how easily Anderson had been beguiled by the woman who purported to be Lorna Gyle. At first Batten was incredulous that Anderson had accepted her story, but then why wouldn't he? He was emotionally primed to empathize with another soul battling their demons. Why would any woman go back to live in the street where she had suffered so much psychological trauma? The blonde, Tamara McMaster, had driven off down Altmore Road after hitting Wyngate and had disappeared. It was only a matter of time. Wyngate had won the bet.

What cards the hands of fate had dealt the real Lorna Gyle were difficult to imagine. She had been strangled and then dismembered, probably by Tamara McMaster and Brian Steele. Costello was pretty sure that Brian had married the real Lorna Gyle, and at some point during the purchase of the house at Altmore Road, Lorna had been murdered, leaving her possessions behind, her fingerprints, her DNA on the hair in the brush.

Had Lorna sensed something? In all her years, she had never visited her dad by her own request, but that Christmas she had tried to see him, but couldn't as he was in the infirmary having suffered that stab wound. If she had spoken to him, would it all have turned out differently? News of her murder was being kept out the media until her dad had been told. He was going to have his liberty; he was going to lose his reason for living. Thank God for Jock.

In Altmore Road, Tamara/Laura was installed with her carefully tattooed scar and her hazy memories. All the time, Lorna was slowly rotting in the culvert, waiting for the Dorcha to revert to its ancient course and dislodge her. Anderson had found the torso. The sinkhole had caught the foot. There would be enough to bury, O'Hare would make sure of that. Brian and Miss McMaster, another *folie à deux*. Costello had enough of them in her career. Were all relationships toxic?

Greed ran through the case like dry rot. Brian Steele had killed Lynda McMutrie while wearing Jock's wellington boots. Those wellington boots, with their telltale puncture repair, had sat in his unlocked porch for anybody to pick up. Shame that Betty was deaf, otherwise she would have heard the boot thief and barked. DNA had been left on the rim of the boots as they had been pulled on, showing it was Brian Steele who had been using them. It was Brian who intrigued Costello; a man who had inveigled his way into Lynda McMutrie's life, no doubt with an eye on buying the house, and never questioning it might not be hers to sell. Had Brian been killed by Tamara because he had been sleeping with Cadena, or was it on the cards all along?

Costello didn't care. Had Brian run over and killed Lorna's adoptive mother so his fiancée could inherit the £500,000 house? It would be impossible to prove who cut the brakes on Helen McNealy's car, an old MGB, but the investigation into her death was being reopened. Steven Melrose had started a relationship with her, and there was no doubt in Costello's mind that Griffin had killed her.

After twenty years in existence, the Braveheart Bangers had respectfully been disbanded. Twenty years after the death of Sue Melrose, Griffin's passion for Steven Melrose was undiminished. That kind of love was toxic.

Melrose had always had his suspicions. That was why he'd left. He could prove nothing, but Costello had the advantage of seeing Griffin with bloodless bands on his wrists in the scene-of-crime pictures, so knew he had been wearing gloves. And that explained the lack of trace transfer. Heidi the dog's toothmarks were visible on Griffin's arm in the selfie he had sent to Brenda via Anderson's phone. Plain for all to see. If anybody had bothered looking at Griffin's shirtsleeves on the evening of the murders, they would have shown the rents and tears made by Heidi's teeth. He had simply put his jumper on to hide the damage, a jumper on a hot summer night. Why did nobody question that?

He was a cop, they had trusted him.

They had checked the travel of noise from the pulpit to the Doon, never from the Doon to the street. Griffin couldn't have heard anything; he had followed Sue in. And twenty-three years later, Jennifer was now between Griffin and Douglas, his new love. No doubt the phone was taken out of Anderson's jacket as he was drunk and used to lure Jennifer to the trap and slipped back in. Anderson had that typical man's habit of hanging his jacket over the back of the chair. That would never make the report, either.

Jennifer Lawson had already started divorce proceedings against Douglas and Douglas was now in therapy for shacking up in Edinburgh with a homicidal lover. Costello hadn't seen that one, but Griffin and McMaster, friends from school, were behind both Jennifer and Brian moving into Altmore Road.

Jennifer and the boys were living on the ground floor of Altmore House, enjoying the company of Betty the dog and the heat from the Aga. Jock was working hard to settle the business of the Altmore estate. He wasn't going to re-dam the Dorcha; he thought it was better to let it run free to the Clyde.

The door of the meeting room opened and Andrew Gyle walked in, still in his prison clothes. He saw Costello and gave her a brief nod of acknowledgement. Then he saw Jock and a warm smile spread across his face, making him look twenty years younger. The two men embraced, then they both sat down. Costello could see Jock's lips moving, no doubt telling Andrew Gyle the dreadful news.

The smile left Andrew Gyle's face and it would be unlikely to return.

EPILOGUE

Professor Michael Batten stood outside the highly polished door. The name plate still said McAlpine Farrell. But that's not who was living inside. He paused for a short moment, then lifted the brass knocker, shaped like a single deer antler, and heard the comforting noise of its gentle rat-tat inside the house. Then a shout that might have been 'I'll get it' drifted through the door, a female voice, the slapping sound of somebody in bare feet hurrying across a hardwood floor. The door opened. The young woman with long dark hair peeked out through the gap, a broad but impersonal smile.

'Hello Claire,' he said.

She narrowed her eyes slightly, recognizing him but not sure where from. 'You work with Dad, don't you?'

'I have that pleasure,' said Batten. So Claire was here – so far, so good.

'You had better come in, he's in the kitchen.' She opened the door further and shouted through the open living-room door, 'Dad? It's for you.' That smile again, and she disappeared up the stairs, leaving him in the downstairs hall with a casualness that suggested to Batten that the machinations of her thought processes were moving towards the norm for 'teenager', i.e. unfathomable.

He walked into the living room, admiring the high-corniced ceiling, the polished floor, marble fireplace, and the white rugs. The house stank of comfort and loneliness. Maybe it wasn't the worst place in the world for Colin to be.

'Prof! How are you?' Colin emerged from the kitchen, hands freckled brown with coffee grains. Dressed in sweatshirt and jeans, he looked tired but happy. Rested. His relaxation now looked to be genuine. Nesbit trotted behind, gave the visitor a quick once-over and disappeared back into the kitchen.

'I was about to ask you the same question.' Batten opened

his arms to the ceiling. 'All this is yours. I take it the family know and they are OK with it. Claire looks fine.'

'Oh they know. All is good.'

'I'm glad.' Batten took a deep breath, 'Look mate, I'd like to apologize. I think I let you down; I let you go back to work too early. It was my mistake, not yours.'

Anderson shrugged. 'I'm not sure that you did, I needed something to sharpen me up, show me where the problems were. And being stuck in that culvert . . . well. It wasn't the worst thing. It proved something to me, about me. Don't analyse that. I have bigger problems.'

'Really?'

'I have no idea how to work a barista coffee machine. I've only been at it half an hour. Helena always had the best, top of the range. The instruction book is bigger than the handbook of a Ferrari. If it was from Argos, I'd have no problem.'

They wandered into the kitchen, boxes lying around, and Nesbit's bed in the corner, where it looked a permanent fixture. Two mugs waiting to be filled. 'Fancy a cup?'

'Do I have time? Half an hour and you haven't found the on-switch yet,' asked Batten, sarcastically.

'I've got Nescafé.' He pulled out another mug, rinsed it under the tap. It had been in the cupboard a long time.

So two mugs: Colin and Claire. One more for him.

Batten leaned over and flicked the switch for the coffee machine on at the wall. 'You had the toaster on instead.' He smiled like an annoying smartarse. 'So is this permanent, this living arrangement?'

'Who knows? Learned not to think about it. The one thing Claire needed was to paint. She's so much better here. So am I. Being away from Brenda. I just needed space, you know.' He flicked the kettle on, checking it was plugged in. 'I think we all did. We went out for dinner last night. As a family. Can't recall when we last did that.'

'So all is good *chez* Anderson.'

'At both of them. They don't want much. Claire wants a prom dress. Brenda wants to chuck work. It's Peter's request I am really struggling with.'

'And what's that?'

'He wants a pet.'

'No harm there; in fact it could be just the thing for him, bring him out his shell a bit. Nice wee dog if you are bringing Nesbit here to live with you.'

'He wants a pet rat.'

'Maybe not then.'